Seven Trips Through Time and Space

Edited by
Groff Conklin

CORONET BOOKS
Hodder Fawcett Ltd., London

Coronet Books Edition 1969
Second impression 1972

Printed and bound in Great Britain for
Coronet Books,
Hodder Fawcett Ltd,
St. Paul's House, Warwick Lane,
London, EC4P 4AH
by Hazell Watson & Viney Ltd,
Aylesbury, Bucks

SBN 340 10866 5

INTRODUCTION

In the September 16, 1967, issue of *The New Yorker*, the department entitled "The Talk of the Town" presented a report on the twenty-fifth annual World Science Fiction convention, held in New York City at the Statler Hilton hotel. The piece opened by stating that *The New Yorker* had "learned that a debate has been going on between the Old Fashioned Futurists, who want science fiction writers to keep on writing about the future as they always have, and the New Wave-icles, who are determined to drag the genre—kicking and screaming, if necessary—into the twenty-first century" where, according to one of the New Wave-icles himself, what's wanted is "total freedom"—"real sex, real drugs, really shocking ideas about society." William Burroughs was mentioned as a model for these "advanced" science fiction writers to follow.

Now, we have nothing against this New Wave in theory, nor against any effective effort to broaden and enrich science fiction with new concepts and materials, always provided the stories are good. The trouble seems to be that the works of many of the avant-garde S.F. writers have little to recommend them except their shock value, and that is not enough.

So let me set your mind at rest: In the present collection of Old (but not tired!) Wave science fiction, there are, of course, some really shocking ideas about society, since that is one of the major concerns of adult science fiction and always has been; but there is little if any of the merely verbally shocking stuff that characterizes much post-adolescent writing today.

Furthermore, every one of these tales is set solidly—not in the twenty-first century (which really will turn out to be little more than the latter third of the twentieth century, carried to extremes), but in various far more distant times in the development of space travel, when men will be skittering out among the stars, investigating unimaginably distant and different societies. What these stories tend to demonstrate is how much these remote polities can logically be expected to reflect the nascent growth, diversification, judgmental errors and suicidal insanities of our own sadly defective world.

The "new" is almost always the old and familiar, dressed up in the seemingly outlandish rigging of future scientific and technological advances. The truly novel, on the other hand, is found in stories of the imagination that extrapolate from the science of today, and describe worlds and peoples of possible tomorrows so that they ring true and at the same time give the reader the unforgettable experience of stretching his imagination's wings. It is that sort of novelty that you will find in the seven exciting tales that comprise the contents of this book.

GROFF CONKLIN

CONTENTS

FLATLANDER

Larry Niven

I

THE MOST BEAUTIFUL GIRL aboard turned out to have a husband with habits so solitary that I didn't know about him until the second week. He was about five feet four and middle-aged, but he wore a hellflare tattoo on his shoulder, which meant he'd been on Kzin during the war thirty years back, which meant he'd been trained to kill adult kzinti with his bare hands, feet, elbows, knees and whatnot. When we found out about each other he very decently gave me a first warning, and broke my arm to prove he meant it.

The arm still ached a day later, and every woman on the *Lensman* was over two hundred years old. I drank alone. I stared glumly into the mirror behind the curving bar. The mirror stared glumly back.

"Hey. You from We Made It. What am I?"

He was two chairs down, and he was glaring. Without the beard he would have had a round, almost petulant face . . . I think. The beard, short and black and carefully shaped, made him look like a cross between Zeus and an angry bulldog. The glare went with the beard. His square fingers wrapped a large drinking bulb in a death grip. A broad belly matched broad shoulders to make him look massive rather than fat.

Obviously he was talking to me. I asked, "What do you mean, what are you?"

"Where am I from?"

"Earth." It was obvious. The accent was Earth. So did the conservatively symmetrical beard. His breathing was unconsciously natural in the ship's standard atmosphere, and his build had been forged at one point zero gee.

"Then what am I?"

"A flatlander."

The glare heat increased. He'd obviously reached the bar way ahead of me. "A flatlander! Dammit, everywhere I go I'm a flatlander. Do you know how many hours I've spent in space?"

"No. Long enough to know how to use a drinking bulb."

"Funny. Very funny. Everywhere in human space a flatlander is a shnook who never gets above the atmosphere. Everywhere but Earth. If you're from Earth you're a flatlander all your life. For the last fifty years I've been running about in human space, and what am I? A flatlander. Why?"

"Earthian is a clumsy term."

"What is WeMadeItian?" he demanded.

"I'm a crashlander. I wasn't born within fifty miles of Crashlanding City, but I'm a crashlander anyway."

That got a grin. I think. It was hard to tell with the beard. "Lucky you're not a pilot."

"I am. Was."

"You're kidding. They let a crashlander pilot a ship?"

"If he's good at it."

"I didn't mean to pique your ire, sir. May I introduce myself? My name's Elephant."

"Beowulf Shaeffer."

He bought me a drink. I bought him a drink. It turned out we both played gin, so we took fresh drinks to a card table. . . .

When I was a kid I used to stand out at the edge of Crashlanding Port watching the ships come in. I'd watch the mob of passengers leave the lock and move in a great clump toward customs, and I'd wonder why they seemed to have trouble navigating. A majority of the starborn would always walk in weaving lines, swaying and blinking teary eyes against the sun. I used to think it was because they came from different worlds with different gravities and different atmospheres beneath differently colored suns.

Later I learned different.

There are no windows in a passenger spacecraft. If there were, half the passengers would go insane; it takes an unusual mentality to watch the blind-spot appearance of hyperspace and still keep one's marbles. For passengers there is nothing to watch and nothing to do, and if you don't like reading sixteen hours a day then you drink.

The ship grounded at Los Angeles two days after I met Elephant. He'd made a good drinking partner. We'd been fairly matched at cards, him with his sharp card sense, me with my usual luck. From the talking we'd done we knew almost as much about each other as anyone knows about anyone. In a way I was sorry to see him leave.

"You've got my number?"

"Yah. But, like I said, I don't know just what I'll be doing." I was telling the truth. When I explore a civilized world I like to make my own discoveries.

"Well, call me if you get a chance. I wish you'd change your mind. I'd really like to show you something of Earth."

"I decline with thanks. Good-by, Elephant. It's been fun."

Elephant waved and turned through the natives' door. I went on to face the smuggler baiters. The last drink was still with me, but I could cure that at the hotel. I never expected to see Elephant again. I really never did.

Nine days ago I'd been on Jinx, I'd been rich. And I'd been depressed.

The money and the depression had stemmed from the same source. The puppeteers, those three-legged, two-headed professional cowards and businessmen, had lured me into taking a new type of ship all the way to the galactic core, thirty thousand light-years away. The trip was for publicity purposes, to get research money to iron out the imperfections in the very ship I was riding.

I suppose I should have had more sense, but I never do, and the money was good. The trouble was that the core had exploded by the time I got there. The core stars had gone off in a chain reaction of novas ten thousand years ago, and a wave of radiation was even then (and even now) sweeping methodically toward known space.

In just over twenty thousand years, we'll all find ourselves in deadly danger.

You're not worried? It didn't bother me much either. But every puppeteer in known space vanished overnight, heading for Finagle knows what other galaxy.

I was depressed. I missed the puppeteers and hated knowing I was responsible for their going. I had time, and money, and a black melancholia to work off. And I'd always wanted to see Earth.

II

EARTH SMELLED GOOD. There was a used flavor to it, a breathed flavor, unlike anything I've ever known. It was the difference between spring water and distilled water. Somewhere in each breath I took were molecules breathed by Dante, Aristotle, Shakespeare, Heinlein, Carter and my own ancestors. Traces of past industries lingered in the air, sensed if not smelled: gasoline, coal fumes, tobacco and burnt cigarette filters, diesel fumes, ale breweries. I left the customs house with inflated lungs and a questioning look.

I could have taken a transfer booth straight to the hotel. I decided to walk a little first.

Everyone on Earth had made the same decision.

The pedwalk held a crowd such as I had never imagined. They were all shapes and all colors, and they dressed in strange and eldritch ways. Shifting colors assaulted the eye and sent one reeling. On any world in human space, any world but one, you know immediately who the natives are. Wunderland? Asymmetric beards mark the nobility, and the common people are the ones who quickly step out of their way. We Made It? The pallor of our skins in summer and winter; in spring and fall, the fact that we all race upstairs, above the buried cities and onto the blooming desert, eager to taste sunlight while the murderous winds are at rest. Jinx? The natives are short and wide and strong; a sweet little old lady's handshake can crush steel. Even in the Belt, within the solar system, a Belter strip haircut adorns both men and women. But Earth—!

No two looked alike. There were reds and blues and greens, yellows and oranges, plaids and stripes. I'm talking about hair, you understand, and skin. All my life I've used tannin secretion pills for protection against ultraviolet, so that my skin color has varied from its normal pinkish-white (I'm an albino) to (under bluewhite stars) tuxedo black. But I'd never known that other skin dye pills existed. I stood rooted to the pedwalk, letting it carry me where it would, watching the incredible crowd swarm around me. They were all knees and elbows. Tomorrow I'd have bruises.

"Hey!"

The girl was four or five heads away, and short. I'd never have seen her if everyone else hadn't been short too. Flatlanders rarely top six feet. And there was this girl, her hair a topological explosion in swirling orange and silver, her face a faint, subtle green with space-black eyebrows and lipstick, waving something and shouting at me.

Waving my wallet.

I forced my way to her, until we were close enough to touch, until I could hear what she was saying above the crowd noise.

"Stupid! Where's your address? You don't even have a place for a stamp!"

"What?"

She looked startled. "Oh! You're an offworlder."

"Yah!" My voice would give out fast at this noise level.

"Well, look." She shoved her way closer to me. "Look, you can't go around town with an offworlder's wallet. Next time someone picks your pocket he may not notice 'till you're gone."

"You picked my pocket?"

"Sure! Think I found it? Would I risk my precious hand under all those spike heels?"

"How if I call a cop?"

"Cop? Oh, a stoneface." She laughed merrily. "Learn or go under, man. There's no law against picking pockets. Look around you."

I looked around me, then looked back fast, afraid she'd disappear. Not only my cash, but my Bank of Jinx draft for forty thousand stars, was in that wallet. Everything I owned.

"See them all? Sixty-four million people in Los Angeles alone. Eighteen billion in the whole world. Suppose there was a law against picking pockets? How would you enforce it?" She deftly extracted the cash from my wallet and handed the wallet back. "Get yourself a new wallet, and fast. It'll have a place for your address and a window for a tenth-star stamp. Put your address in right away, and a stamp too. Then the next guy who takes it can pull out the money and drop your wallet in the nearest mailbox, no sweat. Otherwise you lose your credit cards, your ident, everything." She stuffed two hundred odd stars in cash between her breasts, flashed me a parting smile as she turned.

"Thanks," I called. Yes, I did. I was still bewildered, but she'd obviously stayed to help me. She could just as easily have kept wallet and all.

"No charge," she called back, and was gone.

I stopped off at the first transfer booth I saw, dropped a halfstar in the coin slot and dialed Elephant.

The vestibule was intimidating.

I'd expected a vestibule. Why put a transfer booth inside your own home, where any burglar can get in just by dialing your number? Anyone who can afford the lease on a private transfer booth can also afford a vestibule with a locked door and an intercom switch.

There was a vestibule, but it was the size of a living room, furnished with massage chairs and an autovendor. There was an intercom, but it was a flat vidphone, three hundred years old, restored at perhaps a hundred times its original cost. There was a double door of what looked like polished brass, with two enormous carved handles, and it stood fifteen feet high.

I'd suspected Elephant was well off, but this was too much. It occurred to me that I'd never seen him completely sober, that I had in fact turned down his offer of guide, that a simple morning-after treatment might have wiped me from his memory. Shouldn't I just go away? I *had* wanted to explore Earth on my own.

But I didn't know the rules!

I stepped out of the booth and glimpsed the back wall. It was all picture window, with nothing outside. Just fleecy blue sky. How peculiar, I thought, and stepped closer.

Elephant lived halfway up a cliff. A sheer mile-high cliff.

The phone rang.

On the third ear-jarring ring I answered, mainly to stop the noise. A supercilious voice said, "Is somebody out there?"

"I'm afraid not," I said. "Does someone named Elephant live here?"

"I'll see, sir," said the voice. The screen had not lit, but I had the feeling someone had seen me quite clearly.

Seconds crawled by. I was half minded to jump back in the transfer booth and dial at random. But only half; that was the trouble. Then the screen did light, and it was Elephant. "Bay! You changed your mind!"

"Yah. You didn't tell me you were rich."

"You didn't ask."

"Well, no, of course not."

"How do you expect to learn things if you don't ask? Don't answer that. Hang on, I'll be right down. You did change your mind? You'll let me show you Earth?"

"Yes, I will. I'm scared to go out there alone."

"Why? Don't answer. Tell me in person." He hung up.

Seconds later the big bronze doors swung back with a bone-shaking boom. They just barely got out of Elephant's way. He pulled me inside, giving me no time to gape, shoved a drink in my hand and asked me why I was afraid to go outside.

I told him about the pickpocket, and he laughed. He told me about the time he tried to go outside during a We Made It summer, and I laughed, though I've heard of outworlders being blown away and to Hades doing the same thing. Amazingly, we were off again. It was just like on the ship, even to the end of Elephant's anecdote. "They called me a silly flatlander, of course."

"I've been thinking about that," I said.

"About what?"

"You said you'd give a lot to do something completely original, so the next time someone called you a flatlander you could back him into a corner and force him to listen to your story. You said it several times."

"I didn't say just that. But I would like to have some story to tell, something like your neutron star episode. If only to tell myself. The silly offworlder wouldn't know, but *I'd* know."

I nodded. The neutron star episode he was talking about had been my first meeting with a puppeteer. The puppeteer had blackmailed me into taking one of his ships, a ship with an invulnerable puppeteer-made General Products hull, into a hyperbolic orbit within one mile of the surface of a neutron star. It was the only neutron star ever found, and I was the second man to make that trip. The first, with his wife, had used the same type of ship. They were found crushed shapelessly into its nose by some unknown force. Danger does wonderful things for my well-known mental laziness. With two minutes to spare I had realized what the unknown force was, and had crawled into the repair access tube to avoid it. I'd talked about it over gin cards—a habit I've developed for distracting my opponent—and Elephant had been suitably impressed.

"I've thought of a couple of things you could do," I said.

"Spill."

"One. Visit the puppeteer home world. Nobody's been there, but everyone knows there is one, and everyone knows how difficult it is to find. You could be the first."

"Great." He mused a moment. "Great! And the puppeteers wouldn't stop me because they're gone. Where *is* the puppeteer home world?"

"I don't know."

"What's your second idea?"

"Ask the Outsiders."

"Huh?"

"There's not a system in the galaxy the Outsiders don't know all about. We don't know how far the puppeteer empire extended, though it was way beyond known space, but we do know about the Outsiders. They know the galaxy like the palm of their—uh. . . . And they trade for information; it's just about the only business they do. Ask them what's the most unusual world they know of within reach."

Elephant was nodding gently. There was a glazed look in his eyes. I had not been sure he was serious about seeking some unique achievement. He was.

"The problem is," I said, "that an Outsider's idea of what is unique may not—" I stopped, because Elephant was up and half-running to a tridphone.

I wasn't sorry. It gave me an opportunity to gape in private.

I've been in bigger homes than Elephant's. Much bigger. I grew up in one. But I've never seen a room that soothed the eye like Elephant's living room. It was more than a living room; it was an optical illusion, the opposite of those jittering black-and-white images they show in lectures on how we see. These clinical children of Op Art give the illusion of motion; but Elephant's living room gave the illusion of stillness. A physicist would have loved the soundproofing. Some interior decorator had become famous for this work here, if he hadn't been famous already, in which case he had become rich. How could tall, thin Beowulf Shaeffer fit a chair designed to the measure of short, wide Elephant? Yet I was bonelessly limp, blissfully relaxed, using only the muscles that held a double-walled glass of an odd tasting, strangely refreshing soft drink called Tzlotz beer.

A glass which would not empty. Somewhere in the crystal was a tiny transfer motor connected to the bar; but the bent light in the crystal hid it. Another optical illusion, and one that must have tricked good men into acute alcoholism. I'd have to watch that.

Elephant returned. He walked as if he massed tons, as if any kzin foolish enough to stand in his path would have a short, wide hole in him. "All done," he said. "Don Cramer'll find the nearest Outsider ship and make my pitch for me. We should hear in a couple of days."

"Okay," said I, and asked him about the cliff. It turned out that we were in the Rocky Mountains and that he owned every square inch of the nearly vertical cliff face. Why? I remembered Earth's eighteen billion and wondered if they'd otherwise have surrounded him up, down, and sideways.

Suddenly Elephant remembered that someone named Dianna must be home by now. I followed him into the transfer booth, watched him dial eleven digits, and waited in a much smaller vestibule while Elephant used the more conventional intercom.

Dianna seemed rather dubious about letting him in until he roared that he had a guest and she should stop fooling around.

Dianna was a small, pretty woman with skin the deep, uniform red of a Martian sky and hair like flowing quicksilver. Her irises had the same polished silver luster. She hadn't wanted to let us in because we were both wearing our own skins, but she never mentioned it again once we were inside.

Elephant introduced me to Dianna and instantly told her he'd acted to contact the Outsiders.

"What's an Outsider?" she asked with sudden interest.

"They're hard to describe," I said. "Think of a cat-o'-nine-tails with a big thick handle."

"They live on cold worlds," said Elephant.

"Small, cold, airless worlds like Nereid. They pay rent to use Nereid as a base, don't they, Elephant? And they travel over most of the galaxy in big unpressurized ships with fusion drives and no hyperdrives."

"They sell information. They can tell me about the

world I want to find, the most unusual planet in known space."

"They spend most of their time tracking starseeds."

Dianna broke in. "Why?"

Elephant looked at me. I looked at Elephant.

"Say!" Elephant exclaimed. "Why don't we get a fourth for bridge?"

Dianna looked thoughtful. Then she focused her silver eyes on me, examined me from head to foot and nodded gently to herself. "Sharrol Janss. I'll call her."

While she was phoning, Elephant told me, "That's a good thought. Sharrol's got a tendency toward hero worship. She's a computer analyst at Donovan's Brains, Inc. You'll like her."

"Good," I said, wondering if we were still talking about a bridge game. It struck me that I was building up a debt to Elephant. "Elephant, when you contact the Outsiders, I'd like to come along."

"Oh? Why?"

"You'll need a pilot. And I've dealt with Outsiders before."

"Okay, it's a deal."

The intercom rang from the vestibule. Dianna went to the door and came back with our fourth for bridge. "Sharrol, you know Elephant. This is Beowulf Shaeffer, from We Made It. Bay, this is——"

"You!" I said.

"You!" she said.

It was the pickpocket.

III

My vacation lasted just four days. I hadn't known how long it would last, though I did know how it would end. Consequently I threw myself into it body and soul. If there was a dull moment anywhere in those four days, I slept through it, and at that I didn't get enough sleep. Elephant seemed to feel the same way. He was living life to the hilt; he must have suspected, as I did, that the Outsiders would not consider danger as a factor in choosing his planet. By their own ethics they were bound not to. The days of Elephant's life might be running short.

Buried in those four days were incidents that made me

wonder why Elephant was looking for a weird world. Surely Earth was the weirdest of all. . . .

I remember when we threw in the bridge hands and decided to go out for dinner. This was more complicated than it sounds. Elephant hadn't had a chance to change to flatlander styles, and neither of us was fit to be seen in public. Dianna had cosmetics for us.

I succumbed to an odd impulse. I dressed as an albino.

They were body paints, not pills. When I finished applying them, there in the full length mirror was my younger self. Blood-red irises, snow-white hair, pale transparent skin with a tinge of pink showing beneath: the teenager who had disappeared ages ago, when I was old enough to use tannin pills. My mind wandered far back across the decades, to the days when I was a flatlander myself, my feet firmly beneath the ground, my head never higher than seven feet above the desert sands. . . . They found me there before the mirror and decided my public was ready for me.

I remember that evening, when Dianna told me she had know Elephant forever. "I was the one who named him Elephant," she bragged.

"It's a nickname?"

"Sure," said Sharrol. "His real name is Gregory Pelton."

"O-o-oh." Suddenly all came clear. Gregory Pelton is known among the stars. It is rumored that he owns the thirty-light-year-wide rough sphere called human space, that he earns his income by renting it out. It is rumored that General Products, ostensibly run by the puppeteer species and now defunct in the absence of same, is a front for Gregory Pelton. It's a true fact that his great-to-the-eighth grandmother invented the transfer booth, and that he is rich, rich, rich!

I asked, "Why Elephant? Why that particular nickname?"

Dianna and Sharrol looked demurely at the tablecloth. Elephant said, "Use your imagination, Bay."

"On what? What's an elephant, some kind of animal?"

Three faces registered annoyance. I'd missed a joke.

"Tomorrow," said Elephant, "we'll show you the Zoo."

There are seven transfer booths in the Zoo of Earth. That'll tell you how big it is. But you're wrong; you've forgotten the two hundred taxis on permanent duty. They're there because the booths are too far apart for walking.

We stared down at dusty, compact animals smaller than starseeds or bandersnatchi, but bigger than anything else I'd ever seen. Elephant said, "See?"

"Yah," I said, because the animals showed a compactness and a plodding invulnerability very like Elephant's. And then I found myself watching one of the animals in a muddy pool. It was using a hollow tentacle over its mouth to spray water on its back. I stared at that tentacle . . . and stared. . . .

"Hey, look!" Sharrol called, pointing. "Bay's ears are turning red!"

I didn't forgive her till two that morning.

And I remember reaching over Sharrol to get a tabac stick and seeing her purse lying on her other things. I said, "How if I picked your pocket now?"

Orange and silver lips parted in a lazy smile. "I'm not wearing a pocket."

"Would it be in good taste to sneak the money out of your purse?"

"Only if you could hide it on you."

I found a small, flat purse with four hundred stars in it and stuck it in my mouth.

She made me go through with it. Ever made love to a woman with a purse in your mouth? Unforgettable. Don't try it if you've got asthma.

I remember Sharrol. I remember smooth, warm blue skin, silver eyes half-closed in cool blue loveliness, orange-and-silver hair in a swirling abstract pattern that nothing could muss. It always sprang back. Her laugh was silver too, when I gently extracted two handfuls of hair and tied them in a hard double knot, and when I gibbered and jumped up and down at the sight of her hair slowly untying itself like Medusa's locks. And her voice was a silver croon.

I remember the freeways.

They were the first thing that showed, coming in on Earth. If we'd landed at night it would have been the lighted cities; but of course we came in on the day side. Why else would a world have three spaceports? There were the freeways and autostradas and autobahns, strung in an all-enclosing net across the faces of the continents.

From a few miles up you still can't see the breaks. But they're there, when girders and pavement have collapsed. Only two super-highways are still kept in good repair. Both are on the same continent: the Pennsylanvia Turnpike and the Santa Monica Freeway. The rest of the network is broken chaos.

It seems there are people who collect old groundcars and race them. Some are renovated machines with half the parts replaced; others are handmade reproductions.

I laughed when Elephant told me about them. Seeing them in person was different.

The rodders began to appear about dawn. They gathered around one end of the Santa Monica Freeway, the end that used to join the San Diego Freeway. This end is a maze of fallen spaghetti, great curving loops of prestressed concrete that have lost their strength over the years and sagged to the ground. But you can still use the top loop to reach the starting line. We watched from above, hovering in a cab as the groundcars moved into line.

"Their dues cost more than the cars," said Elephant. "I used to drive one myself. You'd turn white as snow if I told you how much it costs to keep this stretch of freeway in repair."

"How much?"

He told me. I turned white as snow.

They were off. I was still wondering what kick they got, driving an obsolete machine on flat concrete when they could be up here with us. They were off, weaving slightly, weaving more than slightly, foolishly moving at different speeds, coming perilously close to each other before sheering off—and I began to realize things.

Those automobiles had no radar.

They were being steered with a cabin wheel geared directly to four ground wheels. A mistake in steering and they'd crash into each other, or into the concrete curbs. They were steered and stopped by muscle power; but whether they could turn or stop depended on how hard four rubber balloons could grip smooth concrete. If the tires loosed their grip Newton's First Law would take over; the fragile metal mass would continue moving in a straight line until stopped by a concrete curb or another groundcar.

"A man could get killed in one of those."

"Not to worry," said Elephant. "Nobody does, usually."

"Usually?"

He told me. I turned white as snow.

The race ended twenty minutes later, at another angle of fallen concrete. I was wet through. We landed and met some of the racers. One of them, a thin guy with tangled, glossy green hair and a bony white face with a widely grinning scarlet mouth, offered me a ride. I declined with thanks, backing slowly away and wishing for a weapon. This joker was obviously dangerously insane.

I remember flatlander food, the best in known space, and an odd, mildly alcoholic drink called Taittinger Comtes de Champagne '59. I remember invading an out-worlder bar, where the four of us talked shop with a girl rock miner whose inch-wide auburn crest of hair fell clear to the small of her back. I remember flying cross-country with a lift belt, and seeing nothing but city enclosing widely separated patches of food-growing land. I remember a submerged hotel off the Grand Banks of Newfoundland, and a dolphin embassy off Italy where a mixed group of dolphins and flatlanders seemed to be solving the general problem of sentient beings without hands (there are many, and we'll probably find more). It seemed more a coffee-break discussion than true business.

We were about to break up for bed on the evening of the fourth day, when the tridphone rang. Don Cramer had found an Outsider.

I said, disbelieving, "You're leaving *right now?*"

"Sure!" said Elephant. "Here, take one of these pills. You won't feel sleepy till we're on our way."

A deal is a deal, and I owed Elephant plenty. I took the pill. We kissed Sharrol and Dianna good-by, Dianna standing on a chair to reach me, Sharrol climbing me like a beanpole and wrapping her legs around my waist. I was a foot and a half taller than either of them.

Calcutta Base was in daylight. Elephant and I took the transfer booth there, to find that the *ST* ∞ had been shipped ahead of us.

Her full name was *Slower Than Infinity*. She had been built into a General Products #2 hull, a three-hundred-foot-spindle with a wasp waist constriction near the tail. I was relieved. The General Products hull is both invulnerable and impermeable to matter and energy other than visible light, as guaranteed by the puppeteer company and proven over thousands of years of use; but none of the four designs are pretty, and they all look alike. I was afraid Elephant might own a flashy, vulnerable dude's yacht. The two-man control room looked pretty small for a lifesystem until I noticed the bubble extension folded into the nose. The rest of the hull held a one gee fusion drive and fuel tank, a hyperspace motor, a gravity drag and belly landing gear, all clearly visible through the hull, which had been left transparent.

She held fuel, food and aid. She must have been ready for days. We left twenty minutes after arriving.

Now there was plenty of time for sleep. It took us a week at one gee just to get far enough out of the solar system's gravity well to use the hyperdrive. Somewhere in that time I removed my false coloring (it *had* been false; I'd continued to take tannin secretion pills against Earth's sunlight), and Elephant turned his skin back to light tan and his beard and hair back to black. For four days he'd been Zeus, with marble skin and a metal-gold beard and glowing molten gold eyes. It had fitted him so perfectly that I hardly noticed the change.

Hyperdrive—and a long, slow three weeks. We took turns hovering over the mass indicator, though at first quantum hyperdrive speeds we'd have seen a mass at least twelve hours before it became dangerous. I think I was the only man who knew there *was* a second quantum—a puppeteer secret. The Outsider ship was near the edge of known space, well beyond Tau Ceti.

"It was the only one around," Elephant had said. "Number fourteen."

"Fourteen? That's the same ship I dealt with before."

"Oh? Good. That should help."

Days later he asked, "How'd it happen?"

"The usual way. Number fourteen was on the other side of known space then, and she sent out an offer of information exchange. I was almost to Wunderland, and I caught the offer. When I dropped my passengers I went back."

"Did they have anything worthwhile?"

"Yah. They'd found the *Lazy Eight II.*"

The *Lazy Eight II* had been one of the old slowboats, a circular flying wing taking colonists to Jinx. Something had gone wrong before turnover, and the ship had continued on, carrying fifty passengers in suspended animation and a crew of four, presumed dead. With a ramscoop to feed hydrogen to her fusion drive she could accelerate forever. She was five hundred years on her way.

"I remember," said Elephant. "They couldn't reach her."

"No. But we'll know where to find her when the state of the art gets that good."

"That won't be soon."

He was right. A hyperdrive ship would not only have to reach her, but to carry reaction fuel to match her speed. Her speed was just less than a photon's, and she was more than five hundred light-years away, seventeen times the diameter of known space.

"They'll wait for us," I said.

"Did you have any problems?"

"Their translator is pretty good. But we'll have to be careful. The thing about buying information is that you don't know what you've got until you've bought it. They couldn't just offer to sell me the present position of the *Lazy Eight II.* We'd have tracked their course by scope until we saw fusion light, and gotten the information free."

The time came when only a small green dot glowed in the center of the mass indicator. A star would have shown as a line; no star would have shown as no dot. I dropped out of hyperspace and set the deep-radar to hunt out the Outsider.

IV

THE OUTSIDER found us first.

Somewhere in the cylindrical metal pod near her center of mass, perhaps occupying it completely, was the reactionless drive. It was common knowledge that that drive was for sale, and that the cost was a full trillion stars. Though nobody, and no nation now extant, could afford to pay it, the price was not exorbitant. In two or three minutes, while we were still searching, that drive had dropped the Outsider ship from above point nine lights to zero relative and pulled it alongside the *ST*$^{\infty}$.

One moment, nothing but stars. The next, the Outsider ship was alongside.

She was mostly empty space. I knew her population was the size of a small city, but she was much bigger because more strung out. There was the minuscule-seeming drive capsule, and there, on a pole two and a half miles long, was a light source. The rest of the ship was metal ribbons, winding in and out, swooping giddily around themselves and each other, until the ends of each tangled ribbon stopped meandering and joined to the drive capsule. There were around a thousand such ribbons, and each was the width of a wide city pedwalk.

"Like a Christmas tree decoration," said Elephant. "What now, Bay?"

"They'll use the ship radio."

A few minutes of waiting, and here came a bunch of Outsiders. They looked like a black cat-o'-nine-tails with grossly swollen handles. In the handles were their brains and invisible sense organs; in the whip ends, the clusters of mobile root-tentacles, were gas pistols. Six of them braked to a stop outside the airlock.

The radio spoke. "Welcome to Ship Fourteen. Please step outside for conveyance to our office. Take nothing on the outsides of your pressure suits."

Elephant asked "Do we?"

I said, "Sure. The Outsiders are nothing if not honorable."

We went out. The six Outsiders offered us a tentacle each, and away we went across open space. Not fast. The thrust from the gas pistols was very low, irritatingly weak. But the Outsiders themselves were weak: an hour in the gravity of Earth's moon would have killed them.

They maneuvered us through a tangled clutter of silver ribbons, landed us on a ramp next to the looming convex wall of the drive capsule.

It wasn't quite like being lost in a giant bowl of noodles. The rigid ribbons were too far apart for that. Far above us was the light source, about as small and intense and yellowish-white as Earth's sun seen from a moon of Neptune. Shining down through the interstellar vacuum, it cast a network of sharp black shadows across all the thousand looping strands that made up the city.

Along every light-shadow borderline were the Outsiders. Just as their plantlike ancestors had done billions of years ago on some unknown world near the galactic core, the Outsiders were absorbing life-energy. Their branched tails lay in shadow, their heads in sunlight, while thermoelectricity charged their biochemical batteries. Some had root-tentacles dipped in shallow food dishes; the trace elements that kept them alive and growing were in suspension in liquid helium.

We stepped carefully around them, using our headlamps at lowest intensity, following one of the Outsiders toward a door in the wall ahead. There were no rails along the ramps, and nothing but the cold distant stars beneath. Outsiders moved aside if we came too close. Our suits may have been leaking too much heat.

The enclosure was dark until the door closed behind us. Then the light came on. It was sourceless, the color of normal sunlight, and it illuminated a cubicle that was bare and square. The only furnishing was a hemisphere of very dark glass with the coiled shape of an Outsider inside. The hemisphere must have been both evacuated and refrigerated. Only excellent manners could have put him here at all, as if he were the guest instead of us.

"Welcome," said the room. Whatever the Outsider had said was not sonic in nature. "This air is breathable. Take off your helmets, suits, shoes, girdles and whatnot." It was an excellent translator, with a good grasp of idiom and a pleasant baritone voice.

"Thanks," I said, and we doffed our suits, Elephant a little self-consciously.

"Which of you is Gregory Pelton?"

"I am."

"Hi. According to your agent, you want to know how to reach that planet which is most unusual inside the borders of the sixty-light-year-wide region you call known space. Is this correct?"

"Yes."

"We must know if you plan to go there or to send agents there. Also, do you plan a landing, a near orbit, or a distant orbit?"

"Landing."

"Are we to guard against danger to your life or property?"

"No." Elephant's voice was dry. The Outsider ship was an intimidating place.

"Do you plan colonization? Mining? Growth of food plants or animals?"

"I plan only one visit."

"We have selected a world for you. The price will be one million stars."

"That's high," said Elephant. I whistled under my breath. It was: and it wouldn't get lower. The Outsiders never dickered.

"Sold," said Elephant.

The translator gave us a triplet set of coordinates some twenty-four light-years from Earth along galactic north. "The star you are looking for is a protosun with one planet a billion and a half miles distant. The system is moving at point eight lights toward"—he gave a vector direction. It seemed the protosun was drawing a shallow chord through known space; it would never approach human space.

"No good," said Elephant. "No hyperdrive ship can go that fast in real space."

"You could hitch a ride," said the translator. "With us. Moor your ship to our drive capsule."

"That'll work," said Elephant. He was getting more and more uneasy; his eyes seemed to be searching the walls for the source of the voice. He would not look at the Outsider business agent in the vacuum chamber.

"Our ferry fee will be one million stars."

Elephant sputtered.

"Just a sec," I said. "I may have information to sell you."

There was a long pause. Elephant looked at me in surprise.

"You are Beowulf Shaeffer?"

"Yah. You remember me?"

"We find you in our records. Beowulf Shaeffer, we have information for you, already paid. The former regional president of General Products on Jinx wishes you to contact him. I have a transfer booth number."

"That's late news," I said. "The puppeteers are gone.

Anyway, why would that two-headed sharpie want to see me?"

"I do not have that information. I do know that not all puppeteers have left this region. Will you accept the transfer booth number?"

"Sure."

I wrote down the eight digits as they came. A moment later Elephant was yelling, just as if he were a tridee set turned on in the middle of a program. "—hell is going on here?"

"Sorry about that," said the translator.

"What happened?" I asked.

"I couldn't hear anything! Did that monk—Did the Outsider have private business with you?"

"Sort of. I'll tell you later."

The translator said, "Beowulf Shaeffer, we do not buy information. We sell information and use the proceeds to buy territory and food soil."

"You may need this information," I argued. "I'm the only man within reach who knows it."

"What of other races?"

The puppeteers might have told them, but it was worth taking a chance. "You're about to leave known space. If you don't deal with me you may not get this information in time."

"What price do you set on this item?"

"You set the price. You've got more experience at putting values on information, and you're honorable."

"We may not be able to afford an honest price."

"The price may not exceed our ferry fee."

"Done. Speak."

I told him of the core explosion and how I'd come to find out about it. He made me go into detail on what I'd seen: the bright patch of supernovae spreading out as my ship caught up with ancient light waves, until all the bright multicolored ball of the core was ablaze with supernovae. "You couldn't have known this until you got there, and then it would have been too late. You don't use faster-than-light drives."

"We knew from the puppeteers that the core had exploded. They were not able to go into detail because they had not seen it for themselves."

"Oh. Ah, well. I think the explosion must have started

at the back side of the core from here. Otherwise it would have seemed to go much more slowly."

"Many thanks. We will waive your ferry fee. Now, there is one more item. Gregory Pelton, for an additional two hundred thousand stars we will tell you exactly what is peculiar about the planet you intend to visit."

"Can I find out for myself?"

"It is likely."

"Then I will."

Silence followed. The Outsider hadn't expected that. I said, "I'm curious. Your galaxy is rapidly becoming a death trap. What will you do now?"

"That information will cost you—"

"Forget it."

Outside, Elephant said, "Thanks."

"Forget it. I wonder what they will do?"

"Maybe they can shield themselves against the radiation."

"Maybe. But they won't have any starseeds to follow."

"Do they need them?"

Finagle only knew. The starseeds followed a highly rigid migratory mating pattern out from the core of the galaxy and into the arms, almost to the rim, before turning back down to the core. They were doomed. As they returned to the core the expanding wave of radiation from the multiple novas would snuff out the species one by one. What would the Outsiders do without them? What the hell did they do *with* them? Why did they follow them? Did they need starseeds? Did starseeds need Outsiders? The Outsiders would answer these and related questions for one trillion stars apiece. Personal questions cost high with the Outsiders.

A crew was already ringing the *ST* ∞ in to dock. We watched from the ramp, with crewmen sunbathing about our feet. We weren't worried. The way the Outsiders handled it, our invulnerable hull might have been made of spun sugar and sunbeams. When a spiderweb of thin strands fastened the *ST* ∞ to the wall of the drive capsule, the voice of the translator spoke in our ears and invited us to step aboard. We jumped a few hundred feet upward through the trace of artificial gravity, climbed into the airlock and got out of our suits.

"Thanks again," said Elephant.

"Forget it again," I said magnanimously. "I owe you plenty. You've been putting me up as a house guest on the most expensive world in known space, acting as my guide where the cost of labor is——"

"Okay okay okay. But you saved me a million stars, and don't you forget it." He whopped me on the shoulder and hurried into the control room to set up a million-star credit base for the next Outsider ship that came by.

"I won't," I called at his retreating bark. And wondered what the hell I meant by that?

Much later I wondered about something else. Had Elephant planned to take me to "his" world? Or did he think to go it alone, to be the first to see it and not one of the first two? After the Outsider episode it was already too late. He couldn't throw me off the ship then.

I wished I'd thought of it in time. I never wanted to be a batman. My stake in this was to gently, tactfully keep Elephant from killing himself if it became necessary. For all his vast self-confidence, vast riches, vast generosity and vast bulk, he was still only a flatlander, and thus a little bit helpless.

V

We were in the expansion bubble when it happened. The bubble had inflatable seats and an inflatable table; it was there for exercising and killing time, but it also supplied a fine view; the surface was perfectly transparent.

Otherwise we would have missed it.

There was no pressure against the seat of the pants, no crawling sensation in the pit of the stomach, no feel of motion. But Elephant, who was talking about a Jinxian frail he'd picked up in a Chicago bar, stopped just as she was getting ready to tear the place apart because some suicidal idiot had insulted her.

Somebody heavy was sitting down on the universe.

He came down slowly, like a fat man cautiously letting his weight down on a beach ball. From inside the bubble it looked like all the stars and nebulae around us were squeezing themselves together. The Outsiders on the ribbons outside never moved; but Elephant said something profane, and I steeled myself to look up.

The stars overhead were blue-white and blazing. Around us they were squashed together; below, they were turning red and winking out, one by one. It had taken us a week to get out of the solar system, but the Outsider ship could have done it in five hours.

The radio spoke. "Sirs, our crewmen will remove your ship from ours, after which you will be on your own. It has been a pleasure to do business with you."

A swarm of Outsider crewmen hauled us through the maze of basking ramps and left us. Presently the Outsider ship vanished, gone suddenly off, now on its own business.

In the strange starlight Elephant let out a long, shaky sigh. Some people can't take aliens. They don't find puppeteers graceful and beautiful; they find them horrifying, *wrong*. They see kzinti as slavering carnivores whose only love is fighting and killing, which is the truth; but they don't see the rigid code of honor, nor the self-control which allows a kzin ambassador to ride a human city pedwalk without slashing out with his claws at the impertinent stabbing knees and elbows. Elephant was one of these people.

He said, "Okay," in amazed relief that they were actually gone. "I'll take the first watch, Bay."

He did not say, "Those bastards would take your heart as collateral on a tenth-star loan." He couldn't see them as that close to human.

If Elephant's weakness was aliens, mine was relativity.

The trip through hyperspace was routine. I'd been trained to take the sight of the two small windows turning into blind spots, becoming areas of nothing that seemed to draw together the objects around them. So had Elephant; he'd done some flying though he preferred the comfort of a luxury liner. But the Fast Protosun was a week away, and even the best pilot occasionally has to drop back among the stars, to get his bearings and to assure his subconscious that the universe is still there.

And each time it was changed, squashed flat. The crowded blue stars were all ahead; the sparse dim red stars were all behind. Four hundred years ago men and women had lived for years with such a view of the universe. But it hadn't happened since the invention of hyperdrive. I'd never seen the universe look like this. It bothered me.

"No, it doesn't bug me," said Elephant when I mentioned it. We were a day out from our destination. "To me, stars are stars. But I have been worried about something. Bay, you said the Outsiders are honorable."

"They are. They've got to be. They have to be so far above suspicion that any species they deal with will remember their unimpeachable ethics a century later. You can see that, can't you? Outsiders don't show up more often than that."

"Um. Okay. Why did they try to screw that extra two hundred kilostars out of me?"

"Uh—"

"See, the goddam problem is, what if it was a fair price? What if we *need* to know what's funny about the Fast Protosun?"

"You're right. Knowing the Outsiders, it's probably information we can use. All right, we'll nose around a little before we land. We'd have done that anyway, but now we'll do it better."

What was peculiar about the Fast Protosun?

Around lunchtime on the seventh ship's day, a short green line in the sphere of the mass indicator began to extend itself. It was wide and fuzzy, just what you'd expect of a protosun. I let it reach almost to the surface of the sphere before I dropped us into normal space.

The squashed universe looked in the windows. But ahead of us was a circular darkening and blurring of the vivid blue-white stars; and in the center of the circle was a dull red glow.

"Let's go into the extension bubble," said Elephant.

"Let's not."

"We'll get a better view in there." He turned the dial that would make the bubble transparent. Naturally we kept it opaque in hyperspace.

"Repeat, let's not. Think about it, Elephant. What sense does it make to use an impermeable hull, then spend most of our time outside it? Until we know what's here we ought to retract the bubble."

He nodded his shaggy head and touched the board again. Chugging noises announced that air and water were being pulled out of the bubble. Elephant moved to a window.

"Ever seen a protosun?"

"No," I said. "I don't think there are any in human space."

"That could be the peculiarity."

"It could. One thing it isn't, is the speed of the thing. Outsiders spend all their time moving faster than this."

"But planets don't. Neither do stars. Bay, maybe this thing came from outside the galaxy. That would make it unusual."

It was time we made a list. I found a pad and solemnly noted speed of star, nature of star and possible extragalactic origin of star.

"I've found our planet," said Elephant.

"Whereabouts?"

"Almost on the other side of the protosun. We can get there faster in hyperspace."

The planet was still invisibly small where Elephant brought us out. The protosun looked about the same.

A protosun is the foetus of a star: a thin mass of gas and dust, brought together by slow eddies in interstellar magnetic fields or by the presence of a Trojan point in some loose cluster of stars; a mass which is collapsing and contracting due to gravity. I'd found material on protosuns in the ship's library, but it was all astronomical data: nobody had ever been near one for a close look. In theory the Fast Protosun must have been fairly well along in its evolution, not only because it must have formed before acquiring its peculiar velocity, but because it was already glowing.

"There it is," said Elephant. "Two days away at one gee."

"Good. We can do our instrument checks on the way. Strap down."

With the fusion motor pushing us smoothly along, Elephant went back to the scope, and I started checking the other instruments. One thing stood out like a beacon.

"Elephant. Have you noticed in me a tendency to use profanity for emphasis?"

"Not really. Why?"

"It's goddam radioactive out there."

"Could you be more specific, sir?"

"Our suit shields would break down in three days. The extension bubble would go in twenty hours."

"Okay, add it to your list. Any idea what's causing it?"

"Not one." I made a note on my list. We were in no danger; the GP hull would protect us from anything but a heavy impact.

"No asteroid belts," said Elephant. "Meteor density zero, as far as I can tell. No other planets."

"The interstellar gas may clean away anything small, at these speeds."

"One thing's for sure, Bay. I got my money's worth. This is a strange odd peculiar funny system."

"Yah. Well, we missed lunch. Let's get dinner."

"Philistine."

VI

ELEPHANT ATE FAST. He was back at the scope before I was ready for coffee. Watching him move, I was again reminded of a juggernaut; but he'd never shown such determination when I knew him on Earth. If a hungry kzin had been between him and the telescope, Elephant would have left footprints in fur.

But the only thing that could get in his way out here was me.

"Can't get a close look at the planet," said Elephant, "but it looks polished."

"Like a billiard ball?"

"Just that. I don't see any sign of an atmosphere."

"How about blast craters?"

"Nothing."

"They should be there."

"This system's pretty clean of meteors."

"The space around us shouldn't be. And at these speeds—"

"Uh-huh. That better go on your list."

I wrote it down on my list.

We slept in the disaster couches. In front of me were the yellow lights of the control panel; the stars glowed red through one side window, blue through the other. I stayed awake a long time, staring through the forward window into the red darkness ahead. The window was opaqued, but I saw the protosun clearly in my imagination, like a blood droplet spreading in dark, still water.

The radiation held steady all through the next day. I did some more thorough checking, using temperature readings and deep-radar on both sun and planet. Everywhere I looked was a new anomaly.

"This star definitely shouldn't be glowing yet. It's too spread out; the gas should be too thin for fusion."

"Is it hot enough to glow?"

"Sure. But it shouldn't be."

"Maybe the theories on protosuns are wrong."

"Put it on your list."

And, an hour later:

"Elephant—"

"*Another* peculiarity?"

"Yah."

From under shaggy brows. Elephant's eyes plainly told me he was getting sick of peculiarities.

"According to the deep-radar shadow, this planet doesn't have any lithosphere. It's worn right down to what ought to be the magma, but isn't because it's so cold out here."

"Write it down. How many entries have you got?"

"Nine."

"Is any one of them worth paying two hundred kilostars to know about beforehand?"

"The radiation, maybe, if we didn't have a GP hull."

"But," said Elephant, glaring out at the huge, dark disk, "they *knew* we had a GP hull. Bay, can anything get through a General Products hull?"

"Light, like a laser beam. Gravity, like tides crushing you into the nose of a ship when you get too close to a neutron star. Impact won't harm the hull, but it'll kill what's inside."

"Maybe the planet's inhabited. The more I think about it, the more sure I am it came from outside. Nothing in the galaxy could have given it this velocity. It's diving through the plane of the galaxy; it wouldn't have to push in from the rim."

"Okay. What do we do if someone shoots a laser at us?"

"We perish, I think. I had reflective paint spread around the cabin, except for the windows, but the rest of the hull is transparent."

"We can still get into hyperspace from here. And for the next twenty hours. Afterwards we'll be too close to the planet."

I went right to sleep that night, being pretty tired despite the lack of exercise. Hours later I slowly realized that I was being examined. I could see it through my closed eyelids; I could feel the heat of the vast red glare, the size of the angry eye, the awful power of the mind behind it. I tried to struggle away, smacked my hand on something and woke with a shock.

I lay there in the red darkness. The edge of the protosun peeked through a window. I could feel its hostile glare.

I said, "Elephant."

"Mngl?"

"Nothing." Morning would be soon enough.

Morning.

"Elephant, would you do me a favor?"

"Sure. You want Dianna? My right arm? Shave off my beard?"

"I'll keep Sharrol, thanks. Put on your suit, will you?"

"Sure, that makes sense. We aren't nearly uncomfortable enough, just because we closed off the bubble."

"Right. And because I'm a dedicated masochist, I'm going to put my suit on this instant. Now, I hate to enjoy myself alone——"

"You got the wind up?"

"A little. Just enough."

"Anything for a friend. You go first."

There was just room to get our suits on one at a time. If the inner airlock door hadn't been open there wouldn't have been that. We tried leaving our helmets thrown back, but they got in our way against the crash couches. So we taped them to the window in front of us.

I felt better that way, but Elephant clearly thought I'd flipped. "You sure you wouldn't rather eat with your helmet on?"

"I hate suit-food syrup. We can reach our helmets if we get a puncture."

"What puncture? We're in a *General Products hull!"*

"I keep remembering that the Outsiders knew that."

"We've been through that."

"Let's go through it again. Assume they thought we might be killed anyway if we weren't prepared. Then what?"

"Gronk."

"Either they expected us to go out in suits and get killed, or they know of something that can reach through a General Products hull."

"Or both. In which case the suits do us no good at all. Bay, do you know how long it's been since a General Products hull failed?"

"I've never heard of its happening at all."

"It never has."

"You're dead right. I've been stupid. Go ahead and take off your suit."

Elephant turned to look at me. "And you?"

"I'll keep mine on."

Elephant shrugged his shaggy eyebrows and went back to the telescope. By then we were six hours from touch-down, and decelerating.

"I think I've found an asteroid crater," Elephant said presently.

I had a look. "Yah, I think you're right. But it's damn near disappeared."

He took the telescope back. "It's round enough. Almost has to be a crater. Bay, why should it be so eroded?"

"It must be the interstellar dust. If it is, then that's why there's no atmosphere or lithosphere. But I can't see the dust being that thick, even at these speeds."

"Put it——"

"Yah." I reached for my list.

"If we find one more anomaly I'll throw a tantrum."

Half an hour later we found life. By then we were close enough to use the gravity drag. The beautiful thing about a gravity drag is that it uses very little power. It converts a ship's momentum relative to the nearest powerful mass into heat, and all you have to do is get rid of the heat. Since the *ST ∞'s* hull would pass only various ranges of radiation corresponding to what the puppeteers' varied customers call visible light, the ship builders had run a big radiator fin out from the gravity drag and through the hull. It glowed dull red behind us. And the fusion drive was off. There was no white fusion flame to hurt visibility.

Elephant had the scope at highest magnification. At first, as I peered into the eyepiece, I couldn't see what he was talking about. There was a dull white plain, all the same color except for a few bluish blobs. The blobs wouldn't have stood out but for the uniform surface around them.

Then one of them moved. Very slowly, but it was moving.

"Right," I said. "Let's run a temperature check."

The surface temperature in that region was right for helium II. And on the rest of the planet as well; the protosun wasn't putting out much heat, though it was on radiation.

"I don't think they match any species I know."

"I can't tell," said Elephant. He had the telescope and the library screen going at the same time, with a Sirius VIII Blob on the screen. "I've found twenty different species of helium life in this book, and they all look alike."

"Not quite. These must have a vacuum-proof integument. And you'll notice those granules in the——"

"I treasure my ignorance on this subject, Bay. Anyway, we won't find any known species on this world. At these speeds even a stage tree seed wouldn't live through the impact."

I let the subject die.

Once again Elephant ran the scope over "his" planet, this time looking for the blobby life forms. They were big for Helium II life, but not freakishly so. Many cold worlds develop life using the peculiar properties of superfluid helium: but, since such life hasn't much use for complexity, it usually stays in the amoeba stage.

There was one peculiarity, which I duly noted. Every animal was on the planet's backside with relation to its course through the galaxy. They weren't afraid of protosunlight, but they seemed to fear interstellar dust.

Two hours passed.

The red glow of the radiator fin became more pronounced. The planet was closer, but no more detailed.

"Cue Ball," said Elephant.

"No good. It's been used. For Beta Lyrae I."

"Too bad. How about Swoosh?"

"Huh? Oh, *Swoosh*. That isn't bad."

"That's it then. *Swoosh,* discovered by Gregory Zhiv Pelton and Friend."

"Elephant, what are we doing here?"

He turned, startled. "What do you mean?"

"Look, you know by now I'm with you all the way. But I do wonder. You spent a million stars getting here, and you'd have spent two if you had to. You could be home in the Rockies with Dianna, or hovering near Beta Lyrae, which is unusual enough and much better scenery than, uh, Swoosh. You could be sampling oddball drugs and biochemicals in Crashlanding, or looking for mist demons on Plateau, or hunting bandersnatchi and vice versa on a Jinx shoreline. Why here?"

"Because it is there?"

"What the blazes kind of an answer is that?"

"Bay, once upon a time there was a guy named Miller. Six years ago he took a ramscoop-fusion drive ship out of a museum and put a hyperdrive in it and set out for the edge of the universe. He figured he could get his hydrogen in normal space and use the fusion plant to power his hyperdrive. He's probably still going. He may go forever, unless he hits something. So why?"

"A psychiatrist I'm not."

"He wanted to be remembered. When you're dead a hundred years, Bay, what will you be remembered for?"

"I'll be the idiot who rode with Gregory Pelton, who spent two months of his life and more than a million stars to set his ship down once on a totally useless planet."

"Gronk. But do you see? You'll be remembered."

"There must be better things to be remembered for."

"I can't write novels. I'd make a lousy planetary president. A scientist I'm not. What's left?"

"Found a dynasty?"

Elephant's lips tightened, and he glared—not at me, but ahead. "Arrgh," he growled. "I'd make a lousy emperor too. Let's drop it, shall we?"

"Okay," I said. Because something had occurred to me.

That guy named Miller—I'd heard of him. He'd been sterilized while standing too close to a fusion-electric plant the day it decided to leak just a little. There were other heroes, whose names were remembered because they had done strange, difficult, not particularly useful things. Mae Doolin, who had climbed forty miles down the side of Mount Lookitthat in a suit she had designed herself. If she'd spent a couple of extra months on that pressure suit she'd have made it back up. Lynaeus (true name unknown), who fought kzinti with his bare hands, and lived to teach the Hellflare Boys how. Had any of them had families?

Did Elephant have children? Could he?

I could ask the first question, if I phrased it right. I'd have to be subtle.

"Elephant, are you ster——"

There was a muffled, authoritative *boom*, instantly followed by a strangling pressure in my larynx and a cool, puffy sensation over my skin surface and a stabbing pain in the ears.

I heard the bare beginning of an alarm as the air went. Already I was reaching for my helmet. I clamped it down hard, spun the collar, and gave vent to an enormous belch at the same time as the wind went shrieking from my lungs.

VII

THERE WAS NO WAY to realize what was happening, and no time. Vacuum was around us; and air was spraying into my suit, frigid with storage. Iron spikes were being driven through my ears and sinuses; but I was going to live. My lungs held a ghastly emptiness, but my suit was inflating. I would live.

You don't know how selfish your thoughts can be until you've come that close to the Blowout Death. My hands started to shake; I clamped down on myself and turned to Elephant.

The fear of death was naked in his face. He had his helmet down, but he was having trouble with the collar. Mist wreathed his neck ring. I had to force his hands away to fasten his helmet down. The glass misted over, then cleared; he was getting air. Had it come in time?

What had happened was insane.

The hull had turned to dust. Just that. All at once and nothing first, the ship's exterior had disintegrated and blown away on a puff of breathing-air. I'd *seen* it.

And sure enough, the hull was gone. Only the innards of the ship remained. Before me, the lighted control board. A little below that, the manhole to the packed bubble, and the bubble package itself. Above the board, the dull half-disk of Swoosh, and stars. To the left, stars. To the right, Elephant, looking dazed and scared and alive. Beyond him, stars. Behind us, the airlock, the kitchen storage block and dial board, a glimpse of the landing legs and glowing radiator fin, and stars. The *ST* ∞ was a skeleton.

Elephant shook his head, then turned on his suit radio. I heard the magnified *click* in my helmet.

We looked at each other, waiting. There seemed to be nothing to say, no comment that would fit without being obvious.

I sighed, turned to the control board and brought the fusion drive to life. From what I could see of the ship, nothing was missing but the hull. Nothing vital was floating away. Whatever had been attached to the hull had also been attached to other things.

"What are you doing, Bay?"

"Getting us out of here. You can throw your tantrum now."

"Why? I mean, why leave?"

He'd flipped. Flatlanders are basically unstable. I got the drive pushing us at low power, turned off the gravity drag and swiveled to face him. "Look, Elephant. No hull." I swept an arm in a circle. "None. Nothing."

"But what's left of the ship is still mine?"

"Huh? Sure."

"I want to land. Can you talk me out of it?" Behind that intimidating beard he was dead serious and, I was beginning to believe, quite mad. "The landing legs are intact. Our suits can stop the radiation for three days. We could land and take off in twelve hours."

"We probably could, if nothing else happened."

"And we've spent a month and a half getting here."

"Right. Silly, but right."

"I'd feel like an idiot, getting this close and then turning for home. Wouldn't you?"

"I feel like an idiot for getting this close, period. No, cancel that. Yes, I'd feel stupid going home with nothing to show. But we *do* have something to show."

"A skinned ship. All right, so the hull turned to dust and blew away. What does that mean? It means we've got a faulty hull, and I'm going to sue the hind legs off General Products when we get back. But do *you* know what caused it?"

"No. Do you?"

He ignored the question. "So why assume it's some kind of threat?"

He was *wrong*. I knew it. But how to tell him so?

"Tell you what I'll do," I said. I turned the ship until it was tail down to Swoosh. "Now. We'll be there in three hours if you insist on landing. This skinned corpse is your ship, just as you say. But I'm going to talk you out of it."

"That's fair." But his square, bearded mouth had less give in it than a snapping turtle's.

"Have you had astronaut training?"

"Naturally."

"Did it include a history course?"

"All they taught me was how to fly a ship. And a little of the development of the state of the art."

"That's something. You remember that they first explored the System with chemical fuels, and that the first ship to touch an asteroid was built in orbit around the Earth's moon."

"I'll take your word."

"This you may not know. There was a ship before that one, supposed to do the same job. It was launched on a course that took it just inside the moon's orbit, then out and away. About thirty hours after launching, the crew noticed that all their ports were turning to frosted glass. Two of the men wanted to go on and finish the mission. The third man happened to be captain. So they used their rockets and stopped the ship dead.

"Remember, the best materials they had were alloys of iron. The hull was carbon-alloyed iron; the ports were thick glass, two layers. Our heroes stopped the ship 238,000 miles from the moon and called base to say they'd aborted the mission."

"You remember this pretty well. How come?"

"Doc Spinoza drilled these stories into us again and again. Everything he taught us he illustrated with something from history. It stuck. They do a thorough job on passenger-craft astronauts."

"Go on."

"They called base and told them about the windows. Somebody decided it must be dust, lots of dust. Someone else realized that they'd launched the ship straight through the moon's lead Trojan point."

Elephant laughed, then coughed. "Stupid trick. Wish I hadn't breathed so much vacuum. Sir, you're leading up to something."

"If they hadn't stopped the ship the dust would have torn it apart. Trojan points are dust collectors. And the moral of this story is, anything you don't understand is dangerous until you do."

"Sounds paranoid."

"Maybe it does, to a flatlander. You come from a planet so kind to you, so seemingly adapted to you, that you think the whole universe is one big lavish government housing project. You should listen to the Finaglists. The Perversity of the Universe Tends Toward a Maximum. A certain neutron star would have killed me if I hadn't understood that tidal effect in time."

"So it would. So you think all flatlanders are fools?"

Dammit, I'd touched his exposed nerve. "No, Elephant. Just not paranoid enough. And I refuse to apologize."

"Who asked you?"

"I'll land with you if you can tell me what made our hull turn to dust."

Elephant crossed his arms and glared forward. I shut up and waited.

I'd have to land regardless, if he insisted. Not because there was only one ship. Not because I couldn't just wait here for him. But because I'd invited myself along.

Soon he said, "Can we get home?"

"I don't know. The hyperdrive will work, and we can use the gravity drag to slow us when we reach a system. We couldn't have done that with the protosun: too much thick gas going through the system. Physically we should be able to make it."

"Okay, let's go. But I'll tell you this, Bay. If I were alone I'd go down, and damn the hull."

So we turned tail and ran, under protest from Elephant. In ten hours we were far enough from Swoosh's gravity well to enter hyperspace.

I turned on the hyperdrive, gasped and turned it off just as fast as I could. We sat there shaking.

"We can inflate the bubble," said Elephant.

"But can we get in?"

"I don't know. It doesn't have an airlock."

We worked it, though. There was a pressure control in

the cabin, and we set it for zero. The electromagnetic field that folded it would now expand it without pressure. We went in, pressurized it and took off our helmets.

"We're beyond the radiation," said Elephant. "I looked."

"Good." You can go a long way in even a couple of seconds of hyperdrive. "Now, there's one thing I've got to know. Can you take that again?"

Elephant shuddered. "Can you?"

"I think so. I can do all the navigating if I have to."

"Anything you can take I can take."

"Can you take it and stay sane?"

"Yes."

"Then we can trade off. But if you change your mind, let me know that instant. A lot of good men have left their marbles in the Blind Spot, and all they had to face were a couple of covered windows."

"I believe you. Indeed I do, sir. How do we work it?"

"We'll have to chart a course through the least dense regions of known space. The nearest inhabited world is Kzin. I hate to have to trust the kzinti for help, but it looks like our best bet."

"Tell you what, Bay. Let's at least aim for Jinx. I want to use that number of yours to give the puppeteers hell."

"Fine." If it turned out our minds couldn't take it, we could always turn off.

I spent an hour working out a course. When I finished there were precious few gravity wells along our path. We wouldn't have to check the mass indicator more than once every twenty-four hours.

Elephant won the finger-toss. I had won the first watch.

We donned suits and depressurized the bubble. As I crawled through the manhole I saw Elephant making the bubble opaque.

I squeezed into the crash couch, all alone among the compressed stars. The protosun had vanished behind us.

More than half my range of vision was empty space. I found myself looking thoughtfully at the airlock. It was behind and to the left, a metal oblong standing alone at the edge of the deck, with both doors tightly closed. The inner door had slammed when the pressure dropped, and now the airlock mechanisms guarded the pressure inside against the vacuum at both doors. Nobody was inside to benefit; but how to explain that to a pressure sensor?

I was procrastinating. The ship was aimed; I set my jaw and sent the *ST* $^{\infty}$ into hyperspace.

The Blind Spot, they call it. It fits.

There is a way to find the blind spot in your eye. Close one eye, put two dots on a piece of paper and bring the paper toward you, focusing on one of the dots. If you hold the paper just right, the other dot will suddenly vanish.

Let a ship enter hyperspace with the windows transparent, and the windows will seem to vanish. So will the space enclosing them. Objects on either side stretch and draw closer together to fill the missing space. If you look long enough, the Blind Spot starts to spread; the walls and the things against the walls draw even closer to the missing space, until they are engulfed. Covering the windows helps, but after awhile the Blind Spot starts to seep around the covers.

It's all in your mind, they tell me. So?

I turned the key, and half my view was Blind Spot. The control board stretched and flowed. The mass indicator sphere tried to wrap itself around me. I reached for it, and my hands were distorted too. With considerable effort I put them back at my sides and got a grip on myself.

There was one fuzzy green line in the plastic distortion that had been a mass indicator.

And it was behind and to the side. The ship could fly itself until Elephant's turn came. I fumbled my way to the manhole and crawled through.

VIII

SOME TIME LATER, Elephant caught me looking at my list. He took it from me and began to study it.

It said:

1) Velocity of star—.8 lights.
2) Nature of star—protosun. Unique in known space.
3) Origin of star—extragalactic, in all probability.
4) Unusual radiation.
5) Planet has no atmosphere.
6) No sign of blast craters on planet.
7) Protosun shows strangely high temperature.
8) Planet has no lithosphere.
9) Blast crater, vastly eroded. Dust? Why so thick?
10) He II beasts confined to back of planet. Fear Dust?

Elephant nodded to himself, added something and handed it back. The list now read:

11) Hull disintegrated.

Eleven notes. Eleven irregularities with no explanation. They must be connected.

"If we knew more about our hull," I said, "we could probably figure this out."

"Fat chance," said Elephant. "That hull's a puppeteer trade secret."

And there it died.

All our conversations were dying young. Neither of us felt the urge to talk. The hours passed and became days. We took turns at the library screen; if the bubble hadn't had an extension I don't think we would have survived. Every twenty-four hours one of us went out to see if there were dangerous masses around, to drop back to normal space to take a fix and adjust our course. The few hours before each turn, we didn't talk at all; because during these times, one of us would be tense enough to bite.

On my third trip I had no more sense than to look up.

I went more than blind. There was nothing at all in my field of vision, nothing but the Blind Spot.

It was more than blindness. A blind man, a man whose eyes have lost their function, at least remembers what things looked like. A man who has suffered damage to the optic lobe of his brain doesn't. I could remember what I'd come out here for—to find out if there were masses near enough to harm us—but I couldn't remember how to do it. I touched a curved smooth surface and knew that this was the device that would tell me, if only I could guess its secret.

Eventually my neck got sore, so I moved my head. That brought my eyes back into existence.

When we got the bubble pressurized, Elephant said, "Where were you? You've been gone half an hour."

"And lucky at that. When you go out there, just don't look up."

"Oh."

Why the blazes couldn't we find something to talk about? Was it because we'd end up talking about Swoosh? Maybe. The planet had defeated us without ever noticing us. We'd named it, approached it and gone. Two mosquitoes that the mystery world hadn't even had to swat.

We'd left at my insistence.

One day I braced him with it.

"Elephant, there's a word missing from our language."

He looked up from the reading screen. "More than one," he said. "Things have been somewhat silent."

"One word. We're so afraid of using it that we're afraid to talk at all."

"Name it."

"Coward."

Elephant wrinkled his brows, then snapped off the screen. "Okay, we'll talk about it. First of all, you said it, I didn't. Right?"

"Right. Have you been thinking it?"

"No. I've been thinking euphemisms, like 'overcautious' and 'reluctance to risk bodily harm.' But since we're on the subject, why were you so eager to turn back?"

"I was scared." I let the word soak through his brain. "The people who trained me made certain I'd be scared in certain situations. With all due respect, Elephant, I've had more training than you have. I think your wanting to land was the result of ignorance."

Elephant sighed. "You're sure about that?"

"Certainly not. I get less sure every day. Maybe I was bluffed out. Maybe we'd have landed in perfect safety, stepped out, found a good, reasonable answer to these eleven notes here, got back in, took off and arrived at Jinx twelve hours later than we will."

"Maybe. We won't find out here, will we?"

We wouldn't. One of us was right, one wrong. If I was wrong, a pretty good friendship had just gone out the airlock.

I hated that. I wasn't even sure Sharrol wouldn't side with Elephant. And if Sharrol decided I was a coward—

She'd only known me four days.

Was I a coward? I'm no born hero and never claimed to be. This was the first time in my life it had worried me. At times during that trip I actually thought about turning back; and then I'd catch a few minutes of Blind Spot when my turn came around, and I'd go back to just hoping we'd reach Jinx.

We came out of hyperspace near the twin Sirius suns. But that wasn't the end; we still faced a universe moving at point eight lights. It took us almost two weeks to brake down to a normal velocity. The gravity drag's radiator fin glowed orange-white most of the time. I can't guess how many times we circled back through hyperspace for another run through the system's lumpy gravity well.

But at last we were orbiting Jinx.

I broke a silence of hours. "What now, Elephant? You're going back, aren't you?"

"As soon as we get in range, I'm going to call that number of yours."

"Then?"

"Drop you off at Sirius Mater with enough money to get you home. I'd take it kindly if you'd use my house as your own until I come back from Swoosh. I'll get a ship here."

"You don't want me along?"

"I'm going to land, Bay. Wouldn't you feel like a damn fool if you died then?"

"I've spent three months in an extension bubble because of that silly planet. I've made an epic journey through hyperspace with no hull. If you conquer it alone I *will* feel like a damn fool."

Elephant looked excruciatingly unhappy. He started to speak, caught his breath—

If ever I picked the right time to shut a man up, that was the time.

"Hold it. Let's call the puppeteers first. Plenty of time to decide."

Elephant nodded. In a moment he'd have told me he didn't want me along because I was overly reluctant to risk bodily harm. Instead, he turned on the ship phone and dialed.

Jinx was a banded Easter egg below us. To the side was bloated orange Binary, the primary to which Jinx is a moon. We were close enough to talk to Jinx . . . and the puppeteers' transfer booth number would also be their phone number.

Elephant dialed.

A sweet, thrilling contralto voice answered. There was no picture, but I could tell: no woman's voice is quite that good. The puppeteer said, "89346770?"

"My General Products hull just failed." Elephant was getting right to the point.

"I beg your pardon?"

"My name is Gregory Pelton. Twelve years ago I bought a #2 hull from General Products. A month and a half ago, the hull failed. It turned to dust. We've spent the intervening time limping home. May I speak to a puppeteer?"

The screen came on. Two brainless triangular heads looked out at us with one eye each. "This is quite serious," said the puppeteer, looking nothing but silly. With those floppy prehensile lips a puppeteer always looks silly. "Naturally we will pay the indemnity in full. Is that Beowulf Shaeffer?"

"Yes," I said, "but let's take care of this first. Then I'll find out what you wanted to see me about."

"By all means. Gregory Pelton, would you mind detailing the circumstances under which your hull disintegrated?"

Gregory Pelton didn't mind at all. He was quite vehement about it. His ears and neck turned dark red; his thrusting beard seemed to acquire a life of its own. It was a pleasure to listen to him. The diffidence he'd shown the Outsiders was gone; he was treating the puppeteer like a clumsy engineer in his own factory. The alien's silly expressions never wavered, but he was blinking rapidly when Elephant finished.

"I see," he said. "Our apologies are insufficient, of course, but you will understand that we made a natural mistake. We did not think that antimatter was available anywhere in the galaxy, let alone in known space, and in such quantity."

Elephant's bull voice went curiously soft. "Antimatter? Did you say antimatter?"

It was as if he'd screamed the word. I heard it echoing from side to side across my skull.

"Of course. We offer no excuse, but you should have realized it at once. Interstellar gas of normal matter had polished the planet's surface with minuscule explosions and torn away its lithosphere down to the magma, had raised the temperature of the protosun beyond rational expectation, and was causing a truly remarkable radiation hazard. It had swept the protosun's normal collection of gas and dust completely away. Did you not even wonder about these things? You knew that the system was from beyond the galaxy. Humans are supposed to be curious, are they not?"

"The hull," said Elephant.

"Yes. You are entitled to know. A General Products hull is an artificially generated molecule whose interatomic bonds are artifically strengthened by a small power source. The strengthened bonds are proof against any kind of impact, and against heat into the millions of degrees. But when enough atoms had been removed from the molecule by antimatter collisons, the molecule naturally broke down."

Elephant nodded. I wondered if his voice was gone for good.

"When may we expect you to collect your indemnity? I gather no human was killed. This is fortunate. Our funds are low."

Elephant switched off the phone. He gulped once or twice, then started to look me in the eye. I think it took all his strength; and if I'd waited for him to speak, I don't know what he would have said.

"I gloat," I said. I hate sticky scenes. "Verily I gloat. I was right, you were wrong. If we'd landed on your forsaken planet we'd have gone up in pure light. At this time it gives me great pleasure to say, I Told You So."

He smiled weakly. "You told me so. Antimatter."

"Oh, I did, I did. Time after time I said, That Planet's Haunted! It Will Steal Your Life And Soul, I said. There Have Been Signs in the Heavens to—"

"All right, you bastard, don't overdo it. I owe you twice my life plus a million stars, and not a penny more."

"Okay, we'll drop it. But there's one thing I want you to remember."

"If I don't understand it, it's dangerous."

"That's the one thing I want you to remember besides I Told You So."

Half of Elephant's house was buried in the face of Elephant's cliff. The other half projected into space. Without apparent support. A wide balcony ran round that exposed part, also without apparent support, and without a guard rail. The guardian force field at the edge was naturally invisible.

Elephant was somewhere else, off on his own business. He had missed a pretty good dinner.

Sharrol poured us three after-dinner drinks from a

squat green bottle. It was labeled with typical flatlander verbosity: *Rothschild Extra Fine Brandy Napoleon 2680.* The fluid was clear, with a brown tinge.

"One last question," said Dianna. "What did the puppeteers want with you?"

"They wanted me to explore the Clouds of Magellan for them. I turned them down."

The girls stared at me, then at each other. I was a convicted liar. Unfair! I'd told at least half the truth, and the rest was a puppeteer secret. They'd paid me a small "consultant's fee" to make it a privileged communication. I shrugged it off and gulped at my after-dinner drink.

I was trying to cough it out of my windpipe when Elephant breezed in. "The ship's ready!" he shouted from the vestibule. "We take off in a week! What's the trouble, Bay?" By then he was on the balcony.

I got my breathing under control. "Week? Take off? Ship?"

"Didn't I mention any of this? Gronk. I guess I didn't. Bay, I want to go back to the protosun. I've got a GP 2 hull covered a foot deep in foam plastic. There's a foot of glass over the windows; we can ditch that if it frosts up. We'll build up speed with an oversized gravity drag. Want to come along?"

The thing he was carrying was four feet long, metal, covered with rolled cloth which was slightly lumpy. I recognized it as a vacuum flag, with spring wires in it, designed to look as if it's waving where there's no wind.

He must have read my expression correctly. "No, idiot, I'm not going to land. What do you take me for? There's a solid rocket in the mast. I want to plant it on *Swoosh* from a distance. It should make quite a flash, don't you agree?"

"You want me to go along?"

"Sure."

"The ship sounds safe enough. We've got a week?"

"Just about. There's provisioning."

"I'll let you know in plenty of time."

We take off tomorrow. I've got a tridie camera bolted solidly to the control board, and a contract with the biggest broadcasting company in known space. They'll have exclusive rights on the first macroscopic antimatter explosion ever recoded. *This* time I've got a reason for going.

THE CRIME AND THE GLORY OF COMMANDER SUZDAL

Cordwainer Smith

THE BEGINNING

COMMANDER SUZDAL was sent forth in a shell-ship to explore the outermost reaches of our galaxy. His ship was called a cruiser, but he was the only man in it. He was equipped with hypnotics and cubes to provide him the semblance of company, a large crowd of friendly people who could be convoked out of his own hallucinations.

The Instrumentality even offered him some choice in his imaginary companions, each of whom was embodied in a small ceramic cube containing the brain of a small animal but imprinted with the personality of an actual human being.

Suzdal, a short, stocky man with a jolly smile, was blunt about his needs:

"Give me two good security officers. I can manage the ship, but if I'm going into the unknown, I'll need help in meeting the strange problems which might show up."

The loading official smiled at him. "I never heard of a cruiser commander who *asked* for security officers. Most people regard them as an utter nuisance."

"That's all right," said Suzdal. "I don't."

"Don't you want some chess players?"

"I can play chess," said Suzdal, "all I want to, using the spare computers. All I have to do is set the power down and they start losing. On full power, they always beat me."

The official then gave Suzdal an odd look. He did not exactly leer, but his expression became both intimate and a little unpleasant. "What about other companions?" he asked, with a funny little edge to his voice.

"I've got books," said Suzdal, "a couple of thousand. I'm going to be gone only a couple of years Earth time."

"Local-subjective, it might be several thousand years," said the official, "though all the time will wind back up again as you re-approach Earth. And I wasn't talking about books," he repeated, with the same funny, prying lilt to his voice.

Suzdal shook his head with momentary worry, ran his hand through his sandy hair. His blue eys were forthright and he looked straightforwardly into the official's eyes. "What do you mean, then, if not books? Navigators? I've got them, not to mention the turtle-men. They're good company, if you just talk to them slowly enough and then give them plenty of time to answer. Don't forget, I've been out before. . . ."

The official spat out his offer: "Dancing girls. WOMEN. Concubines. Don't you want any of those? We could even cube your own wife for you and print her mind on a cube for you. That way she could be with you every week that you were awake."

Sudzal looked as though he would spit on the floor in sheer disgust. "Alice? You mean, you want me to travel around with a ghost of her? How would the real Alice feel when I came back? Don't tell me that you're going to put my wife on a mousebrain. You're just offering me delirium. I've got to keep my wits out there with space and time rolling in big waves around me. I'm going to be crazy enough, just as it is. Don't forget, I've been out there before. Getting back to a real Alice is going to be one of my biggest reality factors. It will help me to get home." At this point, Suzdal's own voice took on the note of intimate inquiry, as he added, "Don't tell me that a lot of cruiser commanders ask to go flying around with imaginary wives. That would be pretty nasty, in my opinion. Do many of them do it?"

"We're here to get you loaded on board ship, not to discuss what other officers do or do not do. Sometimes we think it good to have a female companion on the ship with the commander, even if she is imaginary. If you ever found anything among the stars which took on female form, you'd be mighty vulnerable to it."

"Females, among the stars? Bosh!" said Suzdal.

"Strange things have happened," said the official.

"Not that," said Suzdal. "Pain, craziness, distortion, panic without end, a craze for food—yes, those I can look for and face. They will be there. But females, no. There aren't any. I love my wife. I won't make females up out of my own mind. After all, I'll have the turtle-people aboard, and they will be bringing up their young. I'll have plenty of family life to watch and to take part in. I can even give Christmas parties for the young ones."

"What kind of parties are those?" asked the official.

"Just a funny little ancient ritual that I heard about from an Outer Pilot. You give all the young things presents, once every local-subjective year."

"It sounds nice," said the official, his voice growing tired and final. "You still refuse to have a cube-woman on board. You wouldn't have to activate her unless you really needed her."

"You haven't flown, yourself, have you?" asked Suzdal.

It was the official's turn to flush. "No," he said, flatly.

"Anything that's in that ship, I'm going to think about. I'm a cheerful sort of man, and very friendly. Let me just get along with my turtle-people. They're not lively, but they are considerate and restful. Two thousand more years, local-subjective, is a lot of time. Don't give me additional decisions to make. It's work enough, running the ship. Just leave me along with my turtle-people. I've gotten along with them before."

"You, Suzdal, are the commander," said the loading official. "We'll do as you say."

"Fine," smiled Suzdal. "You may get a lot of queer types on this run, but I'm not one of them."

The two men smiled agreement at one another and the loading of the ship was completed.

The ship itself was managed by turtle-men, who aged very slowly so that while Suzdal coursed the outer rim of the galaxy and let the thousands of years—local count—go past while he slept in his frozen bed, the turtle-men rose generation by generation, trained their young to work the ship, taught the stories of the earth that they would never see again, and read the computers correctly, to awaken Suzdal only when there was a need for human intervention and for human intelligence. Suzdal awakened from time to time, did his work and then went back. He felt that he had been gone from earth only a few months.

Months indeed! He had been gone more than a subjective ten-thousand years, when he met the siren capsule.

It looked like an ordinary distress capsule. The kind of

thing that was often shot through space to indicate some complication of the destiny of man among the stars. This capsule had apparently been flung across an immense distance, and from the capsule Suzdal got the story of Arachosia.

The story was false. The brains of a whole planet—the wild genius of a malevolent, unhappy race—had been dedicated to the problem of ensnaring and attracting a normal pilot from Old Earth. The story which the capsule sang conveyed the rich personality of a wonderful woman with a contralto voice. The story was true, in part. The appeals were real, in part. Suzdal listened to the story and it sank, like a wonderfully orchestrated piece of grand opera, right into the fibers of his brain. It would have been different if he had known the real story.

Everybody now knows the real story of Arachosia, the bitter terrible story of the planet which was a paradise, which turned into a hell. The story of how people got to be something different from people. The story of what happened way out there in the most dreadful place among the stars.

He would have fled if he knew the real story. He couldn't understand what we now know:

Mankind could not meet the terrible people of Arachosia without the people of Arachosia following them home and bringing to mankind a grief greater than grief, a craziness worse than mere insanity, a plague surpassing all imaginable plagues. The Arachosians had become *un*-people, and yet, in their innermost imprinting of their personalities, they remained people. They sang songs that exalted their own deformity and that praised themselves for what they had so horribly become, and yet, in their own songs, in their own ballads, the organ tones of the refrain rang out,

And I mourn Man!

They knew what they were and they hated themselves. Hating themselves they pursued mankind.

Perhaps they are still pursuing mankind.

The Instrumentality has by now taken good pains that the Arachosians will never find us again, has flung networks of deception out along the edge of the galaxy to make sure that those lost ruined people cannot find us.

The Instrumentality knows and guards our world and all the other worlds of mankind against the deformity which has become Arachosia. We want nothing to do with Arachosia. Let them hunt for us. They won't find us.

How could Suzdal know that?

This was the first time someone had met the Arachosians, and he met the Arachosians, and he met them only with a message in which an elfin voice sang the elfin song of ruin, using perfectly clear words in the old common tongue to tell a story so sad, so abominable, that mankind has not forgotten it yet. In its essence the story was very simple. This is what Suzdal heard, and what people have learned ever since then.

The Arachosians were settlers. Settlers could go out by sail-ship, trailing behind them the pods. That was the first way.

Or they could go out by planoform ship, ships piloted by skillful men, who went into space-two and came out again and found man.

Or for very long distances indeed, they could go out in the new combination. Individual pods packed into an enormous shell-ship, a gigantic version of Suzdal's own ship. The sleepers frozen, the machines waking, the ship fired to and beyond the speed of light, flung below space, coming out at random and homing on a suitable target. It was a gamble, but brave men took it. If no target was found, their machines might course space forever, while the bodies, protected by freezing as they were, spoiled bit by bit, and while the dim light of life went out in the individual frozen brains.

The shell-ships were the answers of mankind to an over-population, which neither the old planet Earth nor its daughter planets could quite respond to. The shell-ships took the bold, the reckless, the romantic, the willful, sometimes the criminals out among the stars. Mankind lost track of these ships, over and over again. The advance explorers, the organized Instrumentality, would stumble upon human beings, cities and cultures, high or low, tribes or families, where the shell-ships had gone on, far, far beyond the outermost limits of mankind where the instruments of search had found an earth-like planet, and the shellship, like some great dying insect, had dropped to the planet, awakened its people, broken open, and destroyed itself with its delivery of newly re-born men and women, to settle a world.

Arachosia looked like a good world to the men and women who came to it. Beautiful beaches, with cliffs like endless rivieras rising above. Two bright big moons in the sky, a sun not too far away. The machines had pre-tested the atmosphere and sampled the water, had already scattered the forms of old earth life into the atmosphere and in the seas so that as the people awakened they heard the singing of earth birds and they knew that earth fish had already been adapted to the oceans and flung in, there to multiply. It seemed a good life, a rich life. Things went well.

Things went very, very well for the Arachosians.

This is the truth.

This was, thus far, the story told by the capsule.

But here they diverged.

The capsule did not tell the dreadful, pitiable truth about Arachosia. It invented a set of plausible lies. The voice that came telepathically out of the capsule was that of a mature, warm happy female—some woman of early middle age with a superb speaking contralto.

Suzdal almost fancied that he talked to it, so real was the personality. How could he know that he was being beguiled, trapped?

It sounded right, *really* right.

"And then," said the voice, "the Arachosian sickness has been hitting us. Do not land. Stand off. Talk to us. Tell us about medicine. Our young die, without reason. Our farms are rich, and the wheat here is more golden than it was on earth, the plums more purple, the flowers whiter. Everything does well—except people.

"Our young die . . ." said the womanly voice, ending in a sob.

"Are there any symptoms?" thought Suzdal, and almost as though it had heard his question, the capsule went on.

"They die of nothing. Nothing which our medicine can test, nothing which our science can show. They die. Our population is dropping. People, do not forget us! Man, whoever you are, come quickly, come now, bring help! But for your own sake, do not land. Stand off-planet and view us through screens so that you can take word back to the Home of Man about the lost children of mankind among the strange and outermost stars!"

Strange, indeed!

The truth was far stranger, and very ugly indeed.

Suzdal was convinced of the truth of the message. He had been selected for the trip because he was good-natured, intelligent, and brave: this appeal touched all three of his qualities.

Later, much later, when he was arrested, Suzdal was asked, "Suzdal, you fool, why didn't you test the message? You've risked the safety of all the mankinds for a foolish appeal!"

"It wasn't foolish!" snapped Suzdal. "That distress capsule had a sad, wonderful womanly voice and the story checked out true."

"With whom?" said the investigator, flatly and dully.

Suzdal sounded weary and sad when he replied to the point. "It checked out with my books. With my knowledge." Reluctantly he added "And with my own judgment. . . ."

"Was your judgment good?" said the investigator.

"No," said Suzdal, and let the single word hang on the air as though it might be the last word he would ever speak.

But it was Suzdal himself who broke the silence when he added, "Before I set course and went to sleep, I activated my security officers in cubes and had them check the story. They got the real story of Arachosia, all right. They cross-ciphered it out of patterns in the distress capsule and they told me the whole real story very quickly, just as I was waking up."

"And what did you do?"

"I did what I did. I did that for which I expect to be punished. The Arachosians were already walking around the outside of my hull by then. They had caught my ship. They had caught me. How was I to know that the wonderful, sad story was true only for the first twenty full years that the woman told about. And she wasn't even a woman. Just a klopt. Only the first twenty years. . . ."

Things had gone well for the Arachosians for the first twenty years. Then came disaster, but it was not the tale told in the distress capsule.

They couldn't understand it. They didn't know why it had to happen to them. They didn't know why it waited twenty years, three months and four days. But their time came.

We think it must have been something in the radiation of their sun. Or perhaps a combination of that particular sun's radiation and the chemistry, which even the wise machines in the shell-ship had not fully analyzed, which reached out and was spread from within. The disaster hit. It was a simple one and utterly unstoppable.

They had doctors. They had hospitals. They even had a limited capacity for research.

But they could not research fast enough. Not enough to meet this disaster. It was simple, monstrous, enormous. *Femininity became carcinogenetic.*

Every woman on the planet began developing cancer at the same time, on her lips, in her breasts, in her groin, sometimes along the edge of her jaw, the edge of her lip, the tender portions of her body. The cancer had many forms, and yet it was always the same. There was something about the radiation which reached through, which reached into the human body, and which made a particular form of desoxycorticosterone turn into a subform—unknown on earth—of pregnandiol, which infallibly caused cancer. The advance was rapid.

The little baby girls began to die first. The women clung weeping to their fathers, their husbands. The mothers tried to say goodbye to their sons.

One of the doctors, herself, was a woman, a strong woman.

Remorselessly, she cut live tissue from her living body, put it under the microscope, took samples of her own urine, her blood, her spit, and she came up with the answer: *There is no answer.* And yet there was something better and worse than an answer.

If the sun of Aracnosia killed everything that was female, if the female fish floated upside down on the surface of the sea, if the female birds sang a shriller, wilder song as they died above the eggs that would never hatch, if the female animals grunted and growled in the lairs where they hid away with pain, female human beings did not have to accept death so tamely. The doctor's name was Astarte Kraus.

THE HUMAN FEMALE could do what the animal female could not. She could turn male. With the help of equipment from the ship, tremendous quantities of testosterone were manufactured, and every single girl and woman still surviving was turned into a man. Massive injections were administered to all of them. Their faces grew heavy, they all returned to growing a little bit, their chests flattened out, their muscles grew stronger, and in less than three months they were indeed men.

Some lower forms of life had survived because they were not polarized clearly enough to the forms of male and female, which depended on that particular organic chemistry for survival. With the fish gone, plants clotted the oceans, the birds were gone but the insects survived; dragonflies, butterflies, mutated versions of grasshoppers, beetles, and other insects swarmed over the planet. The men who had lost women worked side by side with the men who had been made out of the bodies of women.

When they knew each other, it was unutterably sad for them to meet. Husband and wife, both bearded, strong, quarrelsome, desperate and busy. The little boys somehow realizing that they would never grow up to have sweethearts, to have wives, to get married, to have daughters.

But what was a mere world to stop the driving brain and burning intellect of Dr. Astarte Kraus? She became the leader of her people, the men and the men-women. She drove them forward, she made them survive, she used cold brains on all of them.

(Perhaps, if she had been a sympathetic person, she would have let them die. But it was the nature of Dr. Kraus not to be sympathetic—just brilliant, remorseless, implacable against the universe, which had tried to destroy her.)

Before she died, Dr. Kraus had worked out a carefully programed genetic system. Little bits of the men's tissues could be implanted by a surgical routine in the abdomens, just outside the peritoneal wall, crowding a little bit against the intestines, an artifical womb and artificial chemistry and artificial insemination by radiation, by heat made it possible for men to bear boy children.

What was the use of having girl children if they all died? The people of Arachosia went on. The first generation lived through the tragedy, half insane with the grief and disappointment. They sent out message capsules and they knew that their messages would reach earth in 6 million years.

As new explorers, they had gambled on going further than other ships went. They had found a good world, but they were not quite sure where they were. Were they still within the familiar galaxy, or had they jumped beyond to one of the nearby galaxies? They couldn't quite tell. It was a part of the policy of old earth not to overequip the exploring parties for fear that some of them, making violent cultural change or becoming aggressive empires, might turn back on earth and destroy it. Earth always made sure that it had the advantages.

The third and fourth and fifth generations of Arachosians were still people. All of them were male. They had the human memory, they had human books, they knew the words "mama," "sister," "sweetheart" but they no longer really understood what these terms referred to.

The human body, which had taken four million years on earth to grow, has immense resources within it, resources greater than the brain, or the personality, or the hopes of the individual. And the bodies of the Arachosians decided things for them. Since the chemistry of femininity meant instant death, and since an occasional girl baby was born dead and buried casually, the bodies made the adjustment. The men of Arachosia became both men and women. They gave themselves the ugly nickname, "klopt." Since they did not have the rewards of family life, they became strutting cockerels, who mixed their love with murder, who blended their songs with duels, who sharpened their weapons and who earned the right to reproduce within a strange family system which no decent earth-man would find comprehensible.

But they did survive.

And the method of their survival was so sharp, so fierce, that it was indeed a difficult thing to understand.

In less than four hundred years the Arachosians had civilized into groups of fighting clans. They still had just one planet, around just one sun. They lived in just one place. They had a few spacecraft they had built themselves. Their science, their art and their music moved forward with strange lurches of inspired neurotic genius, because they lacked the fundamentals in the human personality itself, the balance of male and female, the family, the operations of love, of hope, of reproduction. They survived, but they themselves had become monsters and did not know it.

Out of their memory of old mankind they created a legend of old earth. Women in that memory were deformities, who should be killed. Misshapen beings, who should be erased. The family, as they recalled it, was filth and abomination, which they were resolved to wipe out if they should ever meet it.

They, themselves, were bearded homosexuals, with rouged lips, ornate earrings, fine heads of hair, and very few old men among them. They killed off their men before they became old; the things they could not get from love or relaxation or comfort, they purchased with battle and death. They made up songs proclaiming themselves to be the last of the old men and the first of the new, and they sang their hate to mankind when they should meet, and they sang "Woe is earth that we should find it," and yet something inside them made them add to almost every song a refrain which troubled even them,

And I mourn Man!

They mourned mankind and yet they plotted to attack all of humanity.

THE TRAP

SUZDAL HAD BEEN DECEIVED by the message capsule. He put himself back in the sleeping compartment and he directed the turtle-men to take the cruiser to Arachosia, wherever it might be. He did not do this crazily or wantonly. He did it as a matter of deliberate judgment. A judgment for which he was later heard, tried, judged fairly and then put to something worse than death.

He deserved it.

He sought for Arachosia without stopping to think of the most fundamental rule: How could he keep the Arachosians, singing monsters that they were, from following him home to the eventual ruin of Earth? Might not their condition be a disease which could be contagious, or might not their fierce society destroy the other societies of men and leave Earth and all of other men's worlds in ruin? He did not think of this, so he was heard, and tried and punished much later. We will come to that.

THE ARRIVAL

SUZDAL AWAKENED IN ORBIT off Arachosia. And he awakened knowing he had made a mistake. Strange ships clung to his shell-ship like evil barnacles from an unknown ocean, attached to a familiar water craft. He called to his turtle-men to press the controls and the controls did not work.

The outsiders, whoever they were, man or woman or beast or god, had enough technology to immobilize his ship. Suzdal immediately realized his mistake. Naturally, he thought of destroying himself and the ship, but he was afraid that if he destroyed himself and missed destroying the ship completely there was a chance that his cruiser, a late model with recent weapons would fall into the hands of whoever it was walking on the outer dome of his own cruiser. He could not afford the risk of mere individual suicide. He had to take a more drastic step. This was not time for obeying earth rules.

His security officer—a cube ghost wakened to human form—whispered the whole story to him in quick intelligent gasps:

"They are people, sir.

"More people than I am.

"I'm a ghost, an echo working out of a dead brain.

"These are real people, Commander Suzdal, but they are the worst people ever to get loose among the stars. You must destroy them, sir!"

"I can't," said Suzdal, still trying to come fully awake. "They're *people.*"

"Then you've got to beat them off. By any means, sir. By any means whatever. Save Earth. Stop them. Warn Earth."

"And I?" asked Suzdal, and was immediately sorry that he had asked the selfish, personal question.

"You will die or you will be punished," said the security officer sympathetically, "and I do not know which one will be worse."

"Now?"

"Right now. There is no time left for you. No time at all."

"But the rules . . . ?"

"You have already strayed far outside of rules."

There were rules, but Suzdal left them all behind.

Rules, rules for ordinary times, for ordinary places, for understandable dangers.

This was a nightmare cooked up by the flesh of man, motivated by the brains of man. Already his monitors were bringing him news of who these people were, these seeming maniacs, these men who had never known women, these boys who had grown to lust and battle, who had a family structure which the normal human brain could not accept, could not believe, could not tolerate. The things on the outside were people, and they weren't. The things on the outside had the human brain, the human imagination, and the human capacity for revenge, and yet Suzdal, a brave officer, was so frightened by the mere nature of them that he did not respond to their efforts to communicate.

He could feel the turtle-women among his crew aching with fright itself, as they realized who was pounding on their ship and who it was that sang through loud announcing machines that they wanted *in, in, in.*

Suzdal committed a crime. It is the pride of the Instrumentality that the Instrumentality allows its officers to commit crimes or mistakes or suicide. The Instrumentality does the things for mankind that a computer cannot do. The Instrumentality leaves the human brain, the human choice in action.

The Instrumentality passes dark knowledge to its staff, things not usually understood in the inhabited world, things prohibited to ordinary men and women because the officers of the Instrumentality, the captains and the sub-chiefs and the chiefs, must know their jobs. If they do not, all mankind might perish.

Suzdal reached into his arsenal. He knew what he was doing. The larger moon of Arachosia was habitable. He could see that there were earth plants already on it, and earth insects. His monitors showed him that the Arachosian men-women had not bothered to settle on the planet.

He threw an agonized inquiry at his computers and cried out:

"Read me the age it's in!"

The machine sang back, "More than thirty million years."

Suzdal had strange resources. He had twins or quadruplets of almost every earth animal. The earth animals were carried in tiny capsules no larger than a medicine capsule and they consisted of the sperm and the ovum of the higher animals, ready to be matched for sowing, ready to be imprinted; he also had small life-bombs which could surround any form of life with at least a chance of survival.

He went to the bank and he got cats, eight pairs, sixteen earth cats, *felis domesticus,* the kind of cat that you and I know, the kind of cat which is bred, sometimes for telepathic uses, sometimes to go along on the ships and serve as auxiliary weapons when the minds of the pinlighters direct the cats to fight off dangers.

He coded these cats. He coded them with messages just as monstrous as the messages which had made the men-women of Arachosia into monsters. This is what he coded:

Do not breed true.
Invent new chemistry.
You will serve man.
Become civilized.
Learn speech.
You will serve man.
When man calls you will serve man.
Go back and come forth.
Serve man.

These instructions were no mere verbal instructions. They were imprints on the actual molecular structure of the animals. They were charges in the genetic and biological coding which went with these cats. And then Suzdal committed his offense against the laws of mankind. He had a chronopathic device on board the ship. A time distorter, usually to be used for a moment or a second or two to bring the ship away from utter destruction.

The men-women of Arachosia were already cutting through the hull.

He could hear their high, hooting voices screaming delirious pleasure at one another as they regarded him as the first of their promised enemies that they had ever met, the first of the monsters from old earth who had finally overtaken them. The true, evil people on whom they, the men-women of Arachosia would be revenged.

Suzdal remained calm. He coded the genetic cats. He loaded them into life-bombs. He adjusted the controls of his chronopathic machine illegally, so that instead of reaching one second for a ship of 80,000 tons, they reached two million years for a load of less than four kilos. He flung the cats into the nameless moon of Arachosia.

And he flung them back in time.

And he knew he did not have to wait.

He didn't.

THE CATLAND SUZDAL MADE

THE CATS CAME. Their ships glittered in the naked sky above Arachosia. Their little combat craft attacked. The cats who had not existed a moment before, but who had then had two million years in which to follow a destiny printed right into their brains, printed down their spinal cords, etched into the chemistry of their bodies and personalities. The cats had turned into people of a kind, with speech, intelligence, hope, and a mission. Their mission was to attack Suzdal, to rescue him, to obey him, and to damage Arachosia.

The cat ships screamed their battle warnings.

"This is the day of the year of the promised age. And *now come cats!*"

The Arachosians had waited for battle for 4,000 years and now they got it. The cats attacked them. Two of the cat craft recognized Suzdal, and the cats reported,

"Oh Lord, oh God, oh Maker of all things, oh Commander of Time, oh Beginner of Life, we have waited since Everything began to serve You, to serve Your Name, to obey Your Glory! May we live for You, may we die for You. We are Your people."

Suzdal cried and threw his message to all the cats.

"Harry the klopts but don't kill them all!"

He repeated "Harry them and stop them until I escape." He flung his cruiser into non-space and escaped.

Neither cat nor Arachosian followed him.

And that's the story, but the tragedy is that Suzdal got back. And the Arachosians are still there and the cats are still there. Perhaps the Instrumentality knows where they are, perhaps the Instrumentality does not. Mankind does not really want to find out. It is against all law to bring up a form of life superior to man. Perhaps the cats are. Perhaps somebody knows whether the Arachosians won and killed the cats and added the cat science to their own and are now looking for us somewhere, probing like blind men through the stars for us true human beings to meet, to hate, to kill. Or perhaps the cats won.

Perhaps the cats are imprinted by a strange mission, by weird hopes of serving men they don't recognize. Perhaps they think we are all Arachosians and should be saved only for some particular cruiser commander, whom they will never see again. They won't see Suzdal, because we know what happened to him.

THE TRIAL OF SUZDAL

SUZDAL WAS BROUGHT TO trial on a great stage in the open world. His trial was recorded. He had gone in when he should not have gone in. He had searched for the Arachosians without waiting and asking for advice and reinforcements. What business was it of his to relieve a distress ages old? What business indeed?

And then the cats. We had the records of the ship to show that something came out of that moon. Spacecraft, things with voices, things that could communicate with the human brain. We're not even sure, since they transmitted directly into the receiver computers, that they spoke an earth language. Perhaps they did it with some sort of direct telepathy. But the crime was, *Suzdal had succeeded.*

By throwing the cats back two million years, by coding them to survive, coding them to develop civilization, coding them to come to his rescue, he had created a whole new world in less than one second of objective time.

His chronopathic device had flung the little life-bombs back to the wet earth of the big moon over Arachosia and in less time than it takes to record this, the bombs came back in the form of a fleet built by a race, an earth race, though of cat origin, two million years old.

The court stripped Suzdal of his name and said, "You will not be named Suzdal any longer."

The court stripped Suzdal of his rank.

"You will not be a commander of this or of any other navy, neither imperial nor of the Instrumentality."

The court stripped Suzdal of his life. "You will not live longer, former Commander, and former Suzdal."

And then the court stripped Suzdal of death.

"You will go to the planet Shayol, the place of uttermost shame from which no one ever returns. You will go there with the contempt and hatred of mankind. We will not punish you. We do not wish to know about you any more. You will live on, but for us you will have ceased to exist."

That's the story. It's a sad, wonderful story. The Instrumentality tries to cheer up all the different kinds of mankind by telling them it isn't true, it's just a ballad.

Perhaps the records do exist. Perhaps somewhere the crazy klopts of Arachosia breed their boyish young, deliver their babies, always by Caesarean, feed them always by bottle, generations of men who have known fathers and who have no idea of what the word *mother* might be. And perhaps the Arachosians spend their crazy lives in endless battle with intelligent cats who are serving a mankind that may never come back.

That's the story.

Furthermore, it isn't true.

OVERPROOF

Johnathan Blake Mackenzie

THE PHOTOGRAPHS WERE SHOCKING—and more than shocking.

To any average human mind, they were nauseating, vile, disgusting, and obscene.

"They make my stomach turn to look at them!" Mrs. Dennis Barlow had said when she had handed the envelope to Dr. Paul Hiroa.

Dr. Hiroa had taken the envelope and slid out the pictures. He was well past the sesquicentennial mark, which made him an "old" man, even by the best of geriatric standards, and he had seen and done many things that probably would have shocked Mrs. Dennis Barlow, so his reaction to the photographs was quite mild by comparison. Nonetheless, he had to admit to himself that they were not the sort of thing one would hang in one's living room.

There were eleven of them, no two alike, and yet all of a pattern. They were ordinary color photographs, taken with a fine-detail lens and printed on nine-by-twelve sheets. They were flats, which made them all the more horrible, since tri-di prints tended to make the subjects of a picture look like little dolls, removing much of the sense of reality that a photograph should evoke.

Dr. Hiroa paused at the fifth picture, knowing that the eyes of both Mrs. Dennis Barlow and her husband were fixed firmly on him.

It was the husband, Dr. Barlow, who spoke. "That's the one that hit me, too, Dr. Hiroa. The rest of them I could take, but a girl like that . . ."

"And that horrible monster!" Mrs. Barlow chimed in.

The "horrible monster" was bad enough to the untutored eye, Dr. Hiroa had to admit. The body was vaguely feline in shape, with legs that might have been a blend of panther and frog. The head might have been part tiger, part shark—although there were only four sharp, tearing teeth; the rest were grinding molars, showing that the creature was omnivorous. The eyes were large, saucerlike, and heavy-lidded.

Instead of shoulders, the thing had a collarlike structure that sprouted eight thick, muscular tentacles.

But that was not the real horror.

The real horror lay in what the tentacles were doing.

The female was hanging by her ankles, which were tied together, from a hook on an overhead beam. She was naked.

In fact, she was far too naked to arouse any emotion other than shock in any sane human male.

She had no skin, and the instruments in the tentacles were flaying knives.

Dr. Hiroa said nothing, but went on to look at the remaining photographs. Like the first five, they were similar scenes in some grim abattoir.

When he had finished, Dr. Hiroa put the photographs flat on his desk, face up, and looked first at Dr. Dennis Barlow and then at his wife, Blanche. Barlow was thirty-eight and rugged-faced—not exactly handsome, but certainly masculine enough to be attractive to most women. Blanche Barlow was six years younger, with gold-blond hair, a magnificent figure, and a strikingly beautiful face. She might easily have passed for twenty-four.

Before he could say anything, the woman spoke. "Were you aware that this sort of thing is going on here on Sandaroth? Had you been informed that this slaughter of human beings was taking place, Dr. Hiroa?"

Dr. Hiroa frowned. "If there has been any killing of human beings by the Darotha, I am certainly not aware of it," he said carefully. "Certainly no deaths of that kind have been reported. There are only some three-quarters of a million human beings on the whole planet, and wholesale slaughter of human beings would certainly have come to light long before now."

"Are you implying that those photographs have been . . . er . . . manufactured? Falsified?" she asked.

Hiroa kept an incipient smile from breaking forth on his lips. He knew that the Barlows had not come two hundred light-years on their investigation simply on the strength of photographs that might have been faked. The woman was trying to see if senile, stupid, feeble old Doc Hiroa would think he could lie his way out of a jam.

Instead of smiling, he raised an eyebrow. "Falsified? Why, no, Mrs. Barlow. Why should they be?"

"You just said that you knew of no such slaughter going on," she pointed out dryly.

All right, madam, he thought to himself, *if you wish to play games, I'll go along with you.* He had been playing such games more than a century longer than she had.

He gestured toward the photographs. "You mean *that* slaughter? I said no such thing, madam. No such thing."

"You said that if any slaughter of human beings by the monstrous Darotha was taking place, it would have come to light long before now." Her blue eyes were angry.

"I believe you have misquoted me, madam," he said with just the right amount of stiffness in his voice. "I am quite certain that I never called the Darotha monstrous." Then his brown-black eyes bored steadily into hers. "And what has that to do with these photographs?"

Her eyes remained angry, and a whiteness appeared at the corners of her mouth. "I see," she said tightly. "You are denying human status to the natives of Sandaroth, then."

"To most of them, yes," Hiroa said. "There is a smallish insectoid creature with all the bad habits of a mosquito, which I would particularly claim to be inhuman."

"Dr. Hiroa!" she exploded suddenly, "don't bandy words with me! You know perfectly good and well what I mean!"

"Blanche——" her husband began.

But Hiroa interrupted him. "No, madam, I do *not* know what you mean! Natives? *What* natives? Very well, I won't bandy words with you any more, if you will stop throwing around undefined terms like 'natives'!"

"I won't be——"

"Blanche, shut up."

Dr. Dennis Barlow didn't speak loudly, but there was firmness and authority in his voice. His wife threw him an angry glance, but she shut up. Dennis Barlow wasn't looking at her, but at Dr. Hiroa.

"Dr. Hiroa, my wife and I have carefully studied the reports concerning the major life forms on this planet. Is it not true that the amphibious, tentacled Darotha have not only enslaved the native humanoids but butcher them and eat them?"

"Butcher and eat them, yes," Dr. Hiroa said calmly. "But enslave them? Hardly. It takes a certain amount of intelligence and a certain amount of tractability to become a slave. You might, by stretching the meaning a little, say that our ancestors enslaved the horse. But never the Bengal tiger or the wolf."

Barlow said: "You are not an anthropologist, Dr. Hiroa?" It was only phrased as a question, not meant as one.

"No," Hiroa said. "My field is political sociology. I'm here to make sure that the colony of *Homo sapiens terrestrialis* doesn't go hog-wild socially, as happened on Vangomar."

"Nor a biologist, either?" Barlow persisted.

"Nor a biologist, either," Hiroa agreed tiredly.

"Hm-m-m. According to the reports, you do not regard the native humanoids as being anything more than animals. The Darlington Foundation does not feel that you or anyone else here on Sandaroth is qualified to make such a judgment. I am a biologist—to be more specific, a zoologist. My wife is an anthropologist. We are both qualified and, if I may say so, well-known and respected in our fields. As you are in yours, of course. The Foundation has sent us here to check scientifically on the plight of the species which we have tentatively named *Homo sapiens sandarothorum*. We had thought to ask your aid, but apparently you, too, are convinced that they are just animals."

"My dear Dr. Barlow," Hiroa said evenly, "I will be perfectly happy to give you whatever aid you desire. Your papers are in order, your commission is explicit. To imply that I would fail to aid you simply because I disagree with your personal bias is to do me an injustice which borders on personal insult."

"I have no bias one way or the other," Barlow snapped. "Nor has my wife. We are here merely to see that justice is done."

"Exactly," he wife agreed. "No personal insult was intended at all, Dr. Hiroa. By the way, may I ask you a question?"

A personal question, of course. Hiroa thought. *That's the only kind that is prefaced by such a remark.* "I am never offended by an honest question," he said aloud, "unless you are offended by a truthful answer."

She ignored that. "You are a New Zealander, I believe, of Maori descent?"

"I am."

"Then I should think that you would have more compassion for the native humans, considering how your own ancestors were treated by the British in the eighteenth and nineteenth centuries."

"In the first place, Mrs. Barlow, my ancestors were never enslaved nor eaten by the British—though I do not deny the possibility that an ancestor or two of mine mightn't have enjoyed English long pig once in a while. In the second place, we won our right to recognition as human beings with human rights by our own ability to learn new ways and by our ability and valor in war. We forced recognition on the British; it was not handed to us on a silver platter by do-gooders. And in the third place, the Maori were human in the first place, if you'll pardon my use of an old wheeze to make a definite, valid point."

Blanche Barlow's lips tightened again, but she said nothing.

"Now," Dr. Hiroa went on, "I see no reason to continue with these arguments. They prove nothing one way or another. Instead of either of us arguing from personal feelings, we should be arguing from scientific facts. You two are here to uncover those facts. Rather than quarrel, let us set up your program. Let us discuss ways and means. Let us establish your needs to carry on this work."

It took him another ten minutes of diplomacy to get the scowls off their faces and replace them with friendly smiles, but he managed it. It took another two hours to make arrangements for the studies they wanted to conduct, but it was accomplished with only the slightest friction.

"He's not such a bad old boy," Dennis Barlow said as he and his wife walked down the hall from Dr. Hiroa's office.

"He is a bigot," Blanche said firmly. "But," she conceded, "I have met many bigots, and some of them are perfectly likeable and rational except in the field of their bigotry."

At the door of the elevator, Barlow tapped the "down" button No gravshafts here; old-fashioned electrics were as yet the best that Sandaroth could offer. The three-quarters of a million Earth colonists had only been on the planet for twenty-five years, although a small group of scientists had been on the planet for nearly thirty-five years before the colonists came. Building a viable colony on an alien planet takes time, money, and effort, and necessities rather than luxuries, basics rather than elaborations, are the primary considerations.

Dennis and Blanche Barlow waited patiently as the indicator crept up toward the figure "6."

When the door slid open and a tentacled horror stepped out, Blanche gave one little scream and fainted. Her husband barely had the presence of mind to grab her and huddle against the wall with her in his arms as the Daroth strode on by with pantherlike steps.

Dr. Hiroa looked up as the knob on his office door turned twice with forceful clatter and then was still.

"Come in and be welcome," he called, knowing that whoever was on the other side was a Daroth. Tentacles, being boneless, are not well adapted for door-knocking, so the Darotha, recognizing the terrestrial desire for privacy, which they themselves did not possess to any marked degree, had adopted their own convention for announcing their presence.

The knob turned again, and the being came in. "Ello, Dr. 'Iroa. I accept your 'ospitality." It was difficult for a Daroth to form a soft aspirate; it tended to come out gargled, like the *ch* in the German *ach*. Some Darotha pronounced it that way; others simply dropped it. It was a matter of taste on the part of the individual.

"Hello, Ghundruth! What brings you here? I thought you were going to be staying at Great Shoals for another hundred days."

"Some things came up, Doctor," Ghundruth said, making little circles with the tips of his foremost pair of tentacles. "I thought it best to discuss them with you. But first, I wish you to convey my apologies to your new people."

"Oh," said Hiroa. "You've met the Barlows."

"In the 'all, yes. Just as I came from the elevator Since they were obviously shocked and frightened, I affected not to notice them."

"I shall convey your apologies," Hiroa said, "although,

of course, such apologies are not at all necessary. It is an automatic reaction of those who are not prepared to meet a Daroth."

"Of course." Ghundruth agreed. "So our people react who 'ave never seen one of you before nor been informed of your existence. 'Ad these people, then, not been informed?"

"Not completely," Hiroa said. The statement, he reflected, was true as far as it went. "Their information was meager and unsatisfactory. My apologies to *you* for that oversight."

"It is as nothing," Ghundruth said, twirling a tentacle-tip. He kept the tips folded, as most Darotha habitually did when they were not being used for delicate work, make the tentacles look like those of an octopus. But, when the work at hand demanded it, each tentacle-tip opened out like a flower, splitting into five tentacular "fingers"—or, more accurately, "thumbs," since each was opposable to every other one. "But that brings a question to mind. I 'ave deduced that there must be a savage life form on your 'ome world w'ich resembles us in many respects. I am curious as to w'ether my deduction is correct."

"It is," Hiroa said carefully. He did not want to lie to Ghundruth. "It is purely an aquatic creature, rather than amphibious as you people are, but it has eight tentacles and is generally dreaded by our people. It is carnivorous, of course." He hesitated, then added: "It is called an octopus."

Ghundruth's shark-tiger mouth curled into a grin and a gurgling chuckle came from deep in his throat. "So *that* is w'y you call us 'Octopussies'!"

"Partly," Hiroa agreed. *Tread carefully now!* "But the word is a . . . what we call a 'portmanteau word' . . . that is, a word made up by blending two words. The other word is 'pussy,' which refers to a small, furry, warm-blooded creature with which some of our people live in a semi-symbiotic relationship."

Ghundruth looked interested. "Indeed? And w'at is the . . . the—mechanism?—trade . . . arrangement?—I do not feel I 'ave the right words."

"The mutual agreement," Hiroa said.

"Yes. W'at does each provide the other, if I do not offend by asking."

"Not at all. A man provides tenderness, security, shelter, and nourishment, while the pussy provides companionship, emotional warmth, and friendship. They are not, you must understand, of high intellectual capacity; their companionship is of a purely emotional character."

"Ah! I see. I thank you for your confidence." Then the tips of each of his two foretentacles split into five finger-length sections and he entwined them in the manner of a man folding his hands over his chest. It was a gesture signifying: "We have exchanged pleasantries; now I wish to speak of important business."

Hiroa lifted his hands and folded them at chest level in reply, indicating that business talk was agreeably in order. Inwardly, he felt a sense of relief. The Darotha had very little sense of physical privacy, but their sense of mental privacy was strong. It was not that they were not curious; their sense of curiosity was highly developed. But their culture forbade permitting that curiosity to invade the personal life of another. A Daroth could, would, and did pry into everything the physical world had to offer. Almost any intelligent adult Daroth could take a device he had never seen before—a mechanical wristwatch, for example—and disassemble it after a few minutes of study, then put it back together in working order. And if such a device was left around untended, a Daroth would proceed to take it apart and study it without asking permission, unless it was actually in use at the time.

Hiroa himself had once watched in faint awe while a Daroth had opened the first safe ever to arrive on Sandaroth, many years ago. It was of old-fashioned design; the newer, personally-attuned, saturated-field devices were too expensive for the economy of Sandaroth's human colony, besides being unnecessary. (The rigid psychological requirements for Sandaroth colonists had kept out those whose mental makeup inclined them away from honest labor and toward felony. The Darotha were the first intelligent extraterrestrial race that man had met, and Hiroa had insisted that Sandaroth be colonized by civilized men, not barbarians.) The safe had not been particularly designed to be burglar-proof; it was designed as a fireproof cache for records. Concrete and steel were still expensive, and most buildings were built of native woods.

Physically, the safe had been a three-foot cube with a door in one side and a simple combination lock set in the door. It was Hiroa's own, and still stood in his office, although the old wooden building had long since been replaced by the present ferroconcrete structure. But twenty years ago, Hiroa had felt that the safe was necessary.

The day after it had arrived, imported at great expense from Earth, a Daroth had come to see Hiroa, and the sociologist had been talking on the phone—still non-vision in those days. He had indicated that the being should wait and went on with his conversation.

The Daroth sat down to wait. (There had been no separate waiting room then, either.) His eyes wandered around the room. He watched Miss Deller, Hiroa's secretary and chief assistant, working assiduously at an electrotyper for a few minutes. Then, having absorbed all the information he could from watching the machine being operated, he turned his eyes to the safe beside her desk.

He looked at it for a long time, apparently fascinated. Miss Deller took a sheet from her typer and left the room. The Daroth rose and walked over to look at the electrotyper and saw that it was still on. "In use," then. Very well. He looked back at the safe. He knelt down to inspect it more closely. Then he looked up at Hiroa to see if he was being observed. Good! He was! He reached out a tentacle-tip and touched the steel structure, his eyes still on Hiroa. Hiroa watched, but went on talking.

The Daroth splayed out his five small tentacles, still watching Hiroa, and rippled them across the top of the safe. No reaction from Hiroa. The Daroth solemnly and slowly closed his eyes and then opened them again. It was the equivalent of a silent nod of thanks from a human being.

"Yes. Certainly, Charlie," Hiroa had said into the phone. "Yes. Bye." But when the click came from the other end, he did not cradle the phone. "Oh. Well, maybe," he said, not knowing how much English the Daroth understood. He wanted to see what the being was up to. He was glad he had so decided.

The Daroth touched and looked: Top, bottom, sides, and back. Then back to the safe door, where he felt around the fine crack between the body of the safe and the door itself. He tried the opening handle. Nothing happened. Then he touched the dial—very cautiously. He looked closely at the markings. He turned it slowly first one way, then the other. He had one tentacle on the handle, one on the knob of the dial, and another near the dial, its sensitive fingerlets touching the rim where the numbers were engraved. The other five tentacles were touching the safe at various other places, sensitive fingerlets attuned to whatever information they might bring. He looked, Hiroa thought, like a starfish opening an oyster, but instead of steady pressure he was using far more potent forces: observation and intelligence.

Hiroa went on making comments into the dead phone. "No, Charlie." "Sure." "If you think so."

Miss Deller returned and stopped just inside the door. She looked at the Daroth and then at Hiroa. Then, understanding and accepting the situation immediately, she went over to her desk and sat down as though nothing unusual at all were going on.

Hiroa had been glancing occasionally at the wall chronometer. When the Daroth finally pulled down on the handle and the safe door swung open, Hiroa looked quickly at the chronometer.

From the time he had started to turn the dial until the opening of the door, something over seventeen minutes had elapsed. In that time, the Daroth had ascertained that the structure was a container, that the handle opened it, and that the dial had to be manipulated in a certain way to release the mechanism that held the door shut. The sensitivity of his fingerlike end-tentacles had done the rest, telling him each time a tumbler fell.

It had been partly luck, of course, but the thinking required had far outweighed the luck.

The Daroth ignored the papers in the safe. He was inspecting the toggle-bolts and the sockets they slid into. Hiroa said: "Fine, Charlie. Good-by" And hung up

The Daroth looked up quickly, then rose to his feet. Without looking at the safe, he closed the door, spun the dial, and tested the handle while he said: "Thanks for chance to self-instruct."

"You are welcome. You wished to speak to me."

"Iess. Iess. Ioo are the *Ch*iroa?" The guttural aspirate was strong.

"Yes."

"I are . . . be? . . . is? . . . Ghundruth. I are . . . *am!* . . . I am *ch*erder of fish. I am told to speak to the *Chi*-roa."

In the twenty years that had passed since then, Ghundruth had lost most of his accent, but his basic personality had remained. Questions about mechanisms; about chemistry, electronics, and physics; about astronomy; about anything the physical world had to offer;—such questions were asked without hesitation. But never personal questions. And, like his fellow Darotha, he considered a question "personal" if it had anything to do with societal relationships; with emotional reactions; with the Earthmen's government, politics, aspirations, desires, intentions, methodology, or purpose; with anything, in fact, that might conceivably be considered subjective, instinctive, or cultural. If information of that sort was volunteered, it was listened to with care—but it was never, *never* asked for.

Hiroa felt it was a measure of the relationship he had with Ghundruth that that reservation had, to some extent, broken down between them in the past few years. Not often, and not without deep apologies, but occasionally, Ghundruth would ask such a question. Even then, his questions were never what the average Earthman would really call "personal."

On the other hand, the questions he had just asked *were*, in a way, personal. There were certain reactions and thought patterns of some human beings that Hiroa did not, as yet, want to reveal to the Darotha. He did not yet want them to know that the seven hundred and fifty thousand human colonists on Sandaroth were a carefully selected group, unlike the average stay-at-home Earthman, and even more unlike the average antisocial malcontent whose numbers formed the bulk of the colonists to the other Earthlike planets, where no alien intelligence had been found.

The Darotha, who were occasionally confronted with the emotional reactions of a few of the new colonists, were inclined to accept it as a non-personal reaction. The situation, they assumed, was analogous to their own reaction when Earthmen had first been seen among them. The Darotha had, individually and collectively, reacted with both fear and loathing when they first saw a human being.

Just so would a group of human beings have reacted if suddenly confronted by a rabid wolf. How long would it take a human being to recognize that, regardless of *appearance*, what at first appeared to be a wolf was, judging by his *behavior*, a rational being? On the average, Hiroa knew, it would take longer than it had taken the Darotha to see that human beings were not Ia*ch*us.

The word "Ia*ch*u" was of English derivation. The preliminary scientific expedition which had first seen the humanoid natives of Sandaroth had immediately dubbed them "Yahoos," thus giving Jonathan Swift another score to rank alongside his prediction of the two moons of Mars. After seeing them, the scientists had felt that the reaction of the Darotha upon seeing an Earthman for the first time was understandable and even justifiable. It was to the credit of the Darotha that they had seen and recognized the differences as well as the similarities between the two races which had been spawned separately on two planets so widely separated in space.

The Darotha were shrewd observers of behavior; they spent the first ten years of their lives as gill-equipped fish-like forms, rather like a small porpoise with tentacles, and one must learn to judge behavior in the sea. Long ago, skin divers in Earthly seas had learned to judge whether a given shark was dangerous or not by watching his behavior. Those who did not had a higher mortality rate than those who did. With the Darotha, that process had been going for millennia, and each individual Daroth had spent more time in the sea by his tenth birthday than a dozen terrestrial skin divers had spent collectively in their entire lives.

The environment of the sea differs qualitatively from the environment of the land. Only the very surface of the sea is troubled by weather; a few fathoms down, the sea is a womb, as far as the non-living environment is concerned. Hail, frost, snow, blistering heat, dehydration, and even the pull of gravity—all negligible or non-existent. Even earthquakes and volcanism, while not unknown, do not take the toll of life that they do on the surface. The dangers faced by marine life are those threatened by other life forms in the sea. On land, death by misadventure is far more prevalent than death by assassination with intent to ingest. In the sea, the reverse is true.

An intelligent marine life form, therefore, learns a different set of lessons than an intelligent land form. An amphibious form, such as the Darotha, has the advantage of learning both.

Little wonder, then, that Ghundruth had deduced the existence of a terrestrial species resembling the Darotha. Why else would an Earthman be startled, frightened by the sight of a Daroth?

Why? thought Hiroa. Simply that human beings used their imagination differently than Darotha did. The Darotha, exposed to dangers on both land and sea, exposed to the voraciousness of marine life and the inanimate, mindless, but nonetheless powerful and deadly natural forces on land, had to use their imaginations to deal with *real* possible dangers. Hiroa was not yet sure whether it was a genetic or a cultural trait—though he hoped it was the atter—but the fact remained that the Darotha were not much given to imaginative fiction—certainly not to the extent that Earthmen were.

Thus, Hiroa would have found it difficult to explain the Barlows' reaction if he had had to admit that, except for the tentacles, a Daroth did not resemble an octopus at all closely, and that the "pussy" part of the tag men had given Darotha was influenced by the end of the word "octopus," and referred, not to the common house cat, but to a resemblance to the greater feline carnivores.

So when he folded his hands to indicate that he was willing to speak of business with Ghundruth, he was happy that the Daroth had not inquired further into "personal" matters. He waited for Ghundruth to speak.

"Dr. 'Iroa," Ghundruth said, "a tragedy is 'appening on the Great Shoals. We do not know 'ow to deal with it."

"What sort of tragedy?" Hiroa asked, narrowing his eyes.

"Our last group of young are—going mad."

Blanche Barlow rubbed her eyes wearily. "Dennis, if I

have to sit through another tape I'll either go blind or crazy. I haven't made up my mind which."

Dr. Dennis Barlow chuckled. "I agree, honey, but we're getting a lot of the data we need." He riffled through a notebook which by now comprised over a hundred pages. "Getting this stuff correlated is going to be our big job."

He reached over to the playback and took out the spool of TV tape. "The next one is—"

"Please, Dennis! No more today! If I see another tape of those pitiful people living like animals . . . I . . . I'll cry. How can they *allow* it?"

Without comment, Barlow touched the cutoff switch, and the glow in the big, two-meter square TV screen they had been watching faded to a dead silver-gray.

"How *can* they *allow* it?" she repeated, her large blue eyes suddenly focused directly on her husband's face.

His wife's question was still rhetorical, Barlow knew, but he also knew she wanted some kind of answer.

"Don't get upset, honey," he said gently. "They've been living like that for tens of thousands of years now, I imagine. Another few months—" He was going to say: *won't hurt anything,* but, seeing the expression that was coming over her face, he rapidly shifted gears, and with hardly a pause finished: "—and we'll be able to change all that."

Before she could say anything, the door of the viewing room opened and a tall, broad-shouldered, dark-haired man with a pronounced widow's peak came in. Then he stopped.

"Oh, I'm sorry," he said. "I didn't realize the screen was in use." He spoke with a British accent that had been modified by years away from England.

"That's perfectly all right, Dr. Pendray," Dennis Barlow said with a smile. "We'd just finished."

Blanche Barlow, too, had allowed her incipient frown to be dissipated by a smile. "Yes, we're through for today, Doctor. Come right on in. Actually, we've taken up rather more time than we should have, I suppose."

"Not at all," Pendray said. "I'm really in no hurry. No urgency about it at all. Just wanted to look at a couple of dissection tapes. The nervous system of the Darotha tentacular complex is quite interesting. If you'd care to watch—" He left the sentence floating as an invitation.

"No, I don't think so; thank you," Blanche Barlow said. Then: "Tell me: how did you get Darotha bodies for dissection?"

The surgeon smiled. "You might say they were willed to us. The Darotha practice sea burial, but they're not dogmatic about it. They have no objections to our studies."

"Natural deaths, then?"

"Or accidental," Dr. Pendray said.

"Have you made dissections of the bodies of any of the humanoids?" the woman asked.

"Oh, yes. Several. I can show you the tapes on them, if you like. I see the ones you've been studying are those taken of them in their native habitat. Very good, aren't they? Some of them go back over fifty years. Hidden cameras, all automatic."

"How do you get the humanoid bodies you dissect? Are they willed to you, too?" Her voice was persistent.

Pendray chuckled. "Well, hardly. Most of them come from the Darotha at round-up time. A few have been shot. And several died in captivity. They don't last long in captivity, you know, so we don't capture them any more. Cruel, I think, to cage any wild beast that way when it simply pines away and dies. And the Yahoos won't breed in captivity, either." He paused, looking at her. "What's the matter, Mrs. Barlow?"

"Yahoos." Her voice was bitter. "All you have to do is put a degrading tag on someone, eh, Dr. Pendray? Call him 'nigger,' or 'chink,' or 'gook'; any nasty label that will take away his dignity! Call him a wild beast, an animal! Then it's all right to shoot him or butcher him or imprison him, isn't it, Dr. Pendray? No, thank you, Dr. Pendray; I do not believe I would like to look at your dissection tapes. Take me out of here, Dennis."

She turned angrily and strode toward the door, with Dennis Barlow following. She did not quite reach the door.

"Mrs. Barlow!"

She stopped, turned slightly, and looked over her shoulder at Pendray. "Yes?"

"You have seen the tapes of the Yahoos in their native

habitat, behaving in their accustomed manner?" His voice was calm on the surface, but there were crackling undercurrents.

"Yes."

"Mrs. Barlow, one cannot take from an organism that which it does not possess. One cannot take dignity from a Yahoo. One cannot even *give* dignity to a Yahoo. If you had learned anything from those tapes, you should have learned that. It would probably be a waste of your time, indeed, to study the dissection tapes, for you would likely learn nothing from *them,* either. Good day, Mrs. Barlow."

Dr. Dennis Barlow's face clouded, but before he could frame any answer, Blanche pulled his arm, and the two of them stalked out without another word.

Dr. Marcus Landau was in the tape stacks, replacing two spools which he had been viewing, when the Barlows came in. He saw them before they saw him.

Uh-oh! he thought to himself. *The Golden Fury is about to launch a billion-volt lightning bolt that will scorch the area for miles around, if that corona effect means anything. I wonder who or what turned her generator on?*

Dr. Landau was a middle-aged man in his early eighties. He had skin the color of burnished bittersweet chocolate, hair like tiny curls of fine, frosted silver wire, and a mellow voice that carried the soft accents of Bermuda. Along with Dr. Paul Hiroa and Dr. James Pendray, he was one of the three ranking scientists of Sandaroth. After observing Blanche Barlow for the first week of her stay, he had tentatively named her "The Golden Fury"; now, at the end of the second week, there was nothing tentative about it. He also had named Paul Hiroa "Old Rawhide" and Jim Pendray "Silk"—but only to himself, and only because it amused him to play mental games with himself. This game he called "Character Tag" and it had strict rules. No one got a tag until Dr. Landau was morally certain that all of the people who knew that person would instantly recognize the tag as fitting and accurate. Like Aristotle, however, he was satisfied with the results of his own cerebration; he never put them to experimental test.

He had not yet made up his mind about Dennis Barlow.

"Blanche," Barlow said in a low, tight voice, "that was uncalled for. You—" Suddenly he stopped and his voice became more normal. "Oh, hello, Dr. Landau."

Aha! Observed! And by a zoologist! "How do you do, Dr. Barlow, Mrs. Barlow," Landau said aloud. "How are your researches coming along? I trust our modest Research Center has supplied you with at least a modicum of pertinent data, eh?"

Evidently the thunderbolt had not been forged for Marcus Landau. She not only didn't unleash it, she put it aside—probably, he decided, for later use. But the coronal discharge that had seemed to crackle soundlessly around her head subsided and vanished.

"Oh, more than that, Dr. Landau," she said with a smile. "There is a fantastic amount of data here. Correlation and interpretation will be the difficult part, I'm afraid. By the way, when do you expect Dr. Hiroa to return from Great Shoals?"

"Why, I don't know. Neither, I'm afraid, does he. I spoke to him over the phone this morning, and he doesn't know how much longer his work will take. Again he asked me to convey his apologies for his precipitate departure so soon after your own arrival. If there is anything you may need or require, of course, you have but to ask."

"Thank you. We will be wanting to make field trips eventually, of course, but it will be some time before we can definitely map out precisely what our plans will be."

Landau bowed his silvery head just a few degrees. "Naturally. Is there anything I can do for you at the moment?"

The Barlows looked at each other. It was Dennis who spoke. "Not just at the moment, Dr. Landau; thanks. Everything's going smoothly so far."

"I am happy to hear it. I wish you every success in your search for truth."

He left them and headed for No. 2 viewing room. Dr. Pendray had not yet turned on the screen. "Busy, Jim?" Landau asked.

"Nothing urgent, Marc. Why?"

Landau came in and closed the door behind him. "I

was just wondering what you'd said to our emissaries from the Darlington Foundation that aroused their wrath," he said with a grin. "Especially hers."

"Oh, that." Pendray repeated the conversation.

"Diplomacy, thy name is Pendray," Landau murmured when he had finished.

"It won't matter a damn anyway," Pendray said with a shrug. "I have a feeling that she's already mentally writing her final report, complete with conclusions. In the back of her mind, she has already decided what she is going to tell the Foundation. Nothing you or I or anyone else could say will change it, and that husband of hers will go right along with her."

"You have no great faith in them as scientific investigators, eh, Jim?"

"Are you kidding? I've seen their kind before. They will gather vast reams of data, make all kinds of carefully tailored experiments, and prepare dozens of pretty little graphs and tables. They will discard the 'anomalies,' of course—any data that doesn't fit in with their preconceived notion. What's left will be neatly pushed and trimmed until it *does* fit. What does Paul think?"

"The same. What can we do about it? The Darlington Foundation will have the report they want. With that and those photographs, the stink they'll raise on Earth will be enough to wreck the whole Sandaroth project, ruining human and Daroth alike."

"One almost wishes," Pendray said, "that the Barlows fail to return from their projected field trip—except that that wouldn't do a bit of good."

"No. The stink that would arise would have a different aroma, but the results would be the same. It's not bad enough that we have this mysterious madness in the last group of Darotha adolescents; we have to have madness of our own race." He put his hand to his forehead and massaged his brows with thumb and middle finger.

"Who's behind it?" Pendray asked. "Do you have any further information?"

"Only what we guessed before. The only man who could have taken those pictures was Finnerly of Industrial Computer Corporation," Landau said. "But they're not the only ones."

"Who else? I thought you said you didn't have any more information."

"I don't. But think about it. ICC isn't trying to get troops sent here to 'protect' the Yahoos just so they can wind up selling us computers and guidance-and-control systems for a few multiphase lathes and shapers."

"You're right." There was anger in Pendray's voice. "Without the Darotha, this planet would be just like any other. Wide open. We'd have fifty million people here within five years. No control."

"No control," Landau agreed. "But plenty of new sales territory for certain unscrupulous lice. We know who *isn't* in on it, too. None of the Big Three in inertiogravitics; they're strictly honest and strictly ethical. The same goes for most of the big, important corporations. You can bet ICC isn't getting any backing from those boys. But there are others. Too many of them."

"It'll be a double play, then," Pendray said. "They'll hit us high and low. Protect the Noble Yahoos on the one hand and open Sandaroth up for full colonization on the other."

"The sound of two hands clapping," Landau said dryly.

"Yeah. While the only extraterrestrial intelligent race we have met gets crushed between them. We might as well pack up and go home."

"You don't have much faith in Paul's plan, then?"

"Frankly, Marc, no." Pendray admitted. "He seems to think that giving the Barlows all the data they can swallow will convince them. But, dammit, Marc, you can't convince a fanatic he's wrong by giving him data. He only believes what he wants to believe."

" 'My mind is made up; please don't confuse me with facts.' " Landau quoted.

"Exactly."

"But there's nothing else we can do, Jim," Landau said. "We can't fight the Darlington Foundation for the Promotion of Human Brotherhood. I doubt if even the Government could fight it. It's got billions behind it—both in money and in people. And it's full of people like the Barlows: honest, dedicated, hardworking fanatics."

"I know. I know." Pendray rubbed his chin with a fingertip. "What about Governor Donovan? What's he going to do?"

"Paul talked to him. He agreed to stay out of the whole mess. If worse comes to worst, and the planet is opened up, he can stay on as Colonial Governor and try to protect the Darotha as much as possible."

"That may help. But not much." Pendray suddenly twisted his mouth into a sardonic grin. "Maybe I'd have been better off if I hadn't come back from the field until this was all over, one way or another. At least one has other things to worry about out in the boondocks. I'm really not a city boy at heart."

Landau grinned back. "Obviously not, or you wouldn't call Point Garrison a city. We're still a village at heart. Forty thousand people could get lost without anyone noticing it in a real city."

"It contains half the human population of the planet," Pendray said. "No city on Earth can make that statement."

"Agreed. Oh, and Jim—"

"Yes?"

"I think we'll be better off if we don't antagonize the Barlows. It just—"

"Just stiffens their resistance. I know, Marc. I'll try to cultivate the 'friendly physician and counselor' attitude. The country doctor bit. But if she gets offended every time she hears the word Yahoo in that context, she's going to feel offended most of the time."

"Well, we can't wrap her in swaddling clothes. I'll let you go back to your tapes now. Thanks, Jim."

Very few of the citizens of Point Garrison were aware of the danger embodied in Blanche and Dennis Barlow. Their names had been mentioned in the newscasts when they arrived, but hardly anyone paid any attention. In certain circles, the word spread that they were studying the Yahoo, but that aroused no particular curiosity. Why should it? It was said by those who had met them that the Barlows—and especially Blanche Barlow—were "a little nutty" on the subject of Yahoos and Yahoo intelligence and most of these people learned to substitute the phrase "humanoid natives" for "Yahoos" in their presence. Except for that quirk, they seemed a pleasant enough couple. Women were attracted to the handsome, personable, Dennis, and men found it difficult to keep their eyes off Blanche's beauty. Even so, they were "foreigners"—visitors, not residents. Somehow, they did not fit well into the social life of Point Garrison. If the truth were known, that didn't bother the Barlows; they didn't even notice it. They were on Sandaroth to work, not to socialize.

At the end of the first month, Dennis decided he'd take a tour of one of the small factories in the city: Garrison Flyer Mfg. Co.

The manager of the plant was a short, round, sandy-haired Scot named Fred Doyle. He met Barlow at the front gate and gave him a hearty handshake.

"Glad to know you, Dr. Barlow! Governor Donovan called me. Said you wanted to look around. Glad to have you. Come in, come in."

After a few minutes of polite amenities, Dennis Barlow was asked where he'd like to start.

"Well, to be perfectly frank, Mr. Doyle—"

"Just call me Fred, Dr. Barlow. Everybody does."

"O.K. Fred. And I'm Dennis. At any rate, I was going to say that I had some free time today, so I thought I'd take a kind of busman's holiday. My wife is feeding stuff into the computer at the Research Institute, and it's a job that only takes one. Actually, I'm interested in your factory as a zoologist rather than from the actual manufacturing point of view."

"Well, if you'll tell me why a zoologist should be interested in the manufacture of inertiogravitic motors from a zoological point of view, I'll be glad to help you, Dennis."

"I understand you have some Darotha working for you, Fred, and I understand they can do jobs that no human being can do."

"Oh!" Fred chuckled. "Why, sure! Come along; I'll take you to the multiplex lathe section. That's the most interesting part, anyway. I'll introduce you to my foreman, Than; he'll be able to show you how these things work."

He led Dennis Barlow to a huge building full of machines. Everything was well-lit, airy, and clean. It seemed more like a kitchen or an operating room than a workshop. It took Barlow a minute or two to realize that, as far as he could see, he and Doyle were the only human beings in the place. All the machines were run by Darotha.

"Than!" Fred called to one of them who was wiping off a big machine with a piece of toweling. "C'mere a minute! I want you to meet a fellow."

The Daroth put the rag down and came toward the two men with panther-like grace. " 'Ow are you this morning, Fred?" His voice carried easily over the low, all-pervading hum of power that was the only noticeable noise in the place.

"Pretty good, Than; pretty good. I'd like you to meet Dr. Dennis Barlow. Dr. Barlow, this is Thannovosh, my general foreman for this section."

"Glad to know you, Dr. Barlow." Then he looked expectantly at Fred.

"Have you got one of the machines free, Than? I'd like you to give Dr. Barlow a little demonstration if you've got the time."

"Sure, Fred; glad to. Just come this way over to number fourteen, Dr. Barlow."

Barlow followed, but he was looking at the other machines in the building. There were about thirty of them, and at each stood a Daroth, all eight tentacles moving at once, turning various verniers, knobs, and control wheels. There was a weird, rhythmic beauty about it that reminded him of seaweed fronds moving in a slow current or the tentacles of a slowly swimming octopus.

At machine number fourteen, Than said: "I've got 'er all set up for a BJF-37, Fred. Will that be all right?"

"Sure. Fine. Show him your check-block, will you, and explain it to him."

From a drawer in the base of the machine, Than took an odd metal shape. It was about the size of a man's fist, but it was surfaced with weirdly undulating curves, complex three-dimensional curves that made queer hills and valleys and swirling grooves.

"This is w'at we call the check-block, Dr. Barlow. It's the same size and shape as the impulse spinner in an inertiogravitic unit. 'Ave you ever looked inside the engine of a flier?"

"Not with the casing off, no."

"Well, the impulse spinner 'as to undergo several different modes of motion at once—depending on w'ether you're moving up or down, right or left, pitching, yawing, rolling, or just 'overing. There are eight of them in an ordinary flier engine. They all move at tremendously 'igh velocities and undergo 'igh surges. And they all 'ave to be synchronized. This is made of 'ardened tool steel instead of Paramag alloy, but the shape is the same. Each one of these surfaces is a control surface for the various modes of motion and each performs a different function as the axis of spin is shifted. That's w'at makes it look so odd." Than chuckled. "It 'as a sort of a shapeless shape, you might say. But it 'as to be that way, and each curve 'as to be just so, or you'll get vibration that'll shake your engine apart."

Two tentacles put the block down. Two more indicated the machine itself. "Now this is w'at we call a multiplex lathe. An impulse spinner can't be cast; it 'as to be forged and machined. You 'ave to be sure it's 'omogeneous and of equal density throughout."

Two more tentacles reached out to a low, wheeled framework nearby and took a lump of metal out of a tray. Than held the lump up for Barlow's inspection. "This is the forged blank. All we 'ave to do is machine it, and this is 'ow it's done."

He fitted the check-block into the multiplex chuck to his left, and the forged blank into the chuck at his right. A guide rod touching the surface of the check-block was exactly matched with a borazon cutting tool that touched the forged blank. As the guide rod followed the curves of the check-block, the tool cut the same curves in the blank. A tentacle touched a switch and both pieces of metal began to spin. Then there was a sudden deadness in the air around the machine, as though someone had thrown a heavy blanket over it. "Got to 'ave the noise suppressors on," Than said, "otherwise this place would be a screaming 'ell."

Than spun two more wheels, and two more borazon tools moved toward the forged blank, each with its corresponding guide rod moving toward the check-block.

Then Than touched another switch and the dance of the tentacles began. There was a grace to it that reminded Barlow of the hand motions of a Hawaiian hula dancer. The tentacles moved knobs and levers, and the borazon tools, all three of them at once, bit smoothly into the spinning blank, slicing off ribbons of bright metal. Than touched the chuck control and the axis of spin changed slightly as the borazon chisels sliced away the unwanted metal. Again the axis of spin shifted, and the tools moved in and out over the blank, cutting, cutting.

Barlow watched in fascination as the impulse spinner took shape beneath the cutting edge of the borazon, transfiguring the lumpy-looking forged blank into a piece of precision machinery.

Then, abruptly, it was finished.

The tools fell away and the spinning stopped. Than released the chuck and took the finished piece out. "Now we'll take 'er over to the comparator and see 'ow she matches the master block." When he was done, he handed the new-formed impulse spinner to Barlow.

"There she is, Dr. Barlow. Correct to a thousandth of a millimeter. Next, she'll go in a similar machine for final polishing, and she'll be done."

"Beautiful," Barlow said in honest admiration.

"Thank you, sir. Was that all you wanted, Fred?"

"That's all. Thanks a lot, Than. Unless Dr. Barlow has some questions."

"The only question I can think of is: How did you do it? It's all I can do to control two arms and ten fingers. The thought of trying to control eight arms and forty fingers appalls me."

Than's shark-tiger face grinned widely. "Just takes practice, Dr. Barlow. And I'll tell you, I don't see 'ow you people do such delicate work with all those bones inside forcing you to bend only at certain places and in certain directions. I saw a man do a steel engraving by 'and once, and I'll never understand 'ow 'e did it. Putting pressure on a burin takes internal bracing w'ich I 'aven't got. It would be like running this machine with my feet, it seems to me."

Barlow glanced at the Daroth's sandaled feet. There were no toes, properly speaking. Each foot came to a point, reminding Barlow of the mail-shod feet of a medieval knight. At the tip was a single, heavy, curving claw.

"He keeps his feet folded in like that for walking on land," Fred said, noticing Barlow's glance. "Dr. Barlow's never met a Daroth before, Than. Show him how your feet unfold for swimming."

"Sure." With three tentacles, he braced himself lightly against the lathe. Two other tentacles pulled the sandal from his right foot. He lifted his leg up and doubled it at the knee, so that Barlow could see the "sole" of the foot. A crease ran from just forward of the heel to the base of the front claw. "W'en I'm in the water, I open out, like this."

The crease widened and the foot folded out, so that the two halves of what had been the sole were now on the upper side of a wide, splayed foot, making a ridge of callous on each side of the upper part. The new sole thus exposed looked membranous and tender.

"Then you can't walk with your feet unfolded that way?" Barlow asked.

"Oh, I could," Than said, refolding his foot and putting it back in the sandal. "But not for very far before my feet 'urt so bad I couldn't take it. That's on solid land, I mean. Walking through swamps, like the brackish swamps down around the Delta Cape, a fellow can unfold 'is feet for walking across thick mud so 'e doesn't sink in. But if the mud is that soft, it doesn't 'urt, you see."

"Very handy," said Barlow. "Or should I say, 'footy'?"

"Ooh!" said Fred, wincing.

Than chuckled. *"Nothing's* 'andy for a Daroth."

"Puns aside," Fred said, "a skilled and trained Daroth comes in handy for running a multiplex lathe. No Earthman could do it. Not even four Earthmen working together could do it. It's been tried. Not only is the coordination lousy, but they get in each other's way. Back on Earth, they use a computer that costs more than the lathe and is damn near as massive. We just bought the lathes and then designed and built the controls ourselves. That saved the cost of the computer and the high interstellar freight charges. It also saves the cost of repairs and of reprogramming the computer when you set up for a different size or type of impulse spinner We pay standard wages for all our employees, Earther or Daroth, so the labor costs run high, but you have to have a certain amount of labor anyway to set up and break down the check-blocks and tools and for maintenance and so on. Besides, the machines are a lot more flexible this way. To set up a computer to make just one piece would cost the same as setting it up for a full run, while a Daroth can interrupt a run, tear down, set up, run a single piece, tear down and set up again, and be back on the regular run in fifteen minutes at no extra cost.

"But the real beauty of the thing is that all the money that would go for freight charges and computer costs stays right here on Sandaroth where it's needed, instead of being funneled back to Earth."

"I'm very 'appy about w'at goes into *my* pocket," said Than, touching a tentacle to his blue work-shorts, the only article of clothing he wore besides the sandals.

Dennis Barlow suddenly realized the change that had come over him in the past twenty minutes or so. He had come in with a sense of horror that had seemed to ride between his shoulder blades. So many Darotha around had brought clearly to mind those terrible photographs. But now he was aware that he thought of Than, not as a tentacled horror, but as a person. Someone you could talk to, laugh with, maybe have a few beers with of an evening. The photos had become dim and lifeless in comparison to the reality that stood before him.

A chime sounded, clearly but not stridently audible over the low hum in the shop.

"Lunchtime," said Fred. "Will you stay and eat with us, Dennis?"

"No, thanks, Fred. Some other time. I appreciate everything, really. I've enjoyed myself tremendously. It was a pleasure meeting you, Than; I hope to see you again sometime."

"The same 'ere, Dr Barlow. Come again w'en you can stay longer. We can show you more."

"That's right," Fred said. "Come around again, early. and I'll show you through the whole plant. Lots of things here I think you might be interested in."

"I'll see if I can't work it in, Fred. But right now, I have a lunch date with a beautiful blonde. My wife."

"O.K. I'll walk you to the gate."

"Me for a *lurgh* sandwich and a cold drink," Than said. "See you again, Dr. Barlow." The Daroth loped off across the shop.

As the two men walked across the yard to the gate, Dennis said: "What was that Than said, Fred? A *lurg* sandwich?"

"Lurgh," Fred corrected. "You've got to sort of gargle that *g* sound."

"Lurghh. I see. What is it?"

"Smoked Yahoo meat. Don't care for it myself, but— Why, what's the matter, Dennis? You sick or something?"

Barlow fought down the wave of horror and nausea that had swept over him. "No," he said. "No. I'm O.K. Just the sun, I guess."

"Yeah. Coming out of that air-conditioned shop into this heat can do that sometimes. You sure you're O.K.?"

"Sure. Just a little wave of dizziness is all. It's gone now. I'm fine."

But he ate no lunch that day, and he did not tell Blanche why.

Dr. James Pendray sat at the controls of the little six-passenger flier and secretly wished he knew what the devil was going on in Paul Hiroa's mind. The old boy was up to something, of that Pendray was certain. But just what it was . . .

Well, whatever it was, Pendray was willing to go along with it. That wise old brain had cooked up some sort of plan, and just because it was Hiroa's plan, it was bound to be a sound one.

In the seat behind him, Dennis and Blanche Barlow were talking in low but not secretive tones, pointing out to each other the various interesting configurations of the terrain below. At a groundspeed of a little less than three hundred thirty kilometers per hour and an altitude of one kilometer, their viewpoint was just right for scenery-gazing.

"Is that the shoreline over there to the south, Jim?" Dennis asked from the back seat.

Pendray had been exercising his diplomacy of late, and the three of them were now on a first name basis.

"That's it. You won't be able to see it too well for a couple of hours yet. We're flying parallel to the sea. After that, it's only another hour to Great Shoals."

"And the humanoid territory is just north of there?" Blanche asked.

"That's right. Less than an hour's flight, even if we're unlucky. Usually, a tribe can be found within ninety kilometers of Grand Shoals."

"Good. We want to get there as quickly as possible."

Too flaming right she does, Pendray thought. The notion of going to the major city of the Darotha did not appeal to her at all. Pendray wasn't quite sure whether she loathed the Darotha, hated them, or feared them, but he suspected it was a blend of all three in various proportions depending on the circumstances.

"I meant to ask you, Jim," Dennis said, "if you know why the Darotha built their city at Great Shoals. I mean, we humans usually build a city near a river or lake or some other water supply, and on Earth the really big cities were near a shipping port. But the Darotha always stay near the sea, and they don't have much shipping, so why should they concentrate around Great Shoals? Just random chance, or is there a reason for it?"

"Didn't you know?" Pendray was actually surprised. "It's one of their major breeding areas."

"Breeding areas?"

"Sure. Great Shoals is an off-shore section of the continental shelf that is practically horizontal. There's nearly a hundred thousand square kilometers of the shelf where the maximum depth is only ten fathoms and the average is about five. It's full of little islands and rocks, sticking above the surface. The edge of the shelf is nearly two hundred kilometers off-shore, but a man could probably wade all the way out if he picked his route carefully. Mightn't even have to get his hair wet. It's just the opposite of an Earthly seaport. Lousy for ship navigation, but a great place for the kiddies."

"How does their reproduction cycle go, anyway?" Dennis asked.

Pendray wondered how a zoologist could have failed to ask that question long before this. Blanche, the anthropologist, wasn't the least bit interested, of course, but Dennis should have been curious from the first. But Blanche had evidently kept him so wrapped up in the Yahoos that he had no time for excursions into other alien life forms.

"Nothing complicated about it," Pendray said. "The Darotha, like man, make love at all seasons of the year, and, as in the human female, the Darotha female's fertility periods are cyclic. But the Darotha cycle is annual rather than monthly. The eggs are laid in the sea about six weeks after fertilization and they hatch about three months after that—about midsummer. At the end of the ninth year, the lungs begin to develop and the gills to disappear. By the spring of the tenth year, the young are ready to come ashore and continue life as air breathers. Like humans, they're ready to reproduce by the time they're fourteen or fifteen, and the cycle begins all over again."

"Um—what sort of family life do they have?" Blanche asked, interested in spite of herself.

"None, if by 'family' you mean blood relationship. The kids are literally on their own for the first ten years. Nobody knows whose is whose or care. The adults keep the big, dangerous predators away, and the females especially will go out and throw food to the little ones. The adults do a great deal of swimming, and they have a great time romping with the kids. The children may not know who their parents are, but they're very much loved. An adult couple will take care of as many of the youngsters as he can afford to, after they have achieved the air-breathing stage."

"If they don't know what the genetic relationships are," Blanche said, "how do they prevent incest?"

"They don't," Pendray told her. "Why should they? The statistical probability that any male and female picked at random will be brother and sister is very low. More often than not, an adult couple who have decided to mate permanently were brought up together in the same household since they were ten. They have no concept of virginity and no bans against premarital experimentation, either. A girl deposits a clutch of eggs every year after her fifteenth birthday; how does she know whether they're fertile or not? And why should she care? The mixing of genetic material is a great deal more random than it is in the human race, believe me."

"Then they have no sexual taboos at all?" Blanche asked.

"Sure they do. No adult would marry anyone more than ten years younger or older. That insures that the generations don't mix. And once a couple decide to marry, they mate for life. Adultery is almost unknown."

"I'm surprised they marry at all," Blanche said with a touch of sarcasm. "I doubt whether animals like that have any real concept of marriage."

Pendray kept his voice level. "Their concept of it isn't the same as ours, of course, but the similarities are surprising. Love, the desire for companionship, the feeling of mutual security, the rearing of a family—those points we have in common. And I doubt that any Daroth couple ever married because she was pregnant or because they had guilt feelings about premarital intercourse. There are some 'forced' marriages, of course. Bachelors and spinsters are frowned upon by society—much more strongly than they are in our own. There are loveless marriages, just as there are quarrels and arguments and lawsuits and so on. They're no more perfect then we are—just different, that's all."

"Different," Blanche said. "Different. Oh, yes. Yes, we're different, all right. Dennis, look over there, to our left! Isn't that a lovely lake?"

She doesn't like Darotha, Pendray thought. *And the only good Indian is a dead Indian. Only she'd never say that about Indians.*

"Then it is not insanity?" Ghundruth said.

"I'm quite certain it isn't," Dr. Hiroa said. "Not in the sense you mean. These children have just learned something that none of your race has ever been exposed to before. It's our fault, of course. We Earthmen have been doing that sort of thing for as far back as we can trace. It's only in the past eighteen months that any sizable group of Earthmen have lived here in Great Shoals, and only during that time have your adolescent children been exposed to them."

"I'm afraid I do not understand," Ghundruth said "These hallucinations, these unreal things w'ich they 'ave made in their own minds. That is not insanity?"

"No. The kids don't believe those things they tell are real. Look, Ghundruth; you can tell a lie, can't you?"

"Yes. When necessary, yes. But w'y do they feel it necessary to tell such outrageous lies?"

"That's the point, the whole point. They *don't* find it necessary. They do it for the fun of it; because they enjoy it."

Ghundruth was silent for a long stretch of seconds Then he burst out: "I don't understand it! 'Ow can they enjoy such a thing? It isn't—it isn't *normal!* That's like enjoying blinking or something. One does it w'en one must, but one doesn't do it for *pleasure.*"

"Do you only eat when you must?"

"No. No."

"And you do enjoy it?"

"Yes. Is there a correlation?"

"Of course. Look at it another way: you use parables and analogies don't you?"

"For instruction. For the purpose of showing an example or for making a generality applicable specifically. Or for showing a similarity or correlation, as you are apparently doing now. But not just for fun. I can't understand that. None of us can."

Hiroa closed his eyes. "Maybe you never will, Ghundruth."

"W'y not? If a child can understand, can't I?" He did not understand; he did not *want* to understand. But he did not like to be told that such understanding might be beyond his capabilities.

"There have been cases, have there not," Hiroa said, "of a Darotha child being lost in a storm during his tenth year and being washed ashore in an uninhabited spot at just the time when the final change is taking place, when his gills have vanished and his lungs are doing all the work?"

"Yes. Occasionally. Not often. Usually 'e will find 'is way back."

"But sometimes he stays there?"

"There 'ave been cases of it. Usually the child dies very soon afterward. Unin'abited places usually 'ave no food available ashore, w'ich means the child would 'ave to live from the sea. But such cases 'ave 'happened, yes."

"What were they like when they were found?"

"Feebleminded. They could not speak and could not learn to speak. Nor could they learn civilized ways. We 'ave assumed that that was the reason w'y they did not return 'ome—because they were feebleminded."

"No. Just the reverse. Because they did not return home, they seemed feebleminded. There is a critical period for learning speech. If one of our children doesn't learn to speak by the time he is five, he never really learns to at all. With your children, that critical five-year period apparently comes immediately after the change.

They don't become symbol users until then. If they're not taught to speak then, they never learn."

"Ahhh," Ghundruth said thoughtfully. "Like swimming."

"Swimming? How's that?"

"Occasionally, a child will 'ave an accident early in 'is tenth year, and 'e must be 'ospitalized. 'Is tail is dissolving and 'is legs are growing. If 'e does not learn to swim with 'is legs during that year, 'e never learns after that. If 'e does not learn to walk during the following year, 'e never learns that."

"Then you can see my point. If I'd known that, I would have used it as my example."

"Is it not the same with you?"

"No. With us, swimming is an art that can be learned at any time, though it is easier to learn it in childhood."

"And w'at 'as this to do with telling lies for fun?"

"Not just with the telling, but with the understanding of *why* they are told for fun. I wonder if it isn't possible that lying for fun is an art that must be learned early or not at all. If it is, then an older Daroth cannot learn it and, therefore, can never understand it. It is my belief that this is true."

"And all Earthmen do this? 'Ow is it that we 'ave never recognized this? 'Ow is it we did not know?"

"You didn't see it because you didn't recognize its existence at all. Ghundruth, both our races have a sense of humor, and in many places they overlap. Puns, for instance. We both enjoy making puns."

"Yes. Because of the theretofore unnoticed cross-correlation between two otherwise unrelated symbols. They are instructive and therefore enjoyable."

Hiroa looked at him. "I'll be damned," he said softly. "I never thought of it that way. Look; you tell jokes, just as we do. We don't enjoy all of yours, and you don't enjoy all of ours, but there are some that we share. Why do you tell jokes?"

"They are instructive. A joke is an instructive parable w'ich 'as an unexpected or theretofore unforeseen result. Is it not?"

"I've just realized, after all these years," Hiroa said, "that we laugh at the same things for entirely different reasons. I'd be willing to bet that the jokes of ours that you didn't get were those which were not instructive. Boy!"

"We learn more about each other every moment, eh, my friend? I wonder if we will ever really understand one another? But you were going to make a correlation between jokes and lies-for-the-fun-of-it."

"I was going to point out that jokes *are* lies-for-the-fun-of-it," Hiroa said. "But evidently they are not, to your way of thinking."

"No. No. I do not understand what you mean. What is the *purpose* of these non-instructive parables? They are meaningless nonsense. Explain to me the meaning of the parable of *Silversheen and the Three Yahoos.*"

Paul Hiroa had to hold back a laugh. Whoever had told that one had made a couple of neat switches. A silvery sheen on the skin of a Daroth female was prized in the same way that blondes were among Earthmen. And the "Three Yahoos" was almost perfect.

"It has no instructive meaning," Hiroa said. "It is an adaptation of a very old children's story. Almost every Earthman has heard it as a child. Where did you hear it?"

"One of my girls told it to me. She asked if I 'ad 'eard it, and I told 'er I 'ad not. I saw that she enjoyed telling it, but I saw no reason for it."

"Tell me: did she use different voice-tones for the three Yahoos? Was Papa Yahoo a deep-voiced person and Baby Yahoo high and squeaky?"

"Yes, that was the way of it."

"And the child enjoyed that particularly?"

"Apparently."

"What was your reaction?"

"I was shocked. I knew she 'ad 'eard it from one of your people, and I could not see w'y anyone would deliberately lie to a child for no reason. I still do not. Yahoos cannot speak, and it is a lie to say that they do."

"And did you explain to her that Yahoos don't speak?"

"Yes. And she said: 'Oh, I know that. It's just a story.' And I didn't understand. I still don't."

"Maybe you will eventually. Someday."

"But you do not think so, eh, friend Hiroa?" He smiled.

"I'd hate to bet on it one way or another. But the children understand it, and that's what led to the next step. They made up their own stories. They made up lies and thought their guardians would understand. And they didn't. You thought they were insane."

"Yes. And I must say frankly that I am not at all sure you are right in your explanation. Even you, wise as you are, do not know 'ow our minds work, any more than we understand you."

"I admit that." *Two countries separated by a common tongue,* he quoted to himself. "We can only wait and see. I shall ask my people not to tell any more stories of that kind to your children if you wish."

"Per'aps it will be better," Ghundruth said thoughtfully. "It 'as caused much disturbance among the older Darotha. I do not like to see 'ard feelings between my people and yours." He paused. "But to be honest, I think the damage 'as already been done. We could forbid the children to tell the stories to each other, but 'ow could we enforce such a rule? It would not be possible. Therefore we will not, for it is foolish to make rules that cannot be enforced."

"I cannot enforce such a rule, either, but I think my people will see the wisdom in acquiescing to my request." *And they'll get quite a laugh out of the idea that Silversheen and the Three Yahoos is a youth-corrupting story which contributes to the delinquency of minors. But they'll understand even* as *they laugh.*

And Ghun is right, he thought, *the damage has been done.*

"Dr. Hiroa," Blanche Barlow said angrily, "I would like to know why you have instructed a flierload of Darotha to follow us north into humanoid country!"

She had knocked on the door of his room, and when he'd said, "Come in," she had burst through the door and snapped out the question.

"I didn't order it, Mrs. Barlow," he said mildly. "That's the law. Not my law. Darotha law. That's protected territory up there."

"But they're going armed!"

"Of course. That's dangerous country, Mrs. Barlow."

"I don't need protection! My husband and I can take

care of ourselves! The humanoids won't hurt us if we show them we come in peace and brotherhood! I won't be followed by armed monsters!"

Hiroa could hear every exclamation point slam into place. "Mrs. Barlow. Listen to me carefully. There is nothing I can do about it. The law cannot be abrogated for me or for you or for anyone else. The game wardens must accompany *anyone* who goes up there. They are not just for your protection; they are there for the protection of the humanoids, too. The game laws must be obeyed."

"*Game* laws!" Her eyes blazed. "So they're just—"

"*Mrs. Barlow!*" Hiroa had an amazingly powerful voice when he chose to use it. "I do not wish to listen to another of your tirades on the rights, privileges, and dignity of the humanoids. The game laws were laid down long before man ever arrived on this world. The wardens will inform you of those laws before you leave. I suggest you listen and obey. If there is nothing else, Mrs. Barlow, then good day."

"I call it a damn fool, damn dangerous stunt!" Dr. Pendray said in a low, harsh whisper.

"My wife knows what she's doing," Dennis Barlow said in the same tone of voice. "Shut up and let her do it. She knows how to handle primitive savages."

"But not wild animals!"

"Shut up!"

The two men were inside the flier. Barlow had a small TV recording camera focused on his wife, who was some thirty yards away, with her back to them, walking slowly forward through the calf-high grass. Twenty yards in front of her, at the foot of a low, rocky hill, a troop of some twenty-five or thirty Yahoos sat silently and watched her.

They looked human. Even James Pendray had to admit that. They were not very clean, but they weren't really filthy, either. They wore no clothes, no decorations of any kind. Their hair was brown and hung in tangled ringlets, but it was not very long. The males had beards, but they were rather sparse and short. They had rather sloping foreheads and rather heavy jaws, but no more so than many human beings. They watched the girl's approach in unmoving silence.

She walked toward them, hands in front of her, fingers outspread, showing that she carried no weapons.

Pendray was silently thankful that four Darotha game wardens were stationed around the area, hidden but alert.

Five yards in front of the statue-like group, Blanche Barlow stopped. She spoke in a voice so soft that the members of her party couldn't hear it, although it was picked up by the directional microphone that Dennis had focused on her. She was not saying words; she was making sounds—gentle, soothing, friendly sounds. They were intended to convey emotion, not intelligence. Her voice was soft, sweet, and tender.

One of the Yahoos growled.

Blanche went on making gentle noises. The only motion was the wriggling of two babies held in the arms of a big-bosomed female. The rest watched Blanche with cautious eyes.

Then one of the males, a broad-shouldered specimen with a mane of graying hair, began walking towards her. Blanche's voice changed a little, became encouraging. She held out her hand to the male.

He grabbed it, jerked her toward him, and slammed a heavy fist against the side of her head. As if at a signal, the rest of the band charged toward her, hands grasping, voices howling and barking.

As Blanche Barlow slumped, there was a ragged chorus of rifle fire. Four high-velocity, heavy-caliber slugs tore into the Yahoos. Two of them slammed into the chest of the male who had struck Blanche. The next two Yahoos got one apiece. More shots crashed through the air.

The Yahoos that remained on their feet spun and fled toward the protection of the rocks. Some picked up stones and began throwing them at Blanche, not knowing where the actual danger had come from, but sniping fire from the four Darotha game wardens kept them from throwing accurately.

Dennis Barlow and James Pendray were already sprinting toward Blanche.

She had only been stunned. She pushed herself to a sitting position and looked groggily around.

"Keep down!" Dennis yelled. *"Keep down, Blanche!"*

She seemed not to hear him. Her eyes were on tragedy.

The big-bosomed female was sprawled nearby, a bullet through her brain. Unhurt, but squalling lustily, the two babies sat near her.

Dennis reached Blanche first, with Pendray only steps behind.

"Come on, honey; let's get out of here!" He helped her to her feet. The stone-throwing had stopped. So had the rifle fire.

"I'm all right," she said weakly. "I can walk. Get the babies, Dennis. Get the babies."

"Aren't they beautiful, Dr. Hiroa? Absolutely beautiful?"

"They are cute," Dr. Hiroa admitted. "I've seen much uglier human babies in my time."

"They aren't more than a month old. Look at the way they take to the bottle! Aren't they darling?" Blanche looked fondly at the two infants in the cribs she had bought for them.

She had had to get a special permit from the Darotha authorities to bring the Yahoo babies back to Point Garrison, but Dr. Hiroa, surprisingly enough, had exercised his influence in her favor. Now, bathed and diapered, the little ones looked as human as any other baby in Point Garrison.

"This will prove my point, Dr. Hiroa. Dennis and I are going to bring them up as though they were our own." She turned away from the cribs to face Hiroa. "The poor things have never had a chance, Dr. Hiroa. For thousands of years, they've been hunted and chivvied, driven like wild beasts by the Darotha. They've had no chance to evolve any sort of stable culture. Their language has remained primitive."

"Are you sure they have a language?" Dr. Hiroa asked.

"Certainly! All human societies have a language. It's one of the things that distinguishes them from animals."

Hiroa nodded. This was no time to point out the circularity of her reasoning.

"It's a matter of environment," Blanche continued. "A human child from Earth, if brought up by the local humanoids, would behave in the same savage manner. He would know no better. After generations of being shot and herded and butchered, they regard every stranger as an enemy. I can hardly blame them for treating me as one.

"But these kids are going to have a chance. They haven't been exposed to that environment long enough for it to make any impression on them—not any deep, lasting impression.

"By bringing them up as we would our own children, they will never know their racial background, never be exposed to the torment their parents had to go through. Instead, they'll learn the way you and I did when we were growing up. They'll learn English instead of the crude tongue of their parents.

"So far as I know, this is the first time this sort of experiment has ever been performed. This is a wonderful chance to add new knowledge to the anthropological field."

Dr. Hiroa nodded slowly. "I believe you're right. I believe you will learn a great deal from this experiment, Mrs. Barlow."

"I'm certain I will. Our research contract with the Institute calls for three years work here. By the end of that time, we will have a great deal of data from the field investigations, and even more from Jane and Michael."

"Jane and Michael, eh? Yes. Yes, I think you'll learn a great deal from Jane and Michael. A great deal."

"Paul," said Dr. Marcus Landau, "I don't know whether your expression indicates disappointment or satisfaction."

Hiroa, Landau, and Pendray were sitting around a conference table in the Research Institute building; cups of coffee, notebooks, pencils, and reports littered the table.

"Neither," Hiroa said. "The fact is there; I merely accept it. I will admit I had hoped—strongly hoped!—that the Darotha would indicate the kind of imaginative streak I was looking for. The indications I got at first made me think that they would. But, as you can see from these reports, the situation has stabilized itself in the past year. Imagination for its own sake, the enjoyment of pure creative imagination, is a passing phase in the Darotha mind. The kids will indulge in it for a little while, but it eventually passes away. By the middle of the second year after they come out of the water, the phase has passed. They look back on it in the same way that an adult human looks back on the days when he or she thought that a cake-candy-and-ice-cream diet was perfect bliss, or that cutting out paper dolls was the greatest pastime in the world."

"But you haven't lost *all* hope, I think," Pendray said.

"No. Certainly not. There will be a few—one or two, maybe, in every generation—who will retain that creative streak. I don't know how long it will take, but I think the time will come when the Darotha will be innovators as well as good learners. I hope that——"

He was interrupted by a rap on the door. "Come in!"

Dr. Dennis Barlow opened the door and entered the room. "Hi, Paul, Marc, Jim. I hope I didn't interrupt anything. You did say fifteen thirty, didn't you?"

"That's right. Come on in. We were just finishing up. Pull up a chair and sit down. There's coffee in the urn over there and a clean cup next to it. Help yourself."

While Barlow got his coffee, Hiroa said: "I think that takes care of everything up to date, then. Next case. Do you have that file on Mike and Janie Barlow, Jim?"

"Right here." Pendray reached for a folder and drew it to him. "We're all learning something from those youngsters."

Dennis Barlow sat down, took one sip of his coffee, and said: "Are they healthy, Doctor?"

"Physically, they're in the prime of condition. Mentally . . . well, who can tell at the age of fourteen months? We haven't got psychology tests that will tell us anything that early. How do they seem to you?"

Barlow grinned wryly. "They sure grow fast, don't they? They're as big and strong as four-year-olds. And the scraps they get into! It's amazing. They don't hurt each other, but they sure slap each other around. Have you been following the tapes?"

All three of the others nodded. "We've seen them," Hiroa said.

"Then you know what I mean. They'll play together nicely most of the time, but if one of them crosses the other, watch out! The other day, Janie was playing with her blocks, and Mike decided he wanted to play, too, so he grabbed a couple of them from her. He got another one right away—bounced off the side of his head. Blanche had to break it up, as usual. Grabbed them and shook them good and gave them a good talking to. She never spanks them, of course. We don't believe spanking is necessary for the proper upbringing of children.

"I think the trouble is that they're still as egocentric as any child of that age, but they're bigger than most kids and can take it out on each other physically, whereas most kids fourteen months old haven't got the strength or coordination to do that."

"Most *Earth* kids, you mean," Pendray corrected gently. "That amount of development at that age is not abnormal for Sandaroth humanoids."

"Really? That wasn't mentioned in any of the tapes."

"Well, we admittedly don't have much to go on," Dr. Landau said. "The adults won't breed in captivity, and——"

"I wouldn't either if I was put in a cage," Barlow interrupted with a grin.

Landau chuckled. "Anyway, as I was saying, we have no definite information. It's hard to follow individuals over a period of years, and this is the first time that any have been raised from infants. But the Darotha say that they mature very rapidly and that these kids are not at all abnormal for their age."

"Hm-m-m. Interesting. You've shown those tapes to Darotha, then?"

"Ghundruth has seen them," said Hiroa. "He's as interested in this experiment as we are."

Barlow's grin had faded away. "He would be. Breeding them like cattle would be easier than driving them to slaughter after rounding them up in the wilds. But you can tell him for me that neither of these kids is going to end up as a slice of *lurgh* on rye. And maybe none of the humanoids will in a few years."

"That, of course, will depend on your report to the Foundation," Hiroa said evenly. "Ghundruth admittedly has an interest. He and his people are as dependent upon the Yahoo herds as the Amerindians of the North American plains were dependent upon the bison herds some centuries back. When the bison herds were reduced to almost nothing, the Amerindian resistance to the white invaders collapsed.

"But Ghundruth isn't thinking of that, odd as it may seem. He is truly interested in knowing whether the humanoids are intelligent—humanly intelligent. The Darotha are an eminently ethical race, Dr. Barlow. Much more so than we are. If they find that the Yahoos are capable of intelligent behavior, there will be no need for us to protect the Yahoos with troops. The Darotha would never kill another one for food. In fact, if they decided that it had been their own fault that the Yahoos had never developed a culture of their own, they would do everything in their power to help them."

"I see." Barlow looked apologetic. "I'm sorry. Forget what I said. But for goodness' sake never say anything like that to Blanche. I'd rather you wouldn't even tell her that Ghundruth is interested or that he's seen the apes."

"We won't," Hiroa said. "We respect your wife's convictions on the subject."

And her temper, Marc Landau thought. *The Golden Fury has become even more touching since she has become a foster mother. Being beaten and stoned hasn't fazed her.*

"What sort of progress are the children making in learning to talk?" Pendray asked, steering the conversation away from the controversy.

"Just 'mama' and 'papa' so far," Barlow said. "But what more can you expect from a fourteen-month-old?"

"Please, Dennis; don't be defensive about it," Pendray said. "I don't *expect* anything. I just want information."

"Sorry. I'll try to keep my foot out of my mouth."

"That's O.K. They call you Papa and Blanche Mama, then, eh?"

Barlow frowned slightly. "No. Not yet. They use the words interchangeably so far." His frown dissolved into a smile. "They know that if they yell either word one of us will come running. I remember once when Mike was inside the playpen and Janie was outside. Something happened, and she grabbed his hair through the bars and started pulling. He couldn't get at her, and he started screaming 'Mama!' at the top of his lungs. I went in and made her quit. I suppose we ought to arrange it so that I only answer to Papa and Blanche only answers to Mama, so they can learn to differentiate."

Pendray nodded. "Yes. I suggest you try that. Otherwise, they have no reason to differentiate. Do they use the words at other times, for other purposes than calling for help?"

"When they're hungry. They come around four or five times a day with 'Mama, mama, papa, papa.' Practically in chorus. It means they're starving. And—boy!—can those kids pack away the food! Of course, they naturally would, growing at that rate. Their anabolism rate must be really high."

"I'm glad you brought that up," said Pendray. "I'd like to have you bring them around for a basal metabolism test sometime soon. Can you do that?"

"Sure. Whenever you like. How about at their regular checkup time, next week?"

"Fine. I'll arrange it. Is there anything else noteworthy?"

"Not that I can think of," Barlow said. "I do think it's a shame they don't have any other kids to play with. But they're far too big and rough for other kids their age, and the four- and five-year-olds are so far ahead of them in education that there's no communication. Besides, the neighbors won't allow it. They're so prejudiced against Yahoos that they're afraid of little babies. I suppose they think Mike and Janie would devour their kids alive or something."

"Probably," Hiroa said. "They have good reason. You saw what happened to the Yahoos that were shot that day as soon as your fliers left the ground. The game wardens got some very good tapes on that."

"Your own ancestors practiced cannibalism at one time, Dr. Hiroa. That didn't mean they weren't human."

"I suppose I should have the grace to blush," Hiroa said. "I don't. All of us have cannibals somewhere back in our ancestry. It's just that the last one of my anthropophagous ancestors lived somewhat later than the last one of yours."

"I might contest with you, Paul," said Dr. Landau with a benevolent smile, "the honor of having had the most recent cannibal on the family tree, but I won't." Then he looked at Barlow with the same smile. "The point that my learned Maori friend was attempting to make, I think, was not the fact of cannibalism *per se*, but the pattern of it. We are not talking now of the rare cases of extreme hunger, where men have been driven to the verge of madness or even beyond it. Those cases are exceptional and we know it. We are talking about cannibalism as a regular, normal practice. In every known case, there was a ritual of some kind connected with it, most especially if the sacrificial victim was a member of the same tribe or family group. Even when an enemy from another group was killed for that purpose, there was a certain amount of dignity and preparation.

"Our *human* ancestors, Dr. Barlow, *did not leap upon their own dead and tear them into gobbets as though they were a pack of wolves.*"

"Not so far as we know, maybe," Barlow said grimly.

"Not so far as we know," Landau agreed. "I admit the evidence is far from conclusive. In itself it proves nothing about the Yahoos. But it must certainly be taken into account, mustn't it?"

"I think the most telling evidence will be Mike and Janie," Barlow said.

"Oh, indeed. Certainly," Landau said.

"I think that is one point upon which we are all agreed," Hiroa said in a carefully neutral tone.

Dr. James Pendray washed his hands in the lavatory in one corner of the surgery. "Janie will be all right, Dennis," he said without looking up. "Just make sure she doesn't pull those stitches loose when she wakes up."

"I hope she doesn't fight when she comes out of the anaesthetic. She's getting to be hell on wheels. I didn't think she'd fight the needle that way." Dennis Barlow's voice sounded both worried and apologetic.

"How's Michael's black eye?" Pendray asked.

"It's O.K. Nothing to worry about. The swelling's almost gone. But where did he ever get the idea of biting his sister on the leg that way? If he'd popped her one on the nose, it wouldn't have been so bad, but those teeth of his inflicted a hell of a nasty wound."

"Yep," Pendray agreed, "he does have a good set of teeth for a two-year-old, doesn't he?"

There was silence while the doctor dried his hands carefully.

"Jim," said Barlow.

"Yes?"

"Don't say anything to Blanche, but I'm beginning to wonder if our hypothesis is as accurate as we thought it was."

"How so?" Pendray was carefully noncommittal.

"Well it's a general rule that the longer the time between puberty and adolescence, the greater the intelligence of the animal. Look at those kids' They look like ten-year-olds!"

"How's their vocabulary?" Pendray knew the answer; he was just pointing something out.

" 'Mama.' 'Papa.' "

"Differentiation?"

"None. They don't seem to know the difference between the words."

"If a chimpanzee is brought up in a human household," Pendray pointed out, "it can usually learn to say a few words. Simple ones."

"I know I know." He paused, and when he spoke again there was anger in his voice. "But, Jim, they're *not* chimpanzees! Look at her!" He gestured toward the surgery table, where Janie lay sleeping under the influence of the injection Pendray had given her. "How can you call a creature as pretty as that an animal?"

"Human beings are animals, I think," Pendray said.

"Don't play around! You know what I mean!"

"Yes, I do. I'm just surprised to hear a zoologist using a word that has a scientific meaning as an emotional tag. They can't dress themselves yet, can they?"

"No, nor undress, either. They don't care whether they're dressed or not. But wouldn't you expect that of a two-year-old?"

"Yes. I'm not arguing with you, Dennis. You're arguing with yourself."

Barlow rubbed a hand across his face. "I know it. Damn! Damn! Damn!"

"What are you going to do about it, Dennis?"

Barlow took his hand away from his face "What? Do about it? I'll go on with the experiment! It isn't over yet; it isn't over by a long shot. It hasn't had time enough yet."

"You and your wife are the sole judges of that, Dennis. It's your experiment. But—" He stopped.

"But what?"

"Getting emotionally involved in an experiment does not tend to make for an unbiased scientific observation of the results. No one can be totally objective about an experiment that is testing his theories, but—a man should try, Dennis. A man should try."

"So you see what we are trying to do, Dr. Barlow," Hiroa said. "Here on this planet, we can begin, for the first time in human history—and in Darotha history—to construct a civilization composed of two non-competing, fully cooperating, intelligent life forms. We are, in comparison with them, high on creative abstract imagination, and low in ethics. The reverse, obviously, is true of them. They can't operate very far from the sea, and they can't stand low humidity; physiologically, they're water wasters. They just aren't built to live in the interior of a continent. They can explore the interior, just as we can go skin diving. But they can't live there. On the other hand, they can do things in the sea that we can't.

"But if this experiment fails, we may never get another chance. That's why I don't want to see this planet opened up to the general run of colonists. I practically handpicked every person here. We used the best psychological tests that we were able to devise to make sure that our people have an ethical standard well above the human average. Not intelligence particularly, but ethics. If the average run of colonists came here, the Darotha would very likely go the way of the Amerindians. We have to give them time to adjust to new technologies, to learn slowly that there are people who can't be trusted. The average colonist is a social misfit, and the ethical standards are actually below the human norm. The Darotha would trust them at first and be robbed and cheated and perhaps enslaved. Then that trust would turn to total distrust of every human being. It would take centuries to straighten the mess out—if, indeed, it ever could be.

"Do you see my point?"

"Certainly, Dr. Hiroa," Dennis Barlow said. "But how would a positive report on the intelligence of the Yahoos affect that?" Now, after three years, Dennis could use the word "Yahoo" without feeling guilty, although he never used it in Blanche's hearing.

Hiroa knew he would have to word his answer carefully. Any suggestion that the Darlington Foundation was a party to chicanery would be rejected out of hand. "There are certain unscrupulous business interests on Earth who want this planet opened up. Your report and those photographs would be used to inflame public sentiment against the Darotha if those unscrupulous men got hold of them."

"But suppose the Yahoos are humanly intelligent?" Barlow asked. "I couldn't falsify a report."

"Of course not! I would never suggest such a thing!" Hiroa said angrily. Then, more calmly: "Let us assume they *are* intelligent, that the experiment with Michael and Jane proves it. I assure you that the Darotha will be absolutely shocked, and will do everything they can to make up for what they have done. It will be up to us to provide a substitute food animal for them, of course, but we could find something—cattle, perhaps. Then we would have *three* intelligent races co-operating.

"In other words, I would like to have your report say that the Darotha no longer kill and eat Yahoos, that the problem *has already been solved!* That will render the information harmless. The unscrupulous interests would no longer be able to use it as a weapon. Do you see?"

"Certainly. I—"

The phone on Dr. Hiroa's desk chimed. He said, "Excuse me," and picked it up. "Dr. Hiroa here. Yes, Jim. *What?*" His eyes came up suddenly, focusing on Barlow's face. "Yes . . . We'll be right there!" He cradled the phone and stood up. "Let's go over to the hospital. There's been an accident."

Dennis Barlow was already on his feet. "One of the kids?"

"No. Your wife. I don't know how serious it is."

It took them five minutes to get to the hospital. Marc Landau was waiting for them in the lobby.

"Where's Blanche?" Dennis half shouted. "What happened?"

"You can't see her now, son. She's in emergency surgery. Jim's working on her. She's in good hands. Just relax."

"What happened? How badly is she hurt?"

"We don't know what happened. She's . . . she's hurt

pretty badly. Her condition is serious, but not critical, Jim says."

Dennis sat down. "Tell me what happened. I have to know."

"One of the neighbors heard her screaming, Dennis. Now, calm yourself. Johnson heard her screaming, and ran over. He had a hunch what it was, so he grabbed a club, a heavy walking stick, before he went." Landau stopped and bit at his lower lip before going on. "Dennis, those Yahoos were trying to kill her. They almost succeeded. Johnson was bitten on the arm, but he managed to knock them both cold. We have them locked up now."

"I can't believe it," Dennis said hollowly. But it was obvious that he did believe it. "Why? Why would they do such a thing?"

"We don't know. We won't know until Blanche can tell us. Was there no indication?"

"No," Dennis Barlow said dully. "No. None. You've read my progress reports. In the past year, the kids have quit fighting one another. You remember how they used to scrap. They don't any more. We thought it was a good sign. Why would a couple of three-year-old kids attack Blanche? Why?" He spoke in a dull monotone, as though he had been drained of emotion.

"They're only three chronologically," Landau said gently. "Physiologically they're about sixteen, if you judge them by human standards. Mentally? Well, I don't know. Johnson said they were screaming *mamapapa*! as they fought. Those are the only words they know, aren't they?"

"Yes." Dully.

"You're a zoologist, Dennis. What would you say was the life expectancy of a mammal that reached pubescence in thirty months?"

"About . . . about twenty years, maximum."

"Intelligence level?"

"Low. Bestial." He glanced up from the floor. "They're baboons, Marc. Baboons. Only worse. Yes! Worse!"

Hiroa looked troubled. "I didn't expect this to happen. I . . . I'm sorry I allowed it, Dennis. Terribly sorry."

"It's not your fault, Dr. Hiroa. It wasn't anyone's fault but mine. I saw it coming, but I wouldn't let myself see it —if you see what I mean. Blanche was even blinder than

I was. I sometimes wondered if she'd ever see. I wonder if she will now. Will she excuse them again, even after this? Will she go on thinking of rationalizations for them?"

It was nearly twenty-four hours before they got the answer to that question.

"She's awake, Dennis," Jim Pendray said. "She's conscious. She'll be all right. She wants to see you."

He led Barlow to the hospital room and let him go inside alone, but he left the door open a trifle so that he and Hiroa and Landau could hear.

"Blanche. Blanche, honey."

She was swathed in sprayed-on bandaging, but she opened her eyes and tried to smile.

"Honey, what happened? Can you talk about it?"

She closed her eyes again. "It was horrible. Horrible."

"What happened?"

"I . . . I was working at my desk. I heard . . . funny noises." Her words came in short gasps. "I got up . . . went into the living room. Michael and Jane were . . . were on the floor. They were—*Oh, Dennis! They were making love!*"

"Yes. And then what?"

"I lost my temper, I . . . I went in and . . . and pushed Michael away from Jane. I . . . I slapped him. They both screamed and snarled and . . . and came at me like . . . like wild animals. I couldn't fight them . . . too strong. They bit and clawed and hit. I . . . I don't remember after that."

She was silent for a moment, then she repeated: "Like wild beasts." Then her eyes opened and she looked at her husband with wide eyes. "They're not human, Dennis! *They're just not human!*"

Outside the door, three men looked at each other with solemn thanks.

POOR PLANET

J. T. McIntosh

I NEVER WAS THE TOUGH he-man lady-killer type of spy, even when I was a lot younger. On the very rare occasions when beautiful girls enticed me into their bedrooms on exotic worlds, the whole operation was only too obviously designed to find out what I'd found out, and the lovely ladies in question not only knew that I knew it, but knew that I knew that they knew it—which tended to remove much of the glamor from the situation, and all the sex.

And by the time I landed at Arneville, capital of the planet Solitaire, to try to solve the enigma of a world that ought to be rich but wasn't, I was still less tough, still less of a he-man, than I had been when I was a mere stripling of thirty-five or forty. By the time I reached Arneville I was forty-eight, married, with three adolescent children. Terran Intelligence had only managed to talk me into going, and Phyllis into letting me go, because I was a historian and the job needed a genuine historian, and because intelligence agents hardly ever failed to return from Solitaire (so named because it was the only planet of its sun).

Solitaire let them come, let them sniff around for a while, and let them go, none the wiser. Occasionally, it was true, agents did not come back. Presumably they'd found out something. But the mortality rate was not high—and Phyllis is a soldier's daughter, complete with stiff upper lip.

The first thing I noticed when I emerged from Arneville spaceport was that it was a cold city. (The fact that I knew this already, having done my homework, did not prevent me from noticing it.) Although the city wasn't bitingly, grindingly cold, it was never far above freezing-point. The previous night's snow was melting as I arrived and crashing in powdery avalanches from the roofs. The overhangs were constructed so that all this soft snow cascaded into the streets, missing the sidewalks. The people hurrying about didn't even look up.

The next thing I noticed about Arneville was that it

was old-fashioned. It was like a twentieth or even nineteenth century Earth city transported many light-years and four centuries to Solitaire. The buildings, vehicles and clothes I saw were all heavy and solid and stolid, with not a hint of frivolity about any of them. Things on Solitaire were made to last, and last, and last.

I had got this far in my observations as I emerged from the spaceport and looked about me when a man came up to me. "Mr. Edwin Horsefeld, from Earth?" the stranger asked diffidently.

"Yes," I said, looking at him. He was the oldest teenager I had ever seen, with the bland innocent fresh-faced look of a kid of fourteen although he must have been thirty-five at least. He was enthusiastic, shy, intense, determined to do his job well. Naturally he must be a counter-espionage agent.

"I'm Tom Harrison," he said eagerly. "I've been asked to contact you and give you any help I can—"

"By whom?" I asked pleasantly.

"Some government department . . . F.R.S., I think it was."

My opinion of Solitaire's counter-espionage division, quaintly named Foreign Relations Security, went up several points. You had to admire a department that told you it knew you were a spy and offered to help you.

But then, Solitaire's counter-espionage division *must* be good. Every other planet in the galaxy, convinced Solitaire had a secret of some kind, had been trying for a long time to find out what it was—and Terran Intelligence would have known if any of them had succeeded, even if it didn't know exactly what they had found out.

We could all guess about Solitaire. None of us *knew*.

"Pleased to meet you, Mr. Harrison," I said, shaking hands. "Are you a historian?"

"No, why?"

"It doesn't matter. Just an idea."

"I'm sorry, Mr. Horsefeld. I guess I can't help you in your work . . . but I can tell you about libraries, hotels, stores—"

"That will be very useful. Hotels first. Where do you suggest I should go?"

Harrison hesitated. "They told me you'd probably want

peace and quiet, a room in a decent, modest hotel where nobody would bother you. Is that right?"

"Exactly right."

"Then maybe you'd like to go to Parkview. It's cheap, clean—"

"Fine. Let's go to the Parkview." I was perfectly happy to let Solitaire's counter-espionage division put me where it liked. It would do that anyway.

Harrison took me to the Parkview, a small inn just off Arne Way, the main street in the city. Then, to my surprise, Harrison seemed not only ready but apologetically anxious to leave me. I'd expected the devil's own job getting out of his sight.

"You can phone me either at Government House or at home," he said, giving me both numbers.

"Just one thing before you go, Tom—may I call you Tom? Where's the nearest music store?"

"Music?" he said vaguely, as if he had never heard the word. "Oh, I guess . . . you could try Prosser's, just round the corner in Arne Way. I think they sell music as well as books."

"Excellent," I said. "That saves me the trouble of asking you where the nearest bookstore is. Thanks, Tom."

"That's all I can do for you just now?"

"I think so. You've been a great help."

He colored. "It's nothing," he said self-consciously. "I'll look in this evening and see how you're making out."

Then he left. F.R.S. had informed me politely that it knew who I was, that it had its eye on me, and then left me to wander about Arneville as I pleased.

It might as well have told me in so many words that I wasn't going to find out anything.

Lunch at the Parkview was excellent. But why the Parkview, I wondered. I'd heard of Arne Park, which was about the only thing in Solitaire most people *had* heard about. The Park must, however, be at least a mile along Arne Way and was not visible even from my top-floor bedroom. Nothing in that direction was visible except the blank wall of a massive office block.

If Solitaire had nothing to hide, I reflected, which was unlikely but not completely impossible, a known Terran spy might well be treated exactly as I was being treated. An intelligent counter-espionage division in a world which had no secrets—if there was any such world—would realize that the only way to convince other nations of this was to let them find it out for themselves.

After lunch I strolled round to Prosser's. By this time most of the snow was brown slush.

It was just as well, I reflected, looking at the people in the streets, that I was forty-eight and no longer interested in girls. For there seemed no prospect of ever seeing a pretty girl in Arneville, at any rate a girl looking pretty. In boots, heavy coats and fur hoods, with faces pinched by the cold, women of sixteen, thirty-six and fifty-six looked much the same. None of them seemed to wear makeup, and since heating in most buildings was only moderately efficient, heavy, unattractive clothes were worn inside as well as out.

The young lady in Prosser's, who might have been attractive if she tried, didn't seem to be trying. On top of a dress which was all right in itself she wore an assortment of woolen jackets in various colors and shapes. None of the latter coincided with hers.

"Opera?" she said. "You must mean *The Arne Story*. That's the only opera I know."

"That's it," I said.

"A score? That's the words and music, isn't it? You want to buy a copy?"

"An original copy, if possible." She went away and returned, after an interminable delay, with a paper-covered score. I looked at the date. It was a new edition published only the year before.

When I tried patiently to explain that what I really wanted was a copy of this opera printed a long time ago, she stared blankly and then brought a small, bald knowledgeable man to talk to me.

"Yes, this *is* a revised edition, sir," he agreed. "Quite extensively revised. You're a foreigner, I take it? Yes, I thought so. You see, since there's only one native opera, and such a great masterpiece at that, it's constantly being revised and improved. I believe the original version of *The Arne Story* was quite different from the version that's performed now—"

"So I understand. That's why I'd like to see the original."

"You could try a library. Or—maybe there would be

an old copy at Jerome's. It's a little place that keeps a lot of old j . . . musical instruments and things like that."

The little knowledgeable man gave me detailed directions, and I trudged through the snow again along streets, which became narrower and shorter and dimmer. I might almost have been in Dickens's London.

At last I found Jerome's, which proved to be a tiny shop with a minute window offering a keyhole view of a startling variety of cornets, trumpets, trombones and mutes. I pushed the door open, stooping to enter, and blinked at the girl in charge.

She was the last, positively the last thing I expected in a place like Jerome's, in a city like Arneville, on a planet like Solitaire. She was very young, a nymphet, very pretty, and she was quite smartly dressed.

"Good afternoon," she said,smiling pleasantly.

"Five minutes ago," I said, "I didn't think so. But now I see it is."

She laughed, being young enough to take naive delight in a frank, sincere compliment. It could only have been a matter of months since men started to pay her compliments; it might be years yet before experience taught her to look gift horses in the mouth.

She was a small brunette with the kind of slim, flawless twinkling legs which only nymphets possess. Above the legs was a short black skirt, and above the skirt a tight white blouse. Above the blouse was a pert, pretty little face which could have passed for the face of a beautiful child if her fully, though recently, developed contours had not been visible.

"I wonder if you have an original score of *The Arne Story?*" I asked.

"You don't want much, do you? It's over two hundred years old. What are you smiling at?"

"You said that as if I'd asked for the Ark's sailing-list in Noah's own handwriting."

She laughed again. And I thought, in italics: *If this lovely little creature really has been placed here by F.R.S., I'm going to enjoy being led up the garden path.*

"Perhaps, if not an original," I said, "you might have an early edition?"

"Well, if you'd like to stick around for about three

hours while I inspect the stock," she said briskly, "I might turn up something."

"It would be a pleasure," I said courteously, "to stick around."

It was. It really did take nearly three hours—the little shop had so many things in such a small space that it was necessary to shift half the stock in order to get at the other half. I soon learned the girl's name—Terry Wood—that her father was alive and her mother dead, that she had no brothers or sisters, that she had a passion for adventure, and that she didn't think I looked very old.

We couldn't help becoming better acquainted, for I had to hold instrument cases for her and move piles of music and stack boxes which she handed down to me. Apparently there was never any rush in Arneville shops; if a purchaser wanted something and you might have it, you thought nothing of spending an hour or two over a two-dollar sale that might not materialize anyway. Certainly Terry was not exactly off her feet. During the time she was searching for the score, there was just one customer, a reedy youth who wanted a clarinet reed.

The pleasure with which I examined Terry's pretty legs clear to the hips as she climbed ladders was neither guilty nor carnal. I had a daughter just Terry's age, and I told her so.

Before Terry at last triumphantly produced a fourth edition score of the opera, dated only three years after the first performance, we had arranged to go together to the opera house that night to see the contemporary *The Arne Story*.

Despite the ease with which this was arranged, I rejected for the moment the possibility that Terry had been planted in Jerome's by F.R.S. For one thing, her knowledge of the stock was remarkable, considering how much of it there was. For another, if F.R.S. had guessed that I would want an early edition of *The Arne Story* and had arranged for me to be directed to Jerome's, they must be even cleverer than I thought them.

In the early evening, before I set out for the opera house, Harrison called to see me. He glanced blankly at the yellowed score lying unopened on the bed.

"*The Arne Story*—two hundred years old!" he said. "What do you want that for?"

"As a historian," I said, "my curiosity is boundless."

Harrison looked at me uncertainly. "Oh, well. I guess you know your business. Is there any way I can help you?"

"Where," I asked, "does one take a girl after the theater?"

Harrison didn't seem to have heard of anyone taking a girl to the theater. He was, I suspected, overacting. Nobody set on me by F.R.S. could be that dim.

"I guess you could bring her back here," he said at last, with a mediocre attempt at a leer.

"That's not what I mean. When one takes a girl to a show in Arneville, isn't there anywhere to go afterwards?"

"Only the Park."

"The Park! To sit holding hands in the snow?"

Harrison blinked. "I meant Arne Park . . . oh, I guess you wouldn't know. It's covered in, heated, and it stretches for miles. It's sort of a summer playground. Night and day."

I should have done my homework better. I knew Arne Park was the showplace of the planet, but I hadn't heard that it was totally enclosed. Vaguely I had imagined a few large hothouses and vast stretches of winter wonderland.

"Thanks, Tom. Maybe we'll take a look at the Park. But not by night, the first time. By the way, have you any idea why this place is called the Parkview?"

"Well . . . I guess it might have been possible to see the Park from here before that office block was built. There are lots of hotels with names like that, you know —Park Hotel, Park Arms, Park Inn, Newpark, Highpark . . ."

"Between Park and Arne you've got all the names you need," I commented.

"Well, Henry Arne was our first premier."

"Yes, Tom," I said gently. "I know."

Harrison tried to be helpful for a few minutes more, and then left. I'd never met anyone connected with spying as uninterested in asking questions.

Terry arrived at the opera house only a few seconds after I did. "Am I late?" she asked breathlessly.

"You're the only girl I ever knew who wasn't," I said.

"Oh, but I'm not sophisticated," she admitted.

"I'm glad you told me. Here I was thinking you were a bored, blasé, langorous woman of the world—"

"Don't pull my leg," she said fiercely. "I don't like it."

So she had a temper. It was a surprise. In the shop that afternoon nothing I had said ruffled her, and when piles of music cascaded on the floor she merely shrugged resignedly.

When she hurried away to the ladies' room I had an opportunity to ponder over the momentary flash of temper and what it meant. I was soon able to make a pretty good guess.

Agents of my type do not move in an atmosphere of blazing guns, flailing fists, exploded safes and chases in fast cars. Rarely had I been in the thick of violent action. I work by keeping my eyes and ears open and fixing on small things that don't seem to fit—like a sudden flash of irritation in a sunny-tempered girl. . . .

The theater was old and dark and massive. If it had only had gas instead of electricity, it would have been a Victorian opera house. I call it a theater and an opera house indiscriminately because the locals do the same. When opera is being performed, it's the opera house. When it's drama or vaudeville, it's a theater.

The cloakrooms were far more extensive and elaborate than in Terran theaters. Since you couldn't sit in a theater and go outside clad the same way anyway, the custom was to make a complete transformation.

Terry came out hesitantly, and not without reason. She wore an ankle-length black satin gown, not particularly revealing, but of a type and cut which on all worlds tacitly proclaims the wearer's profession. If I hadn't known already that Terry's mother was dead and that she had no sisters, that dress would have told me.

As she waited for me to say something, I had an opportunity to check on my guess. In the afternoon, nothing could ruffle her. In the evening, as she arrived for a date she might be expected to enjoy, the gentlest leg-pulling made her snap back. It didn't take a genius to deduce that something had happened in between. Now, what? Row with boyfriend when Terry insisted she was going anyway, so there? Row with Dad when she appeared in dress of which Dad did not approve? My guess was: row with Dad, but not over dress.

I didn't take the opportunity. Terry was inexperienced but intelligent. You couldn't pump her without letting her see she was being pumped.

"You look lovely," I said. And in a way she did. Even in that dress.

She blushed, pleased. I took her in, my gentle touch on her bare arm intended to remind her that I could be her grandfather, very nearly her great-grandfather. It shouldn't have been necessary . . . but then, she had no mother, and seemed to spend her time working in a shop which only had two customers in three hours. In experience she wasn't exactly as old as time.

The opera astonished me. First, it was good, which was odd: opera needs a tradition, and while one of a hundred Italian operas may be a masterpiece, you don't expect much of the only opera native to a planet. I'd expected a sort of *Beggars' Opera,* not a patriotic piece with a strong plot, good dialogue (almost unique in opera), some first-class ballet, fair music (the music was weakest) and really fervent acting.

At the first interval I told Terry how impressed I was, and she was pleased.

The second half was a slight disappointment. The patriotism started high and finished in a frenzy, too idealistic even for opera. The characterization, good at first, fell apart a little when character after character revealed not only impossible patriotism, but the *same* impossible patriotism. The hero, Henry Arne—the Arne who had been Solitaire's first premier—first sacrificed his love of the heroine to Solitaire, and later her life.

The opera was so long, and finished so late, that there was little question of going anywhere afterwards, though we had coffee at the theater before I took Terry home.

I was surprised to find that she agreed with me completely about the opera.

"Dying for love is a beautiful idea," she said, "but dying for a country is crazy, and sacrificing the girl you love for your world is crazier, and whenever it comes to that bit I want to be sick."

"You've seen it often?"

"Not often. Four or five times. They send us from school to see it."

"You don't sound particularly patriotic, Terry," I said lazily.

"I'm not," she admitted frankly. "Oh, if I'd a chance to do something wonderful and romantic and exciting for Solitaire, like . . ."

She blushed and broke off in confusion.

"Like what, Terry," I asked, smiling.

"Anyway, if I'd a chance to do anything like that, I'd do it like a shot. But dying for an ideal . . ."

She went on for quite a while, and I listened. Presently I said quietly: "And you're allowed to get away with that?"

"What do you mean?"

"In most countries and worlds where nationalism is deliberately cultivated, whipped up by propaganda and pieces like *The Arne Story,* people who talk as you've just been doing are liable to . . . disappear."

Terry laughed, at least she started to laugh. Then she looked at me, startled, doubtful, and for a moment I genuinely wished I had not pricked her to see what she would happen.

"Take me home," she said suddenly, breathlessly. "I . . . I have to start early tomorrow."

I took her home.

Next morning after breakfast I went back to my room and had a quick glance through the fourth edition of *The Arne Story.*

The broad outlines of the opera had not changed. A good deal of music was different, and my guess was that the later music was better. Presumably composers in the last two centuries had been encouraged to improve on the original settings if they could.

On the whole the opera had improved a great deal in its two centuries of existence. The early version was crude, rough, even more implausible than the contemporary version.

But the interesting thing about the comparison was that all the changes were designed to make the opera better and more effective patriotic propaganda. And it had been a propaganda piece in the first place.

I pushed the score aside and put my feet up. Later I'd compare the two versions of the opera for my own purposes. Meantime I was here to find out something, and I didn't think *The Arne Story* in versions of ancient or modern could tell me much more than it already had.

The problem was simple. Solitaire had been colonized nearly three centuries earlier. It had never been a particularly attractive world, but its deposits of oil, coal, steel, diamonds, silver and platinum were at least average. Within fifty years there had been a population of nearly a hundred million. So far so good.

Now, over two hundred years later, the population was two hundred million and Solitaire was about the most backward world in the galaxy, with the lowest relative standard of living. (Terry's weekly wage, which she had mentioned when we were discussing Solitaire and Earth, would just about pay for a meal in a New York hotel. And my weekly bill at the Parkview was less than I'd pay to stay one night at the same hotel.)

Why?

Solitaire issued no statistics, and all figures were therefore guesses. Other worlds, however, had figures showing that emigration from Solitaire was negligible.

So why was the population (estimated) so low? Why was the planet so apparently poor? Why only a trickle of exports?

What was Solitaire up to?

The question of a Solitaire *secret* arose only because agents sent to investigate the world on the spot either came back with nothing to report or didn't come back at all. Only a few failed to return—but why should there be any spy casualties on a world which had nothing to hide?

Secret wasn't the right word to apply to the affairs of Solitaire. *Uncertain* was better. Even the precise form of government was uncertain, not because of the kind of iron wall you find in an out-and-out police state, but because hardly anyone seemed to know anything for sure. Although Solitaire was known to have a senate and a premier at its head, less was known of the present premier than of the first . . .

Hence the appearance on the scene of me, Edwin Horsefeld, with one or two tricks up my sleeve. These days spies needed a gimmick more than nerve or brawn.

Having thought for a while I went to the library and found out all I could there. It took me only an hour and a half, and I didn't think I'd missed much of importance.

The library contained only eight thousand books that had been written and published in the whole of Solitaire. Eight thousand in over two hundred years. The rest were reprints of standard texts obtainable anywhere in the galaxy.

Of the eight thousand, four thousand were novels. Three thousand dealt with the natural lore of the planet geography, geology, exploration, fauna and flora. That left me one thousand miscellaneous books to include all the social history, biography, poetry, essays, research, philosophy and psychology of a settlement nearly three centuries old.

It wasn't much.

In the afternoon I met Terry, by arrangement, and let her take me to the Park. It was her afternoon off.

The moment I saw her I knew that once again something had happened between our meetings.

I hoped it wasn't that both times she'd seen her boyfriend—so attractive a girl, however young, simply must have a steady boyfriend, or at least someone who imagined he was—and had now sent him packing, convinced she was in love with me. I thought Terry was too steady and sensible for that, and yet there was no denying that everything I had told her about Earth had seemed to fascinate her and that she already seemed to consider me as something much more than just an elderly male acquaintance.

Although she was evidently going to tell me something that she considered of immense importance, she stuck to trivialities until we were inside the Park.

The dome over the Park was larger than anything on Mars, coated to reflect as little light as possible, and scarcely visible as domes go. Inside was a vast, well-planned, well-maintained garden, warm as July in the northern hemisphere of Earth, cooled and aired by soft breezes. And this is a city where it snowed all the year round.

As I waited for Terry, who was hanging up her coat in the pavilion, I thought: *Terran Intelligence should know more about Arne Park. Anything as untypical of its world as Arne Park is of Solitaire is worth a lot of attention.*

There must be a reason for the Park. Apparently other agents had merely looked at it, said "Very impressive," and taken their cloaks and daggers elsewhere. Well, maybe I was doing them an injustice. Nevertheless, the thought lingered: *On a world like this, in a city like this, there must be a reason for such a vast, expensive, man-made miracle.*

Terry joined me and I saw the reason for the Park. It was a place for her to wear her yellow playsuit, a neat little confection that fitted her as if she'd been born wearing it. After the dreadful unsuitability of her appearance the night before, it was a relief to find her looking like any pretty sun-loving teenager.

"Aren't you going to change too, Edwin?" she asked.

I sighed. "I would if I were about twenty-one. Looking at you I wish I were."

I didn't really; no sensible man of forty-eight really wants to be twenty-one again, unless in possession of all the knowledge, experience and advantages of forty-eight. But Terry was pleased.

We strolled along the walks and lanes of the Park. Practically everyone we saw was gay, exuberant, dressed in bright, frivolous clothes. Arne Park was where the people of Arneville threw off their inhibitions. No city in the galaxy needed such a place more. Yet the Park was anything but crowded. Working hours in Arneville were long.

We must have been about a mile from the pavilion when Terry said: "I want to help you, Edwin."

"To do what?"

She took a deep breath and then said: "I know you're a spy."

"Do you?" I said softly. "Who told you?"

"Just before lunch yesterday somebody called the shop. He didn't give his name. He said you were coming and that I was to make friends with you. He said it wouldn't be dangerous, but I had a chance to prove my loyalty to Solitaire."

So Terry had not been planted. F.R.S. had simply co-opted her.

"What else were you told?" I asked quietly

"Very little, then I guess I was deliberately told practically nothing so I wouldn't dare do anything rash, like asking questions that would tell you what was going on."

"You're very intelligent, Terry."

"Well, I hope so. You know what happened—the way things worked out I didn't have to do or say anything I might not have done anyway. I mean, I've always been interested in Earth, and if there had been no phone call we might still have gone to the opera last night."

I nodded.

If Terry had not been instructed to say to me what she was saying now, she'd made a terrible mistake. However, there was no going back now. I had to hear what she had to say.

"When I went home my father was waiting for me with a tall, thin man. The tall man said he was Mr. Marks and asked me to repeat everything you and I had said to each other. I told him all I could remember, because it couldn't do any harm—could it?"

"No."

"Then . . ." She hesitated.

"Edwin, I think you guessed that my father and I don't get on. He's . . . it's a terrible thing to say about my own father, but he's no good. After a while the atmosphere changed. I was no longer voluntarily cooperating with the police, as I thought. Marks was telling me what to do and warning me that my father would go to jail if I didn't do exactly as I was told that I might go to jail too. And my father was begging me to save him . . ."

I waited. I was very sorry for her. She was very young to be faced with such things.

"They told me you were a spy and it was my duty to report on you. I don't think I let them see I was angry, but I was. I mean—I liked you. I could tell you hadn't done anything bad, and weren't going to do anything bad."

"Yet you knew I was working for Earth," I said, "against your world."

She shrugged. "Earth's never done us any harm, as far as I knew. Maybe if Marks had treated me differently, acted as if he trusted me Anyway, as it was I didn't know what to do. There was no harm in telling Marks exactly what you said and did—unless I suddenly learned something important. If I did, I wasn't sure I wanted to tell Marks."

I nodded. I could understand her attitude, I thought, better than she did herself. She was very young, very inexperienced, and romantic, even sentimental. She had already had to learn that she could not rely on her father. Her world, her environment, her family had never done much for her—yet being sensible and self-reliant she had made the best of everything and managed to be happy.

Then I came along. She liked me—and she was coldly instructed to act like my friend, but report all I said to F.R.S.

F.R.S. was not so clever after all. They should have known what Terry would do. Did they?

"You don't seem surprised," Terry said, a little deflated.

"I'm not. Terry, whenever I land on a strange planet the chances are that anybody who makes friends with me is working for local counter-intelligence. When I find a pretty girl being friendly, I can be practically sure of it."

"That must make you very cynical," she said in a small voice.

"No, why should it? I'm not a character in a fairy story . . . You haven't told me everything yet. That interview with Marks was before we went to the opera, wasn't it? What's happened since?"

"Oh, just more of the same. Marks was waiting when I got home, asked questions again, warned me again. He . . ." She flushed.

"Might as well tell me."

"He said it might be better if I slept with you."

I merely nodded. But I guessed that was what had really decided Terry to confide in me. She had practically no sexual experience—I hadn't lived nearly a half century without being able to discern such things. A young, imaginative girl with romantic notions might easily entertain the exciting thought of a passionate love affair with a spy. But it would have to be a *love* affair. To be coldly instructed to sell her virginity for her world was revolting.

After a pause I said gently: "Do you know the danger you're in, Terry?"

She blinked. "I'm not in any danger. I've warned you.

I'll go on reporting to Marks. But I won't report anything that'll do you any harm."

I sighed. It was probably impossible to make her understand. And no good purpose would be served by trying.

"Who's your boyfriend, Terry?" I asked casually.

She flushed again and started. That was when I knew that she really was beginning to fancy herself in love with me.

To give herself time to think she dropped on the grass, stretched out her legs and lay on her back with her arms behind her head. Then, as an afterthought, she sat up again, unzipped the middle part of her yellow playsuit, tossed it aside and lay down as before.

Between the bottom of her small though well filled halter and the top of the briefs that dipped and rose from one hip to the other, all the fascinating tracery of firm adolescent muscles rippled as she moved. She had the kind of fantastic waist measurement that actresses claim and nymphets really possess.

I sat down beside her.

By this time she was ready to answer: "I don't have a boyfriend."

"You must have, Terry."

"Well, there's Steve. But he . . . oh, he's just a kid."

"Have you seen him in the last twenty-four hours?"

"No. Anyway, there's nothing between us."

For a moment I wished I'd never come to Solitaire. Probably I wouldn't find anything out. And though I expected to leave in one piece, it was now unlikely that Terry had much longer to live.

What she didn't understand was that to F.R.S. loyalty was a deadly serious business. She wouldn't be able to fool F.R.S., either. Sooner or later, whatever I did, Solitaire's counter-espionage department would find out that Terry had (in their estimation) committed high treason.

So she had—unless all this was an act, something I didn't believe for a moment. The fact that Terry couldn't help me was neither here nor there. She had told a spy that she was on his side against her own world.

She sat up suddenly. "Do you think I'm cheap?" she asked bluntly.

I couldn't help looking startled at the sudden challenge.

"Showing myself like this?" she went on. "You've gone quiet. Well, I'm *not* cheap. I don't mind showing myself to you. Steve has meant nothing to me since I met you."

"Terry," I said, "I have two daughters, and one of them is about three years older than you. And I didn't marry particularly young."

"It's true," she said bleakly. "You do think I'm cheap." She reached for the discarded part of her playsuit.

There was no way I could reassure her without abruptly changing the subject. So I changed it.

"Terry," I said, taking the cover-up from her and putting it down again, "I wonder if you really can help me. Have you noticed anything, absolutely anything, about the set-up on your world that puzzles you, or surprises you?"

"What sort of thing?" She was still suspcious and hurt. Probably she felt guilty about Steve—perhaps she'd broken a date with him that afternoon or the night before; perhaps she felt she'd thrown herself at my head and all I did was laugh at her.

"Any sort of thing."

"Well . . . there's one thing I meant to tell you. Only I haven't gotten around to it. It's only a rumor."

"Yes?"

"There may be nothing in it. It's just . . . Well, they say sometimes people disappear."

"Disappear?"

"Oh, they're not supposed to disappear. They're supposed to go somewhere else. But they only write once, or maybe twice, and then nobody ever hears of them again."

"That's very interesting, Terry," I said. But it wasn't. On a hyper-patriotic world like Solitaire there was undoubtedly a secret security service, though we knew nothing about it. Of course people disappeared. It would have been astonishing if they did not . . .

Terry not being dressed for any place in Arneville except the Park, we had a snack at an open-air restaurant inside the dome and then I took her home.

I didn't know yet what to do about her. Pretty soon I'd have to think up something she could tell Marks, something that would convince him Terry was loyal and useful, and that I was nowhere turning up anything. The second part was perfectly true.

For the moment, Terry was to tell Marks everything we'd said with one obvious exception.

Back at the hotel, Tom Harrison, the eager beaver, was waiting for me. He wanted to know if there was anything further he could do to help.

I had an idea. "No, thanks, Tom," I said. "In fact—I can manage by myself now. Thanks for your help earlier. I appreciated it. But I needn't trouble you again."

Harrison nodded awkwardly. "Okay," he said gruffly. "I guess you don't want me hanging around any more, is that it?"

"Well, not exactly. As a matter of fact, the girl I told you about has been showing me around. You're a nice guy, but you must admit you're not a pretty girl."

Harrison's face cleared. "Oh, if it's like that . . . Well, if you want me, you know how to get in touch. So long."

I went upstairs. So long as the gloves were still on, F.R.S. wouldn't crowd me. But they'd still want to keep me under observation. Forcing them to do it through Terry gave her some temporary protection, I thought.

Indeed, within an hour or so I had certain plans worked out, plans I won't bother to detail, for I never had a chance to put them into effect.

It was still fairly early when a porter came to tell me a young lady was waiting for me downstairs.

I went down at once. The visitor could only be Terry. It was a mistake her coming to see me at the Parkview, where everything I did must be under observation and where the walls undoubtedly had ears. The best I could do was act as if I'd been expecting her, and hope she had the sense to wait until we were outside before she said anything that mattered.

She had. She hadn't taken off her coat, and was waiting as if we had arranged to go out together. I thought there was something a little tense aobout her smile.

She waited until we were well away from the Parkview, walking along Arne Way, before she said anything about the reason for her call. It was getting dark, and a soft, fine snow was falling. It was bitterly cold; we breathed out white clouds. Terry, who had never previously shown any sign of feeling the cold, was shivering.

"Edwin," she said suddenly, "it's all gone wrong."

As we walked she told me what had happened. Whenever anyone came close she stalled until we were in effect alone again.

When I left her and she went in, she heard Marks and her father talking. She didn't go straight in to them, but went to her bedroom to change.

In her bedroom she caught one or two words which made her creep quietly into a boxroom to hear better.

Marks was telling her father that in order to be certain that she was telling the truth and the whole truth, he was going to shoot her full of drugs when she came in . . . .

Terry didn't have to tell me how completely this changed the picture for her. Probably she'd had some vague idea appropriate to her years that it would be quite easy to turn awkward questions aside, and that even if later she was tortured in the not too unbearable way reserved for heroines, she'd insist bravely that she had told the truth.

She hadn't seen Marks drugging her to take her will away from her. There was nothing romantic about that. You couldn't fight it . . . .

"I crept out quietly," she concluded, "and came straight to you."

"Don't you realize, Terry," I said, "that you were meant to hear exactly what you did hear, and do exactly what you have done—come running to me in a panic?"

She drew herself up sharply. "I'm not in a panic!"

"You should be. I would be, if I were you."

"Why—what do you mean?"

"I've got some protection. I haven't broken any local or international law."

"But you're a spy!"

"Please don't shout it in the middle of the street, Terry. In a sense I am, but I don't have to go outside the law to do what I want to do. Certainly F.R.S. will put me out of the way if they consider it's got to be done, but they'll know that Earth won't be at all pleased if they do, and might even take the opportunity of clamping down on Solitaire and ordering a full-scale investigation, in the course of which they'll have an excellent chance of finding out what I was sent here to find out. F.R.S. knows all that. But you—"

"What about me?" she asked defiantly.

She could no longer be allowed to deceive herself about her position.

"Well, you see, Terry, only Solitaire has any responsibility for you. No one else can possibly interfere. If your own authorities decide, without trial or any public mention of your case, that you're a traitor, there's nothing whatever to stop them—"

She stared at me in horror. "You mean I'm going to be shot—and there's nothing you can do?"

I pulled her down on a bench at a street corner. It was not a comfortable place to sit, with the snow sifting down, but we were much safer out in the open than in any place where we could be overheard.

The way Terry was shivering made me think of something.

"What are you wearing under your coat?"

"Just—what I wore in the Park. I didn't take time to change."

"That's a great help," I murmured. "That means we can't go anywhere where you'd have to take off your coat."

"Except the Park."

In the afternoon she had told me that the Park was busier by night than by day. And there was no police patrol charged with the duty of protecting public morality. The official view, a more practical one than that of some apparently better organized worlds, was that if no convenient place was provided for young lovers to do what young lovers did, innocent or not so innocent, the only real effect was to drive them into the willing arms of those who made money out of vice.

So we could go to the Park again and not be too conspicuous. F.R.S. could find us there with ease; but then, F.R.S. could find us sooner or later wherever we went.

"Meantime," I said, "is there anybody you can trust, literally with your life? Not your father, evidently."

"Certainly not my father," she said with more bitterness than I had ever heard in her voice.

"Aunts, uncles, cousins?"

"Only Steve," she said in a small voice. "And I don't like——"

"Never mind whether you like it or not. We'll go and see Steve."

First we gave the men trailing us nightmares. There might not be anyone trailing us; still, I had too much respect for F.R.S. to take any chances.

I had failed in my job on Solitaire. All I was trying to do now was to take Terry away with me in one piece, if that was possible. I didn't think it was.

We jumped on and off buses, entered buildings by one doorway and left by another, hurried through crowds, and stayed quietly in cover waiting for anyone following us to overrun us. With my experience and Terry's knowledge of the city, we were soon sure that we were clear.

Then we called at Steve's lodgings. I was fully aware that we might pick up our tail again by calling there. However, I didn't mention this to Terry. She had enough to worry about.

"Why, hello, Miss Terry," said the landlady, faintly surprised. "Didn't Steve call you before he left?"

"Left?" said Terry with foreboding.

"He's gone to Bennerwald. But he must be meaning to write. I guess we'll all be getting a letter from him tomorrow."

Terry was going to say more, a lot more. I gripped her elbow hard. With an effort she thanked the landlady and came away.

"Where's Bennerwald?" I asked.

"On the other side of the planet—ten thousand miles away. He *couldn't* have—"

"Don't talk too much."

We went through another tail-amputating operation. When I considered it safe we sat on another bench, huddled together so that we would be taken for lovers.

"He's disappeared," Terry said flatly.

The emphasis she put on the word made me repeat it interrogatively.

"Disappeared—like the ones I told you about."

"I'm afraid you're right."

She shuddered and clutched me convulsively. Yet the way she took it convinced me that she had never been in love with Steve.

"Was he a rebel?" I asked. "Against patriotism and propaganda, I mean? Did he shoot his mouth off a lot?"

Terry stared. "No. Quite the opposite."

"Really?" I said.

"Yes—we often argued. As I told you, I wouldn't mind loving my country if my country didn't work so hard trying to make me. But with Steve . . ."

She shrugged. "Remember *The Arne Story?* Well, Steve would sacrifice me for Solitaire. That wouldn't have been so bad if he didn't keep boasting about it."

I was beginning to become interested. "Terry, think of all the other people you knew who might have disappeared. What were they like?"

"I told you, nobody can be sure. Maybe nobody disappeared. It may be nothing more than a rumor—"

"I know that. But you can make a guess. The people who go on long journeys, write once or twice and then stop writing—are they young or old? Men or women? Rebels or patriots?"

"Young, mostly. You don't get older people uprooting themselves. Both men and women. And usually—quite patriotic. Anyway, not rebels."

"That's very interesting," I said.

"Edwin—where can we go? Some other town?"

"No, there'll be a watch on all travel depots."

"A hotel?"

"Likewise."

"Then let's go to the Park. I'm freezing."

"All right."

Before we moved, however, a fresh-faced man came past, saluting me cheerfully as he went by.

It was Tom Harrison.

F.R.S. was so efficient that if they lost our trail they could easily pick it up again. More than that, so cocky that they wanted me to know we were being watched.

What, I wondered, were they trying to make me do?

We left our coats at the Park pavilion. Once more we had done our best to give the watchers the slip. After all, we might succeed. They might decide that the Park, which was a trap even if a very large one, was the last place we'd go.

Not that it made any real difference. F.R.S. might or might not let me leave Solitaire when I chose, might or might not let me take Terry with me—and there was nothing I could do about it.

Arne Park by night was wonderful, twice as wonderful as by day—especially to people coming straight in out of the snow.

The dome glowed with electroactinic light matched to some reflecting index which did not interfere with the passage of sunlight the other way. I could not see the source. The light was not bright, only a little stronger than that of a full moon on Earth.

And the huge Park was alive with couples. It must be the longest, widest and busiest lovers' lane in the whole of the galaxy. Soft laughter came from behind every bush.

I was relieved to find that Terry in her yellow playsuit was not unduly conspicuous. The Park was as warm as by day, and since it was a place for the young, the clothes worn were youthful.

We kept walking because when we moved it was scarcely possible that what we said could be overheard.

"Terry," I said. "Have I got this right? The people who disappear are young, of both sexes, and highly patriotic?"

"That's my impression."

"Before they get married and have children?"

"Well, of course. You said that was interesting. Why?"

"Because in this kind of world the people you expect to disappear are the people who disapprove of the setup—the individualists, rebels, intellectuals, anarchists, agitators, reformers."

"Well—it's not like that."

"So they *disappear* . . . they don't die."

"How do you make that out?"

"How much do you know about Henry Arne, the Arne this park and city are named after?"

"Oh, quite a lot. I've been to school, you know. What do you want to know?"

"I don't need to ask you about him, Terry. I'm a historian, you know. Suppose he'd been an individualist himself, a fanatic believer in human freedom, he might long ago have set up a secret but all-powerful organization to weed out the conformists, the yes-men, the people who could be influenced by propaganda."

Terry stopped and grabbed my arm. "That's what happened! Of course it is!"

I shook my head. "No. Arne loved Solitaire so much he was crazy about it. In that way he was a fanatic. He had so much power he was nothing more or less than a dictator. Anything he wanted done was done. So anything he wanted set up *was* set up. Openly or secretly."

"You think he did set up some secret organization?"

"Yes, but not the kind I mentioned. Arne believed passionately that if Solitaire were fully developed it would inevitably be ruined by the predators who are drawn to a rich, successful world, or who are created by it. He believed that if Solitaire were to grow up strong and free and healthy, *it must grow up poor.*"

This time Terry didn't say anything. She was lost. After all, she knew nothing about any world but her own. She had nothing to compare it with.

"Whether Arne was right or not," I mused, "what he wanted for Solitaire has come about. Either by chance or by design, Solitaire hasn't grown strong and rich and successful. It could hardly be by chance, for reasons which I won't go into just now. So it must be by design—almost certainly Arne's design. Which means that he somehow set up a situation, a plan, which is still working two centuries after his death.

"None of this is new, Terry. Anybody who took the trouble could make guesses along these lines without coming near Solitaire. And when you said there were rumors of disappearances, that wasn't any surprise either. The population of Solitaire should be multiplying itself by about six every century. And it's not. At a guess, with no figures to go on, it's only multiplied itself by two in two centuries."

"You can't mean that all these people have disappeared. That they were born and . . . and . . ."

"Died? Were transported? Well, what do you think, Terry? Doesn't nearly everybody get married? Doesn't the average couple have three children?"

"I guess so. But what does that mean?"

"It means," I said, "that in the last two hundred years anything from one to three thousand million people have . . . disappeared."

I expected some reaction from Terry. There was none. Looking around me, I saw why.

Men were approaching us from all directions. They

were so purposeful that it was clear F.R.S. had decided to take us in—if not to shoot us on the spot.

Running was futile. Even Terry realized that. She shrank against me and I squeezed her hand.

Tom Harrison was in charge.

"So you're something quite important in F.R.S., Tom," I said conversationally.

"Quite important," he said drily, with no trace of his former diffident manner. "In fact, I'm the chief."

"I'm honored," I said.

At the gate, Harrison refused to allow us to take our coats. He was right. There was something about my coat that . . . well, anyway, it didn't really matter.

"You're not making Terry go outside like that?" I protested.

"There's a car just outside the door," said Harrison briefly.

There were quite a lot of people about, and naturally they stared as we were hustled into the car. Terry shivered violently as the snowflakes settled on her bare shoulders. But then we were in the car, and she had more to worry about than the cold.

We were taken to a room in Government House, a small room with nothing important in it—no windows, one door, a table, some chairs. Present were Harrison, Terry and I, and two other men, not in uniform.

"We won't do any pretending, shall we?" asked Harrison.

"Not if you'd rather not," I said agreeably.

"Frankly," said Harrison, "I'd rather you simply decided to go away, Horsefeld."

"Taking Terry with me?"

"She stays here, whatever happens." Casually, he looked her up and down, rather as if he were a censor and she were a dirty book.

Terry went pale.

"She never took to Solitaire's nationalism," I said easily. "I think you'd better let her come to Earth with me."

Harrison shook his head. For a moment something hard showed in his eyes: he didn't like traitors. And there was no denying that Terry was a traitor.

"Didn't you expect her to throw in her lot with me?" I asked.

"We did not. We thought either loyalty or sense would keep her from the stupid course she has taken. Not that it greatly matters. You leave Solitaire no wiser than when you came, Horsefeld."

"You're sending me away, then?"

"After you've both been questioned under drugs. You can see the girl die if you like before you go."

"In that case," I said, "I'd better talk now and save time."

"Bluffing is useless. We're using the drugs anyway."

"But questioning under drugs is extremely slow, as we both know very well. When I talk, do you want these two to hear what I say?" I indicated the two guards.

Harrison nodded to them and they went outside. That was interesting. Our chances of escape remained precisely nil, but the fact that Harrison sent them away probably meant that they were not in the secret—that very few were, in fact.

"I've found out quite a lot about the Arne plan," I said, "and guessed the rest. Enough to stop it, I think."

Harrison's reaction was slight, but there was a reaction. I was greatly encouraged. I didn't know the whole story, any more than a fortune-teller did when a client entered. Yet she was trained to make an initial good guess and go on guessing, instantly abandoning a false trail and following up anything that got a reaction.

I was surprised that Harrison let me do this. However, Harrison erroneously thought he held all the cards.

"Everybody always knew about the disappearances," I said, "but that was Solitaire's affair. We thought rebels were simply eliminated. We didn't know they were being saved up, put in the bank, so to speak. We should have known. It's exactly the kind of crazy scheme Henry Arne *would* think up. Anything to put Solitaire on top anything."

Harrison looked back at me as blankly as Terry was doing.

Yet he was still listening. So I went on with a new surge of confidence, knowing that even if I didn't have everything, I had enough. "I admit I don't know where the Arne army is, but once I realized that it was the patriots who were put away, I knew they were in suspended animation somewhere. Probably under the Park. You haven't really been very clever, Harrison. In fact, wasn't it rather stupid to let me know you knew Terry was on my side and that you were watching us, and do nothing until we started wandering around in the Park?"

"Horsefeld," said Harrison quietly, "what are you up to? You know I can't let you go now."

Fool of a man, I thought exultantly. He'd *told* me I was right.

"The end of the plan, I guess," I said, "is that in a few centuries from now Solitaire will gradually waken up. Exports will rise, assets will be converted into cash and machinery. Thousands of young people will be sent to Earth and other planets to attend colleges. They'll come back as trained up-to-the-minute technicians, and they'll start turning Solitaire into a slick, high-powered, efficient world. Then the army will be awakened and trained. By that time it could be as many billion strong as you want. An army of——"

"For what?" Harrison snapped.

"An army that size consisting entirely of patriots could only be designed for one thing—to make Solitaire top dog in the galaxy. Obviously Arne was a megalomaniac. I don't know how he ensured that only other megalomaniacs should be chosen to play their part in the scheme through the centuries, but evidently he succeeded——"

Harrison's gun came up. He wasn't going to argue. He was merely executing Terry and me on the spot, to make sure there were no more mistakes.

"I wouldn't do it if I were you," I said, putting an edge in my voice. "Not long go you asked what I was up to. You knew I must be up to something. You were quite right. I was."

"Well?" said Harrison, his gun pointed straight at my heart.

"You've let yourself get behind technologically here on Solitaire," I said steadily. "So far behind that it probably never even occurred to you that everything that was said in this room was being picked up and recorded for delivery to Earth?"

Harrison didn't try to hide his consternation. If I was bluffing, it wouldn't gain me anything, but a little time. If I wasn't, neither he nor I mattered much any more.

"These buttons," I said, fingering them. "I expect you

had them examined very closely, as you examined everything else—I noticed how thorough the so-called customs examination was. They're simple, ordinary plastic buttons. X-rays would show nothing—you tried all that, of course. If you sawed them up you'd still find nothing. But they happen to be of a new material that resonates with sound vibrations, and on one of the two Terran Navy ships hanging about just clear of Solitaire's atmosphere the most powerful amplifier you ever saw is able to——"

"I don't believe it."

"You don't have to. I can prove it if you like."

"How?"

"Would you like a bomb dropped on Arne Park in ten minutes' time? Or in a more friendly spirit, some colored lights over Arneville? Let me suggest we make it a tender for Terry and me, landing in front of this building in . . . say an hour's time?"

Harrison was staring at me. Suddenly he said: "Get out of those clothes. I want every stitch you're wearing." He turned his head to Terry. "You too."

I laughed. "Shutting the stable door after the horse has bolted only prevents him getting back in."

"Quickly!" said Harrison sharply. "Or I shoot you both, here and now."

Trying hard not to show her fear of the gun waving about at us, Terry stood up straight, defiantly, and started to unfasten her playsuit. I let her go on, because I had thought of something else I'd better tell the Navy ships, although it should hardly be necessary.

"If you have any idea of chasing the ships or trying to blow them out of space," I said, "forget it. The first ship must already be building up acceleration back to Earth. She has all the information she needs. And you'll never catch her . . . Terry, hold it."

"I want those clothes," said Harrison savagely.

"Take the buttons," I said, tearing them off. "Be reasonable, Tom. If I'm lying, there's no point in destroying my clothes, as I presume you're going to do. If I'm not, it's too late—I've said enough already, and anything else that's said will hardly be worth recording."

Harrison hesitated. "All right," he said abruptly. "Tell them to send down the tender. But I'll take those buttons." He did.

Terry, who had taken off the wrap-around part of her suit and was halfway through making the penultimate sacrifice—I caught a quick glimpse of one rosy firm breast—reclaimed her modesty at the moment of surrender.

"You," said Harrison viciously, his cold gaze on Terry, "are not going."

Dropping the buttons in his pocket, he went out.

Terry said: "Edwin, is all that true?"

"All," I said. "Say what you like, Terry, so long as you remember that F.R.S. is taking careful note of everything you say."

The polite hint startled her only for a moment.

"Are they going to let us go?"

Me, yes. Terry, no. Terry had helped to break the Arne plan—for it was certainly broken now. Harrison and F.R.S. wouldn't let her get away with it. Nearly everybody is vicious in defeat.

However, if I put my awareness of this into words, it would finish off any chance I might have of saving Terry.

She had not picked up her wrap and although she was holding her suntop together she had not fastened it. I knew that with the frightening directness of innocence she was trying even at this moment to provoke some reaction from me. Although she had never put it into words, she made no secret of her disappointment and pique that I had never treated her in a way I would not have treated my own teenage daughters.

"That crazy story can't be true, can it?"

"It's crazy but it's certainly true in essence."

"That all these people who disappeared are alive, and can be brought back? Steve too?"

"Yes. In a way it's a heroic plan, from the Solitaire angle. An army of specially selected patriots never existed before. It would fight as no army has ever fought . . ."

"I can't understand why you should be allowed to go."

"Well, I'm here as Earth's semi-official representative. And whatever Solitaire might be in a few hundred years, as of now Earth could crack her like an eggshell. If Harrison shot me, Earth could use my death as an excuse to take Solitaire apart."

Since she apparently wasn't going to do it, I gently fastened her halter by the button in the middle and put the wrap around her.

"Edwin," she pleaded, "don't you care about me at all?"

"I care *about* you very much. Care *for* you—no, not in the way you mean. Terry, there hasn't been much love in your life, that's obvious. You don't really want me as a lover, you want me as a father."

"I don't! I——"

"With me as a father, you'd soon find yourself seeing boys your own age with different eyes. A girl your age needs parents so she can grow out of them."

We talked for an hour. Terry never once mentioned her own danger. In much the same way, patients who know they are going to die make plans for the future.

At last Harrison came back. "A small ship has just landed outside," he said.

"So?"

"So you'd better get on it."

"And what are you going to do? What did the premier say?"

Harrison hesitated, then smiled faintly. "Tell Earth, Horsefeld," he said, "that you can't do a thing to us. As of now, the Arne plan is reversed. If we must—we'll grow rich and fat. We've all the workers we need to transform Solitaire."

I grinned back. "So that's the way of it? That's your business, so long as the original Arne plan is buried. It's nothing to us. Come along, Terry."

"Terry isn't going. I told you."

"Then neither am I."

"Don't be a fool," said Harrison harshly. "Did you ever think there was one chance in a million that we'd let her live?"

Terry tried to hide behind me. As she pressed against me I could feel her heart racing.

"I can make things awkward for you, or easy," I said. "Which is it to be?"

Harrison hesitated again. "I haven't the power to let her go."

"But I'm supposed to go, isn't that so?"

I let the deadlock hang for a few more seconds. Harrison was not really a good actor. His chubby, innocent face might reveal very little; his hesitations and silences revealed a lot.

I was now certain he had been *instructed* to see me off the planet.

"Tell you what," I said at last. "Let us get to the tender, then shoot Terry—and miss. That'll clear you personally."

"Okay," said Harrison instantly.

We walked through Government House, which was silent and empty. We were accompanied not by two but by seven guards, so it was a procession of ten that strode through the empty, echoing building.

We marched out into the night. Again Terry shivered in the snow. The tender was two hundred yards away, a miniature spaceship, sleek, gleaming, and with an air of terrible efficiency.

I hung back to let Terry go first. We were almost at the ship. Terran naval officers were saluting me and eyeing Terry with startled admiration.

She could have stretched out her arms and touched the hull.

Unfortunately it was Harrison I was watching; Harrison did nothing. It was one of the guards who raised his gun suddenly and fired.

The instant before the shot, I pulled Terry's arm and she lurched toward me. Nevertheless, the shot didn't miss. She dropped in the snow with a small red hole in her back.

I swept her up in my arms and leapt inside, knowing Harrison wouldn't let me be shot. Inside the lock I saw familiar faces. "Get off, quick," I said, still holding Terry in my arms. She had not made a sound since the shot. Although I had known she was tiny, she was even lighter than I expected.

There is always a doctor on a tender, by regulation. The doctor stepped forward and led the way to a tiny cabin. I put Terry face down on the bunk.

"Now go away," said the doctor.

In the control room Commander Stimson shook my hand. "Well, you made it, Edwin. Did you ever hear anything so crazy? Would they have gotten away with it?"

"They might," I said. "Depends on our espionage system a few centuries from now."

"I must say," Stimson protested, "I didn't expect you of all people to bring a half naked girl away with you."

I found it hard to be polite. All my thoughts were in the tiny cabin in which Terry lay still with a bullet through her lung certainly, if not through her heart.

"Funny business altogether," said Stimson, who was a good naval officer but not gifted with much imagination. "Hard to believe some of it. In fact, I don't believe it now."

"We'll leave that to Terran Intelligence," I said.

The tender shot up toward its parent ship. The battleship swallowed it neatly and immediately began to pile on acceleration for Earth.

The door in the little cabin in the tender had not yet opened.

I had to make my report to the captain. I had changed my clothes before going back to the tender.

At last the doctor emerged.

"Will she live?" I asked.

"Oh, I shouldn't be surprised. She shouldn't have been moved, you know."

"Can I see her?"

The doctor shrugged.

I went into the cabin quietly. Terry looked ghastly. If I'd seen her like that before seeing the doctor I'd have been sure she was dying. But she was conscious.

"Next stop Earth," I said gently.

"Edwin . . ."

"Don't talk," I said. "And anyway, you're not to call me Edwin any more."

"What am I to call you?"

I said one word very firmly: "Dad."

SHAMAR'S WAR

Kris Neville

I

THE YEAR WAS 2346, and Earth, at the time, was a political democracy.

The population was ruled by the Over-Council and, in order of decreasing importance, by councils, and local councils. Each was composed of representatives duly apportioned by popular vote between the two contending parties. Executive direction was provided by a variety of secretaries, selected by vote of the appropriate councils. An independent judiciary upheld the laws.

A unified Earth sent colonists to the stars. Back came strange tales and improbable animals.

Back, too, came word of a burgeoning technological civilization on the planet Itra, peopled by entirely humanoid aliens.

Earth felt it would be wise for Itra to join in a galactic federation and accordingly, submitted the terms of such a mutually advantageous agreement.

The Itraians declined . . . .

Space Captain Merle S. Shaeffer, the youngest and perhaps the most naive pilot for Trans-Universe Transport, was called unexpectedly to the New York office of the company.

When Captain Shaeffer entered the luxurious eightieth story suite, Old Tom Twilmaker, the president of TUT, greeted him. With an arm around his shoulder, Old Tom led Captain Shaeffer to an immense inner office and introduced him to a General Reuter, identified as the Chairman of the Interscience Committee of the Over-Council.

No one else was present. With the door closed, they were isolated in Olympian splendor above and beyond the affairs of men. Here judgments were final and impartial. Captain Shaeffer, in the presence of two of the men highest in the ruling councils of Earth, was reduced to incoherent awe.

When they were seated, Old Tom swiveled around and gazed long in silence across the spires of the City. Captain Shaeffer waited respectfully. General Reuter fidgeted.

"Some day," Old Tom said at last, "I'm going to take my leave of this. Yes, gentle Jesus! Oh, when I think of all the souls still refusing to admit our precious Savior, what bitterness, oh, what sorrow is my wealth to me! Look down upon the teeming millions below us. How many know not the Lord? Yes, some morning, I will forsake all this and go out into the streets to spend my last days bringing the words of hope to the weary and oppressed. Are you a Christian, Merle?"

General Reuter cracked his knuckles nervously while Captain Shaeffer muttered an embarrassed affirmative.

"I am a deeply religious man," Old Tom continued. "I guess you've heard that, Merle?"

"Yes sir," Captain Shaeffer said.

"But did you know that the Lord has summoned you here today?" Old Tom asked.

"No, sir," Captain Shaeffer said.

"General Reuter, here, is a dear friend. We've known each other, oh, many years. Distantly related through our dear wives, in fact. And we serve on the same board of directors and the same charity committees . . . A few weeks ago, when he asked me for a man, I called for your file, Merle. I made discreet inquiries. Then I got down on my knees and talked it over with God for, oh, it must have been all of an hour. I asked, 'Is this the man?' And I was given a sign. Yes! At that moment, a shaft of sunlight broke through the clouds!"

General Reuter had continued his nervous movements throughout the speech. For the first time, he spoke. "Good God, Tom, serve us a drink." He turned to Captain Shaeffer. "A little drink now and then helps a man relax. I'll just have mine straight, Tom."

Old Tom studied Captain Shaeffer. "I do not feel the gentle Master approves of liquor."

"Don't try to influence him," General Reuter said. "You're embarrassing the boy."

"I—" Captain Shaeffer began.

"Give him the drink. If he doesn't want to drink it, he won't have to drink it."

Sighing, Old Tom poured two bourbons from the bar in back of his desk and passed them over. Martyrdom sat heavily upon his brow.

After a quick twist of the wrist and an expert toss of the head, General Reuter returned an empty glass. "Don't mind if I do have another," he said. He was already less restless.

"How's your ability to pick up languages?" General Reuter asked.

"I learned Spanish and Russian at TUT PS," Captain Shaeffer said apologetically. "I'm supposed to have a real high aptitude in languages, according to some tests I took. In case we should meet intelligent aliens, TUT gives them."

"You got no association with crackpot organizations, anything like that?" General Reuter asked. "You're either a good Liberal-Conservative or Radical-Progressive, aren't you? I don't care which. I don't believe in prying into a man's politics."

"I never belonged to anything," Captain Shaeffer said.

"Oh, I can assure you, that's been checked out very, very thoroughly," Old Tom said.

The general signaled for another drink. With a sigh of exasperation, Old Tom complied.

"Bob," Old Tom said, "I really think you've had enough. Please, now. Our Master counsels moderation."

"Damn it, Tom," the General said and turned back to the space pilot. "May have a little job for you."

Old Tom shook his head at the general, cautioning him.

"Actually," the general said, ignoring the executive, "we'll be sort of renting you from TUT. In a way you'll still be working for them. I can get a million dollars out of the—"

"Bob!"

"—unmarked appropriation if it goes in in TUT's name. No questions asked. National Defense. I couldn't get anywhere near that much for an individual for a year. It gives us a pie to slice. We were talking about it before you came in. How does a quarter of a million dollars a year sound to you?"

"When it comes to such matters," Old Tom interjected hastily, "I think first of the opportunities they bring to do good."

The general continued, "Now you know, Merle. And this is serious. I want you to listen to me. Because this comes under world security laws, and I'm going to bind you to them. You know what that means? You'll be held responsible."

"Yes, sir," Merle said, swallowing stiffly. "I understand."

"Good. Let's have a drink on that."

"Please be quiet, General," Old Tom said. "Let me explain. You see, Merle, the Interscience Committee was recently directed to consider methods for creating a climate of opinion on Itra—of which I'm sure you've heard—which would be favorable to the proposed Galactic Federation."

"Excuse me," General Reuter said. "They don't have a democracy, like we do. They don't have any freedom like we do. I have no doubt the average whateveryoucallem—Itraians, I guess—the average gooks—would be glad to see us come in and just kick the hell out of whoever is in charge of them."

"Now, General," Old Tom said more sharply.

"But that's not the whole thing," the general continued. "Even fit were right thing to do, an' I'm not saying isn't—right thing to do—there's log-lo-lo-gistics. I don't want to convey the impresh, impression that our Defense Force people have been wasting money. Never had as much as needed, fact. No, it's like this.

"We have this broad base to buil' from. Backbone. But we live in a democracy. Now, Old Tom's Liberal-Conservative. And me, I'm Radical-Progresshive. But we agree on one thing: importance of strong defense. A lot of people don' understan' this. Feel we're already spendin' more than we can afford. But I want to ask them, what's more important than the defense of our planet?"

"General, I'm afraid this is not entirely germane," Old Tom said stiffly.

"Never mind that right now. Point is, it will take us long time to get the serious nature of the menace of Itra across to the voters. Ten, maybe fifteen, twenty years . . . Let's just take one thing. We don't have anywhere near enough troop transports to carry out the occupation of Itra. You know how long it takes to build them? My point is, we may not have that long. Suppose Itra should get secret of interstellar drive tomorrow, then where would we be?"

Old Tom slammed his fist on the desk. "General, please! The boy isn't interested in all that."

The general surged angrily to his feet. "By God, that's what's wrong with this world today!" he cried. "Nobody's interested in defense. Spend only a measly twenty per cent of the Gross World Product on defense, and expect to keep strong! Good God, Tom, give me a drink!" Apparently heresy had shocked him sober.

Old Tom explained, "The general is a patriot. We all respect him for it."

"I understand," Captain Shaeffer said.

General Reuter hammered his knuckles in rhythm on the table. "The drink, the drink, the drink! You got more in the bottle. I saw it!"

Old Tom rolled his eyes heavenward and passed the bottle across. "This is all you get. This is all I've got."

The general held the bottle up to the light. "Should have brought my own. Let's hurry up and get this over with."

Old Tom smiled the smile of the sorely beset and persecuted and said, "You see, Merle, there's massive discontent among the population of Itra. We feel we should send a man to the planet to, well, foment change and, uh, hasten the already inevitable overthrow of the despotic government. That man will be strictly on his own. The Government will not be able to back him in any way whatsoever once he lands on Itra."

The general had quickly finished the bottle. "You she," he interrupted, "there's one thing they can't fight, an' that's an idea. Jus' one man goes to Itra with the idea of freedom, that's all it'll take. How many men did it take to start the 'Merican Revolution? Jefferson. The Russian Revolution? Marx!"

"Yes," Old Tom said. "One dedicated man on Itra, preaching the ideas of liberty—liberty with responsibility and property rights under one God. That man can change a world." Exhausted by the purity of his emotions, Old Tom sat back gasping to await the answer.

"A quarter of a million dollars a year?" Captain Shaeffer asked at length.

II

THE ITRAIANS spoke a common language. It was somewhat

guttural and highly inflected. Fortunately, the spelling appeared to be phonetic, with only forty-three characters being required. As near as anyone could tell, centuries of worldwide communication had eliminated regional peculiarities. The speech from one part of Itra was not distinguishable from that of another part.

Most of the language was recovered from spy tapes of television programs. A dictionary was compiled laboriously by a special scientific task force of the Over-Council. The overall program was directed and administered by Intercontinental Iron, Steel, Gas, Electricity, Automobiles and Synthetics, Incorporated.

It took Shaeffer just short of three years to speak Itraian sufficiently well to convince non-Itraians that he spoke without accent.

The remainder of his training program was administered by a variety of other large industrial concerns. The training was conducted at a defense facility.

At the end of his training, Shaeffer was taken by special bus to the New Mexican spaceport. A ship waited.

The car moved smoothly from the Defense Force base, down the broad sixteen-lane highway, through the surrounding slum area and into Grants.

Sight of the slums gave Shaeffer mixed emotions.

It was not a feeling of superiority to the inhabitants; those he had always regarded with a circumspect indifference. The slums were there. He supposed they always would be there. But now, for the first time in his life, he could truly say that he had escaped their omnipresent threat once and for all. He felt relief and guilt.

During the last three years, he had earned $750,000.

As a civilian stationed on a Defense Force base, he had, of course, to pay for his clothing, his food and his lodging. But the charge was nominal. Since he had been given only infrequent and closely supervised leaves, he had been able to spend, altogether, only $12,000.

Which meant that now, after taxes, he had accumulated in his savings account a total of nearly $60,000 awaiting his return from Itra.

Shaeffer's ship stood off Itra while he prepared to disembark.

In his cramped quarters, he dressed himself in Itraianstyle clothing. Captain Merle S. Shaeffer became Shamar the Worker.

In addition to his jump equipment, an oxygen cylinder, a face mask and a shovel, he carried with him eighty pounds of counterfeit Itraian currency . . . all told forty thousand individual bills of various denominations. Earth felt this would be all he would need to survive in a technologically advanced civilization.

His plan was as follows:

1. He was to land in a sparsely inhabited area on the larger masses.

2. He was to procure transportation to Xxla, a major city, equivalent to London or Tokyo. It was the headquarters for the Party.

3. He was to establish residence in the slum area surrounding the University of Xxla.

4. Working through student contacts, he was to ingratiate himself with such rebel intellectuals as could be found.

5. Once his contacts were secure, he was to assist in the preparation of propaganda and establish a clandestine press for its production.

6. As quickly as the operation was self-sufficient, he was to move on to another major city . . . and begin all over.

The ship descended into the atmosphere. The bell rang. Shamar the Worker seated himself, put on his oxygen mask and signaled his readiness. He breathed oxygen. The ship quivered, the door fell away beneath him and he was battered unconscious by the slipstream.

Five minutes later, pinwheeling lazily in free fall, he opened his eyes. For an instant's panic he could not read the altimeter. Then seeing that he was safe, he noted his physical sensations. He was extremely cold. Gyrating wildly, he beat his chest to restore circulation.

He stabilized his fall by stretching out his hands. He floated with no sensation of movement. Itra was overhead, falling up at him slowly. He turned his back to the planet and checked the time. Twelve minutes yet to go.

He spent, in all, seventeen minutes in free fall. At two thousand feet, he opened his parachute. The sound was like an explosion.

He floated quietly, recovering from the shock. He removed his oxygen mask and tasted the alien air. He sniffed several times. It was not unpleasant.

Below was darkness. Then suddenly the ground came floating up and hit him.

The terrain was irregular. He fought the chute to collapse it, tripped, and twisted his ankle painfully.

The chute lay quiet and he sat on the ground and cursed in English.

At length he bundled up the chute and removed all of the packages of money but the one disguised as a field pack. He used the shovel to dig a shallow grave at the base of a tree. He interred the chute, the oxygen cylinder, the mask, the shovel and scooped dirt over them with his hands.

He sat down and unlaced his shoe and found his ankle badly swollen. Distant, unfamiliar odors filled him with apprehension and he started at the slightest sound.

Dawn was breaking.

III

NOTING HIS bearings carefully, he hobbled painfully westward, with thirty pounds of money on his back. He would intersect the major North-South Intercontinental highway by at least noon.

Two hours later, he came to a small plastic cabin in a clearing at the edge of a forest.

Wincing now with each step, he made his way to the door. He knocked.

There was a long wait.

The door opened. A girl stood before him in a dressing gown. She frowned and asked, "*Itsil obwatly jer gekompilp?*"

Hearing Itraian spoken by a native in the flesh had a powerful emotional impact on Shamar the Worker.

Stumblingly, he introduced himself and explained that he was camping out. During the previous night he had become lost and injured his ankle. If she could spare him food and directions, he would gladly pay.

With a smile of superiority, she stepped aside and said in Itraian, "Come in, Chom the Worker."

He felt panic, but he choked it back and followed her. Apparently he had horribly mispronounced his own name. It was as though in English he had said Barchestershire for Barset. He cursed whatever professor had picked that name for whatever obscure reason.

"Sit down," she invited. "I'm about to have breakfast. Eggs and bacon—" the Itraian equivalent—"if that's all right with you. I'm Garfling Germadpoldlt, by the way, although you can call me Ge-Ge."

The food was quite unpleasant, as though overly ripe. He was able to choke down the eggs with the greatest difficulty. Fortunately, the hot drink that was the equivalent of Earth Coffee at the end of the meal, was sufficiently spicy to quiet his stomach.

"Good coffee," he said.

"Thank you. Care for a cigarette?"

"I sure would."

The taste of the cigarette was mild. Rather surprisingly, it substituted for nicotine and allayed the sharp longing that had come with the coffee.

"Let's look at your ankle," she said. She knelt at his feet and began to unlace the right shoe. "My, it's swollen," she said sympathetically.

He winced as she touched it and then he reddened with embarrassment. He had been walking across dusty country. He drew back the foot and bent to restrain her.

Playfully she slapped his hand away. "You sit back! I'll get it. I've seen dirty feet before."

She pulled off the shoe and peeled off the sock. "Oh, God, it is swollen," she said. "You think it's broken, Shamar?"

"Just sprained."

"I'll get some hot water with some MedAid in it, and that'll take the swelling out."

When he had his foot in the water, she sat across from him and arranged her dressing gown with a coquettish gesture. She caught him staring at the earring, and one hand went to it caressingly. She smiled that universal feminine smile of security and recklessness, of invitation and rejection.

"You're engaged," he noted.

She opened her eyes wide and studied him above a thumbnail which she tasted with her teeth. "I'm engaged to Von Stutsman"—as the name might be translated—"Perhaps you've heard of him? He's important in the Party. You know him?"

"No."

"You in the Party?" she said. She was teasing him now. Then, suddenly: "Neither am I, but I guess I'll have to join if I become Mrs. Von Stutsman."

They were silent for a moment.

Then she spoke, and he was frozen in terror, all thoughts but of self-preservation washed from his mind.

"Your accent is unbelieveably bad," she said.

"I'm from Zuleb," he said lamely, at last.

"Meta—Gelwhops—or even Karkeqwol, that makes no difference. Nobody on Itra speaks like you do. So you must be from that planet that had the Party in a flap several years ago—Earth, isn't it?"

He said nothing.

"Do you know what they'll do when they catch you?" she asked

"No," he said hollowly.

"They'll behead you."

She laughed, not unkindly. "If you could see yourself! How ridiculous you look, Shamar. I wonder what your real name is, by the way? Sitting with a foot in the water and looking wildly about. Here, let me fix more coffee and we can talk."

She called cheerily over her shoulder, "You're safe here. No one will be by. I'm not due back until Tuesday."

She brought him a steaming mug. "Drink this while I dress." She disappeared into the bedroom. He heard the shower running.

He sat waiting, numb and desperate, and drank the coffee because it was there. His thoughts scampered in the cage of his skull like mice on a treadmill.

When Ge-Ge came back, he had still not resolved the conflict within him. She stood barefoot upon the rug and looked down at him, hunched miserably over the pan of water, now lukewarm.

"How's the foot?"

"All right."

"Want to take it out?"

"I guess."

"I'll get a towel."

She waited until he had dried the foot and restored the sock and shoe. The swelling was gone. He stood up and put his weight on it. He smiled wanly. "It's okay now. It's not broken, I guess."

She gestured him to the sofa. He complied.

"What's in the field pack?" she asked. "Money? How much?" She moved toward it. He half rose to stop her, but by then she had it partly open. "My," she said, bringing out a thick sheaf of bills. She rippled them sensuously. "Pretty. Very, very pretty." She examined them for texture and appearance. "They look good, Shamar. I'll bet it would cost ten million dollars in research on paper and ink and presses to do this kind of a job. Only another government has got that kind of money to throw around." She tossed the currency carelessly beside him and came to sit at his side.

She took his hand. Her hand was warm and gentle. "Tell me, Shamar," she said. "Tell me all about it."

So this is how easily spies are trapped in real life, Shamar told himself with numb disbelief.

The story came out slowly and hesitantly at first. She said nothing until he had finished.

"And that's all? You really believe that, don't you? And I guess your government does, too. That all we need is just some little idea or something." She turned away from him. "But of course, that's neither here nor there, is it? I never imagined an adventurer type would look like you. You have such a soft, honest voice. As a little girl, I pictured myself being carried off by a tanned desert sheik on a camel; and oh, he was lean and handsome! With the dark flashing eyes and murderously heavy lips and hands like iron! Well, that's life, I guess." She stood and paced the room. "Let me think. We'll pick up a flyer in Zelonip when we catch the bus next Tuesday. How much does the money weigh?"

"Eighty pounds."

"I can carry about 10 pounds in my bag. You can take your field pack. How much is in it? Thirty pounds? That'll leave about forty, which we can ship through on extra charges. Then, when we get to Xxla, I can hide you out in an apartment over on the East side."

"Why would you run a risk like that for me?" he asked.

She brushed the hair from her face. "Let's say—what? I don't really think you can make it, because it's so hopeless. But maybe, just maybe, you might be one of the rare ones who, if he plays his cards right, can beat the system. I love to see them licked!

"Well, I'm a clerk. That's all. Just a lowly clerk in one of the Party offices. I met Von Stutsman a year ago. This is his cabin He lets me use it.

"He's older than I am; but there's worse husband material. But then again, he's about to be transferred to one of the big agricultural combines way out in the boondocks where there's no excitement at all. Just little old ladies and little old men and peasants having children.

"I'm a city girl. I like Xxla. And if I marry him, all that goes up the flue. I'll be marooned with him, God knows where, for years. Stuck, just stuck.

"Still—he is Von Stutsman, and he's on his way up. Everyone says that. Ten, twenty years, he'll be back to Xxla, and he'll come back on top.

"Oh . . . I don't know what I want to do! If I marry him, I can get all the things I've always wanted. Position, security. He's older than I am, but he's really a nice guy. It's just that he's dull. He can't talk about anything but Party, Party, Party.

"That's what I came out to this cabin for. To think things over, to try to get things straightened out. And then you came along. Maybe it gives me a chance for something exciting before I ship off to the boondocks. Does that make sense to you?

"I'll get married and sit out there, and I'll turn the pages of the Party magazine and smile sweetly to myself. Because, you see, I'll always be able to lean forward and say, 'Dear? Once upon a time, I helped hide an Earth spy in Xxla. And that'll knock that silly and self-satisfied look off his face for once . . . Oh, I don't know! Let me alone!" With that, she fled to the bedroom and slammed the door behind her.

He could hear her sobbing helplessly.

In the afternoon, she came out. He had fallen asleep. She shook him gently to waken him.

"Eh? Oh! Huh?" He smiled foolishly.

"Wash up in there," she told him. "I'm sorry I blew up on you this morning. I'll cook something."

When he came back, she was serving them their dinner on steaming platters.

"Look, Ge-Ge," he said over coffee. "You don't like your government. We'll help you out. There's this galactic federation idea." He explained to her the cross-fertilization of the two cultures.

"Shamar, my friend," she said, "did you see Earth's proposal? There was nothing in it about giving us an interstellar drive. We were required to give Earth all transportation franchises. The organization you used to work for was to be given, as I remember it, an exclusive ninety-nine year right to carry all Earth-Itra commerce. It was all covered in the newspapers, didn't you see it?"

Shamar said, "Well, now, I'm not familiar with the details. I wasn't keeping up with them. But I'm sure these things could be, you know, worked out. Maybe, for security reasons, we didn't want to give you the interstellar drive right off, but you can appreciate our logic there. Once we saw you were, well, like us, a peace-loving planet, once you'd changed your government to a democracy, you would see it our way and you'd have no complaints on that score."

"Let's not talk politics," she said wearily. "Maybe it's what you say, and I'm just naturally suspicious. I don't want to talk about it."

"Well, I was just trying to help——"

The sentence was interrupted by a monstrous explosion.

"Good God!" Shamar cried. "What was that?"

"Oh, that," Ge-Ge said, shaking off the effects. "They were probably testing one of their damned automated factories to see if it was explosion-proof and it wasn't."

IV

DURING THE week alone in the cabin, Ge-Ge fell in love with Shamar.

"Oh, my God!" she cried. "What will I do when they catch you? I'll die, Shamar! I couldn't bear it. We'll go to Xxla, we'll hide away as quietly as two mice, somewhere. We won't go out. The two of us, alone but together, behind closed doors and drawn shades. Nobody will ever know about us. We'll be the invisible people."

Shamar protested. "I don't see how we can ever be secure until something's done about your government. As long as you don't reach some kind of agreement with

Earth, I'll be an outlaw. I'll be afraid any minute they'll tap my shoulder and come and take me away. I don't think we could hold up under that. We'd be at each other in no time."

She wept quietly.

The last day in the cabin, they went out and dug up the rest of the money. The trip to Xxla took place without incident. Ge-Ge rented an apartment for him, and he safely checked in. She went shopping for food and clothing.

Thereafter she came nearly every evening. They would eat and she would reveal the inconsequential details of the office regime to which she was daily exposed. After dinner, they would sit in the living room and practice Itraian and neck a little. Then she would go home.

One day, after a month of this routine, she threw herself into his arms and sobbed, "I gave Von Stutsman back his earring today. It was the only fair thing to do. I'm afraid he knows about us. He's had me watched. I know he has. I admitted it was another man."

Shamar held her tensely.

She broke away. "You were born in Zuleb, you suffered amnesia, you woke up in a ditch one morning without papers. You've been an itinerant worker since. Things like that happen all the time. You hit a big lottery ticket a few months ago. I told him that. How can he check it?"

"You told him I didn't have any papers?"

"Millions of people don't have any papers—the drifters, people that do casual labor, the people that don't work at all. The thing is, without papers he doesn't have any way to check on you. Oh, you should have seen his face when I gave him back his earring. He was absolutely livid. I didn't think he had it in him. I suppose I'll have to quit my job now. Oh, if you only had papers so we could be married!"

Ge-Ge's mood, that evening, alternated between despair and optimism. In the end, she was morose, and restless. She repeated several times, "I just don't know what's going to happen to us."

"Ge-Ge," he said, "I can't spend my life in this apartment. I've got to get out."

"You're mad." She faced him from across the room. She stood with her legs apart, firmly set. "Well, I don't care what happens any more. I can't stand things to go on like they are. I'll introduce you to some people I know, since you won't be happy until I do. But God help us!"

After approving his accent, which had improved under her tutelage, Ge-Ge took him to a party the following Saturday.

The party was held in an ill-lighted railroad flat. People congregated cross-legged on the bare floor.

Shamar listened to a man complaining that citizens were being taxed beyond all endurance to support the enforced automation program. "They aren't interested in building consumer goods. They're interested in building factories to build consumer goods and blow them up testing them. Or the factories are always obsolete just as soon as they finish them, and they can't phase into their new production setup and Hundred Year Plan."

Ge-Ge whispered a warning to him to beware of spies.

"Spies?"

"The Party," she said, drawing him to one side.

"But—but—you mean the Party just lets people talk like this?"

"Whatever harm does it do?" she asked. "Everybody benefits from talking out their aggressions. Now, have another drink and relax, and Shamar, be careful! Nobody minds local crackpots, but nobody wants *foreign* crackpots!"

She led him to another drink and left him standing with the host.

"Nice party," Shamar said.

"Thank you," the host said. "I find it very invigorating. As long as there's still people that think and that criticize on this planet, I feel there's hope, don't you? This is your first time? I don't recall your face. I have a study group that meets Wednesday nights. You're welcome to come. We have very stimulating discussions about government and politics. Please do come, any time you can. Just drop in any time after eight. What was your name again?"

"Shamar the Worker."

"Interesting name," the host said. "Another drink?"

Later, Shamar found himself in an intense conversation with a bearded youth of perhaps seventeen.

"A guy's responsible for his own conduct, right? Right! I'm responsible for *their* conduct? Each man goes to hell in his own way, right? Right! I don't want anything to do with them. You can't do anything about it, man, that's what I'm telling you. I don't seem to be getting through. Don't you see, it's a machine . . ."

"But if everybody joined the Party," Shamar suggested.

"So everybody joins? So what's new? Okay, you vote in the Party elections. What do you get? You get these two guys running for office: One is slightly left of center and one is slightly right of center. And both are four-square for the Automated Factory Program. Just suppose you did get a radical—suppose they accidentally let one slip through? He goes off and they argue him into line, and when he comes back, you say, 'Like man, what happened?' And so he tells you, 'Well, I couldn't do anything about it.' That's just what I'm telling you."

"I can't see that," Shamar said. "I just don't believe that."

At another time, Shamar tried to explain free elections to a female. He was informed, "Man, just give me a way to cast a vote against all those crumbs—and then I'll think twice about all this guff you're peddling."

A sober, scholarly man told him, "Join the Party? Whatever for? You join the Party and you're expected to spend all your free evenings at rallies and meetings and speeches and in ceremonial parades in honor of the ground breaking for a new automated factory. No, thank you."

Another told him, "You need a lesson in economics, son. What do you mean by free society? The only way you can run an industrial society is to limit production. If you produce enough for everybody, the government would produce itself out of business. Look here. The Party had millions of tabulating machines of one kind or another clicking happily away day and night arranging production to fit income distribution. They've never been known to goof and produce a surplus of anything. Why, damn it, if every man, woman and child in the world went out to buy a pound of nails apiece, the shortage of nails would be fantastic. But would they produce more nails? You know they wouldn't. 'So you want more nails?' they'd say. 'Well, damn you, work for them!' And the price would go up. See what I mean, son? They'd have another stick to beat us with."

Later, Shamar found himself seated on the floor across from an aesthete in his late thirties. "You see, my friend, force and violence never accomplish their stated ends. We must stand firmly on the principle of non-violence."

"But that's taking it lying down," Shamar protested.

"No! Sometimes I think it goes to the very core of human existence. Perhaps this is the central import of all philosophy: the way things are done is more important than the ends that are obtained."

At that point, Ge-Ge arrived breathlessly. "Shamar, quickly! We must go!"

"Huh? I'm having this interesting little talk—"

She tugged him from the floor. Baffled, he followed her. As he did so, the fighting broke out in the far corner of the room.

"Quickly!" she said. "Let's get out of here before the police come."

They fought their way, hand in hand, to the door. There they paused for a moment to look back.

"It's a couple of rival socialist parties fighting," she explained breathlessly.

"What about?"

"God knows. Hurry."

They were in the street. "Don't run, walk," she cautioned. After a block, she said, "I didn't even need to watch you at the end. Everybody got so drunk nobody noticed you much."

"Even the spies?"

"Oh, they always get the drunkest."

The siren sounded.

"Let's hurry."

When they arrived at Shamar's apartment, she asked, "Well, what did you think of the party?"

"It was an education," he said after a moment.

V

THE FOLLOWING WEEK Shamar spent many hours walking the streets of Xxla. He tried to convince himself that the people he had met at the party were not representative.

They were.

Friday night Ge-Ge announced, "Shamar, I can't stand

much more of this! What's going to happen? What is Von Stutsman going to do? He's onto something. I sometimes wish—oh, God!—I sometimes wish something would happen so we'd know where we stand, so we'd know what to do!" He tried to put an arm around her, but she brushed it away. "Don't! Let me alone!"

She retired to the other side of the room. For a moment, and for no reason, the hostility in the air between them was like ice and fire.

"I'm sorry," Ge-Ge said curtly.

"That's all right," Shamar said, his voice cold and distant.

"Let's talk about something else."

They were silent for a minute. Then he said, "I wanted to ask you. Of all the people I talked to, I couldn't find anyone who seemed to give a damn, one way or the other, about Earth. Why is that? You'd think they'd be at least talking about Earth."

"Why should they be? We've got our own problems."

At that point, the police arrived and took Shamar the Worker away.

They put him in a cell in which there were already three other prisoners.

"What you in for, buddy?"

Shamar studied the prisoner for a moment without answering. His companions looked up.

"No visible means of support," Shamar said.

"I'm Long John Freed."

Shamar nodded.

"They're trying to hook you for evading the productivity tax, huh?"

Shamar declined comment.

Freed settled back on his bunk. "I say take them for all you can. Now, look, you're a little guy. So they bleed us white. Take a factory manager or an important black market operator—you think they pay taxes? You can bet they don't. It's a racket. The poor pay and pay because they can't hire fancy lawyers to lie for them; and the rich take and take. I don't see why the Party puts up with it."

Freed shifted his position, "Say what you will about the Party—and I know it's got it's faults—still, there are dedicated men in it. I may be a small-time crook, but

I'm as patriotic as the next man. The Party's done a lot of good.

"First time for you? How old are you, twenty-seven or so? First time, they usually try to recruit you for the Factory Force.

"It's not such a bad racket. When you start out, they toss you in with lots of kids—usually the draftees. You get six weeks pick-and-shovel, and you're really dragging when you finish that. Then comes specialist school.

"Try to get in as an electrician or plumber. Plasterers or bricklayers have to work too hard. Carpentry's not bad—I'd hold out for cabinet-making, rather than rough carpentry, if I had to go into that. Then there's real specialties. Tile laying. You have to have a personality for that, or you'd go nuts. Demolition's not too bad; you blow up obsolete factories. That would have been right down my alley."

Freed was silent a moment, then he resumed:

"Sometimes I may talk like a radical, and maybe I am a little of a radical, I don't know. You look at the overall picture, things ain't too bad. I've known a lot of thieves and petty crooks in my time. As a class, for pure patriotism, I'll stack them up against anybody you can name; and in a way, you know, I'm kind of proud of that . . . Well, let's shut up and get some shut-eye."

When finally he slept, Shamar dreamed that the Party was a vast, invulnerable pyramid resting on the shifting base of the population. It was constructed to dampen out vibrations. The bottom quivered, and the quiver ran upward a few inches and was absorbed. The top of the pyramid remained stable, fixed and motionless, indifferent even to its own foundation. The pyramid was built like an earthquake-proof tower. It was built to last. The Party was built to govern. It need only devote itself to its own preservation. Any other issue was secondary.

It was an organic machine. The gears were flesh and blood. The people on top were maintenance engineers. Their job was to go around with an oil can that they could squirt when necessary to keep friction to a minimum.

He awakened the following morning ravenously hungry and was hugely disappointed by breakfast. Even discounting his somewhat biased viewpoint, the food was inedible.

Freed accepted Shamar's share eagerly with the comment, "It'll taste better after you miss a few meals. It always does."

An hour later, the jailer came to open the cell.

"Shamar the Worker? Get your stuff. We're going."

Ge-Ge was waiting in the reception room. Her hair had been especially waved for the occasion. She wore a suit newly pressed and gleaming. She had tears in her eyes.

She fled to his arms. "Darling!" she cried, caressing his face with childlike wonder. "Was it awful? Did they beat you?"

"I'm fine."

"Darling, we're going to get you out on bail. I've made all the arrangements. We just have to go to the judge's chambers for a minute, and they'll let you go. Thank God you're going to be out of this horrible place, at least for a little while."

The jailer brought Shamar's belt and his bag of possessions. Shamar signed a receipt for them and they went to the judge.

The judge said, "Please be seated." He had a resonant and friendly voice. He went to his desk and sat down.

Ge-Ge and Shamar seated themselves before him.

"Ah, you young people," he said. "Now, you must be Shamar the Worker, and you——"

"Garfling Germadpoldlt."

"Of course." He turned to Shamar. "I hate to see a fine young person like you in trouble, Shamar. It seems to me such a waste. Man and boy, for sixty years I've been a dedicated worker for the Party. Oh, Shamar, when I think of that glorious paradise to come—that time of wealth and plenty for all—that time when the riches and abundance of Mother Itra will, from automation, overflow alike the homes of the rich and poor. . . ."

They waited.

He continued. "Here I sit, year after year, Garfling and Shamar, judging my fellow men. Judging poor creatures who do not live the Dream. I sometimes feel that this is not the way. I sometimes feel my job is out there on the street corners, preaching the Dream, awakening the souls, telling the story of love and beauty and abundance in the life to come.

"Ah, me. But the world is not yet perfect, is it? And

man's understanding is imperfect. Here you are before me today, Shamar, with no visible means of support and no record of having paid productivity taxes. Oh, what a grim and fearful picture! In all your life have you ever once thought of your obligation to the future? You have failed yourself; you have failed the Party; and failed the future.

"Yet—in a larger sense—although this in no way militates against your own guilt—have we not failed you? How have we permitted a human soul to degrade himself to the point where we must punish him?"

Abruptly, the judge stood up. "Well, I've done the best I can. I remand you to the custody of Miss Germadpoldlt. Your trial will be set at a later date. You are not to leave Xxla without permission of this court. And I hope my lecture today has fallen on fertile soil. It is not too late to correct your ways. And I may say, if I am the one who hears your case, your conduct between now and the trial may have some bearing on the outcome."

They took a taxi back to his apartment. Ge-Ge trembled violently most of the way and nestled against him; they murmured their affection.

After he had been fed, she said nervously, "It was Von Stutsman who was responsible for your arrest. I should have known we couldn't fight the Party. If he digs hard enough, nothing on Itra can save us."

Finally, she went out to canvass lawyers.

She came back at dusk.

"Shamar, darling," she said, "I've located him. I asked a lot of my friends, and he's the best. He's a big lawyer for left-wing people. I talked to him, I told him everything."

"What! You told him everything?"

"Why, yes."

"You, you told him I was an Earthman?" He grabbed her by the shoulders. "Listen, Ge-Ge! I was arrested on a charge I could beat; now look what you've done. What makes you think he won't turn me over to the Party? This is too big, now! This isn't just a tax avoidance matter, this is treason for him."

"It's all right, darling," she said soothingly, breaking free from him. "I had to tell him so he'd take the case Why would a big man like him want to defend a common vagrant?"

Shamar closed his mouth. "But—you mean, he won't tell anyone?"

"Of course not."

"Has the man no patriotism?"

"Look, Shamar," she said in exasperation, "you once asked me why the people in the street aren't upset about Earth. I'm beginning to see the way you think. What you mean is, aren't we *afraid* of Earth? Aren't we afraid Earth would, oh, do something like invade us or something? That's what you mean."

"Of course it is."

"Once upon a time," she said, "when we first got space flight, the Party got all shook up about the possibility of some hostile force out there developing an interstellar drive and coming along and doing their will with us. They asked the computers about it. Invading and conquering a planet is such a vast technological undertaking that the mind just boggles at it. Don't forget, we've got a warning network out there. They're not very alert, or you wouldn't have gotten through, but they wouldn't miss an invasion fleet. There are computer-controlled chemical rockets in orbit, and we've got a few sited on Itra that can blast down anything that slows up to try to land. It wouldn't take one-hundredth, it wouldn't take one-thousandth of the technological resources required to defend Itra that it would to attack her. Earth just simply can't afford to attack us. They'd go broke trying. Every million dollars you spent to get here, we'd spend a thousand to keep you from landing.

"Oh, I suppose if Earth wanted to, they might figure out some way to blow up Itra. But where's the profit in that? We're not bothering you. Why spend all that money when it's not going to get you one damn thing in return?"

The following day, Shamar called on the lawyer, Counselor Freemason.

Counselor Freemason inquired politely as to the state of his financial reserves. Shamar replied reassuringly.

"Good, good. That's most encouraging. Most encouraging indeed. We need not place any limit on our ingenuity, then.

"I've been thinking about your case, Mr. Worker. The thing first to do, in my opinion, is to stir up public sympathy in your favor. It's almost an ideal case. It has no real political overtones. It's not as if you're accused of anything serious. Well, I believe I can interest some friends of mine who are always deeply concerned with cases involving the infringement of an individual's liberty—provided, of course, there are no political overtones. I can think of several good people who would be willing to head up a defense committee. The fact that we have and I'm talking now about as much as, oh, one hundred thousand dollars?" He paused interrogatively.

"I'm prepared to pay," Shamar said.

"Maybe even more," Councilor Freemason continued quickly. "We can come to that later. The important thing right now is to get down to work on your case."

"Counselor Freemason, now, obviously I'm not a lawyer," Shamar said, "and I know it's bad business to tell a professional how to run his job. But I believe Miss Germadpoldlt explained the, ah, rather unusual delicacy of my own position. It would seem to me that the less publicity we got, the better."

Counselor Freemason shook a pen at him. "A very good point, Mr. Worker. It shows you're thinking, and I'm glad of the opportunity to explain the reasons for this recommendation. If I brazenly parade you before them, you see, by implication it means we're not afraid of your background being examined. We have nothing to hide. Consequently, they will not look for anything. If, on the other hand, I'm cautious, fearful, defensive, they'll ask themselves, 'What's Counselor Freemason trying to hide?' And they'll start digging into your past.

"Now, I hope that clears that matter up to your satisfaction? Good. Good. I'll get right to work on your case. Do you have anything else? Miss Germadpoldlt explained rather nicely, I think, yesterday. As far as anyone knows, you're a man without papers. You've never paid any taxes but they have no proof you owe taxes. You won money in the lottery. You collected anonymously; lots of people do for perfectly valid reasons. Let them prove you didn't win. The Party can't be very interested in a man like that.

"So, I'll raise an issue. Maybe we'll suggest that any lottery winner is likely to be persecuted. The Party wants things to go smoothly. The lottery makes the people feel as if, you know, they actually own a piece of things. And too many people don't have papers.

"My job is to take the specific and convert it to a vague general principle that a number of people feel deeply about. The Party will take the easy way out: they're not dumb. They've learned from experience. You're not worth that much trouble to them. Otherwise, there'll be a period of aggravation, people without papers beating up police and things like that."

Three days later, Shamar met with the newly formed Committee of One Hundred for Justice to Shamar the Worker.

There were five members of the Committee and Counselor Freemason in attendance. They briefed him on their initial activities.

They had printed letterheads and were circulating letters to people known to be friendly, with a hastily printed booklet giving the facts of the case.

"As you can see," Counselor Freemason said, "we're off to a very fast start. Um, the question naturally arises as to finances. I have advanced a certain amount out of my own pocket. . . . We will need more than I can conveniently scrape together at the moment, and I'm reluctant to—ah—impose on the Committee for a loan insofar as—"

"I took the liberty of bringing along some cash," Shamar said "For current expenses and, of course, your retainer."

They looked relieved. "Excellent, excellent. I might suggest, Mr. Worker, that we appoint one of the Committee as treasurer—perhaps Mrs. Freetle, here"—the lady smiled—"to take these financial worries off your mind. This will leave you free to devote yourself fully to activities of defense."

"Now that that's out of the way," one of the male Committee members said, "let's get right down to business. As you can see, we're moving fast. Our overall strategy is this. We must first establish a public image for you, Mr. Worker, an image the average man can identify with. Counselor Freemason has described your case to us. I simply don't know what the Party's coming to to permit a man like Von Stutsman to persecute you this way. Oh, I tell you, it makes my blood boil, Mr. Worker!"

Others of the Committee chimed in and the sentiment passed heatedly among them.

"Well," said Counselor Freemason, "I guess that about winds it up for the moment. You all know where to reach me. Any time, day or night. I guess, Mr. Worker, if you'll just turn the money over to Mrs. Freetle. And I think, Mr. Hall, if you'd hire that speech writer—what's his name? McGoglhy?—to work with Mr. Worker on his speeches."

"Speeches?" Shamar asked.

"You're going to be our featured speaker at all the rallies, of course," Mrs. Freetle said. "I know you will do splendidly, just splendidly! Your accent is so captivating. I've never heard anything quite like it."

VI

ON THE EVENING of his first public appearance, Shamar was given a neatly typed speech. He rehearsed it hurriedly, stammers and all.

"Fellow citizens! As I stand here, looking over this sea of faces, hearing your applause and seeing how your hearts go out to one poor man in distress, it—I—well, I'm deeply touched. I can't tell you how much it means to me. I prepared a speech for tonight, but I'm not going to use it. I'm just going to stand here, instead, and tell you, just as the words come out, how I feel." Here he would pause for applause and then continue. "Thank you so very much. Thank you. I know you're all behind me—except for the police agents in the audience." Here he would wait for laughter. "We all know them, don't we? I see about a dozen. A dozen agents have come down here to find out what I'm going to say. Isn't that ridiculous?" Here there would be mixed laughter, applause and cries in the affirmative. "All right! Thank you. I hope they get an earful tonight."

Later in the speech he would demand, "Why are they doing this to me? I want you to tell me why. What have I done? What am I accused of doing? Well, I'll tell you this—I'm not the kind of man who is going to submit meekly to this persecution. I'm going to fight back. I've got a little money left from my lottery winnings, and I'll spend every cent of it to fight these people doing this thing to me." Here he would pause dramatically. "I want to leave you with this point. It's not just Shamar the Worker that's involved. What am I? A poor, itinerant laborer going from town to town. I'm nothing, I have never had anything, and I guess I never will have anything. I'm no rich black marketeer or businessman. I'm no fat politician. I'm just one little man. But it's not me—and this is the point I want to leave you with—it's not Shamar the Worker. He's unimportant. What is important is that if they can do this to me, they can do it to you. If they can do it to Shamar the Worker today, next year one of you will be up here on this platform speaking just the way I am. So you see, this is your fight. It's not me that's important—it's the principle that's important—"

The meeting went brilliantly. Every time he paused, the audience responded just as the speech-writer had indicated. It was as if they were as well rehearsed as he.

The next night, another meeting. And another. And another. He slept no more than four hours a night when the campaign was in full swing. He spoke dozens of times into the bright glare of TV cameras. He paraded down a million streets in an open-topped car. Faces poured in front of his own; on and on they came. People with tears in their eyes cried, "God bless Shamar the Worker!" Once the Committee hired a brass band.

So, for two weeks, it went.

Then the Party threw him back in jail, in an apparent effort to deprive the movement of its momentus.

After three days, during which time Shamar was held incommunicado, Counselor Freemason obtained permission to interview his client.

"We're making marvelous progress! Ge-Ge is turning into a most effective crusader. You should hear her when she cries, 'Give me back my man!' This is a wonderful development for us. It's having the opposite of the intended effect. Von Stutsman has overreached himself this time. The Party is going to have to back down, and it will cost him dearly."

"How's the finances?"

"Ge-Ge has given us some advances—"

"How much have you spent?"

"Well, to tell you the truth, I haven't been keeping

track closely. Perhaps we've run a little more than we anticipated. The response, you see . . ."

Shamar returned to his cell wishing Earth's printing presses had worked a little longer.

It took nearly two weeks to arrange for Ge-Ge to visit him. When she arrived, she was nearly on the point of tears.

"Oh, my darling, how I've missed you!"

She brought him up to date on the progress of his case. As Counselor Freemason had reported, his imprisonment merely increased the vigor of his supporters. Now they were at their highest pitch: a pitch that would be difficult to maintain.

"I'm just worried sick," she said. "If the Party can hold out another week or two. I don't want to worry you, Shamar, but I want you to know how you stand. Counselor Freemason says the worst that could happen would be a short prison sentence, no more than a year, for not filing tax forms. We could keep you out on appeal for quite a while."

"Ge-Ge, how much have we spent so far?"

"About three hundred thousand dollars."

"Good God! They'll have it all when they get through! If I ever get back to Earth——"

"I don't care about money, Shamar! I just want you free!"

He took her shoulders. "Ge-Ge, suppose the Party can't afford to back down? Maybe they feel they have to stand firm to prevent a lot of future trouble. And when Freemason gets all the money . . . then what chance will we stand? They might railroad me for years. They'll make an example out of me. Now, are you willing to gamble? Everybody would jump at the chance to vote them out. If we could——"

"Please, Shamar," Ge-Ge said. "All this voting thing you've always been so sold on is all right, I guess—but it just won't work. To begin with, there isn't any way to vote."

"Maybe there is," he said.

Shamar was still in jail the following day when Ge-Ge appeared on the TV program.

PAMDEN had been reluctant to release time to her.

PAMDEN was Itra's largest industrial cooperative—Plastics, Agricultural Machinery, Detergents, Electricity and Newsprint—and, being the most efficient, was responsible for operating the TV networks.

"Good heavens," said the station executive. "Nobody can say we haven't already given you coverage, Miss Germapoldlt."

"They've ordered you to stop!" she protested.

"They? The Party? Miss Germadpoldlt, do you honestly believe that? Nobody tells a station manager what to program. Believe me. There is no prior censorship whatsoever. But, on the other hand, we can't turn over the TV stations to minority propaganda either."

Ge-Ge argued and pleaded, and in the end the executive sighed wearily. "I think we've been more than fair. But for you—and this is a personal favor, Miss Germadpoldlt, because you are a young and attractive woman—for you, I will phone our program director and see if he can get you on the Noon Interview Show for tomorrow. It gives you the Itra-wide network, which is certainly more than anyone has the right to ask. You'll have ninety seconds to make your case. That's the best I can do."

"Oh, thank you, thank you," Ge-Ge sobbed. "You're so fair and generous." Outside his office she took a deep breath, crossed her fingers and went home to revise her speech. She had only expected sixty.

Ge-Ge arrived at the studio well in advance and was handed over to the makeup department. With deft skill they converted her youth to age and contrived to instill in her face weariness and defeat. Her protests were ignored.

"This is the way you make up for TV," she was told.

They clucked collective tongues in disapproval when they were finished and sent her on her way to a brief chat with the M.C.

The M.C. assured her that she looked divine and hastily scanned her prepared remarks, which had been heavily edited by some anonymous hand in the news department. The M.C. incorporated a few pointless revisions and dispatched the message to the department handling idiot-board material. It was explained that Ge-Ge was to read, word for word, from the electronic prompter.

Ge-Ge watched the program from the wings. When she heard a commercial message in favor of the consumption of a particular variety of candy, her heart ran away with itself. Her courage faltered. But Shamar's face brought it back.

The signal came. She walked into the terrible glare which held up every imperfection to microscopic inspection. She shook hands, turned, and the camera closed in, full face. Beyond the camera lay the largest daytime TV audience on Itra. She felt they were examining her pores with minute and critical attention.

She blinked nervously and began to read. "I am here to tell you about Shamar the Worker." That was as far as she went with the prepared text. Before the horrified ears of the auditors in the studio, she plunged into remarks of another kind entirely.

"If you want to do something to help Shamar the Worker, stop buying candy! Don't buy any more candy. If you want to help Shamar the Worker, don't buy any candy until he's free. If you want to help Shamar, please, *please,* don't buy——"

At this point the technicians cut Ge-Ge out and, with profound mistiming, faded in an oleagenous taped message from the candy manufacturer, which began, "Friends, everybody likes Red Block candy, and millions buy it every day. Here's why—"

Ge-Ge surveyed the surrounding confusion and walked unmolested from the studio.

When she arrived home, an angry Counselor Freemason was waiting on her doorstep. Inside, she allowed the Counselor to present his case.

This new move, he explained, would have terrible consequences. Shamar's good faith would be prejudiced. One simply did not, with impunity, go outside the law in such matters. There were rules you absolutely *must* play the game by. He washed his hands of all responsibility for her conduct. "I hope to God nothing comes of it," he concluded. "I'm having the Committee prepare a denial of——"

The phone rang at this point and without asking permission, Counselor Freemason answered it. "Yes? This is Counselor Freemason, go ahead." He listened a moment, said, "They did," in a weary voice and cradled the phone.

He turned to Ge-Ge. "Now we're in for it. That was Pete Freedle from the Committee."

"Well," said Ge-Ge, "I think we'll just wait a few days and see what happens."

A week later, Ge-Ge was still waiting. Counselor Freemason, deprived of finances, was powerless to move. He saw everything crashing in shambles at their feet.

"But are they selling candy?" Ge-Ge asked.

"That's beside the point!" Counselor Freemason cried. "Look here, every crackpot on the planet will get into the act. They don't care about Shamar. All you're going to prove now is that the Party is unpopular. Everyone already knows that." He struck his forehead in exasperation.

For two weeks, all was quiet. There were no more rallies for Shamar the Worker. Signs were torn down and destroyed. No bulletins were printed. No word passed over the electronic communications network. The Committee, bankrupt, dissolved in mutual recriminations and bickering, convinced that the cause of civil liberties had been set back one hundred years.

But candy was not selling.

It clogged the distribution channels. It piled up in warehouses. It lay untouched in stores. It grew rancid. Mechanically the factories continued to turn it out.

The Party denied the boycott was having any effect. This did not appease the distributors of candy and the sellers of candy and the producers of candy. Their jobs were at stake. They had payrolls to meet.

The Party stopped production of candy. People suddenly found themselves with no jobs to go to.

The economic system was so tightly controlled and organized that the effect was immediate. There was too little money available to purchase the supplies normally purchased. Suppliers cut back on their factory orders. This further reduced the need for supplies.

At this point, the Party decided that the people would, by heaven, eat candy. The Party leader himself went on TV to appeal to the patriotism of the people and to order them to resume buying candy. This was a tactical error. But being the idea of the Party leader himself, who had always crashed headlong into obstacles, none opposed it.

The issue was directly joined. People resented being told that it was their patriotic duty to eat something that all medical opinion held was harmful. Futhermore, people realized that they had somehow stumbled on a fatal flaw in the system, which they could exploit without immediate danger.

They responded by refusing to buy soap.

The people were now in open revolt. At last they had a method for disapproving of things in general.

The economy plummeted. The computers were in a frenzy. Effects of corrective actions were no longer predictable. The Party frantically tried to buy soap and dump it. The people turned to other commodities.

Pressure now mounted from within the Party itself. The supervisor of PAMDEN saw his carefully nurtured empire begin to disintegrate. A massive layoff in Consumer Plastics (badly hit by a running boycott) took with it valuable key personnel. The supervisor of PAMDEN told the Party leader himself that he damned well better do something about the situation, and damned soon, too.

The Party leader himself ordered the release of Shamar the Worker.

But by then no one was interested in Shamar the Worker.

The man came and unlocked Shamar's cell door. Shamar stood up. The guard tossed in Shamar's clothing. "Get dressed." Shamar got dressed. "Come along." Shamar came along.

Shamar had had no word from outside for nearly two months, and it was not until he saw Ge-Ge's face, radiant with joy, that he realized he had won.

"You're free!" she cried excitedly.

Shamar was given back his belt and possessions. As they waited for the judge to make it official, Shamar asked, "I wonder what will happen now?"

"Nobody knows. Everybody says the Party's out for sure. Individual Party members will try to form a new government, but it's going to have to be radically different. They'll try to keep all they can, but the people will wring them dry for every last concession. Maybe now when they build the factories, they'll stay built and actually produce something."

"For a little while," Shamar said.

"Longer than a little while," Ge-Ge said. "We've got a way to vote now, when things get too bad."

The judge, in his red robe, came in. They stood respectfully. He looked at them for a long time and said nothing. Finally, he spoke:

"Well, Shamar the Worker, I guess you've got what you want. You pulled down a whole civilization. I hope you're satisfied. What dream will you give us to replace the dream you have taken from us?"

His face hardened.

"Shamar the Worker," he said, "the Party leader himself has asked us to dismiss the pending charges against you. This I now do. You are free to go."

"Thank you, sir," Shamar said respectfully.

"Shamar the Worker, for your own sake, you better hope that I never see you in my court. You better not get yourself arrested for anything. I will show you no mercy, but justice will be swift and summary. So that you may not rest easily at night, I am having some of my very skillful and competent friends check through your background thoroughly. You should hope, very sincerely, that they find nothing. You may go."

Ge-Ge and Shamar stood. They turned in silence. When they were at the door, the judge called, "Oh, Shamar the Worker!"

He turned, "Yes, sir?"

"Shamar the Worker, I do not like your accent."

Shamar could feel Ge-Ge trembling uncontrollably at his side.

But when they reached the street they were greeted by headlines announcing that a delegation from the planet Earth had arrived.

VII

THE EARTH DELEGATION had taken over a suite in the Party Hotel, grandest and most expensive on Itra. Usually it was reserved for high Party members.

Shamar and Ge-Ge presented themselves at the desk. Shamar wrote out a note in English. "Deliver this to the Earthmen," he instructed.

Shamar and Ge-Ge retired to await results. Less than five minutes passed; the bell hop returned. "Sir and Madam," he said respectfully, "come with me."

When he entered the suite, he felt the personality of Shamar the Worker drop from him into memory.

"Captain Shaeffer! Captain Shaeffer! Oh, what a magnificent job! I'm Gene Gibson from the new Department of Extra-Terrestrial Affairs. Who's this?"

"This is my fiancee."

"Good heavens, man, you intend to marry a *native?"* The man stepped back, shocked.

Captain Shaeffer turned to Ge-Ge and performed bilingual introductions.

They moved from the hallway to the sitting room and arranged themselves on the furniture.

"I must say, Captain Shaeffer, that your success on Itra has surpassed our wildest expectations. The first inkling we had was when, out of the blue, as it were, there was your face looking out at us from the TV screen! You should have been there for our celebration that night! You'd been on Itra just a little over two months! You're going down in history as one of the greatest heroes of all time!"

Captain Shaeffer said, "I think it would be best if Ge-Ge and I were to board your ship immediately. Her life may be in danger. Some old-line Party men might resent her role in the revolution. Actually, she had more to do with it than I did."

"Oh, now, I'm sure you must be exaggerating a bit on that, Captain Shaeffer. Her life in danger? Surely, now! Speaking frankly, Captain—and mind you, I have no personal objection at all; this is none of my business. But she is, after all, an *Itraian*. You know these mixed marriages——"

"I don't give a damn what you personally think," Captain Shaeffer said. "Is that understood once and for all? She goes."

"Of course. I was just—now don't get huffy. Of course she goes. Just as you wish, Captain."

The angry exchange over an unknown but fearfully expected issue caused Ge-Ge to blink back tears.

A week later, Gene Gibson came for the first time to visit them. Captain Shaeffer inquired as to progress.

"Well, Captain, things are progressing. We are establishing a government that will be more responsive to the will of the people of Itra. We've had several very pleasant, informal chats with the Party leader himself. Really a wonderful man. Once he got all the facts—which were kept from him the first time we landed—he strikes me as being quite responsible. I think we may have misjudged him. I'm not too sure but what he isn't just the exact man to head up the new government. We've discussed a few details on trade agreements and, I must say, he's been very reasonable."

Captain Shaeffer said nothing.

"Yes," Gene Gibson said, "he's really an exceptional individual. A wealth of administrative experience. A fine grasp of practical politics. I don't regard him as a typical Itraian at all. He feels that, with us backing him, we can get this whole mess straightened out in a few months."

"Mess?"

"Well, you must admit, I think, Captain Shaeffer, that you did—well—make negotiations extremely difficult, in view of the, ah, present temper of the populace.

"You see, Earth would like to have a stable and responsible government. A government, that is, which can see larger issues in perspective. Not one that must devote its full time to coping with a group of unpatriotic anarchists running loose in the streets."

"What's he saying?" Ge-Ge asked.

"As it is now," Gene Gibson continued, "we do have several rather difficult problems. I think we'll probably have to quarantine Itra for a few months until the Party leader himself can form a stable organizational structure. Somehow news of our trade discussions have leaked out and for some reason has resulted in a general work stoppage. So you see? By God, I'll just come right out and say it: Shaeffer, you've left us one hell of a mess!"

With that, Gene Gibson departed.

"What did he say?" Ge-Ge asked meekly. But Shaeffer only shook his head.

The following day, the ship's captain came to pay a courtesy call.

"A very neat piece of work, Merle. Your new assignment just came in, by the way, on the space radio."

"New assignment? Ge-Ge and I are on our way back to Earth."

"No, you're not. We're to drop you off at Midway for

transhipment to Folger's Hill. It's a new planet. You're to be Earth representative to the people of Folger's Hill. The first shipload of colonists arrived about a month ago."

"I see," Captain Shaeffer said.

"The salary's good," the ship's captain said.

"Suppose I don't want to go?"

"I've got orders to leave you at Midway. I'd want to go if I were you. They want you out of the way for a little while. You can't fight it. You've been appointed a general in the Defense Forces, so you're now under military law—and it's an order."

At this point, Ge-Ge broke in to say, "How are things going in Xxla?"

General Shaeffer choked back his anger and presented the question.

"They don't tell us anything. The crew is confined to the ship."

Shamar the Worker turned to Ge-Ge. "It's going about the same," he said.

A year later, General Merle S. Shaeffer's card popped out of the computer.

"General Shaeffer's up for reassignment."

"Who is General Shaeffer?"

"Never heard of him."

The card passed upward.

"Merle Shaeffer is due for reassignment," a man who knew the name told the Secretary of the Over-Council at lunch the following day. "There's a new planet opened up even further away than Folger's Hill."

"He's the one who butchered the Itra assignment? Send him there. Anything new from Itra recently, by the way?"

"Same as usual. I understand the anarchists have formed some kind of government."

"Terrible. Terrible. Well, the less said about that the better."

A week later, again over lunch, the Secretary was told:

"I guess we needn't worry about Merle Shaeffer any more. Disappeared from his post, he and that Itraian woman of his, a couple of weeks after they arrived on Folger's Hill. Probably a hunting accident got them both.

Their bodies were never found. These things happen on wild new planets."

The Secretary was silent for a long time. Then he said: "Shaeffer dead, eh? I guess it's better that way. Well, a genius has passed, and we'll not see his like again. Perverted, perhaps, but a genius none the less."

They drank solemnly.

"To Merle Shaeffer. You could call him a hero, so let's you and I drink to that. No one else ever will."

They drank again.

Nothing further served to stir the Secretary's memory of Merle Shaeffer, and he retired six months later at the end of his term. The new Secretary was not familiar with the Itraian affair.

He had been in office just a few days less than a year when, one morning, he arrived at his office in a furious rage. "Get me the head of the Defense Forces!"

"I'm sorry, sir, all the phones are tied up," his secretary said.

"What in hell do you mean, all the phones are tied up?"

"I don't know. Maybe all at once everybody just left their phones off the hook or something."

"Why would they do that? That's ridiculous! Get a runner over after him."

Half an hour later, the head of the Defense Forces arrived.

"Do you know," the new Secretary demanded, "that yesterday all the pennies went out of circulation? People apparently have been saving them for the last couple of months. It finally showed up. All at once, there aren't any pennies. You can't make change. Damn it, why would those crazy idiots all decide to save their pennies at the same time? It's not rational. Why did they do it?"

The head of the Defense Forces said nothing.

The Secretary raved at him in anger, but the head of the Defense Forces did not have the heart to tell him that a hero had returned home.

THE TACTFUL SABOTEUR

Frank Herbert

I

"BETTER MEN THAN YOU have tried!" snarled Clinton Watt.

"I quote paragraph four, section ninety-one of the Semantic Revision to the Constitution," said saboteur extraordinary Jorj X. McKie. " 'The need for obstructive processes in government having been established as one of the chief safeguards for human rights, the question of immunities must be defined with extreme precision.' "

McKie sat across a glistening desk from the Intergalactic Government's Secretary of Sabotage, Clinton Watt. An air of tension filled the green-walled office, carrying over into the screenview behind Watt, which showed an expanse of the System Government's compound and people scurrying about their morning business with a sense of urgency.

Watt, a small man who appeared to crackle with suppressed energy, passed a hand across his shaven head. "All right," he said in a suddenly tired voice. "This is the only Secretariat of government that's never immune from sabotage. You've satisfied the legalities by quoting the law. Now, do your damnedest!"

McKie, whose bulk and fat features usually gave him the appearance of a grandfatherly toad, glowered like a gnome-dragon. His mane of red hair appeared to dance with inner flame.

"Damnedest!" he snapped. "You think I came in here to try to unseat you? You think that?"

And McKie thought: *Let's hope he thinks that!*

"Stop the act, McKie!" Watt said. "We both know you're eligible for this chair." He patted the arm of his chair. "And we both know the only way you can eliminate me and qualify yourself for the appointment is to overcome me with a masterful sabotage. Well, McKie, I've sat here more than eighteen years. Another five months and it'll be a new record. Do your damnedest. I'm waiting."

"I came in here for only one reason," McKie said. "I want to report on the search for saboteur extraordinary Napoleon Bildoon."

McKie sat back wondering: *If Watt knew my real purpose here would he act just this way? Perhaps.* The man had been behaving oddly since the start of this interview, but it was difficult to determine real motive when dealing with a fellow member of the Bureau of Sabotage.

Cautious interest quickened Watt's bony face. He wet his lips with his tongue and it was obvious he was asking himself it this were more of an elaborate ruse. But McKie had been assigned the task of searching for the missing agent, Bildoon, and it was just possible . . .

"Have you found him?" Watt asked.

"I'm not sure," McKie said. He ran his fingers through his red hair. "Bildoon's a Pan-Spechi, you know."

"For disruption's sake!" Watt exploded. "I know who and what my own agents are! But we take care of our own. And when one of our best people just drops from sight . . . . What's this about not being sure?"

"The Pan-Spechi are a curious race of creatures," McKie said. "Just because they've taken on humanoid shape we tend to forget their five-phase life cycle."

"Bildoon told me himself he'd hold his group's ego at least another ten years," Watt said. "I think he was being truthful, but . . ." Watt shrugged and some of the bursting energy seemed to leave him. "Well, the group ego's the only place where the Pan-Spechi show vanity, so . . ." Again he shrugged.

"My questioning of the other Pan-Spechi in the Bureau has had to be circumspect, of course," McKie said. "But I did follow one lead clear to Achus."

"And?"

McKie brought a white vial from his copious jacket and scattered a metallic powder on the desktop.

Watt pushed himself back from the desk, eyeing the powder with suspicion. He took a cautious sniff, smelled chalf, the quick-scribe powder. Still . . .

"It's just chalf," McKie said. And he thought: *If he buys that, I may get away with this.*

"So scribe it," Watt said.

Concealing his elation, McKie held a chalf-memory stick over the dusted surface. A broken circle with arrows pointing to a right-hand flow appeared in the chalf. At each break in the circle stood a symbol—in one place the Pan-Spechi character for ego, then the delta for fifth gender and, finally, the three lines that signified the dormant creche-triplets.

McKie pointed to the fifth gender delta. "I've seen a Pan-Spechi in this position who looks a bit like Bildoon and *appears* to have some of his mannerisms. There's no identity response from the creature, of course. Well, you know how the quasi-feminine fifth gender reacts."

"Don't ever let that amorous attitude fool you," Watt warned. "In spite of your nasty disposition I wouldn't want to lose you into a Pan-Spechi creche."

"Bildoon wouldn't rob a fellow agent's identity," McKie said. He pulled at his lower lip, feeling an abrupt uncertainty. Here, of course, was the most touchy part of the whole scheme. "If it was Bildoon."

"Did you meet this group's ego holder?" Watt asked, and his voice betrayed real interest.

"No," McKie said. "But I think the ego-single of this Pan-Spechi is involved with the Tax Watchers."

McKie waited, wondering if Watt would rise to the bait.

"I've never heard of an ego change being forced onto a Pan-Spechi," Watt said in a musing tone, "but that doesn't mean it's impossible. If those Tax Watcher do-gooders found Bildoon sabotaging their efforts and . . . Hmmm."

"Then Bildoon *was* after the Tax Watchers," McKie said.

Watt scowled. McKie's question was in extreme bad taste. Senior agents, unless joined on a project or where the information was volunteered, didn't snoop openly into the work of their fellows. Left hand and right hand remained mutually ignorant in the Bureau of Sabotage and for good reason. Unless . . . Watt stared speculatively at his saboteur extraordinary.

McKie shrugged as Watt remained silent. "I can't operate on inadequate information," he said. "I must, therefore, resign the assignment to search for Bildoon. Instead, I will now look into the Tax Watchers."

"You will not!" Watt snapped.

McKie forced himself not to look at the design he had drawn on the desktop. The next few moments were the critical ones.

"You'd better have a legal reason for that refusal," McKie said.

Watt swiveled sideways in his chair, glanced at the screenview, then addressed himself to the side wall. "The situation has become one of extreme delicacy, Jorj. It's well known that you're one of our finest saboteurs."

"Save your oil for someone who needs it," McKie growled.

"Then I'll put it this way," Watt said, returning his gaze to McKie. "The Tax Watchers in the last few days have posed a real threat to the Bureau. They've managed to convince a High Court magistrate they deserve the same immunity from our ministrations that a . . . well, public water works or . . . ah . . . food processing plant might enjoy. The magistrate, Judge Edwin Dooley, invoked the Public Safety amendment. Our hands are tied. The slightest suspicion that we've disobeyed the injunction and . . ."

Watt drew a finger across his throat.

"Then I quit," McKie said.

"You'll do nothing of the kind!"

"This TW outfit is trying to eliminate the Bureau, isn't it?" McKie asked. "I remember the oath I took just as well as you do."

"Jorj, you couldn't be that much of a simpleton," Watt said. "You quit, thinking that absolves the Bureau from responsibility for you! That trick's as old as time!"

"Then fire me!" McKie said.

"I've no legal reason to fire you, Jorj."

"Refusal to obey orders of a superior," McKie said.

"It wouldn't fool anybody, you dolt!"

McKie appeared to hesitate, said: "Well, the public doesn't know the inner machinery of how we change the Bureau's command. Perhaps it's time we opened up."

"Jorj, before I could fire you there'd have to be a reason so convincing that . . . Just forget it."

The fat pouches beneath McKie's eyes lifted until the

eyes were mere slits. The crucial few moments had arrived. He had managed to smuggle a Jicuzzi stim into this office past all of Watt's detectors, concealing the thing's detectable radiation core within an imitation of the lapel badge that Bureau agents wore.

"In Lieu of Red Tape," McKie said and touched the badge with a finger, feeling the raised letters there—"ILRT." The touch focused the radiation core onto the metallic dust scattered over the desktop.

Watt gripped the arms of the chair, studying McKie with a new look of wary tension.

"We are under legal injunction to keep hands off the Tax Watchers," Watt said. "Anything that happens to those people or to their project for scuttling us—even legitimate accidents—will be laid at our door. We must be able to defend ourselves. No one who has ever been connected with us dares fall under the slightest suspicion of complicity."

"How about a floor waxed to dangerous slickness in the path of one of their messengers? How about a door-lock changed to delay——"

"Nothing."

McKie stared at his chief. Everything depended now on the man holding very still. He knew Watt wore detectors to warn him of concentrated beams of radiation. But this Jicuzzi stim had been rigged to diffuse its charge off the metallic dust on the desk, and that required several seconds of relative quiet.

The men held themselves rigid in the staredown until Watt began to wonder at the extreme stillness of McKie's body. The man was even holding his breath!

McKie took a deep breath, stood up.

"I warn you, Jorj," Watt said.

"Warn me?"

"I can restrain you by physical means if necessary."

"Clint, old enemy, save your breath. What's done is done."

A smile touched McKie's wide mouth. He turned, crossed to the room's only door, paused there, hand on knob.

"What have you done?" Watt exploded.

McKie continued to look at him.

Watt's scalp began itching madly. He put a hand there,

felt a long tangle of . . . tendrils! They were lengthening under his fingers, growing out of his scalp, waving and writhing.

"A Jicuzzi stim," Watt breathed.

McKie let himself out, closed the door.

Watt leaped out of his chair, raced to the door.

Locked!

He knew McKie and didn't try unlocking it. Frantically, Watt slapped a molecular dispersion wad against the door and dived through as the wad blasted. He landed in the outer hall, stared first one direction, then the other.

The hall was empty.

Watt sighed. The tendrils had stopped growing, but they were long enough now that he could see them writhing past his eyes—a rainbow mass of wrigglers, part of himself. And McKie with the original stim was the only one who could reverse the process—unless Watt were willing to spend an interminable time with the Jicuzzi themselves. No. That was out of the question.

Watt began assessing his position.

The stim tendrils couldn't be removed surgically, couldn't be tied down or contained in any kind of disguise without endangering the person afflicted with them. Their presence would hamper him, too, during this critical time of trouble with the Tax Watchers. How could he appear in conferences and interviews with these things writhing in their Medusa dance on his head? It would be laughable! He'd be an object of comedy.

And if McKie could stay out of the way until a Case of Exchangement was brought before the full Cabinet . . . But, no! Watt shook his head. This wasn't the kind of sabotage that required a change of command in the Bureau. This was a gross thing. No subtlety to it. This was like a practical joke. Clownish.

But McKie was noted for his clownish attitude, his irreverence for all the blundering self-importance of government.

Have I been self-important? Watt wondered.

In all honesty, he had to admit it.

I'll have to submit my resignation today, he thought. *Right after I fire McKie. One look at me and there'll be no doubt of why I did it. This is about as convincing a reason as you could find.*

Watt turned to his right and headed for the lab to see if they could help him bring this wriggling mass under control.

The President will want me to stay at the helm until McKie makes his next move, Watt thought. *I have to be able to function somehow.*

II

McKie waited in the living room of the Achusian mansion with ill-concealed unease. Achus was the administrative planet for the Vulpecula region, an area of great wealth, and this room high on a mountaintop commanded a natural view to the southwest across lesser peaks and foothills misted in purple by a westering G_3 sun.

But McKie ignored the view, trying to watch all corners of the room at once. He had seen a fifth gender Pan-Spechi here in company with the fourth-gender egoholder. That could only mean the creche with its three dormants was nearby. By all accounts, this was a dangerous place for someone not protected by bonds of friendship and community of interest.

The value of the Pan-Spechi to the universal human society in which they participated was beyond question. What other species had such refined finesse in deciding when to hinder and when to help? Who else could send a key member of its group into circumstances of extreme peril without fear that the endangered one's knowledge would be lost?

There was always a dormant to take up where the lost one had left off.

Still, the Pan-Spechi did have their idiosyncrasies. And their hungers were at times bizarre.

"Ahh, McKie."

The voice, deep and masculine, came from his left. McKie whirled to study the figure that came through a door carved from a single artificial emerald of glittering creme de menthe colors.

The speaker was humanoid but with Pan-Spechi multi-faceted eyes. He appeared to be a terranic man (except for the blue-green eyes) of an indeterminate, well-preserved middle age. The body suggested a certain daintiness in its yellow tights and singlet. The head was squared in outline with close-cropped blond hair, a fleshy chunk of nose and thick splash of mouth.

"Panthor Bolin here," the Pan-Specchi said. "You are welcome in my home, Jorj McKie."

McKie relaxed slightly. Pan-Spechi were noted for honoring hospitality once it was extended . . . provided the guest didn't violate their mores.

"I'm honored that you've agreed to see me," McKie said.

"The honor is mine," Bolin said. "We've long recognized you as a person whose understanding of the Pan-Spechi is most subtle and penetrating. I've longed for the chance to have uninhibited conversation with you. And here you are." He indicated a chairdog against the wall to his right, and snapped his fingers. The semi-sentient artifact glided to a position behind McKie. "Please be seated."

McKie, his caution re-alerted by Bolin's reference to "uninhibited conversation," sank into the chairdog, patting it until it assumed the contours he wanted.

"Have our egos shared nearness before?" McKie asked. "You appeared to recognize me."

"Recognition goes deeper than ego," Bolin said. "Do you wish to join identities and explore this question?"

McKie wet his lips with his tongue. This was delicate ground with the Pan-Spechi, whose one ego moved somehow from member to member of the unit group as they traversed their *circle of being*.

"I . . . ah . . . not at this time," McKie said.

"Well spoken," Bolin said. "Should you ever change your mind, my ego-group would consider it a most signal honor. Yours is a strong identity, one we respect."

"I'm . . . most honored," McKie said. He rubbed nervously at his jaw, recognizing the dangers in this conversation. Each Pan-Spechi group maintained a supremely jealous attitude of and about its wandering ego. The ego imbued the holder of it with a touchy sense of honor. Inquiries about it could be carried out only through such formula questions as McKie already had asked.

Still, if this were a member of the pent-archal life circle

containing the missing saboteur extraordinary Napoleon Bildoon . . . if it were, much would be explained.

"You're wondering if we really can communicate," Bolin said. McKie nodded.

"The concept of *humanity*," Bolin said, "—our term for it would translate approximately as *com-sentiency*— has been extended to encompass many differing shapes, life systems and methods of mentation. And yet we have never been sure about this question. It's one of the major reasons many of us have adopted your life-shape and much of your metabolism. We wished to experience your strengths and your weaknesses. This helps . . . but is not an absolute solution."

"Weaknesses?" McKie asked, suddenly wary.

"Ahhh-hummm," Bolin said. "I see. To allay your suspicions I will have translated for you soon one of our major works. Its title would be, approximately, *The Development Influence of Weaknesses*. One of the strongest sympathetic bonds we have with your species, for example, is the fact that we both originated as extremely vulnerable surface-bound creatures, whose most sophisticated defense came to be the social structure."

"I'll be most interested to see the translation," McKie said.

"Do you wish more amenities or do you care to state your business now?" Bolin asked.

"I was . . . ah . . . assigned to seek out a missing agent of our Bureau," McKie said, "to be certain no harm had befallen this . . . ah . . . agent."

"Your avoidance of gender is most refined," Bolin said. "I appreciate the delicacy of your position and your good taste. I will say this for now: the Pan-Spechi you seek is not at this time in need of your assistance. Your concern, however, is appreciated. It will be communicated to those upon whom it will have the most influence."

"That's a great relief to me," McKie said. And he wondered: *What did he really mean by that?* This thought elicited another, and McKie said: "Whenever I run into this problem of communication between species I'm reminded of an old culture/teaching story."

"Oh?" Bolin registered polite curiosity.

"Two practitioners of the art of mental healing, so the

story goes, passed each other every morning on their way to their respective offices. They knew each other, but weren't on intimate terms. One morning as they approached each other, one of them turned to the other and said, 'Good morning.' The one greeted failed to respond, but continued toward his office. Presently, though, he stopped, turned and stared at the retreating back of the man who'd spoken, musing to himself: 'Now, what did he really mean by that?' "

Bolin began to chuckle, then laugh. His laughter grew louder and louder until he was holding his sides.

It wasn't that funny, McKie thought.

Bolin's laughter subsided. "A very educational story," he said. "I'm deeply indebted to you. This story shows your awareness of how important it is in communication that we be aware of the other's identity."

Does it? McKie wondered. *How's that?*

And McKie found himself caught up by his knowledge of how the Pan-Spechi could pass a single ego-identity from individual to individual within the life circle group of five distinct protoplasmic units. He wondered how it felt when the ego-holder gave up the identity to become the fifth gender, passing the ego spark to a newly matured unit from the creche. Did the fifth gender willingly become creche nurse and give itself up as a mysterious identity-food for the three dormants in the creche? he wondered.

"I heard about what you did to Secretary of Sabotage Clinton Watt," Bolin said. "The story of your dismissal from the service preceded you here."

"Yes," McKie said. "That's why I'm here, too."

"You've penetrated to the fact that our Pan-Spechi community here on Achus is the heart of the Tax Watchers' organization," Bolin said. "It was very brave of you to walk right into our hands. I understand how much more courage it takes for your kind to face unit extinction than it does for our kind. Admirable! You are indeed a prize."

McKie fought down a sensation of panic, reminding himself that the records he had left in his private locker of Bureau headquarters could be deciphered in time even if he did not return.

"Yes," Bolin said, "you wish to satisfy yourself that the ascension of a Pan-Spechi to the head of your Bureau will pose no threat to other human species. This is understandable."

McKie shook his head to clear it. "Do you read minds?" he demanded.

"Telepathy is not one of our accomplishments," Bolin said, his voice heavy with menace. "I do hope that was a generalized question and no way directed at the intimacies of my ego-group."

"I felt that you were reading my mind," McKie said, tensing himself for defense.

"That was how I interpreted the question," Bolin said. "Forgive my question. I should not have doubted your delicacy or your tact."

"You do hope to place a member in the job of Bureau Secretary, though?" McKie said.

"Remarkable that you should have suspected it," Bolin said. "How can you be sure our intention is not merely to destroy the Bureau?"

"I'm not." McKie glanced around the room, regretting that he had been forced to act alone.

"Where did we give ourselves away?" Bolin mused.

"Let me remind you," McKie said, "that I have accepted the hospitality you offered and that I've not offended your mores."

"Most remarkable," Bolin said. "In spite of all the temptations I offered, you have not offended our mores. This is true. You are an embarrassment, indeed you are. But perhaps you have a weapon. Yes?"

McKie lifted a wavering *shape* from an inner pocket.

"Ahhh, the Jicuzzi stim," Bolin said. "Now, let me see, is that a weapon?"

McKie held the *shape* on his palm. It appeared flat at first, like a palm-sized sheet of pink paper. Gradually, the flatness grew a superimposed image of a tube laid on its surface, then another image of an S-curved spring that coiled and wound around the tube.

"Our species can control its shape to some extent," Bolin said. "There's some question on whether I can consider this a weapon."

McKie curled his fingers around the *shape* and squeezed. There came a pop, and fumeroles of purple light emerged between his fingers accompanied by an odor of burnt sugar.

"Exit stim," McKie said. "Now I'm completely defenseless, entirely dependent upon your hospitality."

"Ah, you are a tricky one," Bolin said. "But have you no regard for Ser Clinton Watt? To him, the change you forced upon him is an affliction. You've destroyed the instrument that might have reversed the process."

"He can apply to the Jicuzzi," McKie said, wondering why Bolin should concern himself over Watt.

"Ah, but they will ask your permission to intervene," Bolin said. "They are so formal. Drafting their request should take at least three standard years. They will not take the slightest chance of offending you. And you, of course, cannot volunteer your permission without offending them. You know, they may even build a nerve-image of you upon which to test their petition. You are not a callous person, McKie, in spite of your clownish poses. I'd not realized how important this confrontation was to you."

"Since I'm completely at your mercy," McKie said, "would you try to stop me from leaving here?"

"An interesting question," Bolin said. "You have information I don't want revealed at this time. You're aware of this, naturally?"

"Naturally."

"I find the constitution a most wonderful document," Bolin said. "The profound awareness of the individual's identity and its relationship to society as a whole. Of particular interest is the portion dealing with the Bureau of Sabotage, those amendments recognizing that the Bureau itself might at times need . . . ah . . . adjustment."

Now what's he driving at? McKie wondered. And he noted how Bolin squinted his eyes in thought, leaving only a thin line of faceted glitter.

"I shall speak now as chief officer of the Tax Watchers," Bolin said, "reminding you that we are legally immune from sabotage."

I've found out what I wanted to know, McKie thought. *Now if I can only get out of here with it!*

"Let us consider the training of saboteurs extraordinary," Bolin said. "What do the trainees learn about the make-work and featherbedding elements in Bureau activity?"

He's not going to trap me in a lie, McKie thought. "We

come right out and tell our trainees that one of our chief functions is to create jobs for the politicians to fill," he said. "The more hands in the pie, the slower the mixing."

"You've heard that telling a falsehood to your host is a great breach of Pan-Spechi mores, I see," Bolin said. "You understand, of course, that refusal to answer certain questions is interpreted as a falsehood?"

"So I've been told," McKie said.

"Wonderful! And what are your trainees told about the foot-dragging and the monkey wrenches you throw into the path of legislation?"

"I quote from the pertinent training brochure," McKie said. " 'A major function of the Bureau is to slow passage of legislation.' "

"Magnificent! And what about the disputes and outright battles Bureau agents have been known to incite?"

"Strictly routine," McKie said. "We're duty bound to encourage the growth of anger in government wherever we can. It exposes the temperamental types, the ones who can't control themselves, who can't think on their feet."

"Ah," Bolin said. "How entertaining."

"We keep entertainment value in mind," McKie admitted. "We use drama and flamboyance wherever possible to keep our activities fascinating to the public."

"Flamboyant obstructionism," Bolin mused.

"Obstruction is a factor in strength," McKie said. "Only the strongest surmount the obstructions to succeed in government. The strongest . . . or the most devious, which is more or less the same thing when it comes to government."

"How illuminating," Bolin said. He rubbed the backs of his hands, a Pan-Spechi mannerism denoting satisfaction. "Do you have special instructions regarding political parties?"

"We stir up dissent between them," McKie said. "Opposition tends to expose reality, that's one of our axioms."

"Would you characterize Bureau agents as troublemakers?"

"Of course! My parents were happy as the devil when I showed troublemaking tendencies at an early age. They knew there'd be a lucrative outlet for this when I grew up. They saw to it that I was channeled in the right directions all through school—special classes in Applied Destruction, Advanced Irritation, Anger I and II . . . only the best teachers."

"You're suggesting the Bureau's an outlet for society's regular crop of troublemakers?"

"Isn't that obvious? And troublemakers naturally call for the services of troubleshooters. That's an outlet for do-gooders. You've a check and balance system serving society."

McKie waited, watching the Pan-Spechi, wondering if his answers had gone far enough.

"I speak as a Tax Watcher, you understand?" Bolin asked.

"I understand."

"The public pays for this Bureau. In essence, the public is paying people to cause trouble."

"Isn't that what we do when we hire police, tax investigators and the like?" McKie asked.

A look of gloating satisfaction came over Bolin's face. "But these agencies operate for the greater good of humanity!" he said.

"Before he begins training," McKie said, and his voice took on a solemn, lecturing tone, "the potential saboteur is shown the entire sordid record of history. The do-gooders succeeded once . . . long ago. They eliminated virtually all red tape from government. This great machine with its power over human lives slipped into high speed. It moved faster and faster." McKie's voice grew louder. "Laws were conceived and passed in the same hour! Appropriations came and were gone in a fortnight. New bureaus flashed into existence for the most insubstantial reasons."

"Fascinating," Bolin said. "Efficient government, eh?"

"Efficient?" McKie's voice was filled with outrage. "It was like a great wheel thrown suddenly out of balance! The whole structure of government was in imminent danger of fragmenting before a handful of people, wise with hindsight, used measures of desperation and started what was called the Sabotage Corps."

"Ahhh, yes, I've heard about the Corps' violence."

He's needling me, McKie thought, but found that honest anger helped now. "All right, there was bloodshed and terrible destruction at the beginning," he said. "But the big wheels were slowed. Government developed a controllable speed."

"Sabotage," Bolin sneered. "In lieu of red tape."

I needed that reminder, McKie thought.

"No task too small for Sabotage, no task too large," McKie said. "We keep the wheel turning slowly and smoothly. Some anonymous Corpsman put it into words a long time ago: 'When in doubt, delay the big ones and speed the little ones.' "

"Would you say the Tax Watchers were a 'big one' or a 'little one'?" Bolin asked, his voice mild.

"Big one," McKie said and waited for Bolin to pounce.

But the Pan-Spechi appeared amused. "An unhappy answer."

"As it says in the Constitution," McKie said. " 'The pursuit of unhappiness is an inalienable right of all humans.' "

"Trouble is as trouble does," Bolin said and clapped his hands.

Two Pan-Spechi in the uniforms of system police came through the creme de menthe emerald door.

"You heard?" Bolin asked.

"We heard," one of the police said.

"Was he defending his bureau?" Bolin asked.

"He was," the policeman said.

"You've seen the court order," Bolin said. "It pains me because Ser McKie accepted the hospitality of my house, but he must be held incommunicado until he's needed in court. He's to be treated kindly, you understand?"

Is he really bent on destroying the Bureau? McKie asked himself in sudden consternation. *Do I have it figured wrong?*

"You contend my words were sabotage?" McKie asked.

"Clearly an attempt to sway the chief officer of the Tax Watchers from his avowed duties," Bolin said. He stood, bowed.

McKie lifted himself out of the chairdog, assumed an air of confidence he did not feel. He clasped his thick-fingered hands together and bowed low, a grandfather toad rising from the deep to give his benediction. "In the words of the ancient proverb," he said, " 'The righteous man lives deep within a cavern and the sky appears to him as nothing but a small round hole.' "

Wrapping himself in dignity, McKie allowed the police to escort him from the room.

Behind him, Bolin gave voice to puzzlement: "Now, what did he mean by that?"

III

"HEAR YE! HEAR YE! System High Court, First Bench, Central Sector, is now in session!"

The robo-clerk darted back and forth across the cleared lift dais of the courtarena, its metal curves glittering in the morning light that poured down through the domed weather cover. Its voice, designed to fit precisely into the great circular room, penetrated to the farthest walls: "All persons having petitions before this court draw near!"

The silvery half globe carrying First Magistrate Edwin Dooley glided through an aperture behind the lift dais and was raised to an appropriate height. His white sword of justice lay diagonally across the bench in front of him.

Judge Dooley was a tall, black-browed man who affected the ancient look with ebon robes over white linen. He was noted for decisions of classic penetration.

He sat now with his face held in rigid immobility to conceal his anger and disquiet. Why had they put him in this hot spot? Because he'd granted the Tax Watchers' injunction? No matter how he ruled now, the likely result would be uproar. Even President Hindley was watching this one through one of the hot-line projectors.

The President had called shortly before this session. It had been Phil and Ed all through the conversation, but the intent remained clear. The Administration was concerned about this case. Vital legislation pended; votes were needed. Neither the budget nor the Bureau of Sabotage had entered their conversation, but the President had made his point—*don't compromise the Bureau but save that Tax Watcher support for the Administration!*

"Clerk, the roster," Judge Dooley said.

And he thought: *They'll get judgment according to strict interpretation of the law! Let them argue with that!*

The robo-clerk's reelslate buzzed. Words appeared on the repeater in front of the judge as the clerk's voice announced: "The People versus Clifton Watt, Jorj X. McKie and the Bureau of Sabotage."

Dooley looked down into the courtarena, noting the group seated at the black oblong table in the Defense ring on his left: a sour-faced Watt with his rainbow horror of Medusa head, McKie's fat features composed in the look of someone trying not to snicker at a sly joke—the two defendants flanking their attorney, Pander Oulson, the Bureau of Sabotage's chief counsel. Oulson was a great thug of a figure in defense white with glistening eyes under beetle brows and a face fashioned mostly of scars.

At the Prosecution table on the right sat Prosecutor Holjance Vohnbrook, a tall scarecrow of a man dressed in conviction red. Gray hair topped a stern face as grim and forbidding as a latter day Cotton Mather. Beside him sat a frightened appearing young aide and Panthor Bolin, the Pan-Spechi complainant, his multifaceted eyes hidden beneath veined lids.

"Are we joined for trial?" Dooley asked.

Both Oulson and Vohnbrook arose, nodded.

"If the court pleases," Vohnbrook rumbled, "I would like to remind the Bureau of Sabotage personnel present that this court is exempt from their ministrations."

"If the prosecutor trips over his own feet," Oulson said, "I assure him it will be his own clumsiness and no act of mine nor of my colleagues."

Vohnbrook's face darkened with a rush of blood. "It's well known how you . . ."

A great drumming boomed through the courtarena as Dooley touched the handle of his sword of office. The sound drowned the prosecutor's words. When silence was restored, Dooley said: "This court will tolerate no displays of personality. I wish that understood at the outset."

Oulson smiled, a look like a grimace on his scarred face. "I apologize, Your Honor," he said.

Dooley sank back into his chair, noting the gleam in Oulson's eyes. It occurred to Dooley then that the defense attorney, sabotage-trained, could have brought on the prosecutor's attack to gain the court's sympathy.

"The charge is outlaw sabotage in violation of this court's injunction," Dooley said. "I understand that opening statements have been waived by both sides, the public having been admitted to causae in this matter by appropriate postings?"

"So recorded," intoned the robo-clerk.

Oulson, leaning forward against the defense table, said: "Your Honor, defendant Jorj X. McKie has not accepted me as counsel and wishes to argue for separate trial. I am here now representing only the Bureau and Clinton Watt."

"Who is appearing for defendant McKie?" the judge asked.

McKie, feeling like a man leaping over a precipice, got to his feet, said: "I wish to represent myself, Your Honor."

"You should be cautioned against this course," Dooley said.

"Ser Oulson has advised me I have a fool for a client," McKie said. "But in common with most Bureau agents, I have legal training. I've been admitted to the System Bar and have practiced under such codes as the Gowachin where the double-negative innocence requirement must be satisfied before bringing criminal accusation against the prosecutor and proceeding backward the premise that . . ."

"This is not Gowachin," Judge Dooley said.

"May I remind the Court," Vohnbrook said, "that defendant McKie is a saboteur extraordinary. This goes beyond questions of champerty. Every utterance this man . . ."

"The law's the same for official saboteurs as it is for others in respect to the issue at hand," Oulson said.

"Gentlemen!" the judge said. "If you please? I will decide law in this court." He waited through a long moment of silence. "The behavior of all parties in this matter is receiving my most careful attention."

McKie forced himself to radiate calm good humor.

Watt, whose profound knowledge of the saboteur extraordinary made this pose a danger signal, tugged violently at the sleeve of defense attorney Oulson. Oulson waved him away. Watt glowered at McKie.

"If the court permits," McKie said, "a joint defense on the present charge would appear to violate . . ."

"The court is well aware that this case was bound over on the basis of deposa summation through a ruling by a robo-legum," Dooley said. "I warn both defense and prosecution, however, that I make my own decisions in such matters. Law and robo-legum are both human constructions and require human interpretation. And I will add that, as far as I'm concerned, in all conflicts between human agencies and machine agencies the human agencies are paramount."

"Is this a hearing or a trial?" McKie asked.

"We will proceed as in trial, subject to the evidence as presented."

McKie rested his palms on the edge of the defense table, studying the judge. The saboteur felt a surge of misgiving. Dooley was a no-nonsense customer. He had left himself a wide avenue within the indictment. And this was a case that went far beyond immediate danger to the Bureau of Sabotage. Far-reaching precedents could be set here this day—or disaster could strike. Ignoring instincts of self preservation, McKie wondered if he dared try sabotage within the confines of the court.

"The robo-legum indictment requires joint defense," McKie said. "I admit sabotage against Ser Clinton Watt, but remind the court of Paragraph Four, section ninety-one, of the Semantic Revision to the Constitution, wherein the Secretary of Sabotage is exempted from all immunities. I move to quash the indictment as it regards myself. I was at the time a legal officer of the Bureau required by my duties to test the abilities of my superior."

"Mmmm," Dooley said. He saw that the prosecutor had detected where McKie's logic must lead. If McKie were legally dismissed from the Bureau at the time of his conversation with the Pan-Spechi, the prosecution's case might fall through.

"Does the prosecutor wish to seek a conspiracy indictment?" Dooley asked.

For the first time since entering the courtarena, defense attorney Oulson appeared agitated. He bent his scarred features close to Watt's gorgon head, conferred in whispers with the defendant. Oulson's face grew darker and darker as he whispered. Watt's gorgon tendrils writhed in agitation.

"We don't seek a conspiracy indictment at this time," Vohnbrook said. "However, we would be willing to separate . . ."

"Your Honor!" Oulson said, surging to his feet. "Defense must protest separation of indictments at this time. It's our contention that . . ."

"Court cautions both counsels in this matter that this is not a Gowachin jurisdiction," Dooley said in an angry voice. "We don't have to convict the defender and exonerate the prosecutor before trying a case! However, if either of you would wish a change of venue . . ."

Vohnbrook, a smug expression on his lean face, bowed to the judge. "Your Honor," he said, "we wish at this time to request removal of defendant McKie from the indictment and ask that he be held as a prosecution witness."

"Objection!" Oulson shouted. "Prosecution well knows it cannot hold a key witness under trumped up . . ."

"Overruled," Dooley said.

"Exception!"

"Noted."

Dooley waited as Oulson sank into his chair. *This is a day to remember,* the judge thought. *Sabotage itself outfoxed!* Then he noted the glint of sly humor in the eyes of saboteur extraordinary McKie, realizing with an abrupt sense of caution that McKie, too, had maneuvered for this position.

"Prosecution may call its first witness," the judge said, and he punched a code signal that sent a robo-aide to escort McKie away from the defense table and into a holding box.

A look of almost-pleasure came over prosecutor Vohnbrook's cadaverous face. He rubbed one of his downdrooping eyelids, and said: "Call Panthor Bolin."

The Achusian capitalist got to his feet, strode to the witness ring. The robo-clerk's screen flashed for the record: "Panthor Bolin of Achus IV, certified witness in case $A0115BD_4gGY74R_6$ of System High Court ZRZ^1."

"The oath of sincerity having been administered, Panthor Bolin is prepared for testifying," the robo-clerk recited.

"Panthor Bolin, are you chief officer of the civil organization known as the Tax Watchers?" Vohnbrook asked.

"I . . . ah . . . y-yes," Bolin faltered. He passed a large blue handkerchief across his forehead, staring sharply at McKie.

He just now realizes what it is I must do, McKie thought.

"I show you this recording from the robo-legum indictment proceedings," Vohnbrook said. "It is certified by System police as being a conversation between yourself and Jorj X. McKie in which . . ."

"Your Honor!" Oulson objected. "Both witnesses to this alleged conversation are present in this courtarena. There are more direct ways to bring out any pertinent information from this matter. Further, since the clear threat of a conspiracy charge remains in this case, I object to introducing this recording as forcing a man to testify against himself."

"Ser McKie is no longer on trial here and Ser Oulson is not McKie's attorney of record," Vohnbrook gloated.

"The objection does, however, have some merit," Dooley said. He looked at McKie seated in the holding box.

"There's nothing shameful about that conversation with Ser Bolin," McKie said. "I've no objection to introducing this record of the conversation."

Bolin rose up on his toes, made as though to speak, sank back.

Now he is certain, McKie thought.

"Then I will admit this record subject to judicial deletions," Dooley said.

Clinton Watt, seated at the defense table, buried his gorgon head in his arms.

Vohnbrook, a death's-head grin on his long face, said: "Ser Bolin, I show you this recording. Now, in this conversation, was Sabotage Agent McKie subjected to any form of coercion?"

"Objection!" Oulson roared, surging to his feet. His scarred face was a scowling mask. "At the time of this alleged recording, Ser McKie was not an agent of the Bureau!" He looked at Vohnbrook. "Defense objects to the prosecutor's obvious effort to link Ser McKie with . . ."

"*Alleged* conversation!" Vohnbrook snarled. "Ser McKie himself admits the exchange!"

In a weary voice, Dooley said: "Objection sustained. Unless tangible evidence of conspiracy is introduced here, references to Ser McKie as an agent of Sabotage will not be admitted here."

"But, Your Honor," Vohnbrook protested, "Ser McKie's own actions preclude any other interpretation!"

"I've ruled on this point," Dooley said. "Proceed."

McKie got to his feet in the holding box, said: "Would Your Honor permit me to act as a friend of the Court here?"

Dooley leaned back, hand on chin, turning the question over in his mind. A general feeling of uneasiness about the case was increasing in him and he couldn't pinpoint it. McKie's every action appeared suspect. Dooley reminded himself that the saboteur extraordinary was notorious for sly plots, for devious and convoluted schemes of the wildest and most improbable inversions—like onion layers in a five dimensional klein-shape. The man's success in practicing under the Gowachin legal code could be understood.

"You may explain what you have in mind," Dooley said, "but I'm not yet ready to admit your statements into the record."

"The Bureau of Sabotage's own Code would clarify matters," McKie said, realizing that these words burned his bridges behind him. "My action in successfully sabotaging *acting* Secretary Watt is a matter of record."

McKie pointed to the gorgon mass visible as Watt lifted his head and glared across the room.

"*Acting* Secretary?" the judge asked.

"So it must be presumed," McKie said. "Under the Bureau's Code, once the Secretary is sabotaged he . . ."

"Your Honor!" Oulson shouted. "We are in danger of breach of security here! I understand these proceedings are being broadcast!"

"As Director-in-Limbo of the Bureau of Sabotage, I will decide what is a breach of security and what isn't!" McKie snapped.

Watt returned his head to his arms, groaned.

Oulson sputtered.

Dooley stared at McKie in shock.

Vohnbrook broke the spell. The prosecutor said: "Your Honor, this man has not been sworn to sincerity. I suggest we excuse Ser Bolin for the time being and have Ser McKie continue his *explanation* under oath."

Dooley took a deep breath and said: "Does defense have any questions of Ser Bolin at this time?"

"Not at this time," Oulson muttered. "I presume he's subject to recall?"

"He is," Dooley said, turning to McKie. "Take the witness ring, Ser McKie."

IV

BOLIN, MOVING LIKE A SLEEPWALKER, stepped out of the ring and returned to the prosecution table. The Pan-Spechi's multifaceted eyes reflected an odd glitter, moving with a trapped sense of evasiveness.

McKie entered the ring, took the oath and faced Vohnbrook, composing his features in a look of purposeful decisiveness that he knew his actions must reflect.

"You called yourself Director-in-Limbo of the Bureau of Sabotage," Vohnbrook said. "Would you explain that, please?"

Before McKie could answer, Watt lifted his head from his arms, growling: "You traitor, McKie!"

Dooley grabbed the pommel of his sword of justice to indicate an absolute position and barked: "I will tolerate no outbursts in my court!"

Oulson put a hand on Watt's shoulder. Both of them glared at McKie. The medusa tendrils of Watt's head writhed as they ranged through the rainbow spectrum.

"I caution the witness," Dooley said, "that his remarks would appear to admit a conspiracy. Anything he says now may be used against him."

"No conspiracy, Your Honor," McKie said. He faced Vohnbrook, but appeared to be addressing Watt. "Over the centuries, the function of Sabotage in the government has grown more and more open, but certain aspects of changing the guard, so to speak, have been held as a highly placed secret. The rule is that if a man can protect himself from sabotage he's fit to boss Sabotage. Once sabotaged, however, the Bureau's Secretary must resign and submit his position to the President and the full Cabinet."

"He's out?" Dooley asked.

"Not necessarily," McKie said. "If the act of sabotage against the Secretary is profound enough, subtle enough, carries enough far-reaching effects, the Secretary is replaced by the successful saboteur. He is, indeed, out."

"Then it's now up to the President and the Cabinet to

decide between Ser Watt and yourself, is that what you're saying?" Dooley asked.

"Me?" McKie asked. "No, I'm Director-in-Limbo because I accomplished a successful *act* of sabotage against Ser Watt and because I happen to be senior saboteur extraordinary on duty."

"But it's alleged that you were fired," Vohnbrook objected.

"A formality," McKie said. "It's customary to fire the saboteur who's successful in such an effort. This makes him eligible for appointment as Secretary if he so aspires. However, I have no such ambition at this time."

Watt jerked upright, staring at McKie.

McKie ran a finger around his collar, realizing the physical peril he was about to face. A glance at the Pan-Spechi confirmed the feeling. Panthor Bolin was holding himself in check by a visible effort.

"This is all very interesting," Vohnbrook sneered, "but how can it possibly have any bearing on the present action? The charge here is outlaw sabotage against the Tax Watchers represented by the person of Ser Panthor Bolin. If Ser McKie . . ."

"If the distinguished prosecutor will permit me," McKie said, "I believe I can set his fears at rest. It should be obvious to——"

"There's conspiracy here!" Vohnbrook shouted. "What about the . . ."

A loud pounding interrupted him as Judge Dooley lifted his sword, its theremin effect filling the room. When silence had been restored, the judge lowered his sword, replaced it firmly on the ledge in front of him.

Dooley took a moment to calm himself. He sensed now the delicate political edge he walked and thanked his stars that he had left the door open to rule that the present session was a hearing.

"We will now proceed in an orderly fashion," Dooley said. "That's one of the things courts are for, you know." He took a deep breath. "Now, there are several people present whose dedication to the maintenance of law and order should be beyond question. I'd think that among those we should number Ser Prosecutor Vohnbrook; the distinguished defense counsel, Ser Oulson; Ser Bolin, whose race is noted for its reasonableness and humanity;

and the distinguished representatives of the Bureau of Sabotage, whose actions may at times annoy and anger us, but who are, we know, consecrated to the principle of strengthening us and exposing our inner resources."

This judge missed his calling, McKie thought. *With speeches like that, he could get into the Legislative branch.*

Abashed, Vohnbrook sank back into his chair.

"Now," the judge said, "unless I'm mistaken, Ser McKie has referred to two acts of sabotage." Dooley glanced down at McKie. "Ser McKie?"

"So it would appear, Your Honor," McKie said, hoping he read the judge's present attitude correctly. "However, this court may be in a unique position to rule on that very question. You see, Your Honor, the alleged act of sabotage to which I refer was initiated by a Pan-Spechi agent of the Bureau. Now, though, the secondary benefits of that action appear to be sought after by a creche mate of that agent, whose . . ."

"You dare suggest that I'm not the holder of my cell's ego?" Bolin demanded.

Without knowing quite where it was or what it was, McKie was aware that a weapon had been trained on him by the Pan-Spechi. References in their culture to the weapon for defense of the ego were clear enough.

"I made no such suggestion," McKie said, speaking hastily and with as much sincerity as he could put into his voice. "But surely you cannot have misinterpreted the terranic-human culture so much that you do not know what will happen now."

Warned by some instinct, the judge and other spectators to this interchange remained silent.

Bolin appeared to be trembling in every cell of his body. "I am distressed," he muttered.

"If there were a way to achieve the necessary rapport and avoid that distress I would have taken it," McKie said. "Can you see another way?"

Still trembling, Bolin said: "I must do what I must do."

In a low voice, Dooley said: "Ser McKie, just what is going on here?"

"Two cultures are, at last, attempting to understand each other," McKie said. "We've lived together in apparent understanding for centuries, but appearances can be deceptive."

Oulson started to rise, was pulled back by Watt.

And McKie noted that his former Bureau chief had assessed the peril here. It was a point in Watt's favor.

"You understand, Ser Bolin," McKie said, watching the Pan-Spechi carefully, "that these things must be brought into the open and discussed carefully before a decision can be reached in this court. It's a rule of law to which you've submitted. I'm inclined to favor your bid for the Secretariat, but my own decision awaits the outcome of this hearing."

"What things must be discussed?" Dooley demanded. "And what gives you the right, Ser McKie, to call this a hearing?"

"A figure of speech," McKie said, but he kept his attention on the Pan-Spechi, wondering what the terrible weapon was that the race used in defense of its egos. "What do you say, Ser Bolin?"

"You protect the sanctity of your home life," Bolin said. "Do you deny me the same right?"

"Sanctity, not secrecy," McKie said.

Dooley looked from McKie to Bolin, noted the compressed-spring look of the Pan-Spechi, the way he kept a hand hidden in a jacket pocket. It occurred to the judge then that the Pan-Spechi might have a weapon ready to use against others in this court. Bolin had that look about him. Dooley hesitated on the point of calling guards, reviewing what he knew of the Pan-Spechi. He decided not to cause a crisis. The Pan-Spechi were admitted to the concourse of humanity, good friends but terrible enemies, and there were always those allusions to their hidden powers, to their ego jealousies, to the fierceness with which they defended the secrecy of their creches.

Slowly, Bolin overcame the trembling. "Say what you feel you must," he growled.

McKie, saying a silent prayer of hope that the Pan-Spechi could control his reflexes, addressed himself to the nexus of pickups on the far wall that was recording this courtarena scene for broadcast to the entire universe.

"A Pan-Spechi who took the name of Napoleon Bildoon was one of the leading agents in the Bureau of Sabotage," McKie said. "Agent Bildoon dropped from sight at the time Panthor Bolin took over as chief of the Tax Watchers. It's highly probable that the Tax Watcher organization is an elaborate and subtle sabotage of the Bureau of Sabotage itself, a move originated by Bildoon."

"There is no such person as Bildoon!" Bolin cried.

"Ser McKie," Judge Dooley said, "would you care to continue this interchange in the privacy of my chambers?" The judge stared down at the saboteur, trying to appear kindly but firm.

"Your Honor," McKie said, "may we, out of respect for a fellow human, leave that decision to Ser Bolin?"

Bolin turned his multifaceted eyes toward the bench, spoke in a low voice: "If the court please, it were best this were done openly." He jerked his hand from his pocket. It came out empty. He leaned across the table, gripped the far edge. "Continue, if you please, Ser."

McKie swallowed, momentarily overcome with admiration for the Pan-Spechi. "It will be a distinct pleasure to serve under you, Ser Bolin," McKie said.

"Do what you must!" Bolin rasped.

McKie looked from the wonderment in the faces of Watt and the attorneys up to the questioning eyes of Judge Dooley. "In Pan-Spechi parlance, there is no person called Bildoon. But there was such a person, a group mate of Ser Bolin. I hope you notice the similarity in the names they chose for themselves?"

"Ah . . . yes," Dooley said.

"I'm afraid I've been somewhat of a nosey Parker, a peeping Tom and several other categories of snoop where the Pan-Spechi are concerned," McKie said. "But it was because I suspected the act of sabotage to which I've referred here. The Tax Watchers revealed too much inside knowledge of the Bureau of Sabotage."

"I . . . ah . . . am not quite sure I understand you," Dooley said.

"The best kept secret in the universe, the Pan-Spechi cyclic change of gender and identity, is no longer a secret where I'm concerned," McKie said. He swallowed as he saw Bolin's fingers go white where they tightly gripped the prosecution table.

"It relates to the issue at hand?" Dooley asked.

"Most definitely, Your Honor," McKie said. "You see, the Pan-Spechi have a unique gland that controls mentation, dominance, the relationship between reason and instinct. The five group mates are, in reality, one person. I wish to make that clear for reasons of legal necessity."

"Legal necessity?" Dooley asked. He glanced down at the obviously distressed Bolin, back to McKie.

"The gland, when it's functioning, confers ego dominance on the Pan-Spechi in whom it functions. But it functions for a time that's definitely limited—twenty-five to thirty years." McKie looked at Bolin. Again, the Pan-Spechi was trembling. "Please understand, Ser Bolin," he said, "that I do this out of necessity and that this is not an act of sabotage."

Bolin lifted his face toward McKie. The Pan-Spechi's features appeared contorted in grief. "Get it over with, man!" he rasped.

"Yes," McKie said, turning back to the judge's puzzled face. "Ego transfer in the Pan-Spechi, Your Honor, involves a transfer of what may be termed basic-experience-learning. It's accomplished through physical contractor when the ego-holder dies, no matter how far he may be separated from the creche; this seems to fire up the eldest of the creche triplets. The ego-single also bequeaths a verbal legacy to his mate whenever possible—and that's most of the time. Specifically, it's this time."

Dooley leaned back. He was beginning to see the legal question McKie's account had posed.

"The act of sabotage that might make a Pan-Spechi eligible for appointment as Secretary of the Bureau of Sabotage was initiated by a . . . ah . . . cell mate of the Ser Bolin in court today, is that it?" Dooley asked.

McKie wiped his brow. "Correct, Your Honor."

"But that cell mate is no longer the ego dominant, eh?"

"Quite right, Your Honor."

"The . . . ah . . . former ego-holder, this . . . ah . . . Bildoon, is no longer eligible?"

"Bildoon, or what was once Bildoon, is a creature operating solely on instinct now, Your Honor," McKie said. "Capable of acting as creche nurse for a time and, eventually, fulfilling another destiny I'd rather not explain."

"I see." Dooley looked at the weather cover of the court arena. He was beginning to see what McKie had risked here. "And you favor this, ah, Ser Bolin's bid for the Secretariat?" Dooley asked.

"If President Hindley and the Cabinet follow the recommendation of the Bureau's senior agents, the procedure always followed in the past, Ser Bolin will be the new Secretary," McKie said. "I favor this."

"Why?" Dooley asked.

"Because of this unique roving ego, the Pan-Spechi have a more communal attitude toward fellow sentients than do most other species admitted to the concourse of humanity," McKie said. "This translates as a sense of responsibility toward all life. They're not necessarily maudlin about it. They oppose where it's necessary to build strength. Their creche life demonstrates several clear examples of this, which I'd prefer not to describe."

"I see," Dooley said, but he had to admit to himself that he did not. McKie's allusions to unspeakable practices were beginning to annoy him. "And you feel that this Bildoon-Bolin act of sabotage qualifies him, provided this court rules they are one and the same person?"

"We're not the same person!" Bolin cried. "You don't dare say that . . . that shambling, clinging . . ."

"Easy," McKie said. "Ser Bolin, I'm sure you see the need for this legal fiction."

"Legal fiction," Bolin said as though clinging to the words. The multifaceted eyes glared across the courtarena at McKie. "Thank you for the verbal nicety, McKie."

"You've not answered my question, Ser McKie," Dooley said, ignoring the exchange with Bolin.

"Sabotaging Ser Watt through an attack on the entire Bureau contains subtlety and finesse never before achieved in such an effort," McKie said. "The entire Bureau will be strengthened by it."

McKie glanced at Watt. The acting Secretary's medusa tangle had ceased its writhing. He was staring Bolin with a speculative look in his eyes. Sensing the quiet in the courtarena, he glanced up at McKie.

"Don't you agree, Ser Watt?" McKie asked.

"Oh, yes. Quite," Watt said.

The note of sincerity in Watt's voice startled the judge. For the first time, he wondered at the dedication these men brought to their jobs.

"Sabotage is a very sensitive bureau," Dooley said. "I've some serious reservations——"

"If Your Honor please," McKie said, "forbearance is one of the chief attributes a saboteur can bring to his duties. Now, I wish you to understand what our Pan-Spechi friend has done here this day. Let us suppose that I had spied upon the most intimate moments between you, Judge, and your wife, and that I reported them in detail here in open court with half the universe looking on. Let us suppose further that you had the strictest moral code against such discussions with outsiders. Let us suppose that I made these disclosures in the basest terms with every four-letter word at my command. Let us suppose that you were armed, traditionally, with a deadly weapon to strike at such blasphemers, such——"

"Filth!" Bolin grated.

"Yes," McKie said. "Filth. Do you suppose, Your Honor, that you could have stood by without killing me?"

"Good heavens!" Dooley said.

V

"SER BOLIN," McKie said, "I offer you and all your race my most humble apologies."

"I'd hoped once to undergo the ordeal in the privacy of a judge's chambers with as few outsiders as possible," Bolin said. "But once you were started in open court . . ."

"It had to be this way," McKie said. "If we'd done it in private, people would've come to be suspicious about a Pan-Spechi in control of . . ."

"People?" Bolin asked.

"Non Pan-Spechi," McKie said. "It'd have been a barrier between our species.

"And we've been strengthened by all this," McKie said. "Those provisions of the Constitution that provide the people with a slowly moving government have been demonstrated anew. We've admitted the public to the inner workings of sabotage, shown them the valuable character of the man who'll be the new Secretary."

"I've not yet ruled on the critical issue here," Dooley said.

"But Your Honor!" McKie said.

"With all due respect to you as a saboteur extraordinary, Ser McKie," Dooley said, "I'll make my decision on evidence gathered under my direction." He looked at Bolin. "Ser Bolin, would you permit an agent of this court to gather such evidence as will allow me to render verdict without fear of harming my own species?"

"We're humans together," Bolin growled.

"But terranic humans hold the balance of power,"

Dooley said. "I owe allegiance to law, yes, but my terranic fellows depend on me, too. I have a . . ."

"You wish your own agents to determine if Ser McKie has told the truth about us?"

"Ah . . . yes," Dooley said.

Bolin looked at McKie. "Ser McKie, it is I who apologize to you. I had not realized how deeply xenophobia penetrated your fellows."

"Because," McKie said, "outside of your natural modesty, you have no such fear. I suspect you know the phenomenon only through reading of us."

"But all strangers are potential sharers of identity," Bolin said. "Ah, well."

"If you're through with your little chat," Dooley said, "would you care to answer my question, Ser Bolin? This is still I hope, a court of law."

"Tell me, Your Honor," Bolin said, "would you permit me to witness the tenderest intimacies between you and your wife?"

Dooley's face darkened, but he saw suddenly in all of its stark detail the extent of McKie's analogy and it was to the judge's credit that he rose to the occasion. "If it were necessary to promote understanding," he rasped, "yes!"

"I believe you would," Bolin murmured. He took a deep breath. "After what I've been through here today, one more sacrifice can be borne, I guess. I grant your investigators the privilege requested, but advise that they be discreet."

"It will strengthen you for the trials ahead as Secretary of the Bureau," McKie said. "The Secretary, you must bear in mind, has no immunities from sabotage whatsoever."

"But," Bolin said, "the Secretary's legal orders carrying out his Constitutional functions must be obeyed by all agents."

McKie nodded, seeing in the glitter of Bolin's eyes a vista of peeping Tom assignments with endless detailed reports to the Secretary of Sabotage—at least until the fellow's curiosity had been satisfied and his need for revenge satiated.

But the others in the courtroom, not having MicKie's insight, merely wondered at the question: *What did he really mean by that?*

MINISTRY OF DISTURBANCE

H. Beam Piper

THE SYMPHONY WAS ENDING, the final triumphant pæan soaring up and up, beyond the limit of audibility. For a moment, after the last notes had gone away, Paul sat motionless, as though some part of him had followed. Then he roused himself and finished his coffee and cigarette, looking out the wide window across the city below—treetops and towers, roofs and domes and arching skyways, busy swarms of aircars glinting in the early sunlight. Not many people cared for João Coelho's music, now, and least of all for the Eighth Symphony. It was the music of another time, a thousand years ago, when the Empire was blazing into being out of the long night and hammering back the Neobarbarians from world after world. Today people found it perturbing.

He smiled faintly at the vacant chair opposite him, and lit another cigarette before putting the breakfast dishes on the serving-robot's tray, and, after a while, realized that the robot was still beside his chair, waiting for dismissal. He gave it an instruction to summon the cleaning robots and sent it away. He could as easily have summoned them himself, or let the guards who would be in checking the room do it for him, but maybe it made a robot feel trusted and important to relay orders to other robots.

Then he smiled again, this time in self-derision. A robot couldn't feel important, or anything else. A robot was nothing but steel and plastic and magnetized tape and photo-micropositronic circuits, whereas a man—His Imperial Majesty Paul XVII, for instance—was nothing but tissues and cells and colloids and electro-neuronic circuits. There was a difference; anybody knew that. The trouble was that he had never met anybody—which included physicists, biologists, psychologists, psionicists, philosophers and theologians—who could define the difference in satisfactorily exact terms. He watched the robot pivot on its treads and glide away, trailing steam from its coffee pot. It might be silly to treat robots like people, but that wasn't as bad as treating people like robots, an attitude that was becoming entirely too prevalent. If only so many people didn't act like robots!

He crossed to the elevator and stood in front of it until a tiny electroencephalograph inside recognized his distinctive brain-wave pattern. Across the room, another door was popping open in response to the robot's distinctive wave pattern. He stepped inside and flipped a switch—there were still a few things around that had to be manually operated—and the door closed behind him and the elevator gave him an instant's weightlessness as it started to drop forty floors.

When it opened, Captain-General Dorflay of the Household Guard was waiting for him, with a captain and ten privates. General Dorflay was human. The captain and his ten soldiers weren't. They wore helmets, emblazoned with the golden sun and superimposed black cogwheel of the Empire, and red kilts and black ankle boots and weapons belts, and the captain had a narrow gold-laced cape over his shoulders, but for the rest, their bodies were covered with a stiff mat of black hair, and their faces were slightly like terriers'. (For all his humanity, Captain-General Dorflay's face was more like a bulldog's.) They were hillmen from the southern hemisphere of Thor, and as a people they made excellent mercenaries. They were crack shots, brave and crafty fighters, totally uninterested in politics off their own planet, and, because they had grown up in a patriarchal-clan society, they were fanatically loyal to anybody they accepted as their chieftain. Paul stepped out and gave them an inclusive nod.

"Good morning, gentlemen."

"Good morning, Your Imperial Majesty," General Dorflay said, bowing the couple of inches consistent with military dignity. The Thoran captain saluted by touching his forehead, his heart, which was on the right side, and the butt of his pistol. Paul complimented him on the smart appearance of his detail, and the captain asked how it could be otherwise, with the example and inspiration of his imperial majesty. Compliment and response could have been a playback from every morning of the ten years of his reign. So could Dorflay's question: "Your Majesty will proceed to his study?"

He wanted to say, "No, to Niffelheim with it; let's get an aircar and fly a million miles somewhere," and watch the look of shocked incomprehension on the captain-general's face. He couldn't do that, though; poor old Harv Dorflay might have a heart attack. He nodded slowly.

"If you please, General."

Dorflay nodded to the Thoran captain, who nodded to his men. Four of them took two paces forward; the rest, unslinging weapons, went scurrying up the corridor, some posting themselves along the way and the rest continuing to the main hallway. The captain and two of his men started forward slowly; after they had gone twenty feet, Paul and General Dorflay fell in behind them, and the other two brought up the rear.

"Your Majesty," Dorflay said, in a low voice, "let me beg you to be most cautious. I have just discovered that there exists a treasonous plot against your life."

Paul nodded. Dorflay was more than due to discover another treasonous plot; it had been ten days since the last one.

"I believe you mentioned it, General. Something about planting loose strontium-90 in the upholstery of the audience throne, wasn't it?"

And before that, somebody had been trying to smuggle a fission bomb into the palace in a wine cask, and before that, it was a booby trap in the elevator, and before that, somebody was planning to build a submachine gun into the viewscreen in the study, and——

"Oh, no, Your Majesty; that was—Well, the persons involved in that plot became alarmed and fled the planet before I could arrest them. This is something different, Your Majesty. I have learned that unauthorized alterations have been made on one of the cooking-robots in your private kitchen, and I am positive that the object is to poison Your Majesty."

They were turning into the main hallway, between the rows of portraits of past emperors, Paul and Rodrik, Paul and Rodrik, alternating over and over on both walls. He felt a smile growing on his face, and banished it.

"The robot for the meat sauces, wasn't it?" he asked.

"Why—! Yes, Your Majesty."

"I'm sorry, general. I should have warned you. Those alterations were made by roboticists from the Ministry of

Security; they were installing an adaptation of a device used in the criminalistics-labs, to insure more uniform measurements. They'd done that already for Prince Travann, the Minister, and he'd recommended it to me."

That was a shame, spoiling poor Harv Dorflay's murder plot. It had been such a nice little plot, too; he must have had a lot of fun inventing it. But a line had to be drawn somewhere. Let him turn the palace upside down hunting for bombs; harass ladies-in-waiting whose lovers he suspected of being hired assassins; hound musicians into whose instruments he imagined firearms had been built; the emperor's private kitchen would have to be off limits.

Dorflay, who should have been looking crestfallen but relieved, stopped short—shocking breach of court etiquette—and was staring in horror.

"Your Majesty! Prince Travann did that openly and with your consent? But, Your Majesty, I am convinced that it is Prince Travann himself who is the instigator of every one of these diabolical schemes. In the case of the elevator, I became suspicious of a man named Samml Ganner, one of Prince Travann's secret police agents. In the case of the gun in the viewscreen, it was a technician whose sister is a member of the household of Countess Yirzy, Prince Travann's mistress. In the case of the fission bomb——"

The two Thorans and their captain had kept on for some distance before they had discovered that they were no longer being followed, and were returning. He put his hand on General Dorflay's shoulder and urged him forward.

"Have you mentioned this to anybody?"

"Not a word, Your Majesty. This court is so full of treachery that I can trust no one, and we must never warn the villain that he is suspected——"

"Good. Say nothing to anybody." They had reached the door of the study, now. "I think I'll be here until noon. If I leave earlier, I'll flash you a signal."

He entered the big oval room, lighted from overhead by the great star-map in the ceiling, and crossed to his desk, with the viewscreens and reading screens and communications screens around it, and as he sat down, he cursed angrily, first at Harv Dorflay and then, after a moment's reflection, at himself. He was the one to blame; he'd known Dorflay's paranoid condition for years. Have to do something about it. Any psycho-medic would certify him; be no problem at all to have him put away. But be blasted if he'd do that. That was no way to repay loyalty, even insane loyalty. Well, he'd find a way.

He lit a cigarette and leaned back, looking up at the glowing swirl of billions of billions of tiny lights in the ceiling. At least, there were supposed to be billions of billions of them; he'd never counted them, and neither had any of the seventeen Rodriks and sixteen Pauls before him who had sat under them. His hand moved to a control button on his chair arm, and a red patch, roughly the shape of a pork chop, appeared on the western side.

That was the Empire. Every one of the thousand three hundred and sixty-five inhabited worlds, a trillion and a half intelligent beings, fourteen races—fifteen if you counted the Zarathustran Fuzzies, who were almost able to qualify under the talk-and-build-a-fire rule. And that had been the Empire when Rodrik VI had seen the map completed, and when Paul II had built the palace, and when Stevan IV, the grandfather of Paul I, had proclaimed Odin the imperial planet and Asgard the capital city. There had been some excuse for staying inside that patch of stars then; a newly won Empire must be consolidated within before it can safely be expanded. But that had been over eight centuries ago.

He looked at the daily schedule, beautifully embossed and neatly slipped under his desk glass. Luncheon on the South Upper Terrace, with the Prime Minister and the Bench of Imperial Counselors. Yes, it was time for that again; that happened as inevitably and regularly as Harv Dorflay's murder plots. And in the afternoon, a Plenary Session, Cabinet and Counselors. Was he going to have to endure the Bench of Counselors twice in the same day? Then the vexation was washed out of his face by a spreading grin. Bench of Counselors; that was the answer! Elevate Harv Dorflay to the Bench. That was what the Bench was for, a gold-plated dustbin for the disposal of superannuated dignitaries. He'd do no harm there, and a touch of outright lunacy might enliven and even improve the Bench.

And in the evening, a banquet, and a reception and

ball, in honor of His Majesty Ranulf XIV, Planetary King of Durendal, and First Citizen Zhorzh Yaggo, People's Manager-in-Chief of and for the Planetary Commonwealth of Aditya. Bargain day; two planetary chiefs of state in one big combination deal. He wondered what sort of prizes he had drawn this time, and closed his eyes, trying to remember. Durendal, of course, was one of the Sword-Worlds, settled by refugees from the losing side of the System States War in the time of the old Terran Federation, who had reappeared in Galactic history a few centuries later as the Space Vikings. They all had monarchial and rather picturesque governments; Durendal, he seemed to recall, was a sort of quasi-feudalism. About Aditya he was less sure. Something unpleasant, he thought; the titles of the government and its head were suggestive.

He lit another cigarette and snapped on the reading screen to see what they had piled onto him this morning, and then swore when a graph chart, with jiggling red and blue and green lines, appeared. Chart day, too. Everything happens at once.

It was the interstellar trade situation chart from Economics. Red line for production, green line for exports, blue for imports, sectioned vertically for the ten Viceroyalties and subsectioned for the Prefectures, and with the magnification and focus controls he could even get data for individual planets. He didn't bother with that, and wondered why he bothered with the charts at all. The stuff was all at least twenty days behind date, and not uniformly so, which accounted for much of the jiggling. It had been transmitted from Planetary Proconsulate to Prefecture, and from Prefecture to Viceroyalty, and from there to Odin, all by ship. A ship on hyperdrive could log lightyears an hour, but radio waves still had to travel 186,000 mps. The supplementary chart for the past five centuries told the real story—three perfectly level and perfectly parallel lines.

It was the same on all the other charts. Population fluctuating slightly at the moment, completely static for the past five centuries. A slight decrease in agriculture, matched by an increase in synthetic food production. A slight population movement toward the more urban planets and the more densely populated centers. A trend downward in employment—nonworking population increasing by about .0001 per cent annually. Not that they were building better robots; they were just building them faster than they wore out. They all told the same story—a stable economy, a static population, a peaceful and undisturbed Empire; eight centuries, five at least, of historyless tranquility. Well, that was what everybody wanted, wasn't it?

He flipped through the rest of the charts, and began getting summarized Ministry reports. Economics had denied a request from the Mining Cartel to authorize operations on a couple of uninhabited planets; danger of local market gluts and overstimulation of manufacturing. Permission granted to Robotics Cartel to— Request from planetary government of Durendal for increase of cereal export quotas under consideration—they wouldn't want to turn that down while King Ranulf was here. Impulsively, he punched out a combination on the communication screen and got Count Duklass, Minister of Economics.

Count Duklass had thinning red hair and a plump, agreeable, extrovert's face. He smiled and waited to be addressed.

"Sorry to bother Your Lordship," Paul greeted him. "What's the story on this export quota request from Durendal? We have their king here, now. Think he's come to lobby for it?"

Count Duklass chuckled. "He's not doing anything about it, himself. Have you met him yet, sir?"

"Not yet. He's to be presented this evening."

"Well, when you see him—I think the masculine pronoun is permissible—you'll see what I mean, sir. It's this Lord Koreff, the Marshal. He came here on business, and had to bring the king along, for fear somebody else would grab him while he was gone. The whole object of Durendalian politics, as I understand, is to get possession of the person of the king. Koreff was on my screen for half an hour; I just got rid of him. Planet's pretty heavily agricultural, they had a couple of very good crop years in a row, and now they have grain running out their ears, and they want to export it and cash in."

"Well?"

"Can't let them do it, Your Majesty. They're not suffering any hardship; they're just not making as much money as they think they ought to. If they start dumping their surplus into interstellar trade, they'll cause all kinds of dislocations on other agricultural planets. At least, that's what our computers all say."

And that, of course, was gospel. He nodded.

"Why don't they turn their surplus into whisky? Age it five or six years and it'd be on the luxury goods schedule and they could sell it anywhere."

Count Duklass' eyes widened. "I never thought of that, Your Majesty. Just a microsec; I want to make a note of that. Pass it down to somebody who could deal with it. That's a wonderful idea, Your Majesty!"

He finally got the conversation to an end, and went back to the reports. Security, as usual, had a few items above the dead level of bureaucratic procedure. The planetary king of Excalibur had been assassinated by his brother and two nephews, all three of whom were now fighting among themselves. As nobody had anything to fight with except small arms and a few light cannon, there would be no intervention. There had been intervention on Behemoth, however, where a whole continent had tried to secede from the planetary republic and the Imperial Navy had been requested to send a task force. That was all right, in both cases. No interference with anything that passed for a planetary government, but only one sovereignty on any planet with nuclear weapons, and only one supreme sovereignty in a galaxy with hyperdrive ships.

And there was rioting on Amaterasu, because of public indignation over a fraudulent election. He looked at that in incredulous delight. Why, here on Odin there hadn't been an election in the past six centuries that hadn't been utterly fraudulent. Nobody voted except the nonworkers, whose votes were bought and sold wholesale by gangster bosses to pressure groups, and no decent person would be caught within a hundred yards of a polling place on an election day. He called the Minister of Security.

Prince Travann was a man of his own age—they had been classmates at the University—but he looked older. His thin face was lined, and his hair was almost completely white. He was at his desk, with the Sun and Cogwheel of the Empire on the wall behind him, but on the breast of his black tunic he wore the badge of his family, a silver planet with three silver moons. Unlike Count Duklass, he didn't wait to be spoken to.

"Good morning, Your Majesty."

"Good morning, Your Highness; sorry to bother you. I just caught an interesting item in your report. This business on Amaterasu. What sort of a planet is it, politically? I don't seem to recall."

"Why, they have a republican government, sir; a very complicated setup. Really, it's a junk heap. When anything goes badly, they always build something new into the government, but they never abolish anything. They have a president, a premier, and an executive cabinet, and a tricameral legislature, and two complete and distinct judiciaries. The premier is always the presidential candidate getting the next highest number of votes. In the present instance, the president, who controls the planetary militia, is accusing the premier, who controls the police, of fraud in the election of the middle house of the legislature. Each is supported by the judiciary he controls. Practically every citizen belongs either to the militia or the police auxiliaries. I am looking forward to further reports from Amaterasu," he added dryly.

"I daresay they'll be interesting. Send them to me in full, and red-star them, if you please, Prince Travann."

He went back to the reports. The Ministry of Science and Technology had sent up a lengthy one. The only trouble with it was that everything reported was duplication of work that had been done centuries before. Well, no. A Dr. Dandrik, of the physics department of the Imperial University here in Asgard announced that a definite limit of accuracy in measuring the velocity of accelerated subnucleonic particles had been established—16.067543333 times light-speed. That seemed to be typical; the frontiers of science, now, were all decimal points. The Ministry of Education had a little to offer; historical scholarship was still active, at least. He was reading about a new trove of source-material that had come to light on Uller, from the Sixth Century Atomic Era, when the door screen buzzed and flashed.

He lit it, and his son Rodrik appeared in it, with Snooks, the little red hound, squirming excitedly in the Crown Prince's arms. The dog began barking at once, and the boy called through the phone:

"Good morning, father; are you busy?"

"Oh, not at all." He pressed the release button. "Come on in."

Immediately, the little hound leaped out of the princely arms and came dashing into the study and around the desk, jumping onto his lap. The boy followed more slowly, sitting down in the deskside chair and drawing his foot up under him. Paul greeted Snooks first—people can wait, but for little dogs everything has to be right now—and rummaged in a drawer until he found some wafers, holding one for Snooks to nibble. Then he became aware that his son was wearing leather shorts and tall buskins.

"Going out somewhere?" he asked, a trifle enviously.

"Up in the mountains, for a picnic. Olva's going along."

And his tutor, and his esquire, and Olva's companion-lady, and a dozen Thoran riflemen, of course, and they'd be in continuous screen-contact with the palace.

"That ought to be a lot of fun. Did you get all your lessons done?"

"Physics and math and galactiography," Rodrik told him. "And Professor Guilsan's going to give me and Olva our history after lunch."

They talked about lessons, and about the picnic. Of course, Snooks was going on the picnic, too. It was evident, though, that Rodrik had something else on his mind. After a while, he came out with it.

"Father, you know I've been a little afraid, lately," he said.

"Well, tell me about it, son. It isn't anything about you and Olva, is it?"

Rod was fourteen; the little Princess Olva thirteen. They would be marriageable in six years. As far as anybody could tell, they were both quite happy about the marriage which had been arranged for them years ago.

"Oh, no; nothing like that. But Olva's sister and a couple others of mother's ladies-in-waiting were to a psi-medium, and the medium told them that there were going to be changes. Great and frightening changes was what she said."

"She didn't specify?"

"No. Just that: great and frightening changes. But the

only change of that kind I can think of would be . . . well, something happening to you."

Snooks, having eaten three wafers, was trying to lick his ear. He pushed the little dog back into his lap and pummeled him gently with his left hand.

"You mustn't let mediums' gabble worry you, son. These psi-mediums have real powers, but they can't turn them off and on like a water tap. When they don't get anything, they don't like to admit it, and they invent things. Always generalities like that; never anything specific."

"I know all that." The boy seemed offended, as though somebody were explaining that his mother hadn't really found him out in the rose garden. "But they talked about it to some of their friends, and it seems that other mediums are saying the same thing. Father, do you remember when the Haval Valley reactor blew up? All over Odin, the mediums had been talking about a terrible accident, for a month before that happened."

"I remember that." Harv Dorflay believed that somebody had been falsely informed that the emperor would visit the plant that day. "These great and frightening changes will probably turn out to be a new fad in abstract sculpture. Any change frightens most people."

They talked more about mediums, and then about aircars and aircar racing, and about the Emperor's Cup race that was to be flown in a month. The communications screen began flashing and buzzing, and after he had silenced it with the busy-button for the third time, Rodrik said that it was time for him to go, came around to gather up Snooks, and went out, saying that he'd be home in time for the banquet. The screen began to flash again as he went out.

It was Prince Ganzay, the Prime Minister. He looked as though he had a persistent low-level toothache, but that was his ordinary expression.

"Sorry to bother Your Majesty. It's about these chiefs-of-state. Count Gadvan, the Chamberlain, appealed to me, and I feel I should ask your advice. It's the matter of precedence."

"Well, we have a fixed rule on that. Which one arrived first?"

"Why, the Adityan, but it seems King Ranulf insists that he's entitled to precedence, or, rather, his Lord Marshal does. This Lord Koreff insists that his king is not going to yield precedence to a commoner."

"Then he can go home to Durendal!" He felt himself growing angry—all the little angers of the morning were focusing on one spot. He forced the harshness out of his voice. "At a court function, somebody has to go first, and our rule is order of arrival at the palace. That rule was established to avoid violating the principle of equality to all civilized peoples and all planetary governments. We're not going to set it aside for the king of Durendal, or anybody else."

Prince Ganzay nodded. Some of the toothache expression had gone out of his face, now that he had been relieved of the decision.

"Of course, Your Majesty." He brightened a little. "Do you think we might compromise? Alternate the precedence, I mean?"

"Only if this First Citizen Yaggo consents. If he does, it would be a good idea."

"I'll talk to him, sir." The toothache expression came back. "Another thing, Your Majesty. They've both been invited to attend the Plenary Session, this afternoon."

"Well, no trouble there; they can enter by different doors and sit in visitors' boxes at opposite ends of the hall."

"Well, sir, I wasn't thinking of precedence. But this is to be an elective session—new ministers to replace Prince Havaly, of Defense, deceased, and Count Frask, of Science and Technology, elevated to the Bench. There seems to be some difference of opinion among some of the ministers and counselors. It's very possible that the session may degenerate into an outright controversy."

"Horrible," Paul said seriously. "I think, though, that our distinguished guests will see that the Empire can survive difference of opinion, and even outright controversy. But if you think it might have a bad effect, why not postpone the election?"

"Well—it's been postponed three times, already, sir."

"Postpone it permanently. Advertise for bids on two robot ministers, Defense, and Science and Technology. If they're a success, we can set up a project to design a robot emperor."

The Prime Minister's face actually twitched and blanched at the blasphemy. "Your Majesty is joking," he said, as though he wanted to be reassured on the point.

"Unfortunately, I am. If my job could be robotized, maybe I could take my wife and my son and our little dog and go fishing for a while."

But, of course, he couldn't. There were only two alternatives: the Empire or Galactic anarchy. The galaxy was too big to hold general elections, and there had to be a supreme ruler, and a positive and automatic—which meant hereditary—means of succession.

"Whose opinion seems to differ from whose, and about what?" he asked.

"Well, Count Duklass and Count Tammsan want to have the Ministry of Science and Technology abolished, and its functions and personnel distributed. Count Duklass means to take over the technological sections under Economics, and Count Tammsan will take over the science part under Education. The proposal is going to be introduced at this session by Count Guilfred, the Minister of Health and Sanity. He hopes to get some of the bio- and psycho-science sections for his own ministry."

"That's right. Duklass gets the hide, Tammsan gets the head and horns, and everybody who hunts with them gets a cut of the meat. That's good sound law of the chase. I'm not in favor of it, myself. Prince Ganzay, at this session I wish you'd get Captain-General Dorflay nominated for the Bench. I feel that it is about time to honor him with elevation."

"General Dorflay? But why, Your Majesty?"

"Great galaxy, do you have to ask? Why, because the man's a raving lunatic. He oughtn't even to be trusted with a sidearm, let alone five companies of armed soldiers. Do you know what he told me this morning?"

"That somebody is training a Nidhog swamp-crawler to crawl up the Octagon Tower and bite you at breakfast, I suppose. But hasn't that been going on for quite a while, sir?"

"It was a gimmick in one of the cooking robots, but that's aside from the question. He's finally named the mastermind behind all these nightmares of his, and who do you think it is? Yorn Travann!"

The Prime Minister's face grew graver than usual. Well, it was something to look grave about; some of these days—

"Your Majesty, I couldn't possibly agree more about the general's mental condition, but I really should say that, crazy or not, he is not alone in his suspicions of Prince Travann. If sharing them makes me a lunatic, too, so be it, but share them I do."

Paul felt his eyebrows lift in surprise. "That's quite too much and too little, Prince Ganzay," he said.

"With your permission, I'll elaborate. Don't think that I suspect Prince Travann of any childish pranks with elevators or viewscreens or cooking-robots," the Prime Minister hastened to disclaim, "but I definitely do suspect him of treasonous ambitions. I suppose Your Majesty knows that he is the first Minister of Security in centuries who has assumed personal control of both the planetary and municipal police, instead of delegating his *ex officio* powers.

"Your Majesty may not know, however, of some of the peculiar uses he has been making of those authorities. Does Your Majesty know that he has recruited the Security Guard up to at least ten times the strength needed to meet any conceivable peace-maintenance problem on this planet, and that he has been piling up huge quantities of heavy combat equipment—guns up to 200-millimeter, heavy contragravity, even gun-cutters and bomb-and-rocket boats? And does Your Majesty know that most of this armament is massed within fifteen minutes' flight-time of this palace? Or that Prince Travann has at his disposal from two and a half to three times, in men and firepower, the combined strength of the Planetary Militia and the Imperial Army on this planet?"

"I know. It has my approval. He's trying to salvage some of the young nonworkers through exposing them to military discipline. A good many of them, I believe, have gone offplanet on their discharge from the SG and hired as mercenaries, which is a far better profession than vote-selling."

"Quite a plausible explanation; Prince Travann is nothing if not plausible," the Prime Minister agreed. "And does Your Majesty know that, because of repeated demands for support from the Ministry of Security, the Imperial Navy has been scattered all over the Empire, and that there is not a naval craft bigger than a scoutboat within fifteen hundred light-years of Odin?"

That was absolutely true. Paul could only nod agreement. Prince Ganzay continued:

"He has been doing some peculiar things as Police Chief of Asgard, too. For instance; there are two powerful nonworkers' voting-bloc bosses, Big Moogie Blisko and Zikko the Nose—I assure Your Majesty that I am not inventing these names; that's what the persons are actually called—who have been enjoying the favor and support of Prince Travann. On a number of occasions, their smaller rivals, leaders of less important gangs, have been arrested, often on trumped-up charges, and held incommunicado until either Moogie or Zikko could move into their territories and annex their nonworker followers. These two bloc-bosses are subsidized, respectively, by the Steel and Shipbuilding Cartels and by the Reaction Products and Chemical Cartels, but actually, they are controlled by Prince Travann. They, in turn, control between them about seventy per cent of the nonworkers in Asgard."

"And you think this adds up to a plot against the throne?"

"A plot to seize the throne, Your Majesty."

"Oh, come, Prince Ganzay! You're talking like Dorflay!"

"Hear me out, Your Majesty. His Imperial Highness is fourteen years old; it will be eleven years before he will be legally able to assume the powers of emperor. In the dreadful event of your immediate death, it would mean a regency for that long. Of course, your ministers and counselors would be the ones to name the regent, but I know how they would vote with Security Guard bayonets at their throats. And regency might not be the limit of Prince Travann's ambitions."

"In your own words, quite plausible, Prince Ganzay. It rests, however, on a very questionable foundation. The assumption that Prince Travann is stupid enough to want the throne."

He had to terminate the conversation himself and

blank the screen. Viktor Ganzay was still staring at him in shocked incredulity when his image vanished. Viktor Ganzay could not imagine anybody not wanting the throne, not even the man who had to sit on it.

He sat, for a while, looking at the darkened screen, a little worried. Viktor Ganzay had a much better intelligence service than he had believed. He wondered how much Ganzay had found out that he hadn't mentioned. Then he went back to the reports. He had gotten down to the Ministry of Fine Arts when the communications screen began calling attention to itself again.

When he flipped the switch, a woman smiled out of it at him. Her blond hair was rumpled, and she wore a dressing gown; her smile brightened as his face appeared in her screen.

"Hi!" she greeted him.

"Hi, yourself. You just get up?"

She raised a hand to cover a yawn. "I'll bet you've been up reigning for hours. Were Rod and Snooks in to see you yet?"

He nodded. "They just left. Rod's going on a picnic with Olva in the mountains." How long had it been since he and Marris had been on a picnic—a real picnic, with less than fifty guards and as many courtiers along? "Do you have much reigning to do, this afternoon?"

She grimaced. "Flower Festivals. I have to make personal tri-di appearances, live, with messages for the loving subjects. Three minutes on, and a two-minute break between. I have forty for this afternoon."

"Ugh! Well, have a good time, sweetheart. All I have is lunch with the Bench, and then this Plenary session." He told her about Ganzay's fear of outright controversy.

"Oh, fun! Maybe somebody'll pull somebody's whiskers, or something. I'm in on that, too."

The call-indicator in front of him began glowing with the code-symbol of the Minister of Security.

"We can always hope, can't we? Well, Yorn Travann's trying to get me, now."

"Don't keep him waiting. Maybe I can see you before the Session." She made a kissing motion with her lips at him, and blanked the screen.

He flipped the switch again, and Prince Travann was

on the screen. The Security Minister didn't waste time being sorry to bother him.

"Your Majesty, a report's just come in that there's a serious riot at the University; between five and ten thousand students are attacking the administration center, lobbing stench bombs into it, and threatening to hang Chancellor Khane. They have already overwhelmed and disarmed the campus police, and I've sent two companies of the Gendarme riot brigade, under an officer I can trust to handle things firmly but intelligently. We don't want any indiscriminate stunning or tear-gassing or shooting; all sorts of people can have sons and daughters mixed up in a student riot."

"Yes. I seem to recall student riots in which the sons of his late Highness Prince Travann and his late Majesty Rodrik XXI were involved." He deliberated the point for a moment, and added: "This scarcely sounds like a frat-fight or a panty-raid, though. What seems to have triggered it?"

"The story I got—a rather hysterical call for help from Khane himself—is that they're protesting an action of his in dismissing a faculty member. I have a couple of undercovers at the University, and I'm trying to contact them. I sent more undercovers, who could pass for students, ahead of the Gendarmes to get the student side of it and the names of the ringleaders." He glanced down at the indicator in front of him, which had begun to glow. "If you'll pardon me, sir, Count Tammsan's trying to get me. He may have particulars. I'll call Your Majesty back when I learn anything more."

There hadn't been anything like that at the University within the memory of the oldest old grad. Chancellor Khane, he knew, was a stupid and arrogant old windbag with a swollen sense of his own importance. He made a small bet with himself that the whole thing was Khane's fault, but he wondered what lay behind it, and what would come out of it. Great plagues from little microbes start. Great and frightening changes—

The screen got itself into an uproar, and he flipped the switch. It was Viktor Ganzay again. He looked as though his permanent toothache had deserted him for the moment.

"Sorry to bother Your Majesty, but it's all fixed up,"

he reported. "First Citizen Yaggo agreed to alternate in precedence with King Ranulf, and Lord Koreff has withdrawn all his objections. As far as I can see, at present, there should be no trouble."

"Fine. I suppose you heard about the excitement at the University?"

"Oh, yes, Your Majesty. Disgraceful affair!"

"Simply shocking. What seems to have started it, have you heard?" he asked. "All I know is that the students were protesting the dismissal of a faculty member. He must have been exceptionally popular, or else he got a more than ordinary raw deal from Khane."

"Well, as to that, sir, I can't say. All I learned was that it was the result of some faculty squabble in one of the science departments; the grounds for the dismissal were insubordination and contempt for authority."

"I always thought that when authority began inspiring contempt, it had stopped being authority. Did you say science? This isn't going to help Duklass and Tammsan any."

"I'm afraid not, Your Majesty." Ganzay didn't look particularly regretful. "The News Cartel's gotten hold of it and are using it; it'll be all over the Empire."

He said that as though it meant something. Well, maybe it did; a lot of ministers and almost all the counselors spent most of their time worrying about what people on planets like Chermosh and Zarathustra and Deirdre and Quetzalcoatl might think, in ignorance of the fact that interest in Empire politics varied inversely as the square of the distance to Odin and the level of corruption and inefficiency of the local government.

"I notice you'll be at the Bench luncheon. Do you think you could invite our guests, too? We could have an informal presentation before it starts. Can do? Good. I'll be seeing you there."

When the screen was blanked, he returned to the reports, ran them off hastily to make sure that nothing had been red-starred, and called a robot to clear the projector. After a while, Prince Travann called again.

"Sorry to bother Your Majesty, but I have most of the facts on the riot, now. What happened was that Chancellor Khane sacked a professor, physics department, under circumstances which aroused resentment among the science students. Some of them walked out of class and went to the stadium to hold a protest meeting, and the thing snowballed until half the students were in it. Khane lost his head and ordered the campus police to clear the stadium; the students rushed them and swamped them. I hope, for their sakes, that none of my men ever let anything like that happen. The man I sent, a Colonel Handrosan, managed to talk the students into going back to the stadium and continuing the meeting under Gendarme protection."

"Sounds like a good man."

"Very good, Your Majesty. Especially in handling disturbances. I have complete confidence in him. He's also investigating the background of the affair. I'll give Your Majesty what he's learned, to date. It seems that the head of the physics department, a Professor Nelse Dandrik, had been conducting an experiment, assisted by a Professor Klenn Faress, to establish more accurately the velocity of subnucleonic particles, beta micropositos, I believe. Dandrik's story, as relayed to Handrosan by Khane, is that he reached a limit and the apparatus began giving erratic results."

Prince Travann stopped to light a cigarette. "At this point, Professor Dandrik ordered the experiment stopped, and Professor Faress insisted on continuing. When Dandrik ordered the apparatus dismantled, Faress became rather emotional about it—obscenely abusive and threatening, according to Dandrik. Dandrik complained to Khane, Khane ordered Faress to apologize, Faress refused, and Khane dismissed Faress. Immediately, the students went on strike. Faress confirmed the whole story, and he added one small detail that Dandrik hadn't seen fit to mention. According to him, when these micropositos were accelerated beyond sixteen and a fraction times light-speed, they began registering at the target before the source registered the emission."

"Yes, I—*What did you say?*"

Prince Travann repeated it slowly, distinctly and tonelessly.

"That was what I thought you said. Well, I'm going to insist on a complete investigation, including a repetition of the experiment. Under direction of Professor Faress."

"Yes, Your Majesty. And when that happens, I mean

to be on hand personally. If somebody is just before discovering time-travel, I think Security has a very substantial interest in it."

The Prime Minister called back to confirm that First Citizen Yaggo and King Ranulf would be at the luncheon. The Chamberlain, Count Gadvan, called with a long and dreary problem about the protocol for the banquet. Finally, at noon, he flashed a signal for General Dorflay, waited five minutes, and then left his desk and went out, to find the mad general and his wirehaired soldiers drawn up in the hall.

There were more Thorans on the South Upper Terrace, and after a flurry of porting and presenting and ordering arms and hand-saluting, the Prime Minister advanced and escorted him to where the Bench of Counselors, all thirty of them, total age close to twenty-eight hundred years, were drawn up in a rough crescent behind the three distinguished guests. The King of Durendal wore a cloth-of-silver leotard and pink tights, and a belt of gold links on which he carried a jeweled dagger only slightly thicker than a knitting needle. He was slender and willowy, and he had large and soulful eyes, and the royal beautician must have worked on him for a couple of hours. Wait till Marris sees this; oh, brother!

Koreff, the Lord Marshal, wore what was probably the standard costume of Durendal, a fairly long jerkin with short sleeves, and knee-boots, and his dress dagger looked as though it had been designed for use. Lord Koreff looked as though he would be quite willing and able to use it; he was fleshy and full-faced, with hard muscles under the flesh.

First Citizen Yaggo, People's Manager-in-Chief of and for the Planetary Commonwealth of Aditya, wore a one-piece white garment like a mechanic's coveralls, with the emblem of his government and the numeral "1" on his breast. He carried no dagger; if he had worn a dress weapon, it would probably have been a slide rule. His head was completely shaven, and he had small, pale eyes and a rat-trap mouth. He was regarding the Durendalians with a distaste that was all too evidently reciprocated.

King Ranulf appeared to have won the toss for first presentation. He squeezed the Imperial hand in both of his and looked up adoringly as he professed his deep honor and pleasure. Yaggo merely clasped both his hands in front of the emblem on his chest and raised them quickly to the level of his chin, saying: "At the service of the Imperial State," and adding, as though it hurt him, "Your Imperial Majesty." Not being a chief of state, Lord Koreff came third; he merely shook hands and said, "A great honor, Your Imperial Majesty, and the thanks both of myself and my royal master, for a most gracious reception." The attempt to grab first place having failed, he was more than willing to forget the whole subject. There was a chance that finding a way to dispose of the grain surplus might make the difference between his staying in power at home or not.

Fortunately, the three guests had already met the Bench of Counselors. Immediately after the presentation of Lord Koreff, they all started the two hundred yards' march to the luncheon pavilion, the King of Durendal clinging to his left arm and First Citizen Yaggo stumping dourly on his right, with Prince Ganzay beyond him and Lord Koreff on Ranulf's left.

"Do you plan to stay long on Odin?" he asked the king.

"Oh, I'd *love* to stay for simply *months!* Everything is so *wonderful* here in Asgard; it makes our little capital of Roncevaux seem so *utterly* provincial. I'm going to tell Your Imperial Majesty a secret. I'm going to see if I can lure some of your *wonderful* ballet dancers back to Durendal with me. Aren't I *naughty,* raiding Your Imperial Majesty's theaters?"

"In keeping with the traditions of your people," he replied gravely. "You Sword-Worlders used to raid everywhere you went."

"I'm afraid those bad old days are long past, Your Imperial Majesty," Lord Koreff said. "But we Sword-Worlders got around the galaxy, for a while. In fact, I seem to remember reading that some of our brethren from Morglay or Flamberge even occupied Aditya for a couple of centuries. Not that you'd guess it to look at Aditya now."

It was First Citizen Yaggo's turn to take precedence—the seat on the right of the throne chair. Lord Koreff sat on Ranulf's left, and, to balance him, Prince Ganzay sat beyond Yaggo and dutifully began inquiring of the People's Manager-in-Chief about the structure of his government, launching him on a monologue that promised to last at least half the luncheon. That left the king of Durendal to Paul; for a start, he dropped a compliment on the cloth-of-silver leotard.

King Ranulf laughed dulcetly, brushed the garment with his fingertips, and said that it was just a simple thing patterned after the Durendalian peasant costume.

"You have peasants on Durendal?"

"Oh, *dear,* yes! Such quaint, *charming* people. Of course, they're all poor, and they wear such *funny* ragged clothes, and travel about in rackety old aircars, it's a wonder they don't fall apart in the air. But they're so *wonderfully* happy and carefree. I often wish I were one of them, instead of king."

"Nonworking class, Your Imperial Majesty," Lord Koreff explained.

"On Aditya," First Citizen Yaggo declared, "There are no classes, and on Aditya everybody works. 'From each according to his ability; to each according to his need.' "

"On Aditya," an elderly counselor four places to the right of him said loudly to his neighbor, "they don't call them classes, they call them sociological categories, and they have nineteen of them. And on Aditya, they don't call them nonworkers, they call them occupational reservists, and they have more of them than we do."

"But of course, I was born a king," Ranulf said sadly and nobly. "I have a duty to my people."

"No, they don't vote at all," Lord Koreff was telling the counselor on his left. "On Durendal, you have to pay taxes before you can vote."

"On Aditya the crime of taxation does not exist," the First Citizen told the Prime Minister.

"On Aditya," the counselor four places down said to his neighbor, "there's nothing to tax. The state owns all the property, and if the Imperial Constitution and the Space Navy let them, the State would own all the people, too. Don't tell me about Aditya. First big-ship command I had was the old *Invictus,* 374, and she was based on Aditya for four years, and I'd sooner have spent that time in orbit around Niffelheim."

Now Paul remembered who he was; old Admiral—now Prince-Counselor—Geklar. He and Prince-Counselor Dorflay would get along famously. The Lord Marshal of Durendal was replying to some objection somebody had made:

"No, nothing of the sort. We hold the view that every civil or political right implies a civil or political obligation. The citizen has a right to protection from the Realm, for instance; he therefore has the obligation to defend the Realm. And his right to participate in the government of the Realm includes his obligation to support the Realm financially. Well, we tax only property; if a nonworker acquires taxable property, he has to go to work to earn the taxes. I might add that our nonworkers are very careful to avoid acquiring taxable property."

"But if they don't have votes to sell, what do they live on?" a counselor asked in bewilderment.

"The nobility supports them; the landowners, the trading barons, the industrial lords. The more nonworking adherents they have, the greater their prestige." And the more rifles they could muster when they quarreled with their fellow nobles, of course. "Beside, if we didn't do that, they'd turn brigand, and it costs less to support them than to have to hunt them out of the brush and hang them."

"On Aditya, brigandage does not exist."

"On Aditya, all the brigands belong to the secret police, only on Aditya they don't call them secret police, they call them Servants of the People, Ninth Category."

A shadow passed quickly over the pavilion, and then another. He glanced up quickly, to see two long black troop carriers, emblazoned with the Sun and Cogwheel and armored fist of Security, pass back of the Octagon Tower and let down on the north landing stage. A third followed. He rose quickly.

"Please remain seated, gentlemen, and continue with the luncheon. If you will excuse me for a moment, I'll be back directly." I hope, he added mentally.

Captain-General Dorflay, surrounded by a dozen officers, Thoran and human, had arrived on the lower terrace at the base of the Octagon Tower. They had a full Thoran rifle company with them. As he went down to them, Dorflay hurried forward.

"It has come, Your Majesty!" he said, as soon as he

could make himself heard without raising his voice. "We are all ready to die with Your Majesty!"

"Oh, I doubt it'll come quite to that, Harv," he said. "but just to be on the safe side, take that company and the gentlemen who are with you and get up to the mountains and join the Crown Prince and his party. Here." He took a notepad from his belt pouch and wrote rapidly, sealing the note and giving it to Dorflay. "Give this to His Highness, and place yourself under his orders. I know; he's just a boy, but he has a good head. Obey him exactly in everything, but under no circumstances return to the palace or allow him to return until I call you."

"Your Majesty is ordering me away?" The old soldier was aghast.

"An emperor who has a son can be spared. An emperor's son who is too young to marry can't. You know that."

Harv Dorflay was only mad on one subject, and even within the frame of his madness he was intensely logical. He nodded. "Yes, Your Imperial Majesty. We both serve the Empire as best we can. And I will guard the little Princess Olva, too." He grasped Paul's hand, said, "Farewell, Your Majesty!" and dashed away, gathering his staff and the company of Thorans as he went. In an instant, they had vanished down the nearest rampway.

The emperor watched their departure, and, at the same time, saw a big black aircar, bearing the three-mooned planet, argent on sable, of Travann, let down onto the south landing stage, and another troop carrier let down after it. Four men left the aircar—Yorn, Prince Travann, and three officers in the black of the Security Guard. Prince Ganzay had also left the table; he came from one direction as Prince Travann advanced from the other. They converged on the emperor.

"What's happening here, Prince Travann?" Prince Ganzay demanded. "Why are you bringing all these troops to the palace?"

"Your Majesty," Prince Travann said smoothly, "I trust that you will pardon this disturbance. I'm sure nothing serious will happen, but I didn't dare take chances. The students from the University are marching on the palace—perfectly peaceful and loyal procession; they're bringing a petition for Your Majesty—but on the way, while passing through a nonworkers' district, they were attacked by a gang of hooligans connected with a voting-bloc boss called Nutchy the Knife. None of the students were hurt, and Colonel Handrosan got the procession out of the district promptly, and then dropped some of his men, who have since been reinforced, to deal with the hooligans. That's still going on, and these riots are like forest fires; you never know when they'll shift and get out of control. I hope the men I brought won't be needed here. Really, they're a reserve for the riot work; I won't commit them, though, until I'm sure the palace is safe."

He nodded. "Prince Travann, how soon do you estimate that the student procession will arrive here?" he asked.

"They're coming on foot, Your Majesty. I'd give them an hour, at least."

"Well, Prince Travann, will you have one of your officers see that the public-address screen in front is ready; I'll want to talk to them when they arrive. And meanwhile, I'll want to talk to Chancellor Khane, Professor Dandrik, Professor Faress and Colonel Handrosan, together. And Count Tammsan, too; Prince Ganzay, will you please screen him and invite him here immediately?"

"Now, Your Majesty?" At first, the Prime Minister was trying to suppress a look of incredulity; then he was trying to keep from showing comprehension. "Yes, Your Majesty; at once." He frowned slightly when he saw two of the Security Guard officers salute Prince Travann instead of the emperor before going away. Then he turned and hurried toward the Octagon Tower.

The officer who had gone to the aircar to use the radio returned and reported that Colonel Handrosan was bringing the chancellor and both professors from the University in his command-car, having anticipated that they would be wanted. Paul nodded in pleasure.

"You have a good man there, Prince," he said. "Keep an eye on him."

"I know it, Your Majesty. To tell the truth, it was he who organized this march. Thought they'd be better employed coming here to petition you than milling around the University getting into further mischief."

The other officer also returned, bringing a portable viewscreen with him on a contragravity-lifter. By this time, the Bench of Counselors and the three off-planet guests had become anxious and left the luncheon pavilion in a body. The counselors were looking about uneasily, noticing the black uniformed Security Guards who had left the troop carrier and were taking position by squads all around the emperor. First Citizen Yaggo, and King Ranulf and Lord Koreff, also seemed uneasy. They were avoiding the proximity of Paul as though he had the green death.

The viewscreen came on, and in it the city, as seen from an aircar at two thousand feet, spread out with the palace visible in the distance, the golden pile of the Octagon Tower jutting up from it. The car carrying the pickup was behind the procession, which was moving toward the palace along one of the broad skyways, with Gendarmes and Security Guards leading, following and flanking. There were a few Imperial and planetary and school flags, but none of the quantity-made banners and placards which always betray a planned demonstration.

Prince Ganzay had been gone for some time, now. When he returned, he drew Paul aside.

"Your Majesty," he whispered softly, "I tried to summon Army troops, but it'll be hours before any can get here. And the Militia can't be mobilized in anything less than a day. There are only five thousand Army Regulars on Odin, now, anyhow."

And half of them officers and noncoms of skeleton regiments. Like the Navy, the Army had been scattered all over the Empire—on Behemoth and Amida and Xipetotec and Astarte and Jotunnheim—in response to calls for support from Security.

"Let's have a look at this rioting, Prince Travann," one of the less decrepit counselors, a retired general, said. "I want to see how your people are handling it."

The officers who had come with Prince Travann consulted briefly, and then got another pickup on the screen. This must have been a regular public pickup, on the front of a tall building. It was a couple of miles farther away; the palace was visible only as a tiny glint from the Octagon Tower, on the skyline. Half a dozen Security aircars were darting about, two of them chasing a battered civilian vehicle and firing at it. On rooftops and terraces and skyways, little clumps of Security Guards were skirmishing, dodging from cover to cover, and sometimes individuals or groups in civilian clothes fired back at them. There was a surprising absence of casualties.

"Your Majesty!" the old general hissed in a scandalized whisper. "That's nothing but a big fake! Look, they're all firing blanks! The rifles hardly kick at all, and there's too much smoke for propellant-powder."

"I noticed that." This riot must have been carefully prepared, long in advance. Yet the student riot seemed to have been entirely spontaneous. That puzzled him; he wished he knew just what Yorn Travann was up to. "Just keep quiet about it," he advised.

More aircars were arriving, big and luxurious, emblazoned with the arms of some of the most distinguished families in Asgard. One of the first to let down bore the device of Duklass, and from it the Minister of Economics, the Minister of Education, and a couple of other ministers, alighted. Count Duklass went at once to Prince Travann, drawing him away from King Ranulf and Lord Koreff and talking to him rapidly and earnestly. Count Tammsan approached at a swift half-run.

"Save Your Majesty!" he greeted, breathlessly. "What's going on, sir? We heard something about some petty brawl at the University, that Prince Ganzay had become alarmed about, but now there seems to be fighting all over the city. I never saw anything like it; on the way here we had to go up to ten thousand feet to get over a battle, and there's a vast crowd on the Avenue of the Arts, and—" He took in the Security Guards. "Your Majesty, just what *is* going on?"

"Great and frightening changes." Count Tammsan started; he must have been to a psi-medium, too. "But I think the Empire is going to survive them. There may even be a few improvements, before things are done."

A blue-uniformed Gendarme officer approached Prince Travann, drawing him away from Count Duklass and speaking briefly to him. The Minister of Security nodded, then turned back to the Minister of Economics. They talked for a few moments longer, then clasped hands, and Travann left Duklass with his face wreathed in smiles. The Gendarme officer accompanied him as he approached.

"Your Majesty, this is Colonel Handrosan, the officer who handled the affair at the University."

"And a very good piece of work, colonel." He shook hands with him. "Don't be surprised if it's remembered next Honors Day. Did you bring Khane and the two professors?"

"They're down on that lower landing-stage, Your Majesty. We're delaying the students, to give your Majesty time to talk to them."

"We'll see them now. My study will do." The officer saluted and went away. He turned to Count Tammsan. "That's why I asked Prince Ganzay to invite you here. This thing's become too public to be ignored; some sort of action will have to be taken. I'm going to talk to the students; I want to find out just what happened before I commit myself to anything. Well, gentlemen, let's go to my study."

Count Tammsan looked around, bewildered. "But I don't understand—" He fell into step with Paul and the Minister of Security; a squad of Security Guards fell in behind them. "I don't understand what's happening," he complained.

An emperor about to have his throne yanked out from under him, and a minister about to stage a *coup d'état,* taking time out to settle a trifling academic squabble. One thing he did understand, though, was that the Ministry of Education was getting some very bad publicity at a time when it could be least afforded. Prince Travann was telling him about the hooligans' attack on the marching students, and that worried him even more. Nonworking hooligans acted as voting-bloc bosses ordered; voting-bloc bosses acted on orders from the political manipulators of cartels and pressure-groups, and action downward through the nonworkers was usually accompanied by action upward through influences to which ministers were sensitive.

There were a dozen Security Guards in black tunics, and as many household Thorans in red kilts, in the hall outside the study, fraternizing amicably. They hurried apart and formed two ranks, and the Thoran officer with them saluted.

Going into the study, he went to his desk; Count Tammsan lit a cigarette and puffed nervously, and sat down as though he were afraid the chair would collapse under him. Prince Travann sank into another chair and relaxed, closing his eyes. There was a bit of wafer on the floor by Paul's chair, dropped by the little dog that morning. He stooped and picked it up, laying it on his desk, and sat looking at it until the door screen flashed and buzzed. Then he pressed the release button.

Colonel Handrosan ushered the three University men in ahead of him—Khane, with a florid, arrogant face that showed worry under the arrogance; Dandrik, gray-haired and stoop-shouldered, looking irritated; Faress, young, with a scrubby red mustache, looking bellicose. He greeted them collectively and invited them to sit, and there was a brief uncomfortable silence which everybody expected him to break.

"Well, gentlemen," he said, "we want to get the facts about this affair in some kind of order. I wish you'd tell me, as briefly and as completely as possible, what you know about it."

"There's the man who started it!" Khane declared, pointing at Faress.

"Professor Faress had nothing to do with it," Colonel Handrosan stated flatly. "He and his wife were in their apartment, packing to move out, when it started. Somebody called him and told him about the fighting at the stadium, and he went there at once to talk his students into dispersing. By that time, the situation was completely out of hand; he could do nothing with the students."

"Well, I think we ought to find out, first of all, why Professor Faress was dismissed," Prince Travann said. "It will take a good deal to convince me that any teacher able to inspire such loyalty in his students is a bad teacher, or deserves dismissal."

"As I understand," Paul said, "the dismissal was the result of a disagreement between Professor Faress and Professor Dandrik about an experiment on which they were working. I believe, an experiment to fix more exactly the velocity of accelerated subnucleonic particles. Beta micropositos, wasn't it, Chancellor Khane?"

Khane looked at him in surprise. "Your Majesty, I know nothing about that. Professor Dandrik is head of the physics department; he came to me, about six months ago, and told me that in his opinion this experiment was desirable. I simply deferred to his judgment and authorized it."

"Your Majesty has just stated the purpose of the experiment," Dandrik said. "For centuries, there have been inaccuracies in mathematical descriptions of subnucleonic events, and this experiment was undertaken in the hope of eliminating these inaccuracies." He went into a lengthy mathematical explanation.

"Yes, I understand that, professor. But just what was the actual experiment, in terms of physical operations?"

Dandrik looked helpless for a moment. Faress, who had been choking back a laugh, interrupted:

"Your Majesty, we were using the big turbo-linear accelerator to project fast micropositos down an evacuated tube one kilometer in length, and clocking them with light, the velocity of which has been established almost absolutely. I will say that with respect to the light, there were no observable inaccuracies at any time, and until the micropositos were accelerated to 16.0675433331⁄3 times light-speed, they registered much as expected. Beyond that velocity, however, the target for the micropositos began registering impacts before the source registered emission, although the light target was still registering normally. I noticed Professor Dandrik about this, and——"

"You notified him. Wasn't he present at the time?"

"No, Your Majesty."

"Your Majesty, I am head of the physics department of the University. I have too much administrative work to waste time on the technical aspects of experiments like this," Dandrik interjected.

"I understand. Professor Faress was actually performing the experiment. You told Professor Dandrik what had happened. What then?"

"Why, Your Majesty, he simply declared that the limit of accuracy had been reached, and ordered the experiment dropped. He then reported the highest reading before this anticipation effect was observed as the newly established limit of accuracy in measuring the velocity of accelerated micropositos, and said nothing whatever in his report about the anticipation effect."

"I read a summary of the report. Why, Professor Dandrik, did you omit mentioning this slightly unusual effect?"

"Why, because the whole thing was utterly preposterous, that's why!" Dandrik barked, and then hastily added, "Your Imperial Majesty." He turned and glared at Faress; professors do not glare at galactic emperors. "Your Majesty, the limit of accuracy had been reached. After that, it was only to be expected that the apparatus would give erratic reports."

"It might have been expected that the apparatus would stop registering increased velocity relative to the light-speed standard, or that it would begin registering disproportionately," Faress said. "But, Your Majesty, I'll submit that it was not to be expected that it would register impacts before emissions. And I'll add this. After registering this slight apparent jump into the future, there was no proportionate increase in anticipation with further increase of acceleration. I wanted to find out why. But when Professor Dandrik saw what was happening, he became almost hysterical, and ordered the accelerator shut down as though he were afraid it would blow up in his face."

"I think it has blown up in his face," Prince Travann said quietly. "Professor, have you any theory, or supposition, or even any wild guess, as to how this anticipation effect occurs?"

"Yes, Your Highness. I suspect that the apparent anticipation is simply an observational illusion, similar to the illusion of time-reversal experienced when it was first observed, though not realized, that positrons sometimes exceeded light-speed."

"Why, that's what I've been saying, all along!" Dandrik broke in. "The whole thing is an illusion, due——"

"To having reached the limit of observational accuracy; I understand, Professor Dandrik. Go on, Professor Faress."

"I think that beyond 16.0675433331⁄3 times light-speed, the micropositos ceased to have any velocity at all, velocity being defined as rate of motion in four-dimensional space-time. I believe they moved through the three spatial dimensions without moving at all in the fourth, temporal, dimension. They made that kilometer from source to target, literally, in nothing flat. Instantaneity."

That must have been the first time he had actually

come out and said it. Dandrik jumped to his feet with a cry that was just short of being a shriek.

"He's crazy! Your Majesty, you mustn't . . . that is, well, I mean—Please, Your Majesty, don't listen to him. He doesn't know what he's saying. He's raving!"

"He knows perfectly well what he's saying, and it probably scares him more than it does you. The difference is that he's willing to face it and you aren't."

The difference was that Faress was a scientist and Dandrik was a science teacher. To Faress, a new door had opened, the first new door in eight hundred years. To Dandrik, it threatened invalidation of everything he had taught since the morning he had opened his first class. He could no longer say to his pupils, "You are here to learn from me." He would have to say, more humbly, "*We* are here to learn from the Universe."

It had happened so many times before, too. The comfortable and established Universe had fitted all the known facts—and then new facts had been learned that wouldn't fit it. The third planet of the Sol system had once been the center of the Universe, and then Terra, and Sol, and even the galaxy, had been forced to abdicate centricity. The atom had been indivisible—until somebody divided it. There had been intangible substance that had permeated the Universe, because it had been necessary for the transmission of light—until it was demonstrated to be unnecessary and nonexistent. And the speed of light had been the ultimate velocity, once, and could be exceeded no more than the atom could be divided. And light speed had been constant, regardless of distance from source, and the Universe, to explain certain observed phenomena, had been believed to be expanding simultaneously in all directions. And the things that had happened in psychology, when psi-phenomena had become too obvious to be shrugged away.

"And then, when Dr. Dandrik ordered you to drop this experiment, just when it was becoming interesting, you refused?"

"Your Majesty, I couldn't stop, not then. But Dr. Dandrik ordered the apparatus dismantled and scrapped, and I'm afraid I lost my head. Told him I'd punch his silly old face in, for one thing."

"You admit that?" Chancellor Khane cried.

"I think you showed admirable self-restraint in not doing it. Did you explain to Chancellor Khane the importance of this experiment?"

"I tried to, Your Majesty, but he simply wouldn't listen."

"But, Your Majesty!" Khane expostulated. "Professor Dandrik is head of the department, and one of the foremost physicists of the Empire, and this young man is only one of the junior assistant-professors. Isn't even a full professor, and he got his degree from some school away off planet. University of Brannerton, on Gimli."

"Were you a pupil of Professor Vann Evaratt?" Prince Travann asked sharply.

"Why, yes, sir. I—"

"Ha, no wonder!" Dandrik crowed. "Your Majesty, that man's an out-and-out charlatan! He was kicked out of the University here ten years ago, and I'm surprised he could even get on the faculty of a school like Brannerton, on a planet like Gimli."

"Why, you stupid old fool!" Faress yelled at him. "You aren't enough of a physicist to oil robots in Vann Evaratt's lab!"

"There, Your Majesty," Khane said. "You see how much respect for authority this hooligan has!"

On Aditya, such would be unthinkable; on Aditya, everybody respects authority. Whether it's respectable or not.

Count Tammsan laughed, and he realized that he must have spoken aloud. Nobody else seemed to have gotten the joke.

"Well, how about the riot, now?" he asked. "Who started that?"

"Colonel Handrosan made an investigation on the spot," Prince Travann said. "May I suggest that we hear his report?"

"Yes indeed. Colonel?"

Handrosan rose and stood with his hands behind his back, looking fixedly at the wall behind the desk.

"Your Majesty, the students of Professor Faress' advanced subnucleonic physics class, postgraduate students, all of them, were told of Professor Faress' dismissal by a faculty member who had taken over the class this morning. They all got up and walked out in a body, and gather outdoors on the campus to discuss the matter. At the next class break, they were joined by other science students, and they went into the stadium, where they were joined, half an hour later, by more students who had learned of the dismissal in the meantime. At no time was the gathering disorderly. The stadium is covered by a viewscreen pickup, which is fitted with a recording device; there is a complete audiovisual of the whole thing, including the attack on them by the campus police.

"This attack was ordered by Chancellor Khane, at about 1100; the chief of the campus police was told to clear the stadium, and when he asked if he was to use force, Chancellor Khane told him to use anything he wanted to."

"I did not! I told him to get the students out of the stadium, but—"

"The chief of campus police carries a personal wire recorder," Handrosan said, in his flat monotone. "He has a recording of the order, in Chancellor Khane's own voice. I heard it myself. The police," he continued, "first tried to use gas, but the wind was against them. They then tried to use sono-stunners, but the students rushed them and overwhelmed them. If Your Majesty will permit a personal opinion, while I do not sympathize with their subsequent attack on the administration center, they were entirely within their rights in defending themselves in the stadium, and it's hard enough to stop trained and disciplined troops when they are winning. After defeating the police, they simply went on by what might be called the momentum of victory."

"Then you'd say that it's positively established that the students were behaving in a peaceable and orderly manner in the stadium when they were attacked, and that Chancellor Khane ordered the attack personally?"

"I would, emphatically, Your Majesty."

"I think we've done enough here, gentlemen." He turned to Count Tammsan. "This is, jointly, the affair of Education and Security. I would suggest that you and Prince Travann join in a formal and public inquiry, and until all the facts have been established and recorded and action decided upon, the dismissal of Professor Faress be reversed and he be restored to his position on the faculty."

"Yes, Your Majesty," Tammsan agreed. "And I think it would be a good idea for Chancellor Khane to take a vacation till then, too."

"I would further suggest that, as this microposito experiment is crucial to the whole question, it should be repeated. Under the personal direction of Professor Faress."

"I agree with that, Your Majesty," Prince Travann said. "If it's as important as I think it is, Professor Dandrik is greatly to be censured for ordering it stopped and for failing to report this anticipation effect."

"We'll consult about the inquiry, including the experiment, tomorrow, Your Highness," Tammsan told Travann.

Paul rose, and everybody rose with him. "That being the case, you gentlemen are all excused. The students' procession ought to be arriving, now, and I want to tell them what's going to be done. Prince Travann, Count Tammsan; do you care to accompany me?"

Going up to the central terrace in front of the Octagon Tower, he turned to Count Tammsan.

"I notice you laughed at that remark of mine about Aditya," he said. "Have you met the First Citizen?"

"Only on screen, sir. He was at me for about an hour, this morning. It seems that they are reforming the educational system on Aditya. On Aditya, everything gets reformed every ten years, whether it needs it or not. He came here to find somebody to take charge of the reformation."

He stopped short, bringing the others to a halt beside him, and laughed heartily.

"Well, we'll send First Citizen Yaggo away happy; we'll make him a present of the most distinguished educator on Odin."

"Khane?" Tammsan asked.

"Khane. Isn't it wonderful; if you have a few problems, you have trouble, but if you have a whole lot of problems, they start solving each other. We get a chance to get rid of Khane, and create a vacancy that can be filled by somebody big enough to fill it; the Ministry of Education gets out from under a nasty situation; First Citizen Yaggo gets what he thinks he wants—"

"And if I know Khane, and if I know the People's

Commonwealth of Aditya, it won't be a year before Yaggo has Khane shot or stuffs him into jail, and then the Space Navy will have an excuse to visit Aditya, and Aditya'll never be the same afterward," Prince Travann added.

The students massed on the front lawns were still cheering as they went down after addressing them. The Security Guards were conspicuously absent and it was a detail of red-kilted Thoran riflemen who met them as they entered the hall to the Session Chamber. Prince Ganzay approached, attended by two Household Guard officers, a human and a Thoran. Count Tammsan looked from one to the other of his companions, bewildered. The bewildering thing was that everything was as it should be.

"Well, gentlemen," Paul said, "I'm sure that both of you will want to confer for a moment with your colleagues in the rotunda before the session. Please don't feel obliged to attend me further."

Prince Ganzay approached as they went down the hall. "Your Majesty, what *is* going on here?" he demanded querulously. "Just who is in control of the palace—you or Prince Travann? And where is His Imperial Highness, and where is General Dorflay?"

"I sent Dorflay to join Prince Rodrik's picnic party. If you're upset about this, you can imagine what he might have done here."

Prince Ganzay looked at him curiously for a moment. "I thought I understood what was happening," he said. "Now I—this business about the students, sir; how did it come out?"

Paul told him. They talked for a while, and then the Prime Minister looked at his watch, and suggested that the session ought to be getting started. Paul nodded, and they went down the hall and into the rotunda.

The big semicircular lobby was empty, now, except for a platoon of Household guards, and the Empress Marris and her ladies-in-waiting. She advanced as quickly as her sheath gown would permit, and took his arm; the ladies-in-waiting fell in behind her, and Prince Ganzay went ahead, crying: "My Lords, Your Venerable Highnesses, gentlemen; His Imperial Majesty!"

Marris tightened her grip on his arm as they started forward. "Paul!" she hissed into his ear. "What is this silly story about Yorn Travann trying to seize the throne?"

"Isn't it? Yorn's been too close the throne for too long not to know what sort of a seat it is. He'd commit any crime up to and including genocide to keep off it."

She gave a quick skip to get into step with him. "Then why's he filled the palace with these blackcoats? Is Rod all right?"

"Perfectly all right; he's somewhere out in the mountains, keeping Harv Dorflay out of mischief."

They crossed the Session Hall and took their seats on the double throne; everybody sat down, and the Prime Minister, after some formalities, declared the Plenary session in being. Almost at once, one of the Prince-Counselors was on his feet begging His Majesty's leave to interrogate the Government.

"I wish to ask His Highness the Minister of Security the meaning of all this unprecedented disturbance, both here in the palace and in the city," he said.

Prince Travann rose at once. "Your Majesty, in reply to the question of His Venerable Highness," he began, and then launched himself into an account of the student riot, the march to petition the emperor, and the clash with the nonworking-class hooligans. "As to the affair at the University, I hesitate to speak on what is really the concern of His Lordship the Minister of Education, but as to the fighting in the city, if it is still going on, I can assure His Venerable Highness that the Gendarmes and Security Guards have it well in hand; the persons responsible are being rounded up, and, if the Minister of Justice concurs, an inquiry will be started tomorrow."

The Minister of Justice assured the Minister of Security that his ministry would be quite ready to co-operate in the inquiry. Count Tammsan then got up and began talking about the riot at the University.

"What did happen, Paul?" Marris whispered.

"Chancellor Khane sacked a science professor for being too interested in science. The students didn't like it. I think Khane's successor will rectify that. Have a good time at the Flower Festivals?"

She raised her fan to hide a grimace. "I made my schedule," she said. "Tomorrow, I have fifty more booked."

"Your Imperial Majesty!" The Counselor who had risen paused to make sure that he had the Imperial attention, before continuing: "Inasmuch as this question also seems to involve a scientific experiment, I would suggest that the Ministry of Science and Technology is also interested, and since there is at present no minister holding that portfolio, I would suggest that the discussion be continued after a minister has been elected."

The Minister of Health and Sanity jumped to his feet.

"Your Imperial Majesty; permit me to concur with the proposal of His Venerable Highness, and to extend it with the subproposal that the Ministry of Science and Technology be abolished, and its functions and personnel divided among the other ministries, specifically those of Education and of Economics."

The Minister of Fine Arts was up before he was fully seated.

"Your Imperial Majesty; permit me to concur with the proposal of Count Guilfred, and to extend it further with the proposal that the Ministry of Defense, now also vacant, be likewise abolished, and its functions and personnel added to the Ministry of Security under His Highness Prince Travann."

So that was it! Marris, beside him, said, "Well!" He had long ago discovered that she could pack more meaning into that monosyllable than the average counselor could into a half-hour's speech. Prince Ganzay was thunderstruck, and from the Bench of Counselors six or eight voices were babbling loudly at once. Four Ministers were on their feet clamoring for recognition; Count Duklass of Economics was yelling the loudest, so he got it.

"Your Imperial Majesty; it would have been most unseemly in me to have spoken in favor of the proposal of Count Guilfred, being an interested party, but I feel no such hesitation in concurring with the proposal of Baron Garratt, the Minister of Fine Arts. Indeed, I consider it a most excellent proposal——"

"And I consider it the most diabolically dangerous proposal to be made in this hall in the last six centuries!" old Admiral Geklar shouted. "This is a proposal to concentrate all the armed force of the Empire in the hands of one man. Who can say what unscrupulous use might be made of such power?"

"Are you intimating, Prince-Counselor, that Prince Travann is contemplating some tyrannical or subversive use of such power?" Count Tammsan, of all people, demanded.

There was a concerted gasp at that; about half the plenary session were absolutely sure that he was. Admiral Geklar backed quickly away from the question.

"Prince Travann will not be the last Minister of Security," he said.

"What I was about to say, Your Majesty, is that as matters stand, Security has a virtual monopoly on armed power on this planet. When these disorders in the city—which Prince Travann's men are now bringing under control—broke out, there was, I am informed, an order sent out to bring Regular Army and Planetary Militia into Asgard. It will be hours before any of the former can arrive, and at least a day before the latter can even be mobilized. By the time any of them get here, there will be nothing for them to do. Is that not correct, Prince Ganzay?"

The Prime Minister looked at him angrily, stung by the realization that somebody else had a personal intelligence service as good as his own, then swallowed his anger and assented.

"Furthermore," Count Duklass continued, "the Ministry of Defense itself, is an anachronism, which no doubt accounts for the condition in which we now find it. The Empire has no external enemies whatever; all our defense problems are problems of internal security. Let us therefore turn the facilities over to the ministry responsible for the tasks."

The debate went on and on; he paid less and less attention to it, and it became increasingly obvious that opposition to the proposition was dwindling. Cries of, "Vote! Vote!" began to be heard from its supporters. Prince Ganzay rose from his desk and came to the throne.

"Your Imperial Majesty," he said softly. "I am opposed to this proposition, but I am convinced that enough favor it to pass it, even over Your Majesty's veto. Before the vote is called, does Your Majesty wish my resignation?"

He rose and stepped down beside the Prime Minister, putting an arm over Prince Ganzay's shoulder.

"Far from it, old friend," he said, in a distinctly audible voice. "I will have too much need for you. But, as for the proposal, I don't oppose it. I think it an excellent one; it has my approval." He lowered his voice. "As soon as it's passed, place General Dorflay's name in nomination."

The Prime Minister looked at him sadly for a moment, then nodded, returning to his desk, where he rapped for order and called for the vote.

"Well, if you can't lick them, join them," Marris said as she sat down beside her. "And if they start chasing you, just yell, 'There he goes; follow me!' "

The proposal carried, almost unanimously. Prince Ganzay then presented the name of Captain-General Dorflay for elevation to the Bench of Counselors, and the emperor decreed it. As soon as the session was adjourned and he could do so, he slipped out the little door behind the throne, into an elevator.

In the room at the top of the Octagon Tower, he laid aside his belt and dress dagger and unfastened his tunic, then sat down in his deep chair and called a serving-robot. It was the one that had brought him his breakfast, and he greeted it as a friend; it lit a cigarette for him, and poured a drink of brandy. For a long time he sat, smoking and sipping and looking out the wide window to the west, where the orange sun was firing the clouds behind the mountains, and he realized that he was abominably tired. Well, no wonder; more Empire history had been made today than in the years since he had come to the throne.

Then something behind him clicked. He turned his head, to see Yorn Travann emerge from the concealed elevator. He grinned and lifted his drink in greeting.

"I thought you'd be a little late," he said. "Everybody trying to climb onto the bandwagon?"

Yorn Travann came forward, unbuckling his belt and laying it with Paul's; he sank into the chair opposite, and the robot poured him a drink.

"Well, do you blame them? What would it have looked like to you, in their place?"

"A *coup d'état*. For that matter, wasn't that what it was? Why didn't you tell me you were springing it?"

"I didn't spring it; it was sprung on me. I didn't know a thing about it till Max Duklass buttonholed me down by the landing stage. I'd intended fighting this proposal to partition Science and Technology, but this riot blew up and scared Duklass and Tammsan and Guilfred and the rest of them. They weren't too sure of their majority—that's why they had the election postponed a couple of times—but they were sure that the riot would turn some of the undecided counselors against them. So they offered to back me to take over Defense in exchange for my supporting their proposal. It looked too good to pass up."

"Even at the price of wrecking Science and Technology?"

"It was wrecked, or left to rust into uselessness, long ago. The main function of Technology has been to suppress anything that might threaten this state of economic *rigor mortis* that Duklass calls stability, and the function of Science has been to let muttonheads like Khane and Dandrik dominate the teaching of science. Well, Defense has its own scientific and technical sections, and when we come to carving the bird, Duklass and Tammsan are going to see a lot of slices going onto my plate."

"And when it's all cut up, it will be discovered that there is no provision for original research. So it will please My Majesty to institute an Imperial Office of Scientific Research, independent of any ministry, and guess who'll be named to head it."

"Faress. And, by the way, we're all set on Khane, too. First Citizen Yaggo is as delighted to have him as we are to get rid of him. Why don't we get Vann Evaratt back, and give him the job?"

"Good. If he takes charge there at the opening of the next academic year, in ten years we'll have a thousand young men, maybe ten times that many, who won't be afraid of new things and new ideas. But the main thing is that now you have Defense, and now the plan can really start firing all jets."

"Yes." Yorn Travann got out his cigarettes and lit one. Paul glanced at the robot, hoping that its feelings hadn't been hurt. "All these native uprisings I've been blowing up out of inter-tribal knife fights, and all these civil wars my people have been manufacturing; there'll be more of them, and I'll start yelling my head off for an adequate Space Navy, and after we get it, these local troubles will all stop, and then what'll we be expected to do? Scrap the ships?"

They both knew what would be done with some of them. It would have to be done stealthily, while nobody was looking, but some of those ships would go far beyond the boundaries of the Empire, and new things would happen. New worlds, new problems. Great and frightening changes.

"Paul, we agreed upon this long ago, when we were still boys at the University. The Empire stopped growing, and when things stop growing, they start dying, the death of petrifaction. And when petrifaction is complete, the cracking and the crumbling starts, and there's no way of stopping it. But if we can get people out onto new planets, the Empire won't die; it'll start growing again."

"You didn't start that thing at the University, this morning, yourself, did you?"

"Not the student riot, no. But the hooligan attack, yes. That was some of my own men. The real hooligans began looting after Handrosan had gotten the students out of the district. We collared all of them, including their boss, Nutchy the Knife, right away, and as soon as we did that, Big Moogie and Zikko the Nose tried to move in. We're cleaning them up now. By tomorrow morning there won't be one of these nonworkers' voting blocks left in Asgard, and by the end of the week they'll be cleaned up all over Odin. I have discovered a plot, and they're all involved in it."

"Wait a moment." Paul got to his feet. "That reminds me; Harv Dorflay's hiding Rod and Olva out in the mountains. I wanted him out of here while things were happening. I'll have to call him and tell him it's safe to come in, now."

"Well, zip up your tunic and put your dagger on; you look as though you'd been arrested, disarmed and searched."

"That's right." He hastily repaired his appearance and went to the screen across the room, punching out the combination of the screen with Rodrik's picnic party.

A young lieutenant of the Household Troops appeared in it, and had to be reassured. He got General Dorflay.

"Your Majesty! You all right?"

"Perfectly all right, general, and it's quite safe to bring His Imperial Highness in. The conspiracy against the throne has been crushed."

"Oh, thank the gods! Is Prince Travann a prisoner?"

"Quite the contrary, general. It was our loyal and devoted subject, Prince Travann, who crushed the conspiracy."

"But—but, Your Majesty—!"

"You aren't to be blamed for suspecting him, general. His agents were working in the very innermost councils of the conspirators. Every one of the people whom you suspected—with excellent reason—was actually working to defeat the plot. Think back, general; the scheme to put the gun in the viewscreen, the scheme to sabotage the elevator, the scheme to introduce assassins into the orchestra with guns built into their trumpets—every one came to your notice because of what seemed to be some indiscretion of the plotters, didn't it?"

"Why . . . why, yes, Your Majesty!" By this time tomorrow, he would have a complete set of memories for each one of them. "You mean, the indiscretions were deliberate?"

"Your vigilance and loyalty made it necessary for them to resort to these fantastic expedients, and your vigilance defeated them as fast as they came to your notice. Well, today, Prince Travann and I struck back. I may tell you, in confidence, that every one of the conspirators is dead. Killed in this afternoon's rioting—which was incited for that purpose by Prince Travann."

"Then—then there will be no more plots against your life?" There was a note of regret in the old man's voice.

"No more, Your Venerable Highness."

"But—What did Your Majesty call me?" he asked incredulously.

"I took the honor of being the first to address you by your new title, Prince-Counselor Dorflay."

He left the old man overcome, and blubbering happily on the shoulder of the Crown Prince, who winked at his father out of the screen. Prince Travann had gotten a couple of fresh drinks from the robot and handed one to him when he returned to his chair.

"He'll be finding the Bench of Counselors riddled with treason inside a week," Travann said. "You handled that just right, though. Another case of making problems solve each other."

"You were telling me about a plot you'd discovered."

"Oh, yes; this is one to top Dorflay's best efforts. All the voting-bloc bosses on Odin are in a conspiracy to start a civil war to give them a chance to loot the planet. There isn't a word of truth in it, of course, but it'll do to arrest and hold them for a few days, and by that time some of my undercovers will be in control of every nonworker vote on the planet. After all, the cartels put an end to competition in every other business; why not a voting cartel, too? Then, whenever there's an election, we just advertise for bids."

"Why, that would mean absolute control——"

"Of the nonworking vote, yes. And I'll guarantee, personally, that in five years the politics of Odin will have become so unbearably corrupt and abusive that the intellectuals, the technicians, the business people, even the nobility, will be flocking to the polls to vote, and if only half of them turn out, they'll snow the nonworkers under. And that'll mean, eventually, an end to vote-selling, and the nonworkers'll have to find work. We'll find it for them."

"Great and frightening changes." Yorn Travann laughed: he recognized the phrase. Probably started it himself. Paul lifted his glass. "To the Minister of Disturbance!"

"Your Majesty!" They drank to each other, and then Yorn Travann said, "We had a lot of wild dreams, when we were boys; it looks as though we're starting to make some of them come true. You know, when we were in the University, the students would never have done what they did today. They didn't even do it ten years ago, when Vann Evaratt was dismissed."

"And Van Evaratt's pupil came back to Odin and touched this whole thing off." He thought for a moment, "I wonder what Faress has, in that anticipation effect."

"I think I can see what can come out of it. If he can propagate a wave that behaves like those micropositos, we may not have to depend on ships for communication. We may be able, some day, to screen Baldur or Vishnu or Aton or Thor as easily as you screened Dorflay, up in the mountains." He thought silently for a moment. "I don't know whether that would be good or bad. But it would be new, and that's what matters. That's the only thing that matters."

"Flower Festivals," Paul said, and, when Yorn Travann wanted to know what he meant, he told him. "When Princess Olva's Empress, she's going to curse the name of Klenn Faress. Flower Festivals, all around the galaxy, without end."